KU-495-469

Aftershock

Quintin Jardine

headline

Copyright © 2008 Portador Ltd

The right of Quintin Jardine to be identified as the Author
of the Work has been asserted by him in accordance with the
Copyright, Designs and Patents Act 1988.

First published in 2008
by HEADLINE PUBLISHING GROUP

2

Apart from any use permitted under UK copyright law, this publication
may only be reproduced, stored, or transmitted, in any form, or by any means,
with prior permission in writing of the publishers or, in the case of
reprographic production, in accordance with the terms of licences issued
by the Copyright Licensing Agency.

All characters in this publication are fictitious and any
resemblance to real persons, living or dead, is purely coincidental.

Cataloguing in Publication Data is available from the British Library

978 0 7553 2912 0 (Hardback)
978 0 7553 2913 7 (Trade paperback)

Typeset in Electra by Avon DataSet Ltd,
Bidford-on-Avon, Warwickshire

Printed and bound in the UK by
CPI Mackays, Chatham ME5 8TD

Headline's policy is to use papers that are natural, renewable and
recyclable products and made from wood grown in sustainable forests.
The logging and manufacturing processes are expected to conform
to the environmental regulations of the country of origin.

HEADLINE PUBLISHING GROUP
An Hachette Livre UK Company
338 Euston Road
London NW1 3BH

www.headline.co.uk
www.hodderheadline.com

Aftershock

Also by Quintin Jardine and available from Headline

Bob Skinner series:
Skinner's Rules
Skinner's Festival
Skinner's Trail
Skinner's Round
Skinner's Ordeal
Skinner's Mission
Skinner's Ghosts
Murmuring the Judges
Gallery Whispers
Thursday Legends
Autographs in the Rain
Head Shot
Fallen Gods
Stay of Execution
Lethal Intent
Dead and Buried
Death's Door

Oz Blackstone series:
Blackstone's Pursuits
A Coffin for Two
Wearing Purple
Screen Savers
On Honeymoon with Death
Poisoned Cherries
Unnatural Justice
Alarm Call
For the Death of Me

This book is for Allan Campbell Reid Jardine, my main man, my son. Although this dedication will embarrass the hell out of him, the world needs to know just how proud of him I am.

One

'How's she doing?' asked Neil McIlhenney.

'Maggie?' Mario McGuire's heavy black eyebrows rose. 'For a woman who's just had her womb and ovaries removed because of cancer, and who's in the middle of follow-up chemotherapy, she's doing bloody well. But why are you asking me? Why haven't you been to see her yourself?'

'I haven't been given the okay.'

'Come again?'

'Her sister said she would phone me when she was ready for visitors.'

'Her sister?' Mario snorted. 'Look, Bet's only just come back into her life after fifteen years or so. She doesn't know who's who. You're not bloody "visitors"; you're family, as near as damn it. Phone her first, just to make sure she'll be in, then get your arse down to Gordon Terrace and pay her a visit.'

'Will do. How's the baby?'

A big smile creased McGuire's swarthy features. 'Stephanie Margaret is blooming. She's up to six and a half pounds, and she's absolutely drop-dead gorgeous.'

'Who does she take after?'

'Her mother, mostly; it looks like she's going to have the same red hair. But if you look closely, around her eyes, you can see her dad in her: you can see Stevie.'

Neil frowned. 'Will that be good for Maggie? It's only a couple of months since he was killed.'

'Wee Steph can't be anything but good for her. She's what her life's all about now; she's her reason to beat this damn disease. And she will, too.'

'What if she doesn't?'

Detective Chief Superintendent Mario McGuire's face had always been his weakness as an interrogator. Invariably, his feelings were written across it. At his friend's question, it darkened. 'That's not an option,' he growled.

'That's what I said about my Olive, when she was in treatment. The trouble is, mate, sometimes strength of will isn't enough. I know that the surgeon was optimistic after the operation, but you can never take anything for granted. So I'm asking you. What if she doesn't make it? How will you feel?'

'What do you mean, how will I feel? How the fuck do you think I'll feel?'

'Like you're feeling now: guilty. Only ten times worse.'

Mario's mouth opened, but the words of denial died in his throat. He shrugged his shoulders helplessly. 'Wouldn't you, in the same circumstances? Suppose you had walked out on Olive and the kids . . . not that I'm saying you ever would have . . . and then she'd taken ill.'

McIlhenney nodded. 'Sure, if that had happened I'd have torn myself apart . . . but I'd have done it anyway, for having been such an idiot. Chum, our circumstances, yours and mine, can't ever be the same. Your marriage was over, yours and Maggie's. Splitting up was the biggest favour you could have done each other. You let her enjoy the happiest time of her life with Stevie, and she let you and Paula get together as you should have done years before.'

'Her happiness didn't last long, though, did it?'

'No, but what the hell has that to do with you? You didn't set the booby-trap that Stevie walked into: you didn't kill him. Dražen Boras did that, beyond a shadow of a doubt. If I'd been on duty at that time, it could just as easily have been me that went through the door and triggered the grenade. If you'd been nearest the scene, it would have been you. Suppose it had been, and Stevie was still alive, would Mags be going on a guilt trip right now? Would she hell!'

'But that's not what happened.'

'Aw, for fu . . . Look, Mario, before you give yourself any more grief, go back and see Maggie, and ask her whether she harbours the slightest grudge against you for leaving her. Know what she'll do? First she'll laugh, and then she'll thank you for it.'

'Maybe.'

'No "maybe" about it. Know what you really should do?'

McGuire shrugged again; a small, slightly sheepish grin crossed his face. 'Seems like you're in the fucking *Mastermind* chair, so you'd better tell me.'

'You should go home to Paula, give her a very large hug and thank your luckiest star that it wasn't you went through that door.'

'That's advice I don't mind taking.' He checked his watch. 'Or, I should say, I won't in about seven hours. But for now, is this just a social call, or do you have something to tell me? Is Edinburgh ablaze with crime?'

Detective Superintendent McIlhenney looked at the head of CID, then rolled his eyes. 'In the second week of the July Trades Holiday? You have to be kidding. If you didn't insist on the two of us meeting at ten o'clock every Monday morning, then I wouldn't be here. I'd have gone fishing,' he paused, 'or maybe I'd have gone out and pulled off a couple of robberies, just to give my people something to do.'

'Are you telling me that we're victims of our own success?'

'That's a nice way of putting it. I don't have a single serious unsolved crime on my books. I've got detectives sitting on their hands in every office in the city. I can't even send them out to do crime-prevention lectures, because the schools are on holiday, and just about every other bugger along with them.'

'How are the burglary stats? Holidays mean empty houses, ready to be broken into.'

'That's become a problem for the uniforms, rather than us.

3

Nowadays empty houses mean burglar alarms going off in the middle of the night, but nine times out of ten . . . no, that's not true, it's more like nineteen out of twenty . . . it's been caused by a spider walking across a sensor.'

'Tell me about it,' McGuire grunted. 'Ours went off the other night because Paula left a window open in the living room; the wind got up in the middle of the night and blew a door shut. The alarm company called it in but, thank Christ, the control room recognised the name and address, and called me to check it out before they despatched a car.'

'That would have looked good in the *Evening News*. But no,' McIlhenney continued, 'even burglary's going out of fashion. And street muggings are down too: Brian Mackie's extra patrols in high-risk areas seem to be doing the job there.'

'Good for the new ACC. A few more like him and we'll be hearing the word "redundancy" around this building.'

'It won't come to that.' The superintendent chuckled. 'Our deputy chief constable will be back from his sabbatical soon; Bob Skinner attracts trouble like a magnet attracts pins.'

'True. He's got another fortnight off, hasn't he?'

'That's right, but he's thinking about coming back next week.'

'Is he at home?'

'No. His kids are off to spend the summer with their mum in the US and he's at his place in Spain for a couple of weeks.'

'Alone?'

'No, the Scottish Parliament's in recess, so Aileen's gone with him.'

'Do you think this new relationship will last?'

'Bob and the First Minister? Yeah, I reckon it will. She's been great for him, just when he's needed it. I was really worried about him for a while, after that armed incident up in St Andrews. I even thought we might have lost him; with that and his marriage break-up coming so close together, I was afraid he might have walked away from the job. Thank God for Aileen de Marco, I tell you; she helped him through it, and got him refocused. Now, six months on, he's as contented as I've ever seen him.'

McGuire made a small sound of agreement. 'Identifying Boras as the man who killed Stevie,' he said, 'that helped him too, I reckon. You should have seen him interrogate the key witness. He even scared me shitless, and I was on his side of the table.'

'He'd get a bigger lift if we actually caught the bastard. Have you had any more feedback on that?'

'I make a point of asking every week. I wish to Christ it was our inquiry, not the Northumbrian force's . . . and I think they're beginning to feel that way too. I'm becoming a nuisance to them . . . not that I'm apologising for it . . . but the story I'm getting hasn't changed. "We believe that Dražen Boras is in the USA and we've asked the FBI to assist in tracking him down." Big help that is! I bloody well know he's in the USA: it was the DCC and me who told them so. We also told them they'd need political pressure to stir the FBI into action, and that's where they're failing. Maybe we'll get some movement when the big man gets back from Spain. He knows the buttons to push.'

'Sure,' said McIlhenney, grimly, 'but nothing's going to happen in a hurry . . . if it ever does. Boras will be well under cover by now; he'll have a new identity, maybe even a surgically altered appearance. He'll never come within our reach again.'

He started, as the mobile phone in his pocket began to vibrate. He took it out and flipped it open. 'Yes?' he said.

'Sir, it's Jack McGurk,' a voice replied. 'I'm in Corstorphine, up the hill, in a wooded area just above Murrayfield golf course.'

'Crime scene?'

'Maybe, sir; a suspicious death for now. I'm looking at the body of a young woman, fully clothed, lying on her back. Her eyes are closed and there's no sign of a struggle.'

McIlhenney felt a prickling in the short hair on the back of his neck. 'Jack,' he ordered, 'take a photo with your mobile and send it to me, on this number.'

'Is that secure, sir?'

'It's as secure as we need for now. Do it.' He closed the phone and held it in his hand.

'What's that?' McGuire asked, his curiosity underlined by his expression.

'Maybe nothing. Wait.'

After a few seconds the mobile vibrated once again. The superintendent opened it, and accessed the incoming picture message. He stared at the image, then whistled softly, and handed the open phone to McGuire.

The head of CID's eyes widened. 'Jesus,' he whispered.

'Yes,' said McIlhenney. 'Does that look familiar or what? We'd better get out there.'

Two

Andy Martin had a secret: well, maybe no longer a secret, as he had shared it with Karen, his wife, and with Bob Skinner, his closest friend, but it was definitely something that, with those two exceptions, he kept strictly to himself. The subject had not come up during the interview that had taken him to chief officer rank in the Tayside force. If it had, he doubted that he would be wearing the extra braid on his uniform.

The young Martin had been raised in a Christian family. He had been baptised and confirmed in the Roman Catholic Church; its values had been instilled in him throughout his childhood, and carried with him into his adult life. Yet he was in no way a prude. He had played rugby at near international level, and had been as ruthless as the game required. As a single man he had gathered a reputation as something of a swinger, with a succession of partners leading up to an ill-fated engagement to Alexis Skinner, Bob's daughter. For a while, he had endured his friend's wrath, but eventually they had been reconciled, and the bond between them renewed. In fact it was stronger than ever, and had survived the acrimonious break-up of that relationship.

Its ending had been due entirely to the influences that had moulded Martin's character. He had loved Alex, but when she had terminated a pregnancy without consulting him, he had found it unforgivable. His Christianity was founded on the principles of the Ten Commandments, and although he and Alex had laughed about coveted asses,

7

when it came to 'Thou shalt not kill', he could find no room for compromise.

They had split and he had drifted into a couple of dangerous liaisons, before finding security with Karen Neville, a serving officer herself at that time. They were happy together, with Danielle, their toddler, and with another on the way, and if a small part deep within him still yearned occasionally for Alex, he managed to keep it suppressed. He felt a warm contentment as he glanced at his wife, sitting beside him at the coffee-table in their conservatory, enjoying a rare Monday together after Andy had spent the weekend supervising the policing of an outdoor music festival.

His secret? No, not that: the world knew he had carried a torch for Alex for a while. No, the elephant hiding in Andy Martin's briefcase, the truth that might have constrained his career if he had brought it out into the open, had to do with drugs.

For much of his police service in Edinburgh, he had been involved in the suppression of the illegal trade, and in the pursuit and prosecution of users and dealers alike. In his time he had met a few cops who had been known to smoke a wee bit of grass, and he had let it be known quietly that if they ever indulged around him, he would do them, just like any other punter. On his arrival in Dundee, to take over the deputy chief's post, he had made it just as clear that, however liberal public attitudes had become, any of his serving officers caught with cannabis, or any other proscribed drug, would be sacked.

And yet although he enforced the law on illegal narcotics as stringently as any officer in Scotland, privately Andy Martin did not agree with it. He had searched the teachings of his faith for grounds to justify the control or prohibition of what people might choose to take into their bodies, and had found none. There was nothing in the Ten Commandments that said, even by implication, 'Thou shalt not take drugs'. And in his view, if there was no moral basis for a law, then that law was flawed.

While he recognised the terrible effects that hard drugs could have on users and their families, he knew that control by prohibition was proving to be globally unsuccessful. His core belief was 'prescription not proscription'. He felt, instinctively, that legalisation and licensing was the only long-term way to rid the streets of dealers and the world of their brutal suppliers. The US had proved in the Twenties and Thirties that legal prohibition of alcohol, another narcotic, was untenable, and governments around the world continued to draw much of their revenue from the taxation of tobacco. Therefore, as he saw it, if the same was recognised to be true of the narcotics trade, and it was legalised, regulated and taxed, with the resources currently devoted to the pursuit, prosecution and imprisonment of those involved in it being diverted to health education, society could only be improved.

Martin believed, sincerely, this to be true. But he knew with equal certainty that if he ever said so, publicly, he would be putting his career on the line. This had been brought home to him forcefully by Bob Skinner, a natural politician for all that he had said about the breed over the years.

'Many people would agree with you, Andy,' he had said, in one of their after-dinner discussions of the subject. 'To be honest, when you put it like that, it's difficult to see the counter-argument. The trouble is that many more people would disagree with you, vehemently, because that's the way they've been conditioned to think. The truth is that you and I and the entire Association of Chief Police Officers could stand up and argue the case and it wouldn't make any differ-ence. Even if we did secure majority support in this country, even if decriminalisation became government policy, even if it became the goal of the entire European Union, it wouldn't matter a damn. Any about-face of that size would have to be implemented internationally. First and foremost, the Americans would have to be on board, and believe me when I tell you that there is not the slightest chance of that happening. If you want my advice, keep your mouth shut and get on with the job.'

Martin smiled as he remembered Skinner's finger jabbing into the table to emphasise every point.

'What are you grinning at?' Karen asked.

'I'm recalling a lecture from my old mentor,' he told her.

'Which of the many?'

'Something to do with this.' He picked up a large white envelope from the table and handed it across to her, watching as she opened it and read the contents.

'Director, Scottish Crime and Drug Enforcement Agency,' she said. 'It's an application form. Did you send for it?'

'No. Somebody in the Executive decided to circulate it to all assistant and deputy chief constables.'

'Including Bob Skinner?'

'I suppose so.'

'Are you going to go for it?'

'I dunno. What do you think?'

'It's a big job, high profile. A few years in there and you'd be favourite for the Strathclyde chief's job when it comes up again . . . and that's the biggest of the lot.'

'That's if there is a Strathclyde.'

'What do you mean?' asked Karen, intrigued.

He looked at her. 'Within these glass walls . . . there's a rumour that the Executive might consider merging all the Scottish forces and creating a single national constabulary.' He paused. 'Only it isn't a rumour; it's true. Aileen de Marco's asked Bob to do a feasibility study, highly confidential, her eyes only. That's how he's spent a lot of his sabbatical. He's done a potential command structure already. It stands up. I know because I've seen it; Bob's been taking soundings among those senior colleagues he can trust to keep it to themselves. If it happens, it'll even swallow the SCDEA; that's part of the plan. It might still exist as a unit, but there would be no need for it to be a separate agency; its commander would report to the new commissioner.'

'Commissioner? As in the Metropolitan?'

Andy nodded. 'Yup. Bob's thinking is that if this is to happen it's best if the old structure changes completely. The posts of chief constable, deputy and assistants would disappear, or at least the titles would. There would be a commissioner and a deputy operating nationally, and assistant commissioners at regional level, running uniformed policing and community relations. There would be two criminal investigation units, each headed by another assistant commissioner. One of those would be the SCDEA, and the other would be an amalgamation of existing CID units, with a regional structure, but reporting to a national commander.'

'All based in Edinburgh, I suppose. The Glaswegians will love that.'

'No. The central command won't be in either of the main cities. Bob's plan is that it should be physically separated from the politicians. He's proposing that it should be centred in Motherwell.'

'Motherwell?' Karen exclaimed.

'Why not?' Andy retorted. 'It's Bob's home town.'

'So there are no prizes for guessing who the first commissioner will be.'

Her husband laughed. 'You can stop right there,' he told her. 'This is a study, that's all. It works in principle. Greater London's twice the size of Scotland in population terms, and it has a single force . . . if you ignore the City of Westminster force, which is small by any standard, an anomaly, really. Ontario's another good comparison: bigger than us, but with a single police force. Bob's done some research over there. But putting it into practice, that's another thing altogether.'

'Who's to stop it?'

'Aileen de Marco. She's a tremendously powerful figure just now. She may lead a coalition administration, but what she says goes. If she wants it to happen it will, if not . . . forget it.'

'And where does Bob stand on it?'

'As far as I know, he's neutral. He's done it because Aileen asked him, that's all.'

'So,' Karen continued, 'while we're waiting for the revolution, what's going to happen?' She picked up the form. 'Are you going to apply for this? Because I'm damn sure you'd get it.'

'What about Bob?'

'Come on, you know there's no danger of him going after it.'

'That's true, so would you like me to?'

'Your career, your decision. I'll support you, either way.'

'In that case . . . I won't bother.' He ran his fingers through his thick blond hair. 'It sounds glamorous, but I doubt whether my heart would be in it, for a reason which will remain between you and me.'

'Ah, Andy's drugs philosophy, is it? I can see how that might make it difficult. Does that mean you've settled for this nice quiet backwater?'

His green eyes drilled into her until his face creased into a smile. 'That will be the day, my love. No, there's something in the wind for me, and it might not be too long till it blows to our door. Until then, we'll both have to be patient and bide our time in leafy Tayside.'

Three

'How long has she been here?' the head of CID asked.

'The doc reckoned about ten days, sir,' Jack McGurk replied, his voice muffled by his face mask. The space in the copse was restricted by overhanging branches, forcing the towering detective sergeant into an awkward crouch. 'He can't be certain, though,' he continued. 'He was going by maggot infestation, mostly. It's been hot for the last week, and he did say that could have affected it. Poor lass,' he murmured, 'she's not a pretty sight.'

'That went without saying,' Neil McIlhenney growled. The ears, mouth and nasal cavities of the body were filled with pupae, and with black crawling insects that were feeding on them in turn. He turned to McGuire. 'You're in no doubt, now you've seen her close up?'

'None,' said the chief superintendent. 'The way she's been left, been laid out. It's . . . it's very similar to the others. Come on, let's get the smell out of our nostrils, and let the crime-scene people back in.' Stripping off his mask, he led the way out of the small clearing and on to the green hillside below. A woman dressed in a white tunic, like the three men, stood waiting for them on the edge of the golf course. She was in her mid-thirties, tall and slim with dark, close-cropped hair.

'Is it what you thought?' she asked McGurk.

McGuire answered for him. 'No, Inspector, it's as Superintendent McIlhenney and I suspected when we saw the image on the mobile. Jack wasn't at any of the earlier crime scenes. The body's laid out in exactly the same way as they were. It looks like an overdose, a suicide

13

or a natural death, except there's no sign of drug use, no empty pill bottles, and the victim was young and apparently healthy. The only difference is that the others were in fairly public places and were all found immediately after the kill. This girl's off the beaten track.'

'Are we sure about that?' McIlhenney asked him. 'Don't people walk through these woods?'

'I've never imagined so, but maybe I'm wrong. There is a path by the fence, but it's pretty much overgrown.' He looked at McGurk. 'How was she found?'

'By a golfer,' the sergeant told him. 'He hit a big hook off the tee, and knocked his ball into the woods. It's out of bounds, but he went looking for it just the same.'

'He hit it that far off line?' McIlhenney exclaimed.

'No. The ball was just inside the tree-line. He said to the uniforms it was the smell that attracted him, once he got in there.'

'Have you spoken to him?'

McGurk winced. 'I thought I'd leave that to you, sir. He's a High Court judge.'

'Who?'

'Lord Archibald. I was in the witness box before him once. He gave me a hard time.'

McGuire laughed. 'Archie Nelson gives everybody a hard time; it's what makes him a great judge. Did you learn from the experience?'

'Yes indeed, boss. I learned never to cross his path again if I can avoid it.'

'I'll interview him, if you like,' said the woman.

The head of CID nodded. 'You do that, Becky,' he said. 'You should be getting to know landmark figures like him. How are you settling in at Torphichen Place, by the way? I do plan to come and visit you there, honest.'

'I like it,' Detective Inspector Becky Stallings replied. 'It's a change from Charing Cross and no mistake, but it's so much more civilised.' Stallings was a newcomer to the Edinburgh force. She had been seconded from the Metropolitan Police to assist the internal inquiry into Stevie Steele's death, and had applied for a permanent transfer shortly afterwards.

'Do you understand what we're talking about here? You know all about the Boras investigation, but are you up to speed with everything that went before?'

'Not completely,' she admitted.

'That's okay,' said McGuire. 'There's no reason why you should be: those cases were all closed. Let me give you a run-down. Earlier this year, a young artist named Stacey Gavin was found dead near South Queensferry. There was no sign of a struggle, and the body was . . . how do I put it? . . . composed, as if she had simply laid down to die, just like that girl in there. This caused the officers who attended the scene to . . .' he paused '. . . I'll use a technical police term here . . . to fuck up, and assume that Stacey had either ODed accidentally or topped herself. This led to the autopsy being given low priority, so it was over twenty-four hours before she was properly examined and we discovered that she'd been killed by a single shot to the back of the head.'

He sighed. 'Almost as soon as the fan started dispersing the shit, we pulled out all the stops . . . and came up blank. Stacey was a genuinely nice girl, and if she had an enemy in the world, we couldn't find him, at that point at any rate. No blame was attached to Stevie Steele, who led the team; once all the available lines of enquiry were exhausted, he had nowhere else to go. He did a reconstruction, even got it on *Crimewatch*, but there was no arrest, not even a viable suspect.' He glanced at McIlhenney. 'Does that sum it up accurately, Neil?'

The superintendent nodded. 'Yes. Stevie reported to me. He didn't miss anything; former boyfriends, family members, life-sentence prisoners out on licence, he checked them all out. And then . . .'

'A couple of months later,' McGuire continued, 'a second body, another young woman, was found on a beach near Gullane, killed and laid out in exactly the same way as Stacey had been. There was nothing on her to tell us who she was . . . nor was there on Stacey, by the way. By sheer chance, the driver of the vehicle that came to collect the body had been at school with her.

'It took some time, some forensic evidence and a bus driver with a good memory to help us identify the second victim as Zrinka Boras, another artist, the daughter of the businessman Davor Boras, address, a flat just off Princes Street. We found the tent that she'd camped in the night before she was killed, and a short while later we also found the body of her boyfriend, a poor lad called Harry Paul. There was nothing neat about his death. He was killed and his body stuffed away in the bushes for the foxes to get at.'

'Was there any sign of a struggle this time, near the woman's body?' Stallings asked.

'None at all. We decided, in the absence of any evidence, that she had left young Harry asleep and gone for a walk, or maybe to wash herself in the sea . . . they'd had sex. The killer tracked her and shot her. Maybe he killed Harry first, or maybe he went back and did it.'

'Probably the latter,' McIlhenney interjected. 'It must have taken him some time to dispose of the lad's body.'

'True,' McGuire conceded. 'Anyway, this time, we had something to go on. Zrinka's mother told us about an ex of hers, a man named Dominic Padstow. They'd had a thing until she'd dumped him. Straight away, this opened a lot of doors for us. We took the name to the Gavins and discovered that Padstow and Stacey had also had a relationship, post-Zrinka, serious enough for her to have painted him in the nude. We also found out that Zrinka and Stacey knew each other.'

Stallings frowned. 'The parents didn't mention this?'

'No. Doreen Gavin was deeply shocked by her kid's death, plus she's a bit unworldly at the best of times. As for her husband, it turned out that he'd been giving Zrinka one on the side, so he wasn't for volunteering much. To be fair, though, he might not even have known about Padstow. Whatever, our information on Zrinka led us to a third woman, a hairdresser called Amy Noone. She'd met Padstow, and couldn't stand him; she told us that Zrinka and Stacey fell out over him, and that eventually Stacey binned him too. We started looking for Padstow, and when we did, we discovered that he didn't exist; the name was a phoney.'

The head of CID sighed again, even more heavily. 'I've been kicking myself ever since. Neil was on leave, and Stevie was reporting to me. Amy was a key witness, the only person who could place him with both women. I should have given her protection, straight away, but I didn't, and she was killed too, shot dead in her flat and laid out in the same way as Stacey and Zrinka. The only difference was that she was naked.'

'Had she been sexually assaulted?'

'No. He wasn't into that, it seems.' McGuire paused. 'But this is more or less where you came into the story, Becky. We identified Padstow as a fairly seedy investigative journalist called Daniel Ballester, out to dig the dirt on the dealings of Davor Boras . . . and there was dirt in plenty. Then you and Stevie Steele traced him to a cottage in Wooler, in what's now called Northumbria, and Stevie went up there, alone. When he looked through a window, he saw Ballester, hanged by the neck from a light fitting. He charged in there, but the door was booby-trapped: end of Stevie.'

'Only it wasn't Ballester who rigged the door, was it?' McIlhenney growled grimly. 'The Borases knew where he was too, before we did, thanks to a very iffy security firm that Davor had on his payroll. Dražen went up there; he beat Stevie to it. He killed Ballester, made it look like a suicide, right down to a goodbye note on his computer confessing to the four murders, then he rigged the door, not to get Stevie but to eliminate the security guys his dad had sent up there: the only people who could put the two of them in the frame. It was meant to look like a last vicious killing by Ballester, one that could never be pinned on them.'

'Or so they thought,' said McGuire, 'until Bob Skinner got involved, and found a witness, and some DNA evidence that nailed Dražen fair and square. It did hand us Ballester as our multiple murderer, though. We found all the evidence we needed hidden around the cottage: the gun, personal effects from all three women, including a couple of Zrinka's paintings that had vanished from the scene of her death. It all went to prove that Daniel Ballester committed all four murders; we reported our findings, the case was written up by the procurator fiscal, and signed off, closed.'

Becky Stallings looked at him. 'And now?' she murmured.

'And now we've got a body in that wood, not as fresh as the others, but laid out in more or less the same way. Neil and I have going on for forty years' police service between us; I know he's as worried as I am that the pathologist is going to find a bullet in the back of that woman's head.'

McIlhenney nodded, firmly, in agreement.

The inspector took a breath. 'You're saying we've got a copycat killer on our hands.'

'That I am, Becky; that I am.'

Four

Maggie Rose Steele passed her daughter to her sister, and stood up from the sofa. 'I need to stretch,' she said, as she stood the baby's empty feeding bottle on the coffee-table. 'In fact, I need to exercise. My abdominal muscles are still weak from the surgery.'

'Margaret,' Bet reminded her unnecessarily, 'you're having chemotherapy; you're supposed to be taking it easy.'

Maggie raised her right hand and touched her head. Much of her hair had gone; that which was left felt rough under her fingers. 'I know,' she admitted. 'You don't have to lecture me. The drugs are holding me back anyway: I'm truly knackered.' She looked across the room, catching her reflection in a mirror. 'One thing I am going to do, though; I'm going to take the hospital up on its offer of a wig. My treatment nurse gave me a form today, and told me where to go for a fitting. Tomorrow morning I'm going to look out Stevie's grooming set and crop this lot right down with the clippers, then I'm off to the hair studio.'

Bet smiled. 'What colour do you fancy?'

Her sister made a face. 'I've always had a secret notion that I'd have liked to be a blonde, like you.'

'You know I fake it.'

'And a wig is real? Hell, I'll see what they've got. I don't imagine they'll have a colour chart.' She moved back to the sofa and sat down again.

'Margaret, go to bed,' Bet urged her.

'I'm okay, really. I seem to be getting used to the stuff they're pumping into my belly. I haven't been sick this time, nor even felt like it. Mr Ronald my consultant's chuffed with me, you know. I saw him today and he gave me a rave review.' She said it casually, but a tremor in her voice betrayed her.

'You didn't tell me that. What did he say?'

'He showed me the pictures they took at my scan the other day. The cancer's completely gone. They're going to complete the chemo, but he told me that my prognosis is entirely positive.' She reached out and touched baby Stephanie's wispy red hair. 'I've got this wee one to thank for it. If I hadn't been carrying her, the disease wouldn't have presented . . . his word . . . until it was much more advanced, and I'd have . . . I'd have had much less chance of survival.' She hesitated. 'He said something else too. I've been working up to telling you about it; that's why I didn't mention it earlier.'

'What?'

'He asked about you, what age you were and so on, whether you were married, had children, et cetera.'

'What the hell has that got to do with him?'

'Apparently we've always been high risk, Bet, you and me. It runs in the family.'

'So?'

'So he'd like you to go and see him. His inclination, that's how he put it, no stronger than that, is that you should maybe have your womb and ovaries removed as well, as a precaution.'

'Jesus, would they do that?'

'It's not uncommon, so he said.'

'Bloody hell. That would mean I couldn't have kids, Margaret.'

'Since when did you want kids? You don't even have a partner.'

'I'd be hollowed out inside.' She blurted out the words thoughtlessly, then bit her lip as she saw the look on her sister's face. 'Oh, God, I'm sorry. Me and my bloody mouth.'

'It's all right.' Maggie grinned, quickly, to put her at her ease. 'It doesn't feel like that, honest. It's not the end of the world. It's not as if they stitch your fanny up. You can't have kids, but you can still have sex, as normal.'

'Best of both worlds, eh?'

'I wouldn't say that.'

'No, maybe not,' said Bet, quietly. 'Do you think you will again?'

'What?'

'Have sex.'

Maggie wrinkled her nose. 'It won't bother me if I don't. I was never any good at it, apart from with Stevie. I did it because . . . well, we just did, didn't we?'

'I know what you mean. I had this bloke once, not so long ago, a real Aussie charmer. He told me I was the worst shag he'd ever had.'

'Bastard.'

'Yeah, he surely was. He said I was a walking advert for necrophilia.'

'Did you shoot him, stab him, or rip his balls off with red-hot pincers?'

'No, I told him that word had three more syllables than I'd ever heard him use before; then I told him to go and fuck himself, since I wasn't up to the job.'

Maggie began to laugh, then cut it off short as the baby stirred in Bet's arms. 'Good for you, Sis. But it just takes the right man, you know, even for ladies with our repressed background.'

'I can't imagine how much you must miss Stevie.'

'I hope you never know the feeling. But it's not for that I miss him most. It's for everything else. The companionship, the laughs, the . . . I don't even know how to say it. The way he made me feel. The peace he brought to me when we were alone together.' Her face set hard. 'And that's all gone; even in my dreams I can only see him dead. You know my big ambition, now that it looks as if I still have a life? I want to find the man who killed him. Oh, I know that Bob Skinner and Mario feel the same way, and they're in a far better position to do it than I am, but I want the personal satisfaction of finding him.'

21

'And what will you do when you have him?'

'Hand him over. Let him take what's coming, a life sentence with a high tariff. Then I'll think of him, every morning for the next thirty years, waking up in a locked room, with someone else holding the key. I'll think of him, a rich and powerful man, banged up like an animal. I'll think of him, growing old in there, waiting for the day when the gate is finally opened. And then, only then, when he steps back into the outside world, aged about sixty, free again to enjoy all the stuff that his wealth brings him . . . then I'll kill him.'

Five

'You're new, aren't you?' Lord Archibald asked.

'New to Edinburgh, sir, yes,' DI Stallings replied. 'Until recently I was with the Met.'

'I thought so. I'd be surprised if there's a senior officer in this city that I don't know.' He smiled, and his eyes twinkled. 'You chose to come here? You weren't banished to the north for some unspeakable offence?'

'My choice, sir.'

'*Cherchez l'homme?*'

'Partly,' she admitted, returning his smile, 'but if I hadn't liked the place when I got here, he'd have had to transfer south.'

'Does that imply that he is also a serving police officer?'

'Yes, it does. His name's Ray Wilding, detective sergeant. I expect you know him too.'

'Yes indeed,' the silver-haired judge replied. 'He's not one to forget. Last time I saw him in the witness box he was a detective constable. A very confident chap; in fact you'll forgive me if I call him a cocky beggar. He gave defence counsel such a ripping that I considered holding him in contempt.'

'That sounds like Ray.'

Stallings had found Lord Archibald in the clubhouse, seated in an upstairs lounge with a view of the first and eighteenth fairways. From what she had heard of Scottish Supreme Court judges, she had expected an austere firebrand; instead she had been greeted by a

23

friendly man of middle age, who might have been an early-retired banker or businessman.

'I bet you're wondering how a duffer like me could hit the ball so far off the tee, even if it wasn't exactly straight. It's this modern equipment,' he continued, forestalling her reply that the question had not crossed her mind, as she had never been on a golf course in her life before that morning. 'Metal drivers with great big bouncy heads. They've transformed the game with the extra distance they give you. Unfortunately, they also magnify your errors. We never used to bother about those damned trees, but that's the third time I've been in them this year.'

He paused, as the club steward arrived at their table with a coffee for Stallings. 'I almost carried on, you know, after I found my ball. I noticed the smell right away, of course; you couldn't miss it.'

'I know,' said the inspector. 'I've been up there.'

'Of course you have. My first reaction was the normal one: that it was an animal, that a dog or a cat had died in there. I was going to play on, and report it to the first green-keeper I saw . . . not that it's the club's responsibility: that land isn't ours . . . until it occurred to me that to smell that bad it had to be a pretty large creature, maybe something that had slipped out of the zoo over the hill. Then I remembered going to an exhumation once, when I was Lord Advocate, a body that had to be dug up for DNA testing. So I went in for a look.' He shuddered at the memory. 'Wish I hadn't. When I saw that it was indeed human, I confess that I bolted. A photograph in an evidence book, that's one thing; up close is another matter. What was it? Male or female?'

'It's the body of a woman.'

'Dead for how long?'

'More than a week; the autopsy will give us a more accurate time.'

'Post-mortem examination, Inspector,' he said, gently. 'We're traditionalists in Scotland . . . at least I am. The influence of Patricia Cornwell has not yet reached my court.'

'I'll bear that in mind, sir. Do you often see people on the path at the edge of the woods, Lord Archibald?'

'Not often. Used to be never, but since all this right-to-roam stuff came in, we get a few. I argued against it, you know, lobbied my successor in the Crown Office, but Aileen de Marco was handling the Bill and she won the day.' The eyes twinkled again. 'You won't report me to Bob Skinner, will you? I imagine that criticism of the First Minister is off limits now.'

'Politics are none of my business,' Stallings replied tactfully.

'Nor mine, constitutionally,' the judge murmured. 'But if I see a bad law being proposed, I'm going to try and stop it.'

The detective pressed on: 'Have you ever seen anyone on the path that you knew or recognised?'

'No.' The reply was immediate and unequivocal. 'I take that to mean that there's no identification on the body.'

'Correct.'

'Do you know how she was killed?'

'What makes you think she was, sir?'

Lord Archibald looked at her almost benevolently. 'My dear inspector,' he said, 'I was head of this country's criminal prosecution service for three and a half years. Before that I was in practice at the Bar for more than twenty years. I know a crime scene when I see one. People are not cats; they don't crawl away to die somewhere they're not going to be found. When they decide to end it all, they do it in bed or their favourite chair with a bottle of whisky and a handful of pills, or in the bath with a razor, or they go into the garage with the engine running. In my experience, suicides want their body to be found . . . unless they chuck themselves in the sea, and that isn't the case here. No, that poor woman was killed, and somebody put her there.'

Stallings's silence signalled her agreement.

'Good luck with your inquiry,' Lord Archibald exclaimed. 'But do one thing for me, if you can. When you apprehend the killer, persuade him, if you can, that a guilty plea would be in his interests, rather than going to trial. The last thing any judge wants is to find himself in the witness box; counsel on both sides would have an absolute field day.'

Stallings smiled. 'I'll do my utmost, my lord.'

'Good. Now can you answer the question I'm going to be asked by everyone I meet in this place? When can we have our golf course back?'

'That's one I'll need to pass up the line.'

'Oh, God!' Lord Archibald sighed, as she turned to leave. 'That means McGuire and McIlhenney, and neither of them are golfers!'

Six

'I'm goïng to need a list of members,' Neil McIlhenney told the golf club manager, a prickly little man who had introduced himself as Major Leo Fullbright as he entered the mobile police station that had been set up in the car park. 'We'll have to interview everyone to establish whether the woman was seen just before her death.'

'Am I obliged to provide that?'

'Is there any reason why you shouldn't?'

'Data Protection Act.'

'And general get-out excuse,' McIlhenney growled. 'Technically, Major, this isn't a criminal investigation, not yet. It's an inquiry into a suspicious death. However, I could argue in court that the general administration of justice exemption applies here. Do you want me to get a warrant from the court?'

'For my own protection,' the man smirked, 'as well as for the protection of the data.'

'This isn't funny, but if that's what you want, that's what you'll get. Of course, I can't proceed until I have it,' he paused as the door opened and Becky Stallings stepped into the van, 'and until I can proceed, this course stays closed.'

He looked over at the inspector. 'Did you see Lord Archibald?'

'Yes, I've just left him.'

'He's still here?'

'I think so. He hadn't finished his coffee.'

'In that case, I want you to get back in there and ask him if he'll put on his wig, metaphorically, and hear a formal application for authority to access the membership records of this club for the purpose of interviewing potential witnesses. You can tell him that the club manager's worried about his personal position.'

'I'm on my way.' She headed for the door.

'You can tell him also that once he gives me the authority I need, and once the forensic people are finished, I'll cordon off the area around the scene and the course can be reopened. If his lordship has any doubt about being able to hear our application, that should sway him.' He turned back to the club manager. 'All that should take about ten minutes, tops. I want those records here as soon as I have the judge's written order in my hand.'

'Very good.' Fullbright followed Stallings out of the office.

'Well, Jack,' said McIlhenney to McGurk as they left, 'how do you see our priorities?'

'Number one, identify the victim; no question about it.'

'Absolutely; we have to put a name to her soonest, so get on to Missing Persons, here and nationally. You were at the scene for longer than I was: can you set search parameters?'

'Dark hair, approximately five feet four, slim build; the doc estimated her age as mid-twenties.'

'We can't rely on that, given the state she was in. Ask for details of all women reported missing in the last month, aged between twenty and thirty-five.'

'The last month? She's been dead for a fortnight at most.'

'So maybe she was abducted, and reported missing before she died. Let's overlook nothing, Jack. If we don't find her listed we're in trouble. We're not going to have a photograph to publish, not without doing a facial reconstruction from her skull.'

'Can't we use dental records?'

'Not until we've got a name, or a list of names to match against them. We'll try that route, sure, and the national DNA database, but I don't fancy our chances.'

'Okay, boss. First off, I'll get on to Missing Persons.'

'Good. When you've done that, there's another area I want to explore. I hope to Christ I'm wrong, but if the pathologist does say, "murder," and we are looking at a copycat, what's the betting he's continuing to prey on artists?'

Seven

'I was expecting to see Gregor Broughton,' said Detective Superintendent McIlhenney, surprise written on his face as he stepped into the room.

'I'm sorry,' replied the dark-suited, bespectacled woman who sat behind the desk. 'He's away. I'm his assistant.' As she stood and extended a hand, he realised that they were almost eye to eye. 'Joanna Lock. You're the CID gaffer in the city, aren't you?'

He nodded, sighing inwardly; he had made the journey to the procurator fiscal's office in Chambers Street expecting to see Broughton himself, and he never appreciated wasted time, especially not in the early hours of an investigation. 'How far away is he?' he asked. 'If he's in court, I'll wait for him.'

'No, he's not. He's part of a liaison visit to our opposite numbers in the Catalan government; I'm filling in for him. Why did you want to see him?'

McIlhenney eased himself into a chair. 'I wanted to share something with him.'

'That's intriguing. What could that be?'

'The ton and a half of grief that I've just had dropped into my life; I didn't see why I should carry it all.'

The assistant fiscal frowned. 'Let me take some of the load. I was brought up in Drumchapel; I'm tougher than I look.'

'How long have you been here?'

'I moved through from Glasgow in April.'

'Are you familiar with the Zrinka Boras–Harry Paul murder inquiry?'

'Of course; and Amy Noone . . . and Stacey Gavin too. I wasn't here when that one happened, but I read it up. All four homicides officially attributed to the late Daniel Ballester, dead by his own hand in Wooler, Northumbria. I helped to draft the final report with Gregor.'

'What?' the detective exclaimed. 'Your submission said that Ballester killed himself?'

'Calm down, it didn't; that's just what I'm saying to you. It was absolutely factual; it said that the circumstances of his death were the subject of a coroner's inquest in England. That's not relevant anyway: all we cared about was that he was found with overwhelming evidence of his guilt. Are the cops in Northumbria now telling us that he wasn't a suicide?'

'It's pretty clear that the Northumbrian force isn't telling you anything, Ms Lock.'

'Joanna, please.'

'Joanna, then. The fact is, they're in possession of a report, based on some forensic work done in our lab, that indicates quite clearly that there was somebody else in Ballester's cottage at the time of his death.'

'Who?'

'That doesn't matter; as you said, it has nothing to do with your remit. Gregor knows about it. He wouldn't have signed off on your document if it hadn't been legally correct. If he hasn't chosen to share it with you . . . that's between the two of you. Forget all that; I asked if you were familiar with the cases, that's all.'

'And I am.' The assistant fiscal's tone had become curt.

'To hell with it.' McIlhenney sighed. 'I'll leave this until Gregor gets back.'

He was in the act of rising when Lock held up a hand. 'I'm sorry,' she said. 'Let's start again.'

The big detective relented; he sank back into his chair. 'Okay,' he continued. 'I asked the question because I've just come from a post-mortem on the body of a woman found dead this morning in woodland on the east side of Corstorphine Hill.' He took a photograph from his pocket and passed it across the desk. 'That's how she was found,' he said. 'Trust me, you don't want to see the close-ups. Anything strike you about it?'

Lock's eyes narrowed as she looked at the print. 'How long?' she murmured.

'Ten to twelve days, the pathologists reckon.'

'Cause of death?'

'Single shot to the back of the head from a small-calibre weapon.'

The lawyer leaned back in her absent boss's chair and stared at the ceiling. 'Oh, no,' she moaned. 'There's another of them.'

'It looks that way, doesn't it?'

Her eyes switched back to the detective. 'You don't think so?' she asked.

'Oh, yes, I do. We're agreed that Daniel Ballester was responsible for the other four murders. The confession contained in his suicide note on his lap-top was almost certainly faked, or he was forced to write it, but there was so much evidence in and around his house that it had to be him. The real clincher, though, were death photos of all the victims: they were found on the computer too.'

'What about the man you think killed him? Couldn't he have planted it all?'

'No,' McIlhenney replied firmly. 'We've checked that out. The man who did Ballester, and who set the trap that killed Detective Inspector Steele, couldn't have committed any of the four murders. When Stacey Gavin died he was in Taiwan, and when the other three were killed he was in Jamaica. We're pretty much certain of that.'

'So why did he kill Ballester?'

The detective superintendent smiled. 'There's an even better question than that, if you think about it.'

Lock gazed back at him, puzzled, then her forehead creased in concentration. 'How did he know to kill Ballester? I remember now:

your team didn't identify him until very late in the day. They were looking for him under another name. Are you saying that he was Ballester's accomplice, and that he did him in to protect himself?'

'No, I'm not. The guy didn't have any accomplice. The man who killed him had his own sources of information. His father had dealings with him before; as soon as he saw his image, he knew who he was, and put specialists on to tracing him.'

'You're talking about Zrinka's brother, aren't you?'

'Yes, and we can prove it. Forget him: let's address the things that are troubling me.'

'What are they?'

'For a start, the degree of similarity, and the speed with which this copycat's appeared. It took almost a century for the second Ripper to emerge. Ballester's last kill was less than three months ago.'

'They didn't have electronic media in the eighteen eighties.'

'No, nor police officers smart enough to keep the details of those murders from the press that did exist at the time. We did, though, or at least we held on to some of them; we released the cause of death, but we didn't say anything about the calibre of weapon used. Nobody ever described the way the three women were killed, or the way their bodies were laid out. Yet this new murder differs in only one respect, the fact that the body appears to have been concealed.'

'What do you know about the victim?'

'Nothing. We haven't linked her to any missing person yet. We don't know who she is.'

'So you don't know if she's an artist?'

'That goes without saying, doesn't it?'

'I suppose so, but if she is that would tie it up, wouldn't it?'

'Tie what up? In the Ballester investigation, we started off looking for a serial killer with a down on female artists, and wound up with a disillusioned hack who'd murdered two women with whom he'd had affairs and who'd dumped him, and who'd taken out two other people just because they were in the way. What have we got here? What's the motive? So far, all I can see is that we might have someone who's taking the piss!'

'Or someone who doesn't know what Ballester's real motive was, and who thinks he's carrying on his mission in some bizarre way.'

'That may well be so,' McIlhenney conceded. 'Meanwhile . . . and this is the real reason I wanted to see Gregor . . . I need something from you. I want you to identify everybody who could possibly have seen your report to the Crown Office. I'm doing the same thing at my end. It may all be a coincidence, but it looks to me as if this second killer might have had access to inside information.'

Eight

'That list of members looks pretty formidable,' said Becky Stallings. 'There must be a few hundred of them.'

'Yes,' DS McGurk agreed, 'but I can shrink it if I cross-reference it against playing records to identify those people who're known to have been on the course in the period when the woman was killed.'

'Do that, Jack, but I doubt if it'll be that simple. Sure, we might get lucky and find an eye-witness who saw the woman and her killer and can give us a description, but still, our first job is just to identify her. So we need to find out from the members, not just those who were on the course that day, whether she used that path regularly, and if she did, whether any of them knew who she was.'

'That's assuming she walked it at all. Maybe she was taken there at gun-point.'

'Across the golf course?'

'Through the woods: you can get in there from the other side of the hill, off Clermiston Road.'

'From what I've been told, they're pretty thick. They're also bounded by the zoo to the north. No, let's start with the premise that she went there of her own accord.'

'Regularly.'

'Why?'

The detective stretched his long body in his chair. 'As I see it, she either knew her killer, and he was with her, or he followed her. If he did that, my gut tells me that he didn't pick her at random. He was watching her, he got to know her movements, and he chose his moment. From what we've been told, Daniel Ballester was meticulous in his preparation for each kill. He caught his targets off-guard every time, with nobody else around. I'd say we assume that the mark-two version is doing the same.'

'Then let's get after him, and let's be meticulous ourselves. Prioritise if you want, but we need to interview all the members and staff as quickly as we can. Luckily we have telephone numbers for all of them, so we can do it that way. I want a dozen uniforms and a dozen phones, mobiles if necessary; give them each a batch of names and a question template.'

Stallings turned to look at a young officer seated at a desk behind her, a telephone held to his ear. She waited for him to finish. 'Sauce,' she said, when he had, 'how are you getting on with putting together that list of artists?'

'I'm getting there, ma'am,' Detective Constable Harold Haddock replied. 'I've contacted seven art galleries so far and built up a list of female painters on their books aged between twenty and thirty-five. So far I have eleven names.'

'Did you factor in hair colour, given that our victim's was jet black?'

'She was female. Who knows what colour it was the day before she died?'

'Are you cheeking me, son?'

'No, ma'am. I didn't think it was worth doing at this stage, that's all. I'll call them all back, if you want.'

Stallings grinned. 'Don't bother, Sauce; you're right. And don't mind me either. I'll jump to the defence of my gender at a moment's notice. Anything else to tell me?'

'Yes. I've spoken to Mrs Dell at High-end Talent; she was Zrinka Boras's agent. She has several other painters on her books; four of them are on my list, and she's seen three of those within the last week, so I can score them off. I'm also just off the phone with the principal's secretary up at the Edinburgh College of Art. She's going to put together a list of female painting graduates over the last ten years, plus current mature students in the age-group we're looking at, and email it to me. She made another suggestion, too.'

'What's that?'

'Schools. She said we shouldn't forget art teachers either. I explained that we were actually looking at working artists, but she said that many teachers supplement their income if they can.'

'What's the nearest school?' the inspector asked.

'The Royal High,' Haddock replied, 'on the other side of the Queensferry road.'

'No,' McGurk interposed, 'not quite. You're forgetting Mary Erskine.'

Stallings frowned. 'Who's she?'

'It: one of the oldest girls' schools in the world, one of three run by the Edinburgh Merchant Company. It's just across the road from the entrance to the golf club, not much more than a hundred yards away.'

'Would it have an art department?'

'Bound to have.'

'Okay.' Stallings turned back to Haddock. 'Sauce, close the gap. Ask the education authority for a list of all female art teachers within the age limit, then contact this Merchant Company thingie, and ask them for the same information.'

Nine

'Do you think I'm a hypocrite?'

She looked up at him, unable to contain her surprise. 'Do I what?' she gasped, spluttering as she failed to suppress her laughter.

'You heard. Do you think I'm a hypocrite?'

'And why the hell should I think that?'

Bob Skinner gazed at her.

A new Bob Skinner, she thought, yet again. He was sun-bronzed, and his blue eyes sparkled. He was ten years older than her, nearer fifty than forty, yet he seemed to have grown younger in the time they had been together. The network of care lines around his eyes had faded until they were barely noticeable. He was slimmer in the waist, thicker in the chest, and the tension that had emanated from him in waves a few months before had gone, replaced by an air of easy relaxation. She thought back to the man he had been in the depths of winter and marvelled at the change in him. And yet, for all that, he looked sombre.

His right hand lay on the restaurant table, his fingers toying with the stem of his wine glass, the big vein that ran down his bicep from beneath the sleeve of his short-sleeved shirt twitching with the movement. 'Because I do,' he murmured.

Aileen de Marco chuckled. 'You'll need to run that one past me again, love,' she said, in her soft Scots tone. 'You are a very complicated guy, sure, but strip all that away, and you're also the straightest, most honest man I've ever met. You've done some serious things in your life, but I'll bet you've never done anything that you didn't believe was right. You and hypocrisy don't belong in the same bed . . . unlike you and me,' she added. 'Knowing how you feel about the double standards of politics, there are still times when I wonder how you and I got together.'

He grinned. 'Fishing for them, are you? Aileen, my darling, you are the one politician I know who confounds all the stereotypes, and you're the only one I've ever admired, apart, maybe, from Bill Clinton and Barack Obama. You do not have a duplicitous bone in your body.'

'Well, if you have,' she retorted, 'I've never found it . . . and I've been over all the territory by now. Come on, where's this nonsense coming from?'

'That reminds me of a joke I heard in Canada at Easter,' he said, as he picked up his glass and drained the last of the Raimat Clamor, his regular choice from the wine list of Trattoria La Clota. 'There's this Saskatchewan girl, on a plane out of Toronto, sat next to a power-dressed big-city woman. Once they've taken off, the Saskatchewan girl, being friendly and all, says to her neighbour, "Where you from?" The power lady replies, "From a place where they know not to end a sentence with a preposition." The Saskatchewan girl thinks about this for a few seconds and then she says, as friendly as before, "Where you from, bitch?" '

Aileen's laugh caused the heads of the couple at the next table to turn in their direction. She waited until they had returned to their own conversation, then moved closer to him. 'Very funny,' she murmured, 'but now you've come out with that bolt from the blue, don't think you can kick my question under the table. Explain yourself, Deputy Chief Constable Skinner. That's an order from the First Minister.'

'Hey,' he exclaimed. 'We've been through that one. The First Minister can't give coppers direct orders.' He paused. 'On the other hand, my partner . . . I suppose that's a different story.'

She blinked. 'You've never called me that before.'

'You don't like the term?'

'No. I mean, yes. I mean, I've got nothing against it.' Her eyes met his. 'Sounds more official than girlfriend; more dignified, too, more suited to our age and station.'

'Wouldn't you prefer "wife"?' he asked her.

They looked at each other for a long, lingering moment, locked in the kind of silence that brooks no interruption. John, the proprietor, read the sign, and his move towards their table was aborted in mid-stride. 'Was that a proposal?' Aileen whispered eventually.

'I suppose it was. Not the most gracious one I've ever made, I'm afraid. I'm sorry, it wasn't planned. It just slipped out.'

'Then slip it back in again,' she said. 'I am very happy as we are, love. We've been together for little over half a year: there's no need to rush fences. Let's just enjoy being together and let things take their course.'

'I'll take that as a "no", then.'

'Take it as a "not yet". Take it as a "maybe". Take it as "You're the man I love, we're a couple, and that's all I've ever hoped for." Besides, you're still coming down off your sabbatical. Wait till you get back to work; you'll be too busy to think about things like that.'

'You're supposed to be pro-marriage,' he challenged, smiling broadly as if to reassure her that he had not been wounded by her rejection. 'Isn't that the party line?'

'The party line is toleration of all sorts of permanent relationships: formal, informal, straight, gay . . .'

'Sheep, chickens . . . ?'

Her giggle was girlish, unlike her; in that instant he felt privileged, knowing that he was seeing her as no-one else ever did. 'We're not that modern,' she replied.

'So are you saying that I'd be a high-risk husband?'

'No!' she protested. 'I wasn't saying that at all.'

'If you were, you'd be right. Look at my track record. On that evidence, I'm terrible at husbanding. That's where I fear my hypocrisy lies.'

'Explain.'

Bob leaned forward, until they were only a matter of inches apart. They were sitting at right angles to each other at the small square table so that each could have a view across L'Escala's moonlit marina. The night was hot and the air was heavy; he swatted a buzzing fly away from his face as he gazed at the throng of boats, side by side on their moorings.

'I've been married twice,' he began. 'If I say that Myra, my first wife, played around, I'd be understating things. She was international class, as I discovered years after her death. Yet in truth, even if I'd known the whole story, everything, as it was happening, I'd have forgiven her. Why? Because I worshipped the damn ground she walked on, that's why. There was one blip, when we were engaged and very young, but I was faithful to her all through our marriage and, in truth, for quite a while after she was dead. I was never there for her, though: I was too busy career-building. Don't let anyone tell you that success came my way by accident. I had my eyes fixed on command rank from the day I joined the force, and I worked my arse off getting there. Myra suffered for it, Alex suffered . . .'

'That's not what she says.'

'Uh?' The trademark eyebrow rose.

'Your daughter told me that you were the best single parent she's ever encountered. She says that she never once felt excluded, or starved of your time and your love, and she never once felt that she was any sort of a burden to you.'

'Alex is loyal.'

'Alexis Skinner is a straight-shooter, just like her dad.'

'When did she tell you this?'

'About three months ago, one day we had lunch together.'

'You and my kid do lunches? I never knew that.'

'As often as we can. I didn't bring the subject up either, she did. She said that I shouldn't be surprised to find you missing the kids while they're with their mother in America, even though they're with you all the rest of the year. She said that's the kind of dad you are. So Alex didn't suffer at all; that's not a stick for your back. As for Myra, from what you've told me, and from what Alex has let slip, she was a danger junkie.'

'That's true,' Bob conceded, 'but it's beside the point. If I'd known I'd have lived with it.'

'If you'd known, you'd probably have scared off any potential partners. No, delete "probably".'

He let out a wry snort. 'You'd be amazed at the courage that a hard-on can give a normally timid bloke.'

She laughed. 'No, I wouldn't, but there's courage and then there's a death-wish.'

'Be that as it may, I'd still have stuck with her; I chose her over Louise Bankier, for Christ's sake.'

'What? Neil McIlhenney's wife?'

'Yes, but long, long ago. Lou was my blip, at university. It taught me that Myra and I were joined at the heart. From that point on, I never contemplated life without her.'

He shook his head. 'I should never have married Sarah, though. I never treated her as I did Myra; I never even thought of her that way. I drove the wedge between us; when she had her flings, I should have been able to live through them too, but I couldn't. Not that I was the only wronged half of that marriage. I've told you, I strayed a couple of times too, once very indiscreetly. That must have humiliated her when it all got out, yet, do you know, I don't recall ever telling her that I was sorry? No, Aileen, I should never have married her . . . and here I am having the bloody nerve to threaten you with the same. I apologise, that was hugely presumptuous of me. No, it was downright bloody cruel!'

He paused, but only for a second or so. 'Now do you see why I feel like a hypocrite? The way I treated Sarah, it was unforgivable.'

Aileen put a hand on his. 'Can I stop you there, just for a moment? The way I understand it, again from Alex, because I promise I haven't been checking up on you, there was someone in Sarah's student life too, someone she was in love with. For whatever reason, they broke up, and then, years later, they met up again in America, and she found that maybe she still was. But then he died.'

'Yes,' he agreed, 'that pretty much sums it up. But through it all, I showed her no understanding, I showed her no compassion. I wouldn't even let her go to his funeral. Do you see what I'm saying now?'

'I understand it, but I don't agree with your self-analysis. If you really want to know, I'd say that there was a lack of compassion on both sides. Maybe the two of you shouldn't have married, but that's not how you saw it at the time, and you've got three fine kids to show that there was some purpose to it.' She drew his eyes to hers once more. 'Now, do you feel better for getting all that off your chest, DCC Skinner?'

'I suppose so.'

'In that case, will you please promise that you'll stop beating yourself over the head with it?'

He grinned, reproved. 'I'll do my best. But you do see what a lousy risk I am, don't you?'

Aileen's expression grew serious. 'Why do you love me?' she asked. 'I warn you, though, if you say it's because I remind you of Myra, I'll knock you backwards out of that chair, big and all as you are.'

'I believe you. It won't stop me saying, though, that there's a facial resemblance, in profile, no more. But that's not the answer. I love you because you're different, you're special, beautiful, all that stuff. And there's more: I love what's on the inside, your goodness, your commitment, your courage. And here's the clincher: every time I've been with a woman since Myra died, she's been there with us. But not with you: when we're together we're unaccompanied. There's nobody else in the room, or in the bed. You haven't made me forget her, but with you, I'm finally able to put her behind me, and get on with the rest of my life. How's that?'

'It's what I wanted to hear.'

'I don't scare you?'

43

She showed him a mock frown. 'I don't scare; when I have to I scare other people. And that's just one of the many qualities that you and I have in common. You do know we could take over the world if we wanted, don't you?'

'Yeah. Just as well we're happy with what we've got. You are happy, aren't you?' he asked her earnestly. 'This isn't just an interlude, is it?'

'No, my big awkward love, it's for keeps, I promise. You may think you're hard to handle, but you're in the process of learning otherwise.'

'In that case,' he murmured, 'let's ask John for *la cuenta* and get out of here. It may be time for my next lesson. Going back to something I said earlier, suddenly I'm feeling tremendously courageous.'

Ten

'What have we got?' asked Becky Stallings, as she draped her light jacket over the back of a chair in the mobile police station. The clock showed twenty-five minutes after eight a.m., but even that early in the day the confined space was stuffy, with the promise of more to come as the temperature neared the forecast high seventies. 'Has the team finished calling the members?'

'They've gone as far as they can go,' McGurk told her. 'Just under twenty per cent of them were no-response, as you would expect at this time of year. In a couple of weeks it would have been nearer fifty per cent.'

'I thought this was the Edinburgh holiday fortnight.'

'Yes, it's the Trades, but that's mostly manual workers; builders and the like. The professionals tend to take theirs later; as you'll have noticed, this isn't exactly an artisan golf club.'

'If Lord Archibald's typical, I see what you mean.'

'Hey,' McGurk exclaimed, 'don't let his title fool you. He doesn't come from one of the legal families; he came up the hard way. My old boss, Dan Pringle, told me that in his first year as an advocate, when he was making his name and had little or no money coming in, he wasn't too proud to do the odd shift behind the other sort of bar.'

'They should make that compulsory for judges . . . at least for some of the English ones I've appeared before. They have no idea about the lives of ordinary people.' She drew a breath. 'I don't suppose the call-round turned up anything?'

'Surprise, it did. There's a group of four retired members who play a couple of times a week, in the afternoon, when it tends to be quiet. Three of them said that they'd seen a dark-haired woman using that path.'

'Regularly?'

'More than once, anyway. One of them told the officer who interviewed him that she annoyed them by not standing still while they were playing.'

'Do you reckon that's grounds for murder?'

'I've known flimsier,' Haddock muttered, in the corner.

'When they saw her, in what direction was she heading?'

'Always south; that's from the green to the tee,' said McGurk.

'The green's where the flag is?'

'I see you're learning the game, ma'am.'

Stallings laughed lightly. 'I'll leave it to you boys.'

'Don't count me among them,' the sergeant advised her. 'I'm too tall. They don't make clubs for people who are six feet eight.'

She turned to Haddock. 'How about you, Sauce?'

The young DC nodded. 'I play at Newbattle.'

'Are you any good?'

'Mmm,' he mumbled.

'What does that mean?' said McGurk. 'What's your handicap? Twenty-eight?'

'Actually, it's two, Sarge. By the way, it wouldn't be difficult to get clubs to suit your size. I'm sure if you asked the pro here he'd fix you up.'

'But before then . . .' Stallings interrupted.

'Yes, ma'am.' Haddock seemed to come to attention in his chair. 'I spent all yesterday evening working through my list of artists and art teachers, checking them all out. I've eliminated most of them, but there are four I still haven't been able to contact by phone. Their names are Maeve O'Farrell, Ghita Patel, Josie Smout and Sugar Dean.'

46

'Sugar?'

'That's the name I was given by the secretary of the Merchant Company. She's on the art staff at the Mary Erskine school.'

'I reckon you can take Ghita Patel off the list,' McGurk told him. 'The dead woman wasn't Asian.'

'Do we have addresses for the other three?' Stallings asked.

'Yes. O'Farrell stays in North Berwick, Smout's in Pennywell Medway, and Sugar Dean lives in Meriadoc Crescent.'

'Where?' The sergeant's voice was suddenly sharp.

'Meriadoc Crescent, number eight.'

'That's just on the other side of the hill.'

Haddock was out of his chair in a flash. 'I'll get round there.'

'I'm coming with you,' said Stallings. She led the way out of the office. 'My car.'

'You know the way there, ma'am?' The inspector stared at him. 'I'm sorry,' he stammered. 'It's just that, you being new to the city . . .'

'Ever heard of satellite navigation, Sauce?'

She programmed the address into her TomTom, and let its voice guide her out of the car park, and down towards Queensferry Road, then left on to Clermiston Road. Less than five minutes later she drew up outside number eight Meriadoc Crescent, a semi-detached bungalow that stood on a steep incline. As the two detectives stepped out into the quiet street, they saw, between two houses on the crest of the hill, a lane that seemed to lead straight into the woods.

Stallings was frowning as she walked up the path to the front door of number eight, and pressed the buzzer. She waited for thirty seconds, then pressed it again. 'Bugger,' she swore quietly.

'Excuse me.'

The voice came from the doorway of number six, the other half of the semi. It belonged to a lady of mature years, and fixed habits; even at ten to nine she was dressed for the day, in tweed skirt and cardigan. Her grey hair showed all the signs of being regularly permed. She gazed at them severely. 'Are you looking for the Deans?' She barked on without waiting for a reply: 'You won't find them in, you know. They're on holiday, up at their cottage in Appin.'

'Actually,' said the inspector, firmly, to break her flow, 'we're looking for Miss Dean.'

'Sugar?' Her forehead seemed to acquire an extra ridge. 'And you are?'

'We're police officers, Mrs . . .'

'Holmes.' No forename was offered. 'Police officers, indeed.' She stopped short of a sniff of disapproval, but favoured them with a look of distaste. 'We're not used to having police at the doors in this street. What's Sugar been up to?'

'Nothing at all. We simply want to establish her whereabouts.'

'Well, she's not here,' Mrs Holmes snapped, as if she was anxious to move them on before other residents observed the encounter.

'Could she be with her parents?'

'She might be. More likely off with that boyfriend of hers.' The woman's lips pursed. 'She's asking for trouble, that lass: the lad's barely out of short trousers, and her a teacher too. I thought there were laws against that sort of thing.'

'There might be,' said Haddock. 'What age is he?'

'He can't be any more than eighteen. He's only left school last month.'

'It's all legal and above board in that case,' the DC told her cheerfully. She replied with a glare that reminded him of the Sunday when his Free Presbyterian grandmother caught him listening to Radio Forth.

'But she does live with her parents?' asked Stallings, distracting her from her prey.

'Yes, she does. She moved back in with them last year when she got the job at Mary Erskine. I must say, it surprised me that she was taken on there. My granddaughter's at George Watson's; they don't have types like her there.'

'Can you describe Sugar for us, Mrs Holmes? We've never met her.'

'Describe her? There's her hair, for a start, pure black; I'm sure she dyes it. She's a pretty girl, I suppose, but the way she dresses, the mini-skirts these girls wear nowadays . . .'

'She wears a mini-skirt to work?'

'Oh, no. She wouldn't get away with that at Mary Erskine.'

'Do you know how she goes to work? Does she drive?'

'In the winter John, her dad, takes her. But in the summer, I think she's been walking. I've seen her going up the lane there in the morning, and coming back in the evening.' In that moment, Mrs Holmes's expression began to change; her eyes went somewhere else for a few seconds, then focused again on Stallings. 'There was a body found yesterday, wasn't there?' she said, in a different, softer voice. 'You don't think that was Sugar, do you?'

'We don't think anything at the moment,' the inspector replied. 'Right now, we're trying to identify her, which is why we need to establish where Sugar is, and that she's all right. Do you have a telephone number for Mr and Mrs Dean's cottage? Or an address, even?'

'I've got both. Just you wait there a minute.' She turned and went back indoors.

As they stood on the path, Stallings looked up at Haddock. 'Bloody hell, Sauce,' she murmured. 'I fear, I really do . . .'

'Me too, ma'am.'

'Here you are!' Mrs Holmes re-emerged, brandishing a slip of paper. She made her way across a small lawn to the low wall that divided the two properties and reached out to hand it across. Haddock stretched a long arm and took it from her.

'Thanks, Mrs Holmes,' said Stallings. 'I'm sure she'll be up there with them, but we need to make sure.'

'Let's hope so.' It was as if she had become a different woman. 'The poor lass. She's not that bad, you know. She's always got a cheerful smile about her, at least.'

'When did you see her last? Can you remember?'

'Just before the schools broke up; in fact, it was that very day, yes, the Friday before last. She was heading up the hill to the lane, as usual.'

Eleven

There were occasions when Mario McGuire regretted not having chosen the other career paths that had been open to him, not only as a youth but through most of his adult life. His mother had been of Italian stock, the daughter of one of Edinburgh's most successful businessmen, and he had been the only boy among three grand-children.

Before diversifying into the delicatessen and importing business, his grandfather's fortune had been built up through a chain of fish-and-chip shops. His mother's attitude to the young Mario's career choice may have been coloured by her own childhood memories of the smell of cooking fat, as she had fought a protracted battle with her father over her son's future.

In the event, Papa Viareggio had died when Mario was sixteen, and the running of the business had passed to his uncle, Beppe, who had no desire to take a young *protégé* on board, especially as he had the ambition that at least one of his daughters would join him.

That did not mean that all opportunity had been ripped from the teenager's grasp. His father, big Eamon McGuire, had been a modestly successful building contractor, while his mother, Christina, had set up a recruitment consultancy, and had shown her Viareggio genes by building it into one of the most successful in Edinburgh. Neither parent had put any pressure on him to join them, but each had made the offer.

There were two photographs on the head of CID's desk. One was of Paula, the silver-haired cousin he had loved for years; they had been inseparable as children, and had come to realise, eventually, in the wake of the collapse of Mario's marriage to Maggie Rose, that there was no reason, legal or moral, why they should be separated as adults either. He smiled as he looked at her image, and blew it a kiss.

The other frame enclosed his parents. He reached out and picked it up; the picture had been taken at a wedding, when they were both in their mid-forties, his mother slim, dark and beautiful, his father massive and unforgettable in a white dinner jacket. They had both gone from his life, although Christina was not too far away, having sold her business a few years before and retired to Italy. Eamon, though, had gone on a longer journey, having died of cancer in his early fifties. Mario tried not to think about him too often although, in fact, a day never passed when he did not. He had loved his father, and had looked forward to his companionship well into his own middle age. He was a big man in every respect, with a personality to match his physique. While he had more or less grown up on building sites and, they said, was not a man to cross in business, he had left that side of his life behind him the moment he had taken off his work boots. His son, grown hard as nails himself, regarded him, and always would, as the gentlest man he had ever known. More than ten years after his death his memory could bring a lump to his throat.

He replaced the frame and turned to the item at the top of the pile in his in-tray, the final paperwork covering the transfer of Becky Stallings from the Met, sent up by Human Resources. He was about to pick it up when there was a soft knock on his office door. He looked up, expecting it to open, but nothing happened. After a few seconds, the knock was repeated.

'Come in,' he called out.

The door opened and a strikingly blonde woman stepped into the room. She wore baggy red denims and a T-shirt with a big rocking-horse symbol on the chest. She carried a bag, slung over her shoulder.

'Yes,' he began, frowning, 'what can I do . . .' and then he saw the smile spread slowly across her face. 'Maggie, for fuck's sake!'

'How long were we married?' she exclaimed, as she took a seat. 'How many years was it? You used to say you could recognise me in the dark. Now all I have to do is put on a blonde wig and I could be just another young detective constable making a nuisance of herself.'

'And a very nice blonde wig it is. When did you decide to go for it?'

'Yesterday, not long after Mr Ronald finally put his reputation on the line by telling me that I'm not going to die any time soon.' She reached up and touched her new coiffure. 'Not bad, is it? I thought I'd have to be measured for it, and have to wait for a while before it was ready, but no, they fixed me up right there and then; this is an Irish jig straight off the peg. I went in there virtually baldy, and came out a foxy blonde babe.'

'You'll be beating the men off with a club.'

'Damn right I will,' she agreed, 'if any of them are insensitive enough to come near me. Neil said I can expect that.'

'He's been to see you?'

'Yes. He called in last night, with a present for the baby and flowers for me. I asked him what it's like being a widow. It's something I haven't considered until now. I've been fully focused on staying alive. He told me that people will be falling over themselves to be kind to me, and that if quite a few of them are men, I shouldn't be surprised.'

'Don't be offended either. Maybe I didn't tell you this as often as I should have, but you're a very attractive woman.'

'Maybe I didn't need you to tell me,' she said archly. 'But you can add another adjective: a very attractive, menopausal woman.'

'Menopausal? But you're still well shy of forty.'

'That matters not: I've stopped ovulating, on account of having no ovaries any more. I've had my first hot flush already.'

'What can you do about it?'

'Grin and bear it. After what's happened to me, do you think I care?'

Mario shook his head solemnly. 'No, love, I don't suppose you do.'
He looked across the desk. 'Want a coffee?' he asked.

'No, thanks.' She delved into her bag and produced a bottle of
water. 'I'll stick to this; I have to drink plenty just now, with the chemo.'

'How did you get here? You're not cleared to drive yet, are you?'

'Not quite; I'll give that another week or so. No, I came by taxi; a
real one this time. I've been taking Bob Skinner and Brian Mackie up
on their offer of using police transport, but I caught a cab from the hair
studio along here.'

'It's good to see you out and about again.'

'After thinking you never would?' A look in his eyes told her that she
had hit the mark. 'It's okay,' she said. 'There were moments when I
thought the same, more than a few of them.' She drank some of her
water, straight from the bottle. 'Mario, can I ask you something?'

'Of course. What?'

'Remember at my going-away do, when I went on maternity leave,
when I shocked the world by saying that I wouldn't be coming back to
the job?'

He chuckled softly. 'Who will ever forget it?'

'In that case, do you think that I would have any credibility among
my colleagues if I went back on my word, once I'm ready?'

Mario leaned back in his chair and gazed at her. 'Mags,' he
murmured, 'I don't remember you ever asking a stupid question, until
now. I can't think of a senior officer who doesn't expect you to do just
that. When you do, you'll be welcomed back with open arms. We all
miss you like hell.'

'I might put Mary Chambers's nose out of joint. She probably
expects to succeed me permanently, on promotion.'

'Mary's not so petty. Besides, I wouldn't let that happen; I wasn't best
pleased when she was moved out of CID, but in the circumstances I
couldn't say so. I was promised a period of stability, but with
Mackenzie crashing and burning and Mary being moved into your
job, my divisional commanders are going down like ninepins.'

'Mackenzie? How is the Bandit?'

'We don't call him that any more. He wants to put those flash Harry days behind him. He's Chief Inspector David Mackenzie now, back in uniform as staff officer in the command corridor.'

'Does that mean that Jack McGurk's staying at Torphichen Place?'

'Yes, with DI Stallings, our new arrival from the Met.'

'You've put her in there?'

He raised his eyebrows. 'I could hardly send her to the Leith office, since she's shagging Ray Wilding.'

'What?'

'He was part of the reason for her move, probably the main reason.'

'God, I really am out of the loop! All this office gossip I've been missing out on. I've got to get back.'

'Yes, but not before you're ready.'

She held up a hand. 'I know, I know: it'll be a few months yet. But still . . .' She frowned. 'Mario,' she continued, in an untypically tentative voice, 'if I called on everything we've been to each other over the years, would you do me a favour?'

He stared back at her, wondering what was to come. 'Jesus, when you put it like that it must be a big one. Spit it out.'

'Okay. It has to do with Dražen Boras, the man who killed Stevie.'

'What about the bastard?'

'He's still on the run, isn't he?'

Mario nodded. 'I'm afraid so,' he admitted. 'By the time the boss and I tied him to it, and the Met went to pick him up, he was gone. He and his Bosnian father were mixed up in some serious Balkan stuff, running people in there for the CIA, and for us. He has contacts in the States and we're pretty sure he used them to help him disappear.'

'I'd like to try and find him.'

He sat bolt upright. 'You'd what?'

'I mean it. I'd like to run a wee private-enterprise search for him. I don't mean physically; I know I'm tied down for a while. But, as you'll imagine, I've spent a lot of time thinking about Mr Boras. That's not good for me: it makes me obsessive. So I need to do something proactive.'

'Such as?'

'I don't actually know. For openers, I'd like to see the file you have on him, the one that you and Bob Skinner put together, and I'd like to know everything that Bob found out about him in London.'

'I don't have that: it's not on paper. It came from MI5. I've just given you the outline.'

'Okay, I'll talk to him.'

'But what are you going to do with this information?'

'I told you, I don't know yet. I just want to read it, to think about it, and to see if I can come up with any ideas about where he might be. Even if I can't, I'll feel better for having tried.'

'Mags, you realise that this isn't even our thing, don't you? He didn't commit any crime on our patch.'

A look of real pain settled on her face. 'It may not be "our thing", as you put it,' she said slowly, 'but it sure as hell is mine. It was my husband he killed: that gives me jurisdiction.'

'Okay.'

Her eyes brightened. 'You'll do it?'

'I'll do what I can. That means I'll give you a copy of the report the boss and I handed over to Les Cairns in Northumberland; I don't have anything else for you to go on. Yes, you should talk to the DCC and see what he's prepared to tell you. I'll give you his phone number out in L'Escala. Promise me one thing, though, Mags.'

'Maybe.'

'If he tells you to drop it, you'll do just that.'

Her smile returned. 'Yes,' she said, 'I'll promise you that. Because I don't think there's a chance he'll try to stop me. You know Bob Skinner; you know how he'll feel about Dražen Boras getting away with killing one of his people. I bet you he gives me all the help he can.'

Twelve

'I'm sorry about the hour, Mrs Brown,' said Becky Stallings.

A volley sounded in her ear.

'Yes, I appreciate that it's only half past four in Boston.'

The voice on the line did not sound mollified.

'Yes, I know you're on holiday and, no, I'm not a market researcher. I'm a police officer.' Pause. 'Yes, I said police officer, Detective Inspector Stallings, from Edinburgh. First of all, can you confirm that I am speaking with Mrs Grace Brown, the principal of Mary Erskine School? ... I am. Good. I was given this number by your school administrator, but you can't be too careful.'

'I suppose not,' the drowsy voice replied. 'Now that you have interrupted my sleep, what can I do for you? Has there been an incident at the school?' A note of concern crept in. 'Has something happened to one of the kids?'

'No, to both questions,' Stallings told her. 'I want to talk to you about one of your teachers, Miss Dean. I believe she's in your art department.'

'Sugar? Yes, that's right. What's up?'

'When did you see her last?'

'The day before school broke up. That would make it the Thursday before last. I remember that, because she didn't turn up on the Friday. Our last morning assembly of the session is a big event. All the staff are expected to be there, but Sugar wasn't. I asked her department head whether she had called in, and he said that she hadn't. I meant to call her myself, to see if she was sick, but the day got filled up, and it slipped my mind.'

'Did she have any history of absenteeism?'

'No, not at all. She was an exemplary staff member, but having been brought up in a teaching household, you'd expect that. Now, why have you woken me up to ask me this?'

'Because the body of a young woman was found yesterday morning, in woods near Murrayfield golf course.'

Stallings heard a gasp. 'Sugar?'

'We don't know. But the body had been there for some time; it would be consistent with the date you're talking about.'

'The school will give you a photograph; we have one on file.'

'That won't be enough, Mrs Brown.'

'Oh, God!'

'Let's not jump to conclusions,' said Stallings. 'At the moment we're trying to contact Miss Dean's parents in the hope that she's with them.'

'She won't be,' the woman told her. 'Sugar was planning to go to the South of France to paint. She told me that she had rented an apartment in a place called Collioure.'

'Was she going alone?'

'She didn't tell me, but I suspect not.'

'Why?'

'She was friendly with a young man; she called him her apprentice. He was a pupil at our companion school Stewart's-Melville. I use the past tense because he left at the end of term.'

'She was in a relationship with a pupil? Is that allowed?'

'Of course not, but it wasn't regarded as a relationship. The boy is a very promising painter, and Sugar was giving him spare-time tuition, with the full knowledge of his parents and with my approval. However, I did hear that they were seeing a lot of each other.'

'Did you do anything about it?'

'I had a gentle word with her. She wasn't upset. She told me, "Mrs

Brown, I promise you that I'm not breaking any rules with Davis, nor will I." Those were her very words.'

'Davis?'

'Davis Colledge, with a "d". That's his name. Very good-looking young man; and he didn't have a girlfriend, hence the gossip.'

'If it was only gossip, what makes you think they were planning to go off together?'

'The way that she said it. I may be wrong but I took her to be implying that once he was no longer a pupil . . .'

'There would be no rules to break?'

'Exactly.'

'Where can we find this young man?'

'You don't think he'd anything to . . .'

Stallings cut her off. 'Until we identify the dead woman I'm not thinking anything, but if it is Sugar, we're going to need to speak to him.'

'In that case, you'll have to contact the school, either directly or through the Merchant Company. I believe that Davis was a boarder.'

'They do that?'

'Of course, Inspector; so do we. We have a mix of day pupils and boarders.'

'I see. Thank you, Mrs Brown. That's all I need to ask you. Again, I'm sorry to have disturbed your holiday. I'll let you get back to sleep now.'

'Fat chance. Look, Inspector, you will let me know, won't you, one way or another, once you identify this poor woman?'

'Yes, I promise. 'Bye for now.' She hung up and turned to Jack McGurk. We need an address,' she told him. 'Lad named Davis Colledge . . . with a "d". Until the week before last he was a pupil at Mary Erskine's partner school.'

'I'm on to it,' the sergeant replied.

She turned to Haddock; he was standing solemnly by her desk, as if he had been waiting for her to finish. 'Sauce?'

59

'I've just spoken to John Dean, Sugar's dad. He and his wife were at the shops when I called earlier; that's why there was no reply. His understanding is that Sugar's in France. In a place called . . .'

'Collioure?'

'That's it, ma'am.'

'When did they see her last?'

'The last day of term, when she left to walk to work. He and Mrs Dean are both primary-school teachers; he's a headmaster. They both finished at lunchtime that day, and headed straight up to Appin. As they understood it, Sugar was flying to Perpignan next morning.'

'But they haven't heard from her since?'

'No.'

She looked at him. 'Did you tell him why you were calling?'

'I had to. He didn't buy "routine enquiries" for a second. He and his wife are heading home straight away.'

'Okay, Sauce, that's well done. Breaking news like that is tough for me, and I'm longer in the tooth than you are.'

'There's something else, ma'am. Once we had got past that I asked him if there was anything in Sugar's medical record that would help us eliminate her. He said she had her appendix out when she was ten, and broke her left arm falling off her bike when she was fifteen.' The young detective constable frowned. 'I've just checked the post-mortem report. It's her, no doubt about it.'

Thirteen

'Let me ask you again,' said Bob Skinner. 'Are you absolutely sure about this?'

'Yes, I am. I don't expect to achieve anything, apart from the comfort of knowing I made the effort, but I feel that I have to do it.'

'Maggie, my dear, you're on sick leave, maternity leave and compassionate leave all at the same time. It would be against justifiably established police practice for me to let you do this.'

'Yes, it would, wouldn't it?' They were a thousand miles apart, yet he could see her smile as she spoke.

'Ah, to hell with it,' he exclaimed. 'Go for it. Mario's already called me to let me know, and I think to seek my approval after the event. The report we put together was typed up by a Special Branch secretary; that's how confidential it is. But I've agreed with his rash promise to give you a copy.'

'Thanks, boss.' There was a moment's silence on the line. 'Mario said there was other information, stuff that only you have.'

'There is,' said Skinner, 'but I'm not going to give you it over an insecure telephone line. If you think you need it, I'll visit you when I get back, although I'm not sure that any of it will be any good to you.'

'In that case, I'll start with the report, and see what I can glean from that.'

'You do that.' He paused. 'Let's be professional about this, Maggie, rather than just plain personal. What are you bringing to this investigation . . . apart from your obvious motivation, that is?'

61

'A fresh eye. I won't say objectivity, but I've held high rank in CID, so I should know what I'm doing.'

'And that's why I'm giving you the go-ahead, albeit on one condition.'

'What's that?'

'That should you find it becoming too much for you to handle, emotionally or physically, you hold your hand up at the very first moment it does and tell me. I'll pick up whatever progress you've made and take it on from there myself. Deal?'

'Deal.'

'Good. Now, I've been thinking as we've been speaking. If you're going to do this, you'd better have official status. Your study, as we'll call it, will be part of the internal investigation into Stevie's death, and for its purpose, you are temporarily attached to Special Branch. You won't use its office, and you won't get in the SB commander's way, but if at any time you need access to sensitive information, you can use the clout that department gives you.'

'Thanks, sir. I appreciate the leverage, even though I don't imagine I'll use it.'

'Don't be so sure. If you make any progress, I reckon you will. All the best now, I'll see you when you get back. Oh, and one other thing, Chief Superintendent Steele. I can't begin to tell you how pleased I am that you've changed your mind about leaving the force. It can't afford to lose you.'

As he hung up, Aileen came into the room. 'Who was that?' she asked.

'That? I reckon it was the awakening of a sleeping tigress. Maggie Rose Steele is on the prowl, on the scent of Dražen Boras.'

'Judging by the look on your face that's good, but is she up to it yet?'

'It's probably the best therapy she could have,' said Bob. 'I've told Mario to monitor her closely, but I'm sure she'll be fine. Who knows? Maggie being Maggie, she might even get a result.'

Fourteen

'Do you want to make this call, ma'am?' asked Detective Constable Haddock. 'I've finally traced Davis Colledge's family, through the office at the Merchant Company. I thought there was something familiar about the name. His father's a Member of Parliament . . . Westminster, not Holyrood.'

'Michael Colledge?' DI Stallings exclaimed. 'The shadow Defence Secretary?'

'That's the man.'

'In that case, Sauce, yes; you'd better leave that one to me. In fact, I'd better check further up the line myself.'

She picked up the phone and dialled Neil McIlhenney: as commander of all CID operations in Edinburgh, he was her operational boss. All day, she had been keeping him briefed on the progress of the inquiry. She heard him sigh as she gave him the latest update. 'Do you want to take it on from here, sir?' she asked. 'Given that he's a VIP?'

'Do you want me to?'

'I'm not asking,' she replied, 'if that's what you mean.'

'In that case, go ahead. You've got the rank; you don't need me. Anyway, the guy's not a VIP; he's a Tory.'

She laughed. 'I won't tell anyone you said that.'

'It wouldn't hurt my career if you did. This is Scotland: we've got more dinosaurs left than we have Tories.'

Stallings opened her bag and took out her Filofax. It was one of her most treasured possessions. It had been an eighteenth-birthday gift

63

from her boyfriend of the moment, but its value was far more than sentimental. Within its brown-leather cover was every telephone number she had called since then, personal and professional, listed alphabetically on well-thumbed pages. She opened at 'C', and drew a blank, but switched to 'H' and found the main number for the House of Commons.

It took several minutes for the switchboard to locate the Member of Parliament for Newtown Mowbray through his researcher. When he came on line, he sounded distinctly out of breath. 'My assistant says that you're the police,' he gasped.

'Yes, Mr Colledge,' the DI began, pushing thoughts of MPs and their researchers to the back of her mind. 'Becky Stallings, detective inspector, Edinburgh, CID. I need to contact your son, Davis. I wonder if you can tell me how I can reach him.'

'Dave? Why do you want Dave? What the hell's he been up to? I've had no reports from his school of any incidents.'

'He hasn't been up to anything, sir. I need to speak to him in connection with an investigation we have going up here.'

'What's it about?'

'The death of a woman. We haven't confirmed her identity formally, but we believe she was your son's art tutor.'

'Jesus! Sugar? You are absolutely certain that it's her?'

'We'll need to use DNA to confirm it, but I'm in no doubt.'

'How did she die? Did she have a heart condition? Or was it some sort of an accident?'

'She was shot in the head, at close range.'

'And you're looking for Dave?' the MP exclaimed.

'It's okay,' said Stallings, quickly. 'I'm not saying he's a suspect. We're going to be speaking to everyone who knew Miss Dean.'

'Jesus!' Colledge murmured again. 'It's unbelievable. Such a vivacious girl. Who'd . . .'

'You've met her?'

'Yes, a couple of weeks ago. My wife and I visited Edinburgh to attend the school prize-giving. Dave won the art prize. We arranged to take him to dinner the night before, and he asked if he could bring a friend. We were expecting another lad; we got quite a shock when she arrived. That was Thursday evening; and you're saying that she was . . . That's just awful.'

'You called her vivacious, sir.'

'Yes, and I meant it literally: full of life, that's how she struck my wife and me. We took to her, once we had got over the initial surprise.'

The MP was being more talkative than Stallings had expected. She decided to move the discussion on, further than she had intended when it began. 'Did Davis . . . did they . . . discuss the nature of their relationship?'

'He introduced her as his art tutor. He told us that they had met at an inter-school event and that she had been impressed by his work, enough to have offered to coach him in her spare time.'

'So they were simply pupil and tutor.'

She heard Michael Colledge take a deep breath. 'That was how he introduced her. However, it became clear during the evening that they were very good friends.'

'Intimate?'

'There was nothing said to confirm it, but from something my son let slip, I wouldn't have been surprised.'

'Would that have worried you?'

'It might have worried Irma, Dave's mother, but I wouldn't have been too concerned. My son is a grown man: he's approaching nineteen, a mature nineteen, I think you'd say. He's had girlfriends since he was fifteen, at school and at home. Yes, I could see him being attracted to an older woman, and she to him.' He paused. 'Inspector, the fact is, he and Sugar were planning to go to France together.'

'To Collioure?'

'Yes. How did you know?'

'I was told that Sugar was supposed to be going there.'

'It's true. Dave told me that they had rented a place for July, through an agency, and that they were going to spend the time painting. It's a favourite spot for artists, apparently; Charles Rennie Mackintosh, among others. I asked him how much they were paying. The figure he gave me didn't sound very much for that part of the world, so I surmised that it didn't run to a bedroom each.'

'Do you know where your son is now?' Stallings asked.

'I assume he's in France. He travelled back to our home in Buxton with us after the school closed. We drove, as he had to move all his stuff out of the boarders' residence. The arrangement was that Sugar would fly there on the Saturday, that's . . . what? . . . ten days ago now, and that Dave would follow her a couple of days after that. He left for Collioure last Monday; he flew to Perpignan and planned to take the bus from there.'

'Have you heard from him since then?'

'No. Not a word. I've been assuming that the two of them were painting away, or whatever. The last thing he said when I dropped him at Stansted was that he'd send me a postcard. Those can take for ever to get here from Europe, so I haven't been bothered.'

'Do you have an address?'

'No, he didn't give me one. I don't think he knew it himself.'

'Do you have a means of contacting him?'

'He has a mobile. And as soon as we're finished, Inspector, I'll be calling him. Be sure of that.'

'I think it might be better if I speak to him first,' Stallings ventured.

'You can think what you like,' Colledge snapped, 'but you're not going to forbid me to call my son. I'll be happy to give you the number, but I want a few minutes' grace before you use it.'

'If that's how you want it, you're right, I can't stop you. But please, be careful what you say to him. Mature he may be, but it's not the sort of news he'll be expecting.'

'I'm not without experience of such matters,' the MP told her. 'I'm a barrister by profession. I've handled Privy Council appeals for a couple of Caribbean clients in my time, in capital cases; unsuccessful appeals, I should add. It's never easy to tell a chap they're going to hang him in the morning. Here's the number, if you're ready. It's a UK mobile, as I say. You won't need to use the French code.'

She entered the eleven digits into her Filofax, under 'C', then followed it with Michael Colledge's personal House of Commons and mobile numbers. 'I expect to be kept informed,' he told her.

'I promise to do so,' said Stallings. 'Does your son have the means to get back to Britain?'

'He has a return ticket; plus he's not short of cash. He has a decent allowance, and a couple of pieces of plastic.'

'Mr Colledge, one final question. Let's assume that your son got to France to find that Sugar wasn't there. How would he react?'

'In any number of ways, Inspector. Because we've been apart for most of Dave's growing up, I might not know him as well as I should. But I can tell you this. He will handle it; if he's worried or hurt or anything else, he will not turn to anyone else for help . . . not even me.'

Fifteen

As Becky Stallings walked up the path towards number eight Meriadoc Crescent, she saw the curtains twitch at number six, and guessed that Mrs Holmes was at her post.

On her second visit to the bungalow, there was no need to ring the bell. The door was opened as she approached by a tall, middle-aged man in a checked shirt and faded jeans. His face bore an expression that managed to combine shock and trepidation. 'Ms Stallings?' he asked. 'I'm John Dean.'

They shook hands, and the inspector introduced DC Haddock, who was following her. 'Thank you for letting me know you were back,' she said. 'I wasn't expecting to hear from you till this evening.'

'Don't ask how fast I drove,' Dean replied, as he led them into a thoroughly conventional living room, one of thousands of its type in Edinburgh's middle-class suburbia. A woman sat in an armchair, a glass full of a brownish liquid clutched tightly in her hand. 'My wife, Greta.' He caught Stallings's glance. 'I'm sorry, after the journey we both felt the need of a drink. Would you like one?'

'No, thanks. I know it's a cliché, but we're on duty.'

'Have you sorted this thing out?' the anxious mother asked harshly. 'Have you found out who this woman is? It can't be Sugar: we'd have . . . We'd just have known.'

Unbidden, Stallings sat on the couch close to her. 'Mrs Dean,' she began, but got no further. The woman bent forward, putting her hands to her face and pressing the glass against her forehead, as if she was trying to hide inside it from the truth. Her shoulders began to shake with sobs.

Her husband came and stood beside her, as if he was standing guard. 'There's no doubt?' he whispered, colour draining from his cheeks.

'The medical history you gave us,' Stallings told him, 'appendectomy scar, healed radial fracture: they're both present on the dead woman.'

Dean was shivering as he stared blankly at the wall. Sauce Haddock stepped across to the sideboard, picked up his discarded glass and a bottle of Famous Grouse, and poured a large measure. 'Here, sir,' said the young man, as he handed it to him.

'Thanks,' he murmured. He took a swallow, then another. 'You'll want me to identify her, I take it. I'd be grateful for an hour or two to prepare myself.'

'In the circumstances,' the inspector replied, 'that won't be necessary. We can confirm your daughter's identity by DNA, if you can give us personal samples.'

Greta Dean had recovered some composure. 'That's very kind of you.' She paused for a strengthening breath. 'But we'd like to see for ourselves that it's true.'

Stallings looked up at John Dean, hoping that he had read her meaning.

He had. 'No, Gret,' he told his wife. 'What the officers are saying is that there's no legal requirement for a formal identification, and that it will be better for us to see Sugar in a funeral home, rather than in the mortuary. In that case, that's what we'll do.'

The inspector nodded, hoping that they chose the most skilled mortician in the city. Dean motioned her towards the back of the room, then through an open door that led into the kitchen. 'What happened?' he asked quietly. 'I'm aware now, from the radio, that this is a murder investigation.'

'Sugar was shot in the back of the head. Her death bears strong similarities to a series of murders committed earlier this year.'

Dean frowned heavily. 'Yes, I remember. Sugar knew one of those poor girls, Stacey Gavin. They were at art college at the same time. But I thought that you'd caught the person who did those.'

'We did. He was found dead, and those investigations are closed.'

'So this might be the sincerest form of flattery? Is that what you think?'

'It's an unavoidable possibility.'

'So there may be more on the way?'

'Let's hope not. But we're not there yet. The first thing we have to try to do is establish a motive for Sugar's death. If we can't, then we may come to the conclusion that it was random.'

'I understand.'

'You thought your daughter was in France, sir?' she continued.

'Yes, that's true. Off on the Picasso trail, as she put it, with her young friend.'

'Davis Colledge?'

'That's him.'

'Friend? Or boyfriend?'

'Moving towards the latter status, I'd say. My daughter is well aware of the duties and responsibilities of a teacher towards pupils . . . all pupils, that is, not only her own. But Davis is off to art school now, and a studio apartment, as she told me they'd booked, doesn't really allow for young people being just good friends.'

'Art school? That's where he's going?'

'Yes. He has a place at Edinburgh. He's a very committed young man, and very talented, Sugar says.'

'Is there anyone else in Sugar's life? Another man?'

'That's how you're thinking, is it? A lover cast aside?'

'That's one of the first directions we take in an investigation like this,' Stallings admitted.

Dean frowned. 'I doubt if it will get you far. Her last serious involvement was two years ago, with a bloke called Theo Weekes. The fact is, they were engaged, but he broke it off.'

'Do you know why?' asked Stallings.

'He went off with someone else, Sugar told me. She didn't volunteer any more, but I could tell that she was hurt very badly. Now that I think about it, it's only since she's been friendly with Davis that she's been back to her old self.'

'Did she ever see Mr Weekes after the engagement ended?'

'Not that I know of.'

'Have you any idea where we could find him?'

'Probably by checking with your personnel department. He's a police constable; or, at least, he was then . . . or at least that's what he said he was. Us dads, we tend to accept our daughters' involvements regardless of personal feelings: if we have reservations we keep them to ourselves. I never took to Weekes, and I was secretly pleased when it ended. The man was such a shit that I wouldn't put it past him to have made the police thing up.'

'Where was he stationed? Or, rather, where did he tell you he was stationed?'

'Livingston.'

'Thanks.'

'About boyfriends,' Dean mused. 'If you look at old flames routinely, what about new ones?'

The inspector frowned. 'We will be interviewing Davis,' she replied, 'as soon as we can find him. He was last seen heading for France to meet Sugar. Why do you ask? Did you have doubts about him?'

The teacher shook his head. 'No. He's a very impressive young man. But when something like this happens . . . I'm just discovering that you see the devil in everyone.'

'I know. In my career, I've met too many people in your situation.'

'Then, if I can be brutal,' the bereaved father asked, 'in how many of those cases did the boyfriend do it?'

Stallings sighed. 'Mr Dean, I'm new to this force, so I'm still moving cautiously. It could be more than my job's worth to give you a straight answer to that question.'

'Then forget I asked.' He drew his shoulders back. 'These DNA samples; how do we give them?'

'I'll send forensic officers round as soon as possible; they'll do it. A saliva swab from each of you is all they'll need.'

'Okay.' As Dean led her back towards his wife, the inspector saw that Haddock was seated on the couch, speaking to her quietly. For the first time she understood why he had been fast-tracked into CID.

As they stepped out into the crescent, she thanked him.

'What for, ma'am?'

'Comforting the mother. Not many people can do that. Most of us just stand stiff and stare ahead.'

'It's how I was brought up,' he replied.

'What did you talk about?'

'Sugar. You know how she got the name? Mrs Dean's favourite film is *Some Like It Hot*. Poor woman was almost embarrassed to tell me that she called her daughter after Marilyn Monroe's character.'

Sixteen

Maggie Steele, as she always thought of herself now, smiled at her daughter, asleep in the carry-cot that was part of something called by its manufacturer a 'baby travel system'. They were alone, Bet having gone to a late-afternoon movie.

'It's an easy life being two months old, isn't it?' she whispered. Stephanie made a small noise, but dozed on, as her mother walked over to the desk that she and her father had once shared.

A brown envelope lay there: it had been delivered half an hour earlier by a uniformed constable from police headquarters at Fettes. She took a deep breath, then opened it and removed its contents.

The document was slimmer than she had expected, but as she looked at the list of sections she realised that it dealt only with events directly related to Stevie's death, and did not include the detailed investigation into the Ballester murders. Also, if the original had contained crime-scene photographs showing her husband's body, as she guessed it would have, they had been omitted from the copy.

'You might have given me one of Boras, Mario,' she murmured. 'You might have let me see his face. Or did you think that might upset me?'

She opened the report and began to read, slowly and carefully, taking note of every detail, even those that were seemingly insignificant. Twenty minutes later she finished. 'There's nothing there that I didn't know already,' she said, to no-one other than her sleeping daughter.

Dražen Boras, tycoon son of a tycoon father, had been very clever. He had set up two unwitting detective constables to provide his alibi. It would have stood, too, but for the tenacity of Bob Skinner and Mario McGuire, and the investigative skill, bordering on genius, of Detective Inspector Arthur Dorward, the force's senior scene-of-crime officer. Thanks to them, the case against Boras had been made.

But to no avail: the killer had evaded capture. He had fled the country in a private plane, just as the net was being readied to close around him. 'Or, rather,' Maggie whispered, 'they assumed that he fled the country.'

She picked up the phone and called McGuire's private number at Fettes. 'Mario,' she said urgently, as he answered, 'thanks for the report. I've just finished reading it. Tell me something: how did the Met establish that he had left the country?'

'His father's company jet was missing from its hangar. Davor Boras said that he had no idea where it had gone, and nobody could prove different.'

'What about the flight plan?'

'There was none, but the plane had the range to cross the Atlantic.'

'So that's where the Met assumed he was headed?'

'Yes, but they had other reasons to believe that.'

'Did anyone search for him in England? Were commercial flights and ferry crossings monitored? Was the Channel Tunnel checked?'

'No. They were dead sure he's gone to the US.'

'And what if they were wrong? What if he didn't head for America? What if the plane was simply moved somewhere else?'

McGuire sighed. 'Then he could have gone anywhere.'

'He could still be in Britain.'

'Risky.'

'He's used an assumed name in the past, to distance himself from his father. Okay, he can't call himself David Barnes any more, but what if he had a third identity, ready and waiting?'

'It would be typical behaviour for him, but, Mags, don't count on him being in Britain.'

'I'm not, but at least I've got somewhere to go from here.'

Seventeen

'Any joy, Jack?' asked Stallings, as she stepped back into the mobile police station, which was still parked outside the golf club. 'Have you managed to contact Davis Colledge?'

'No, boss,' McGurk replied. 'I've tried the mobile number you gave me, but the network says it's switched off. There's no voicemail available either. The best I've been able to do with it is send him a text, asking him to contact us about Sugar Dean.'

'That could alarm him.'

'Frankly, I don't care. We need to talk to him; if I have to give him a shake to make him call us, so be it.'

'Kid gloves, Jack; his dad's important.'

'I've spoken to his dad. He's had no luck with the mobile either. He's getting worried about him; he was talking about flying down there. I advised him not to, not yet at any rate, till we've exhausted all our channels. However, I did persuade him to give me the numbers for his son's debit and credit cards, and the account details. The issuers told me that he used the credit card to buy eighteen quid's worth of books in WHSmith at Stansted airport last Monday, and in a supermarket in Collioure on Thursday, to buy goods worth forty-seven euros. On Saturday, he withdrew three hundred euros from an ATM, again in Collioure.'

'Have you told Mr Colledge about this?'

'Not yet. The bank only just called me back.'

'Okay. You can ring him when you have a minute.'

'Will do.' The DS frowned. 'You know, it really would help if we had an address.'

'We do,' said Haddock, who had returned to his desk beside the wall, and was leaning over a lap-top computer. 'After a fashion. Sugar's mum told me that she booked the place on the Internet, through a letting agency called "franceabroad.com". I'm just looking it up now.' He waited. 'Yes, here it is; and there's a phone number.'

'Get on it,' Stallings ordered. 'While you're doing that I'm going to call Mr McIlhenney. I'm not waiting for young Dave to pick up your text, Jack. For all we know his battery's dead and he's left his charger at home. It's time we asked the local gendarmes for help.'

She picked up her phone and dialled the superintendent's number. It was engaged.

Eighteen

'The boy's father's an MP,' McGuire exclaimed. 'Is that going to be a problem?'

'Not so far, from what Becky told me,' McIlhenney replied. 'She says that the man's concerned, fair enough, but that he gave her all the help he could. Longer term, that'll depend on how things go with the boy. If he has someone who can vouch for where he was at the time of the murder, there's no problem. If not, it might become a bit trickier; if we have to treat the kid as a suspect. I trust Becky to handle the dad, though. She's lived and worked in his environment for years.'

'Sure, but this is a homicide investigation.'

'She's had plenty experience of those too. Remember, she was a DS in the East End of London before she moved to Charing Cross. What's making you so twitchy anyway?'

'This situation; the idea of some nutter copying Ballester.'

'We don't know that it is. We've only just IDed the victim; we hardly know anything about her. She could have had people in her private life queuing up to bump her off. We still have to find that out.'

'Maybe so, but my money's on this being down to that nutter I'm worrying about. Come on, you've seen the crime-scene photos, and you've seen the PM report. You had the same pathologist who did the autopsies on Zrinka and Amy Noone handle this one. What did he say? That in his opinion the methods of execution were identical. Are you telling me that you don't believe, in your heart of hearts, that we've got a copycat?'

McIlhenney shook his head. 'No. I admit it, I agree with you. But I'm hoping we're both wrong, because chances are a head-banger won't stop at one. Ballester wasn't really a serial killer, but this one might well be. We could be out on a limb here.' He looked his colleague in the eye. 'Should we seek the advice of our absent friend and mentor?'

'I rather think we should,' said McGuire. 'I've already called him once today, about something else, but I don't think we should put this off. Tell you what, let's try an Internet link; I know he's on line in his Spanish house. I'll call him and ask him to switch on.'

'Okay; you do that and I'll e-mail him some of the crime-scene pics, so that he can see what we're talking about.'

As the head of CID left his room, McIlhenney turned to his computer terminal and opened the folder he had set up for the Dean murder inquiry, then switched on his e-mail link and clicked the 'write message' command.

He was about to begin when the phone rang. He snatched it up. 'McIlhenney,' he said evenly, conquering his impatience.

'Superintendent,' a woman's voice replied. 'Joanna Lock.'

'What can I do for you?'

'Nothing,' she said coolly. 'I have a message for you, from the Crown Agent, Joe Dowley. I went to see him after our discussion and I told him what you wanted me to do. He went ballistic. I am to tell you, on his instructions, that there is no way that anybody in the Crown Office leaked the contents of that report, and that if you ever again make the slightest implication that there might be, he will have your guts for garters. He says that the buck stops with you and if you have a problem with that he'll go to Sir James Proud, your chief constable.'

Neil McIlhenney could count on the fingers of one hand the number of times that he had lost his temper in his adult life. At that moment he knew that he would have to bring the other hand into play.

'He said what?' he exploded. 'You tell Mr Dowley from me that I didn't ask for his opinion, nor do I give a fuck about it. I'm engaged in a murder investigation and I require the assistance of his office. And tell him this too, Joanna, word for word. If he ever threatens me again I will head straight up to Chambers Street and rip his nuts off!'

'He's not going to like that.'

'Too fucking true he's not!' He slammed the phone back into its cradle.

Nineteen

Becky Stallings picked up the phone and tried again, for the third time in ten minutes. Third time lucky.

'Yes!' Neil McIlhenney snapped. In his unofficial introduction to the Edinburgh force and its senior figures, her boyfriend, Detective Sergeant Ray Wilding, had described the city's CID controller as 'the soothing influence on Mario McGuire and Bob Skinner'. Both the head of CID and the deputy chief constable were famously volatile, he had told her, seriously hard men, never to be taken lightly. On the other hand McIlhenney, while no soft touch, was invariably calm and heavily relied on by his two senior officers, both of whom were close friends as well as colleagues. 'McGuire and McIlhenney are blood brothers,' Ray had said. 'When they were younger, they used to call them the Glimmer Twins; you know, as in Mick Jagger and Keith Richards. Some still do.'

And so, when the detective superintendent bit her head off, it came as a complete surprise.

'Sorry, sir,' she replied. 'Bad time?'

It was as if she had pressed a reset button; immediately, normal service was restored. 'No, excuse me, Inspector; I was expecting a call from my bank manager. How are things? Have you found the MP's son yet?'

'We know where he was last Saturday and, thanks to young Sauce, we've got an address for him in France.'

'What does your instinct tell you about this lad? Is he our killer, and is he sitting out there pretending to wait for her?'

'He has to be a suspect, sir. He's her boyfriend, and one of the last people to see her alive.'

'So was his father,' McIlhenney pointed out. 'You told me they all had dinner together the night before Sugar was murdered. Why would the boy kill her? They were just about to go off to France for some serious art and probably some serious horizontal jogging.'

'If you want a reason, maybe he took cold feet.'

'I doubt that; teenage boy, older woman? Now, can we go back to my question? What does your instinct say?'

'That he didn't do it,' Stallings replied instantly.

'Then we're agreed. He has to be interviewed, for sure, as a priority, but we won't expect that to close the case.'

'No. He's not the only person on the suspect list either. Have you ever heard of a PC named Weekes, Theo Weekes?'

The line went quiet. 'The name's familiar,' said McIlhenney, eventually. 'One of ours?'

'So I'm told by Sugar's father. He and Sugar were engaged, but he dumped her a couple of years ago. John Dean was pleased: he didn't like him.'

'Would he take to any of his daughter's men? Fathers can be possessive.'

'Do you speak from experience?'

The superintendent laughed. 'Ask me in two or three years.'

'John Dean isn't. He likes Davis Colledge, for all that he's nearly eight years younger than Sugar.'

'How would Dean be as a judge of character?'

'I hope he'd be good; he's a head teacher.'

'Let's take a look at PC Weekes, in that case, formally.'

'How hard do you want me to look at him?' she asked.

'As hard as you have to. But don't do anything about him just yet. Let's set him a test. I'm about to give a press briefing at which I'll announce that we've identified the victim as Sugar Dean. There's no last lingering doubt about that, is there?'

'No. Jack's just had a call from the mortuary: her dental records are a match, to back up the scar and the broken arm.'

'Right. I'll release her name, and confirm that this is a murder investigation, as the media are saying already. I'll ask for people who knew Sugar to come forward with information. In these circumstances I'd expect a serving officer to come forward without being asked. If we haven't heard from Weekes by midday tomorrow, we'll pull him in.'

'Where? Torphichen Place?'

'No. We'll rattle his cage harder than that. I'll see him in my office, two o'clock. If DCS McGuire's free, I might even ask him to sit in. Mario's bad-cop act is something to see.'

Stallings heard a soft chuckle. 'You've got me hoping that Weekes doesn't volunteer information, sir,' she said.

'If Dean's right about him, he probably won't. Between now and then, I want you to contact as many of Sugar's colleagues and friends as you can. Mention Weekes's name to them and see what comes up.'

'What about Dave Colledge? Should we ask about him?'

'Of course. Okay, our gut says it's not him, but I've been wrong before, and I'll bet you have too.'

'Maybe, but I'm a woman, so I'm not going to admit it.'

'God, you sounded just like my late wife there. And her successor, for that matter.'

'Thank you; I'll take that as a compliment.'

'You should, Becky. Now, how do we get hold of the boy Davis?'

'I was going to ask you for permission to have the French police locate him and hold him for questioning.'

'That could be dangerous; they might bang him up in some dirty local police cell for a couple of days. I doubt if Daddy would fancy that much. No, we need somebody on the ground there when the contact is made. Remind me, where is Collioure, exactly?'

'It's on the French Mediterranean coast. According to the map, it's practically on the Spanish border.'

'In that case,' said McIlhenney, 'leave finding the boy to me. Mr McGuire and I are having a meeting soon that might provide a solution to the problem.'

Twenty

Maggie gazed at the computer screen as the web page unfolded. 'Weird name for a company,' she murmured to the still-dozing Stephanie. 'Fishheads dot com. But you know what? Your dad worked out where it came from.

'That's right, Steph,' she continued. 'Your father had a photographic memory for apocrypha of all sorts. There was hardly a useless fact that wasn't filed away in his brain. I remember he told me what Dražen Boras's company was called, just after the name had come up in the investigation. I said to him what I've just said to you, and he looked at me, shrugged his shoulders and said, "Barnes and Barnes." I said, "What?" and he told me that there was an iconic ... his word ... American rock band in the seventies whose only hit was a song called "Fishheads". And since Dražen had changed his name to David Barnes, to get out from under his father's shadow, there was the connection. Imagine, wee one, your dad knowing that sort of stuff off the top of his head.'

Which was where the grenade fragment that killed him went in. The thought thrust itself at her, bringing with it the images that still haunted her on her many sleepless nights. She focused her gaze on the screen until they vanished and all she could see was the bizarre Fishheads logo.

The company sold office supplies, exclusively over the Internet, to business and domestic customers. Its major selling point, emphasised on the page, was its cost structure, with cheap or even free delivery for relatively small quantities, clearly aimed at home businesses and at other self-managed enterprises.

Ignoring the display of headlined products, which included paper, furniture and even a water-cooler, she looked at the site contents, listed at the bottom of the screen. Using the mouse, she moved the cursor to 'About Us' and double-clicked. Within seconds a new page appeared, with a second set of choices: 'Our People', 'Our Depots', and 'Our Terms and Conditions'. She selected the first, and watched as a list of names and designations appeared.

The absence of a name registered, just as another caught her eye. There was no David Barnes, or Dražen Boras, anywhere to be seen. She guessed that when the company had been set up he had been listed as its chairman or chief executive, or possibly as both. But now he was gone, into the dark world she was setting out to probe.

In his place, she saw the name Sanda Boras. 'So his mum stepped in,' Maggie whispered. 'A stooge, I suppose. But where do her orders come from?'

She picked up her mobile and scrolled the stored numbers, until she found 'Goode, M.'. She hit the green button and waited.

'*Scotsman* business desk,' a tired voice answered.

'You sound like you can't wait for the school bell to ring,' she said. 'Maurice, it's Maggie Steele here . . . Maggie Rose, as was. Remember me from when you did the crime beat?'

'Maggie, of course.' The journalist switched back to working mode. 'How are you? Sorry about Stevie. That was just wicked. I heard you've got a daughter now. Is that right?'

'Yes, and if I sound quiet, that's why. She's not far from me, and she's asleep.' As she spoke, she realised that he had not asked about her illness. She took that to mean that word had not leaked out into the wider world: Maurice Goode knew most of what was going on in town.

'So how can I help you, Chief Superintendent?' he asked. 'How are you going to brighten up this drab world they promoted me into?'

'I want to talk to a retail analyst, one of the best. It's a personal thing,' she added, choosing her words carefully.

'Which retail sector?'

'Office supplies.'

'Office supplies; let me think.' She let him. 'You probably want Jacqui Harkness,' he said eventually. 'She's Glasgow-based, works for a stockbroker firm called Levene and Company; it's a small outfit, but don't let that put you off. Jacqui's as good as there is; you can tell her I said so, too.' He recited her telephone number from memory.

'Thanks. I'll be on maternity leave for a while yet, but when I'm back at work, I'll owe you one.'

'I'll remember that. Look after yourself, and the youngster.'

She hung up and dialled Levene and Company, hoping that the firm did not close at the same time as the London Stock Exchange, four p.m., relieved when her call was answered swiftly. She asked for Jacqui Harkness. 'Who's calling?' the telephonist asked.

'My name's Margaret Steele, Mrs. Tell her I'm a friend of Maurice Goode and that he says she's the best in the business.'

'They all say that.' The girl laughed. 'Hold on.'

She waited, for almost a minute.

'Sorry I took so long.' The woman who came on the line had a strong Glasgow accent, and sounded middle-aged. 'So you're a pal of Mo B. Goode, are you? How do you know him, smarmy bastard that he is?'

'From his days as a crime reporter; I'm a police officer.'

'Polis?' exclaimed Jacqui Harkness. 'Fraud Squad?'

'No. I'm a chief super, in uniform mostly, but just now I'm on secondment to Special Branch.'

'The secret police? Magic. I've never had a call from you lot before. What are you after? Where Al Qaeda have their money stashed? I can't tell you for sure, but I've got some ideas. For example, if I were you I'd be looking at businesses with a strong Jewish base and blue-chip American corporations for two reasons: one, they usually do bloody well, and two, it's the last place you'd expect Islamic terrorists to hide money.'

'I'll pass that on,' Maggie told her, 'but that's not why I'm calling. I want to ask you about a company called Fishheads.'

'Ah!' the analyst exclaimed. 'You want to talk about Star Wars: young Dražen Boras's strike against his dad's evil empire.'

'That's right; or David Barnes as he became when he set the company up.'

'Yes, but it didn't fool anybody. Dražen's got a bloody big ego; he wanted everybody to know who he was, so his advisers leaked his real identity early on. It did no harm when it came to raising finance either. The family-at-war thing helped too. It all gave him an instant profile in the marketplace, where another new-start business would have had a growth period that would have lasted for years, and might have ended in failure.' Harkness paused. 'So, Mrs Steele, are you trying to solve the great mystery?'

'Which one's that?'

'Where's Dražen gone?'

'Yes, I am. What's your view?'

'I don't have one; I don't deal in guesses, hen. The market doesn't have much of a clue either. It's all gossip, but the most popular theory is that he's got some terminal disease, and that he's away to die somewhere. There is a much darker notion too, that his old man's had him encased in concrete and dumped at sea.'

'Do you mean there are people in the business community who'd believe that of Davor Boras, that he'd kill his own son?'

'There are indeed. Their theory goes that Davor couldn't stand his daughter being dead and Dražen being alive so he corrected the situation. He had some people down in London used to work for him; a so-called security firm. They disappeared off the face of the earth at the same time as Dražen did.'

'And which of these theories do you favour, Jacqui?'

'Neither of those. If you press me to give you my opinion, not a guess, but not offered as fact either, I'd say he's on the run. I'd say that you lot are after him.'

'But if he'd broken any company laws, that would be the subject of a very open investigation.'

'I don't mean company laws, Margaret.'

'Everyone except my sister calls me Maggie. You mean another sort of criminality?'

'Yes. Am I right?'

'Will you take silence for an answer?'

'I often do.'

'Do you know who's running Fishheads now? I know that his mother's taken over the chair, but who's in charge?'

'Ostensibly, it's the CEO, Godric Hawker. He was Dražen's finance director.'

'Ostensibly?'

'That's the other open question. Is he really in charge or is he still taking orders from Dražen? Or even from Davor? Is the evil emperor pulling the strings now?'

'Or might he have been pulling them all along?'

Harkness drew a breath. 'Are you saying that the family-at-war thing was a hoax?'

'Has Davor's business suffered?'

'A bit.'

'Put the two of them together and how does it look in terms of total market share? Positive or negative?'

'Heavily in the black. But you know what? The City doesn't care; all it sees are two very successful companies. Ethical investment is a load of shite, Maggie; you'd better believe that.'

'I wish I didn't, but I'm one of nature's cynics too. A couple more questions, Jacqui, then I'm done. When Dražen was around, how close were he and Hawker?'

'They were always side by side at City presentations; that's all I can tell you.'

'Apart from him, was Dražen close to anyone else in the company?'

'Ifan Richards, the third executive director, had the authority to speak for the company when he wasn't around. You might talk to him.'

'I might very well,' said Maggie. 'Thanks, Jacqui; Maurice was right.' She hung up, just as Stephanie began to stir in her cot.

Twenty-one

'I hope Aileen's not too pissed off,' said Neil McIlhenney. 'I wouldn't fancy being in her bad books.'

'Nah,' said Skinner. 'She's okay. But I promised her we wouldn't take more than fifteen minutes, so bear that in mind.' He paused. 'Can you guys see me all right at your end? You're fine on my screen.' Two figures nodded in reply.

He, McIlhenney and Mario McGuire were making their first stab at a video conference over the Internet. 'I didn't give Aileen any details,' he went on, 'beyond that there's been a crime in Edinburgh and you need my input. How's your investigation going?'

'It's complicated,' McGuire told him.

'How are the media playing it?'

'As a straightforward murder so far. Nobody's made the art connection yet; all Neil said at the press briefing was that the victim was a member of staff at Mary Erskine.'

'They will, though. Three dead artists inside five months, the latest after the perpetrator of the first two topped himself . . . or, rather, was topped, although they don't know that yet either.'

McIlhenney leaned towards the web cam. 'Sugar Dean was a teacher, though, not really an artist.'

'Don't you believe it,' Skinner countered. 'I've been doing some digging of my own, through a lecturer I know. She was a prize-winner at the art school, then she moved on to her teaching qualification. While she was doing that, she was commissioned by the Scottish

91

Executive, on the back of her final-year work, to paint a series of pictures under the theme "justice". There are four in all; one hangs in the High Court in Glasgow, one's in the Crown Office, one's in the Parliament building, and the fourth is about two hundred yards away from you two, in the conference room at Fettes. Fucking detectives, eh?'

McGuire and McIlhenney looked at each other, in the same moment. 'You guys are on borrowed time,' said Skinner. 'If this connection doesn't break before tomorrow, I'll be surprised. What are your priorities?'

'At the moment, Sugar's background is,' McIlhenney told him. 'We've got a nasty ex-fiancé in her past, who just happens to be a serving police officer.'

'What's his name?'

'PC Theodore Weekes, aged twenty-eight, been on the job for five years, currently stationed at South Queensferry, resident in west Edinburgh.'

'How nasty?'

'We don't know yet,' McGuire interposed. 'I've spoken to his inspector, Chippy Grade, and to Jock Varley at Livingston, where he used to be stationed. Chippy doesn't like him, but has nothing against him. Varley said that he had a reputation for being a bit heavy-handed.'

'All police officers need to be able to handle themselves.'

'Not when tackling a five-foot-four-inch law student whose only crime is throwing a fag packet at a bin and missing.'

'No,' Skinner conceded. 'Has he volunteered information about his past relationship with the victim?'

'No,' McIlhenney replied, 'but to be fair, he's hardly had time. He's got until midday tomorrow, then he's being pulled in here for interview.'

'If it comes to it, don't go easy on him.'

'Don't worry about that, boss.' The superintendent paused. 'But before that, there's something else to be done.'

'In due course,' said Skinner, 'but let's talk basics first. It appears that the Dean murder has many of the hallmarks of the Gavin and Boras killings. Right?'

'Yes,' McGuire agreed.

'The full details of the murders carried out by Daniel Ballester, they've never been revealed, to my knowledge.'

'No, they haven't.'

'So we might be looking at a leak, in our own organisation or in the Crown Office.'

'Yes,' said McIlhenney. 'We're addressing that, don't worry. Mario's putting together a list of all officers who were part of the overall Ballester inquiry, and who might know the whole story. I've been to the fiscal's office to ask them to do the same.'

'Did you see Gregor Broughton?'

'No, he's away just now. I spoke to his new assistant, a woman called Lock. As soon as I'd closed the door behind me she went running off to Gregor's boss, the Crown Agent.'

'Joe Dowley? I don't like that man.'

'Me neither,' the superintendent growled. 'He had Lock call me back and threaten me with the chief's carpet if I didn't back off.'

'What did you threaten him with?' asked Skinner, laconically.

'Emasculation, and I don't think I was kidding.'

'Pointless. Inappropriate. If the guy had any balls he'd have phoned you himself, not got a junior to do it. Bugger him; my time's limited so let's get on with it. Run through all the points of coincidence between the Dean murder and the others.'

'One, the method of execution: single shot, back of head. Two, the victim is an artist. Three, the way the body was laid out, although after ten days we can't be so sure about that.'

'Points of diversion from the Ballester killings.'

'The body was hidden. Stacey Gavin and Zrinka Boras were left in the open.'

'Amy Noone wasn't.'

'Amy Noone was killed in her flat. She wasn't an artist either: she was a potential witness. We believe that's why Ballester killed her, and it's why he killed Harry Paul, Zrinka's boyfriend. Boss, you're working up to asking us whether we think Sugar Dean was killed by a copycat with inside knowledge of the earlier murders. I know I speak for Neil when I say that, on balance, we do. Yes, the body was hidden and that's different from the pattern, but this girl was shot around eight in the morning on the edge of a golf course. There were golfers out there already; they hadn't reached that part of the course yet, but the green-keepers could have turned up at any time, so he had to get the body into the woods and out of sight.'

'Yes, that's about a fair assumption. So what about Weekes? What else do we know about him?'

'He's just one lead,' McIlhenney reminded Skinner. 'But we have checked him out. He was off shift when Sugar was killed. We know that much. We-also know that he's engaged again, this time to a fellow police officer, a woman called Mae Grey. They met when he was at Livingston; she's still there. The problem with Weekes has to be motive; he and Sugar split two years ago. It might have been acrimonious then, but there's no obvious reason for him to go back and kill her now.'

'Not obvious, but it may be there, nonetheless.'

'Yes, and we'll look for it, unless he can give us a stonewall alibi. The thing that interests me most about him is that he's stationed at South Queensferry; that's where Stacey Gavin's death was first reported. It's possible that he was at the scene, and saw the body; Chippy Grade's checking the duty rosters to find out.'

'Okay. What else?'

'Sugar's most recent boyfriend, and he's the real reason we needed to brief you on what's happening.'

Skinner grinned. 'I'd like to think that you'd be briefing me anyway, but I suppose it serves me right for promoting two independent-minded bastards like you. What about the man?'

'Only just a man,' said McIlhenney. 'He's eighteen, and until the week before last, he was a pupil at Stew-Mel. A promising artist, and she was coaching him in her spare time.'

'Coaching him in what?'

'Nothing against the rules, or so her head teacher and parents believe, but it's pretty clear they were about to move on to that part of the tutorial.'

'Is the boy a suspect?'

'He's somebody we have to interview.'

'So?'

'So his dad's in the shadow fucking cabinet,' McGuire drawled. 'The boy's name is Davis Colledge.'

'Aah,' said Skinner. 'Son of Michael, last of the Conservative tough guys among the new user-friendly breed. Making waves?'

'Not as yet; he's been co-operative with Becky's team in helping us try to reach his son.'

'You can't find the boy? Does that make him prime suspect?' Pause. 'God, I hate that fucking series!'

'Me too,' said McIlhenney, 'but it doesn't. Davis was last seen when he left to meet up with Sugar. They were supposed to spend a month together, painting.'

'Cut the euphemisms and get to the point.'

The superintendent grinned. 'Point is, we've located him, in France. Now we need to interview him, to take him out of the frame altogether.'

'I'm with you. If you contact the French police, they'll treat it as a "detain for questioning" request, and lift him, running the risk of Colledge senior becoming uncooperative, and sending in lawyers.'

'Exactly, and then it could all go pear-shaped. Worst case, we might need to extradite him just to ask him where he was when Sugar was killed. Whereas . . .'

It was Skinner's turn to smile for the camera. 'Whereas if you had a man on the ground, ready to interview the lad informally, maybe without the gendarmerie even being involved . . .'

'. . . someone of sufficient seniority to impress even his dad . . .'

'Where is he?'

'We have an address for him in a town called Collioure. He used his bank card there on Saturday.'

'Collioure's just up the road,' said Skinner. 'I've been there. Nice place; it'll be crawling with punters at this time of year. I'll do it, but it has to be with the knowledge of the French authorities.'

'If it's only an informal interview . . .' McGuire began. 'Private investigators don't ask permission when they cross frontiers.'

'No, they don't, but if things don't go right for them they're in trouble. Suppose young Davis proves you wrong? Remember, boys, I don't do friendly chats. Suppose when I find him and ask him the straight questions that I'll have to, he bursts into tears and says, "It was me, guv, wot dun it"? What can I do then? No, I'll need someone with me with power of arrest, just in case.'

'Point taken,' the head of CID conceded. 'We'll make an arrangement and get back to you. When can you get up there?'

'Now, if I have to.'

'Let's hold on that until tomorrow morning; I may not be able to tie up the French end before then.'

'Okay, I'll leave here at eleven, ten o'clock your time, whether I've heard from you or not. After that you can raise me on the mobile. Meantime, send me the address by e-mail, and a local map showing me where it and the local police office are. So long for now.'

Skinner clicked on the exit symbol on his screen to end the conference, then closed the lap-top and walked out into the evening heat. Aileen was lying on a lounger on the terrace, face down. He sat beside her on the tiles, picked up a bottle of Piz Buin and began to massage the lotion into her back.

'Mmmmmm,' she murmured languidly.

'Feeling good?' he asked.

'Am I ever . . .' She twisted her head round and peered at him through a half-closed eye.

He beamed. 'In that case,' he said, 'do you fancy coming with me to France tomorrow, while I interview a suspect in a murder investigation?'

Twenty-two

Sir James Proud had a hidden shame: it was known only to himself and to his wife, Lady Chrissie . . . No-one ever addressed her by her proper name, Christine. None of their children were privy to it, and neither was Bob Skinner, his deputy, nor any other senior colleague. The truth, if it ever emerged, would not end his career, but it would make it impossible for him to see out its final months without the suspicion, even the certainty, that those who offered him smart salutes in the corridors of the headquarters building would be exchanging winks and smirks as soon as his back was to them.

Sir James Proud was an addict.

He knew well enough, because his rank required him to know, that he was not the only police officer to be in the grip of a private vice, or to have a skeleton from the past so serious, to its owner if no-one else, that it had to be hidden not in a cupboard but in a safe.

There was Assistant Chief Constable Brian Mackie, whose meticulous personal grooming could not disguise the fact that outside the office he was an incurable cigar smoker. Chief Inspector David Mackenzie, the new executive officer on the command corridor, had just recovered from an illness that had had as much to do with alcohol as the stress to which it had been publicly attributed. Detective Inspector Dorothy Shannon, who ran Special Branch, had had a fling with the married DS George Regan that had put an end to her relationship with the then single Stevie Steele. Chief Superintendent Margaret Rose Steele, and Bet her sister, had been sexually abused as children by their father. Gerry Crossley, his secretary, suspected by half the force of being gay because he was a man in what was perceived to be a woman's job, kept a collection of girlie magazines in his desk.

And there was Skinner himself; his strength was his weakness, expressed in an obsession with physical fitness that had become even greater since the fitting of a pacemaker to counter an unpredictable heartbeat, and which was rooted, according to his last psychological profile, in a sense of shame at his own infirmity.

The chief constable's secret was not as dark as any of those; it was more of an embarrassment.

Proud Jimmy was addicted to *The Bill*, a twice-weekly police drama that had been running on Scottish Television for almost as long as *Coronation Street*. He found many of the story lines ludicrous, and barely a week went by without him muttering to Chrissie that 'any officer on my force who behaved that way would be out the door in two seconds flat'. Nonetheless he watched it whenever he could, as he had done for almost a quarter of a century, back when June, Tony and Reg were rookies, before Carver went on the booze and when Meadows was still on the beat in another part of London.

The week's first episode was five minutes old when the phone rang. It was six feet away from his chair, but he made no move to answer. Lady Chrissie frowned at him, sighed and went to pick it up.

'Let it ring,' he grunted at her. 'They can leave a message.'

'They can do no such thing,' she replied. 'Press your "pause" button. That's what you got it for.'

He snatched up the remote and pressed it, freezing DI Manson's scowl on screen as she picked up the handset from its charging socket. He heard her recite their number, as she always did when she took a call.

'Yes,' she said, 'he is, but he's rather busy. Is this urgent? Can it wait till morning, or can he call you back in an hour or so?' She waited, listening as the caller spoke into her ear. 'In that case, if you'll just hold on a second. Jimmy, it's Mr Dowley, the Crown Agent; he says it's very important.' She held the phone out for her husband.

Sir James almost snarled as he took it from her. 'Proud,' he said stiffly.

'Sir James, it's Joe Dowley, Crown Agent.'

'So Lady Proud tells me. What's the crisis?'

'Crisis it is, Sir James,' the man replied, his voice rising. 'I find myself in an impasse with your force and I'm not having it. I've been told by your man McIlhenney that I have to conduct an inquiry within the Crown Office into a potential leak of information. That's bloody outrageous. Information does not leak from the Crown Office; the organisation is tight as a drum when it comes to confidentiality. I'm not having us called into question. I've tried to contact Skinner, but your new executive officer insists that he's incommunicado, so in his absence I'm coming to you.'

'I beg your pardon, Mr Dowley?' Chrissie Proud looked at her husband. When his voice dropped to a level just above a whisper it was a sure sign of a gathering storm. 'Did I hear you correctly? You couldn't contact my deputy, so you're coming to me in his absence?'

'I think . . .'

Proud cut him off. 'And suppose you had contacted DCC Skinner,' he said, 'what would you have said to him?'

'I'd have demanded that he order McIlhenney to desist. He's obviously forgotten that in criminal matters the police report to the Crown Office, not the other way around.'

'Have you expressed this sentiment to Detective Superintendent McIlhenney yourself?'

'I instructed a colleague to tell him as much.'

'And did he respond?'

Chrissie Proud read the menace in the chief's tone. Dowley did not. 'Yes, he did, in most offensive terms, and that's something else I want to complain about. I want him disciplined.'

Proud chuckled. 'What would you like me to do with him?'

'An official reprimand at the very least.'

'Mmm. One more question, Mr Dowley. After I've told you to fuck off, where do you go next?' Sir James was oblivious of Lady Proud's glare.

The Crown Agent spluttered, but the chief continued, 'You and I disagree profoundly about our relationship, sir. It's the job of my force, like any other, to investigate crimes and to do what is necessary in pursuit of its enquiries. Once we're finished, we report to the procurator fiscal, but until we've done that, any person who obstructs us wilfully is committing an offence himself. I repeat, any person, wherever he might be. No doors are closed to us. I know about your exchange with McIlhenney; my head of CID told me all about you being on your high horse. I endorse Neil's position entirely, and I even have some sympathy with his language.'

'I'm not taking this,' Dowley hissed.

Finally Proud exploded. 'For God's sake, man!' he roared. 'If he'd been available Gregor Broughton would have sorted this with a couple of phone calls. Instead you want to start an interdepartmental war. Well, you go ahead. See if you can find somebody who has the authority to tell me to back down.'

He cut the Crown Agent off and tossed the handset back to his wife. 'If that bloody thing rings again, Chrissie,' he said, 'you do not answer it. Understood?'

'Yes, dear,' she replied. 'Not until *The Bill*'s finished.'

He settled back into his chair, and picked up the digi-box remote, then paused. 'You know what?' he said. 'I've had enough.'

Lady Proud stared at him. 'Enough of *The Bill*?'

'No, love,' he replied. 'I've had enough of being one of Edinburgh's bloody institutions. I've had enough of our evenings being interrupted by pillocks like him. My time's up. The truth is, it's been up for a while now, and I'm the only man on the force who hasn't seen and acknowledged the same. That guy there just told me I was his court of second resort after Bob Skinner. He didn't put it in so many words, but that's what he meant.'

'Oh, Jimmy, he didn't.'

'He did. And the thing is, he's right. Bob's where the power lies now. Everybody knows that if he takes a decision I won't countermand it, and equally they know that I won't make a major decision myself without talking to him about it. I'm drawing the salary under false pretences. And why? We don't need the money, that's for sure. My pension will be the equivalent of Mario McGuire's salary, give or take.'

'Yes, but you're due to go in less than a year anyway.'

'Too long. I need to go now. Tomorrow I set the retirement wheels in motion, once I've spoken to Bob and told him that I'm getting out of his way.'

Chrissie Proud frowned. 'I know you've always wanted him to succeed you. But will he apply for the job?'

'He has to make up his mind about that, and I'm not delaying the moment for him any longer. It's bloody well time he did.'

Twenty-three

Bet Rose looked at her sister from the doorway. 'Are you on that bloody computer already?' The question was pointless since Maggie was staring at the monitor, with her right hand on the mouse.

She twisted round in her chair. 'Sorry. Do you need to go on line?'

'No, that's all right. I can work on my lap-top and copy stuff across for transfer later. It would help if you had a wireless network, though. Then we could both access the Net at the same time if we needed.' She paused. 'But Margaret, it's not even quarter to nine yet; you're up, dressed, Steph's fed and changed, and you're at it already. This is not what recuperation's supposed to be like.' She peered at the screen. 'What are you doing anyway?'

'Working on my memoirs. Now bugger off and get designing.'

'Okay, you old charmer. By the way,' she called out, as Maggie turned back to her computer, 'you've got your wig on back to front.'

'No, I haven't.' She laughed. 'I checked where the label was when I put it on.'

Alone again, she focused on the screen once more; she was logged on to the Fishheads website once more and, when Bet had interrupted her, had just clicked on the biography of Godric Hawker, BSc (Acc), CPFA, the chief executive officer.

There was a photograph at the top of the page, showing a clean-cut, immaculately groomed young man in his early thirties. He was pictured, jacketless, in an open-necked shirt, seated on the arm of a chair, rather than in it. Clearly, she thought, the company's publicity advisers believed that their clients should look like young politicians rather than business leaders.

Hawker's biography told her that he was a graduate of the University of Southampton, and that he had completed his professional training with a leading, but unnamed, firm of London accountants. He had spent three years as a manager, specialising in corporate finance, before being head-hunted by Fishheads to become its finance director. He had been chief executive for only a month. The section gave minimal career information and said nothing about the man.

On impulse, Maggie went to the foot of the screen and clicked on 'Press Releases'. A list of announcements made by the company over the previous twelve months unrolled before her eyes. Two of the most recent were headed, 'First major order from Hong Kong', and 'Fishheads.com climbs suppliers' league table', but when she scrolled up, at the top of the list was one titled 'Board Appointments'. She checked the date and saw that it had been posted that morning. She opened it.

It read:

The directors of Fishheads plc wish to confirm a number of boardroom changes, which have been in place on a provisional basis for the last two months. These follow the decision of David Barnes, the founder of the company, to withdraw from business life, and are designed to ensure continuity in the upper tier of management.

Mrs Sanda Boras has been confirmed as a director and as non-executive chair of the company.

Mr Godric Hawker has been confirmed as chief executive officer, with day-to-day responsibility for all operations. With Mrs Boras, he will exercise oversight of all financial matters and will continue to act as finance director.

Mr Ifan Richards continues as an executive director, assuming responsibility for investor relations and corporate communications.

The board also wishes to announce that agreement has been reached on the acquisition of the shareholding of David Barnes by the LTN Trust. In consequence of the sale Mr Ignacio Riesgo is appointed as a non-executive director of the company.

'Who the hell is he?' Maggie murmured. She returned to the biography section. The name of the new director was listed there; she clicked on it, and read:

Mr Ignacio Riesgo, 30, is the son of the late Hilario Riesgo. He was born in Panama, and was educated there and in the United States. He is a trustee of the LTN Trust, which is based in Bermuda, where he is resident.

'That tells me precisely fuck all,' she said. 'But I suppose . . . Dražen has to disappear, so he cashes up by selling his fifty-one per cent share in Fishheads, which is worth, going by the company's current market value, about two hundred million. Where does the money go?'

She picked up the phone and dialled the number of Levene and Company, hoping that Jacqui Harkness was an early starter. She was.

'Who's Ignacio Riesgo?' Maggie asked, not spending time on pleasantries.

'Hah.' The analyst laughed. 'I thought I'd be hearing from you this morning, once you caught up with the Fishheads announcement. The answer is that I haven't a clue who the bugger is, other than that he's tied into the LTN Trust. It has investments around the world, in computing, property, and even football.'

'Is Ignacio a director of those companies?'

'Not that I know of, but most of them aren't in my sector so I don't study them.'

'Will this make it more difficult for me to locate Dražen?'

'If he doesn't want you to find him, and it seems clear that he doesn't, it makes it bloody near impossible. These old Bermuda trusts are very difficult to penetrate. Dražen's money will be locked up in Switzerland by now, and you'll never pick up the trail.'

'He'll be long gone, with a new identity anyway,' said Maggie, gloomily. 'What do you know about the LTN Trust?'

'Nothing, other than it's an investment vehicle that's been around for years. There are loads like it, there and in other offshore places. It'll be legit, though; I'd vouch for that. Bermuda isn't lawless; investment is its main industry and it's regulated. You have to be these days, or the G8'll shut you down. Sorry, Maggie, you're stuck. You'll have to try something else.' Harkness chuckled. 'How about tapping his mother's letters, phones and e-mails?'

'I could do all that. I could follow her every movement, and Davor's too. But, Jacqui, this man is way too smart to be sending his mum postcards from exotic locations, or dropping her a quick call on the mobile, and his folks aren't going to put him at risk by meeting him.' She paused. 'Have you got any literature on Fishheads, anything that goes back to the time he was there?'

'I've got a copy of the last annual report. I'll send you that. Where do you want it?' Maggie gave her the Gordon Terrace address. 'That doesn't sound like a police station,' she said.

'It's not. It's my home; I told you, I've got Special Branch status on this, but I'm working on my own, with my boss's approval.'

Harkness whistled. 'Wow! Go on, Maggie, tell me what's he done? I won't breathe a word, I promise.'

As she spoke, Stephanie stirred in her carry-cot, and began to cry.

'Do you hear that wee one in the background?' her mother asked.

'Couldn't fail to. Yours?'

'Yes. Just before she was born, Dražen killed her dad.'

Twenty-four

Inspector Grade had carried his nickname from childhood, having inherited it from several generations of male forebears, since his official Christian name, Joyner, had been introduced by marriage to his family in the mid-eighteenth century. In his infancy he had been known as 'Wee Chippy', until, in his seventh year, his grandfather had died and the sobriquet 'Young Chippy' had passed to him. He still wore it within his circle of relations, friends and neighbours in and around the town of Broxburn, where he had been born and where he still lived. His father . . . plain 'Chippy'; the term 'senior' was never used . . . was a hearty sixty-nine. Grade hoped that he would still be 'Young Chippy' long after he had given up work, and that his older son, aged fourteen and six feet tall, would have to wait far longer than he had before the time came for him to move up the pecking order.

In fact, when the current 'Wee Chippy' had been born, he and his wife had considered breaking the chain by naming him William, but had bottled out in the face of his father's silent glare when they had broached the subject.

So, when the call was put through, he replied automatically, 'Chippy Grade.' 'Young' was beyond the pale at work and his given name had simply disappeared from the public domain.

'Good morning, Inspector,' said Detective Superintendent Neil McIlhenney.

Grade tried to read his tone, but failed. He barely knew the recently appointed Edinburgh CID commander, or his boss, DCS McGuire, but their formidable reputations had spread throughout the force: they were to be treated with caution.

'And the same to you, sir.' He carried on, briskly, 'I've looked out those rosters Mr McGuire asked me about. PC Weekes was indeed on duty the day that Stacey Gavin's body was found. But without asking him directly, I've no way of telling whether he was at the scene or not. I do know this, though: less than two hours after it was reported, he was at the scene of a traffic accident on the A90. So if he did respond to the Gavin call . . .'

'He wasn't there long,' McIlhenney concluded. 'That's fine, Inspector; at least we know he was in the vicinity. He's on shift now, yes?'

'Yes, sir. He clocked on at eight.'

'And the poster we circulated, the one asking for information about Sugar Dean, with her photograph, that's on prominent display in your station?'

'You can't miss it,' Grade assured him. 'You can't walk into this building without coming face to face with the poor woman. It's in the locker room too, as DCS McGuire asked.'

'Has Weekes reacted?'

'In what way?'

'Has he said anything about it, to you or his sergeant?'

'No.' Grade drew a deep breath. 'Look, sir,' he sighed, 'what's this about?'

'Maybe nothing, but we've discovered from the woman's folks that Weekes was engaged to her a couple of years back.'

'And he hasn't volunteered the fact? I'll have him on the carpet right now.'

'No, Inspector, don't do that. We've got other plans for him. Say nothing to him, unless he walks into your office and asks to make a statement about the relationship. If he does that, let me know at once. If he doesn't, make sure that at midday he's somewhere we can get our hands on him double quick.'

Twenty-five

Skinner checked his watch: it showed one minute to eleven, Central European Time. There had been no call from McGuire with the name and location of a contact with the French police.

'Let's hit the road,' he said to Aileen testily, 'if you still want to come, that is.'

'Of course I do,' she replied, 'but don't you want to give Mario another half-hour?'

'Fifteen minutes, maybe.'

'Which force will your contact be from?'

'The gendarmerie, I suppose, since it's a rural area. The Police Nationale, the lot that used to be called the Sûreté, operate in the cities and larger towns.'

'See?' She smiled. 'National police forces.'

'The gendarmerie is under the control of the French defence ministry,' he pointed out. 'They're bloody soldiers in all but name. Do you want Scotland to have riot police like they've got . . . the CRS, bussing in heavies in uniform from Aberdeen when there's trouble in Glasgow, so there's less chance of them knowing any of the heads they crack open?'

'Okay, okay,' Aileen assured him. 'I'm not jumping the gun; we still have to discuss your report. Now, are you going to tell me why you're on edge all of a sudden?'

'Ach, it's nothing.'

She raised an eyebrow. 'Bob.'

His grin had a boyish look to it. 'You know,' he said, 'when you put on that face, I understand how the guy who leads your opposition in the Parliament must feel, when he gets his weekly hammering. I'm sorry, love. When you were in the shower I had a phone call I wasn't expecting.'

'Who was it from?'

'Jimmy, the chief; telling me that he's chucking it. Retiring. Taking his pension. Now.'

'But he's not supposed to go until next year.'

'Not quite. He has to go next year, but with his service, he could have retired years ago on full whack.'

'What's made him change his mind?'

'The tank's empty, he says. He also said that he's been feeling like a spare prick in the command corridor for the last two or three years, although I don't know what he meant by that. Jimmy's been a great chief constable; there won't be another like him.'

'Oh, no?'

'No, there won't, ever,' he insisted. 'Jimmy's unique.'

'And so will you be.'

'That's what he said too. He also told me that he'll take it as a personal affront if I don't apply for the job.'

'So will I . . .' said Aileen. She paused. 'Well, maybe not quite as strongly as that, but I'll be disappointed.'

'Maybe you're the very reason why I won't apply. The First Minister's partner in a chief constable's uniform? The tabloids will have a field day.'

'Excuse my English, but fuck the tabloids. What's my job got to do with yours or yours with mine? If I thought that I was preventing you from being all you should be, I'd get out of the way.'

He stared at her. 'You'd leave me?'

She smiled. 'Don't be so bloody silly. I'll never leave you. But I'm only a politician, a glorified committee chair. I could be replaced tomorrow, as my predecessor found out the hard way, and it wouldn't hurt me to walk away. You, my love, are different; you're a leader . . . born and bred, from what you've told me about your father. This is something you've got to do.'

'I'm a hands-on cop, Aileen,' he said quietly.

'Then be a hands-on chief constable; break the bloody mould. I've seen all of them, you know; I've met all the Scottish chiefs. We don't need yet another bureaucrat among them. We need you. And if I do start a debate about a national police force, I'll need you . . . on the right side.'

He slid his arms around her waist. 'You know what? I need you too, Ms de Marco, much more than I need any career; you've been the salvation of me. Tell you what: I'll do you a deal. You marry me, and I'll apply for Jimmy's job.'

Her mouth fell open. 'You . . .' she gasped. 'Don't think you can wriggle out of it like that. You've got a responsibility to the people.' She paused. 'However, if that's what it takes . . . okay, you've got a deal.'

He raised her on her toes and kissed her. 'When?' he murmured.

'In six months,' she replied, 'if we both still want it. Let's get you in the chair first, let some time elapse, and then do it quietly. When does Sir James go?'

'In a couple of months; he'll give a period of notice and take accrued leave. End result, he'll be gone before September. The selection process will take longer than that, though; much of the six months you were talking about.' He put his forehead against hers. 'By the way, that was serious nonsense you were talking back there. No way are you just a glorified committee chair. It's people like you who make people like me decide not to take over the country, not just yet.'

Aileen laughed. 'You will let me know when you change your mind, won't you, so I can have you arrested?'

Bob checked his watch. 'Come on,' he said, 'let's get on the road. I've got a witness to track down and interview.'

He was in the act of picking up the car keys when the phone rang. 'At last,' he exclaimed, snatching it up. 'Mario?' he said.

'Mr Skinner?' asked a female voice.

'Yes.'

'Is the First Minister with you?'

'That depends. Who is this, and how did you get this number?'

'It's the Lord Advocate's office, and Lena McElhone, her private secretary, gave it to me.'

He ignored the stiffness in the woman's voice. 'She's here,' he conceded. 'What's the panic?'

'The Lord Advocate would like to speak to Ms de Marco.'

He could feel Aileen's eyes on his back. 'Please tell the Lord Advocate she'll call him back in a couple of minutes. I have your office number.'

'That's all right. I'll hold on.'

'No,' he said firmly. 'The First Minister will call you back.'

'I could have taken it,' she said, as he turned to face her.

'And possibly found yourself talking to the news editor of the *Daily Star*. She could have been anyone. Basic security, love, that's all. I'll call Johnson back now.' He flipped through his directory, found the number and dialled it. 'I have the First Minister on the line for the Lord Advocate,' he told the switchboard. 'He's expecting the call.'

He handed over the white handset.

'This is Aileen de Marco,' he heard her begin; then add, a few seconds later, 'Gavin, you're not one of my regular callers. What can I do for you?'

Although she had never asked him to, Bob preferred to leave her to make her business calls in private; he strolled outside, on to the terrace, and waited. Almost fifteen minutes later, she came out to rejoin him. Her expression was troubled.

'What's set my Lord Advocate's wig spinning?' he asked her.

'You have, or at least your force has. Gavin Johnson's new in the job, even newer than I am in mine, so he's anxious not to stand on anyone's toes. He's got the Crown Agent up in arms. Apparently, there was a report on the Daniel Ballester murders, by your force, to the Crown

Office. It led to the inquiry being closed. Now we've got this new killing in Edinburgh. It bears a strong similarity to some of the others and Neil McIlhenney's insisting that the Agent ... What's his name again?'

'Dowley. Joe Dowley.'

'That's it. Neil wants the Crown Office to have a leak inquiry, and Dowley is having none of it.'

'What do you mean, having none of it?' Bob demanded.

'I'm quoting Gavin Johnson.'

'But we're entitled to ask him to do that.'

'Dowley says you're not, that his office is at the top of the pyramid.' ·

'I always knew that man was a fool.'

'He's an adamant fool, though. When Neil stood his ground, he phoned Sir James at home and, again according to Gavin, he was told to eff off.'

Bob winced. 'He must have riled him: that's not the chief's style.' He frowned. 'I'll bet that's what's behind it, this sudden decision of his to go. He's had enough of intransigent idiots interrupting his private life. What's Johnson doing about it? Why's he bothering you?'

Aileen wrinkled her nose. 'I think he's a bit afraid of the Crown Agent.'

'I'm not,' Bob growled. 'I'll deal with the bastard.'

'Gavin's afraid of that too. He's asked me to persuade you to back off.'

'Jesus! What did you tell him?'

'That I couldn't possibly interfere in an operational police matter.'

'But, still, you've been caught in the middle of this. Aileen, I can't tell Neil to walk away. Apart from the loss of face involved, the guy's right. If we don't eliminate the possibility of a leak within the Crown Office, we could have an investigation with a big hole in it. Dowley should never have got involved.'

'But he did, and now he's threatening to resign, publicly, if he's overruled.'

'And now,' said Bob, 'he'll know that Johnson's spoken to you, so if I persist and he does resign, he could well claim that by staying out of it, you took my side against him: or, worse, that I told you to stay out of it. I can't let any of that happen.'

'We're not going to let him win, though. Are we?'

He fell silent. He sat on a lounger and gazed into the pool until, finally, he shook his head. 'No,' he declared, 'we're not. Here's what we're going to do.'

Twenty-six

Andy Martin scowled across the desk at Detective Chief Superintendent Rod Greatorix, the Tayside force's head of CID. 'You can't be serious,' he said.

'I can,' the detective replied. 'I wish I wasn't, but I was there and I witnessed the whole fucking shambles. I was ready, the other police witnesses were ready, the pathologists were there, the jury was empanelled and in place, and the judge was on the bench. The only thing that was fucking empty was the dock. The prisoner wasn't with us.'

'Where the hell was he?'

'In Edinburgh, in a cell, in the remand section of Saughton Prison. Somebody in the Crown Office got the dates mixed up. They had the trial down to begin next Wednesday, not this morning.'

'Who was the judge?'

'Lady Broughton, one of the new ones. Remember? She used to be Phyllis Davidson, QC.'

'I know Phil. How did she react?'

'Like the lady she is. When Herman Butters, the Advocate Depute, finally stood up, half an hour late, and said that he wasn't ready to proceed, and wouldn't be until tomorrow morning, she just smiled at him, and said, "That is unfortunate, isn't it? In that case, we all might as well go home." You should have seen the look of relief on wee Butters's face, until she dropped the bomb, that is.'

'What bloody bomb?'

'Butters asked her if she wanted to start early tomorrow, to make up time, and she said, "You misunderstand me. The case is deserted, *pro loco et tempore*. The jury is discharged." Then she thanked them all for their service, short though it had been, as she put it. As if that wasn't bad enough, Grandpa McCullough's counsel, Sally Mathewson, stood up and asked that her client be formally acquitted and released.'

'He wasn't, was he? Don't tell me that.'

'No, Phil was too smart for that. She pointed out that what she had done didn't amount to an acquittal, and that the Crown could bring the case back to court. But she did say that he could have bail until they were ready to do that.'

Martin pushed himself out of his chair and stepped towards the window of his office. 'Bloody hell,' he exclaimed. 'It's taken you . . . what? . . . more than half of your career to nail McCullough for something serious, and now he's out on the street. We'll have to lock the key witnesses up, or they'll both wind up as dead as the guy he killed.'

Greatorix held up a hand, as if in reassurance. 'It's okay. It's not as bad as that. Remember, we're proceeding with the murder charge separately from the Class A possession indictment. I had him rearrested on that so he never got out of Saughton.'

'Thank Christ for small mercies, Rod. Have you told the chief?'

'He's not back from his meeting yet. If I know him he'll want to write to the Solicitor General. Black day for wee Butters, eh?'

'Too right.' Martin snorted. 'I've got a feeling that he'll spend the rest of his stint as a prosecutor in places like Wick, Dumfries and Ayr. Maybe even Lerwick, if they can find a reason to have the High Court sit up there.'

'It can't be far enough away,' said the chief superintendent. 'See you later.'

The deputy chief constable returned to his desk with mixed emotions, a small part of him wanting to laugh at the farcical scene that had played out in court, the rest appalled by the consequences that might have flowed from the prosecution's mistake, but for Greatorix's quick thinking. Knowing that Graham Morton, his chief constable, would consult him about a formal complaint to the Solicitor General, he began to draft a letter. It was almost complete when his assistant opened his door.

'I've got Sir James Proud on the line, sir,' he said. 'He'd like a word.'

'Then put him through,' Martin replied at once. 'Chief,' he said, as he heard the click of the connection.

'Not for much longer, son.'

'So I hear. Nine months, is it?'

'Less than nine weeks. I've moved the date forward. Mind you, as of this moment, you, Bob and my human-resources director are the only three people outside my house who know.' He paused. 'But maybe not. I imagine that Bob has had a heart to heart with his lady by now.'

'Has he said whether he'll apply?'

'No, but I believe that he'll be told to.'

'And she must be obeyed?'

'No again, unless she's right, as she usually is.'

'You know that if he does apply, I won't?'

'I guessed as much. That'll be your decision, Andy. I'd respect it either way.'

'Thanks, Chief,' said Martin. 'And thanks for letting me know too. I appreciate that. I'll look forward to your leaving do.'

'Ah, but that's not the only reason I called.' A new, mysterious tone came into Sir James's voice. 'I want to make you a formal request, one of the last I'll make in office, so if you turn me down you'll feel really guilty about it.'

'If it comes to that,' Martin chuckled, 'I'll go to confession and seek absolution. But go on, you've got my attention.'

'A situation has developed in Edinburgh. It's a difference of view that's developed into a confrontation between senior CID officers and Joe Dowley, the Crown Agent.'

Martin listened, as Proud described how the problem had arisen, and how it had escalated. 'Dowley doesn't have a leg to stand on,' he said, when the chief constable had finished. 'If the Lord Advocate's too chicken to back you, and you want to take it all the way, couldn't you apply to the court for a compliance order?'

'Yes,' Sir James agreed, 'I could; I've already had legal advice to that effect. But for various reasons, I don't want to go there. I've discussed this with Bob, and it's our considered view that the best way to defuse the situation is by appointing an officer from another force to carry out an objective inquiry into the possibility of a leak of sensitive information from the Ballester report.'

'Why has it gone this far so fast?' asked Martin. 'There's no certainty that the Dean homicide is a copycat.'

'No, but the investigating officers believe that to be a possibility, so it has to be checked out. To answer your question, if Gregor Broughton, the Edinburgh fiscal, hadn't been off at a conference somewhere, he'd have talked to a few people quietly and either come up with a culprit or given McIlhenney an assurance that his office was clean. But he wasn't, so Neil asked his assistant to look into it. She's new, so she took it all the way up to Dowley, and war broke out.'

'Why didn't she go to the deputy Crown Agent?'

'On holiday.'

'So what's Dowley's angle?'

'The Lord Advocate thinks that he's trying to make a name for himself, with a view to becoming a judge. Having a reputation for not being a soft touch for the police might not do him any harm with the judicial appointments board.'

'Why make such a fuss? The Crown Agent's pretty much assured of going on to become a sheriff.'

'Gavin Johnson reckons he's more ambitious, that his sights are set on the Supreme Court. But,' said Sir James, 'you haven't asked me why I'm speaking to you about this.'

Martin smiled. 'I have a terrible feeling that I know.'

'You're right, then. I want you to conduct the investigation. You know this force, you're familiar with the workings of the Crown Office, and with a spell in Special Branch on your CV, your discretion is assured. This has to be completely confidential. I've spoken to Graham Morton, and given the time of year he's okay with it, as long as it doesn't take more than a couple of weeks, which it won't, since there aren't that many people in the chain. So, Andy, will you take the job on?'

Martin sighed. 'Hell's teeth, Chief; rattling cages in the Crown Office and investigating former colleagues is not my idea of a fun time.'

'As a favour to me?'

'Ah, shit. Put like that . . . Give me a quiet room on the command corridor, and your exec as my leg man, if I need him. I'll be there tomorrow morning.'

Twenty-seven

'How are we going to play this? The usual way?' McIlhenney was gazing from McGuire's office window down the driveway that approached the entrance to the force headquarters building. 'It does no harm to be able to see who's coming and who's going,' Bob Skinner always maintained. As he watched the uniformed figure walking up the slope from the patrol car that had dropped him off, the detective superintendent understood what he meant.

He recognised Constable Theodore Weekes from the photograph in the personnel file that lay open on the head of CID's desk. Even from that distance he read the look of uncertainty on his face, and detected his hesitancy as he walked up the rising pavement. Chippy Grade had told him he was wanted at Fettes, no more than that, and had detailed a car to take him straight there, with a colleague beside him in the back seat as if he were a prisoner.

'You nice guy, me nasty guy, you mean?' McGuire replied. His eyebrows came together in a frown. 'No, let's change the act; let's give this man no comfort at all.'

'Treat him as a suspect from the off, you mean?'

'He's more than a suspect: he's guilty of failing to report information that might be relevant to a murder investigation. So let's not offer him as much as a single smile, from either of us. The best that's going to happen to him is that he walks out of this room with a reprimand on his record stiff enough to end any hopes he might have of ever making sergeant.'

'Fine by me.' McIlhenney's face set hard as he took a seat beside the chief superintendent, facing the door, watching and waiting.

The reception staff had been ordered to say nothing to Weekes as he arrived, to answer no questions he might ask, but simply to escort him to his final destination.

There was no name on McGuire's door, only a number. When, finally, the two detectives heard their visitor's knock, they waited. The knock was repeated, louder this time.

'Come in,' McIlhenney shouted. The door was opened slowly and PC Weekes stepped inside.

In the days of heavy serge uniforms, all police officers had had a substantial look to them. The modern tunic may suit some better than others, but Weekes filled his impressively. He was over six feet tall, with strikingly good looks, enhanced by a honey-brown complexion that would have suggested at least one parent of Caribbean origin, had McGuire and McIlhenney not known already from his file that his mother was Barbadian.

He stared at them, patently puzzled.

'Cap off,' McGuire snapped. His briskness broke the constable's trance. Instantly, he swept his cap from his head and tucked it under his arm as he stepped up to the head of CID's desk and came to attention.

They let him stand there for over a minute, rigid and staring straight ahead, until McIlhenney, in an even tone, with just a hint of menace, asked him, 'Do you know who we are?'

Without easing his stance, Weekes swept his eyes from one seated man to the other. 'No, sir,' he replied.

'Then why the fuck are you standing to attention?' the super-intendent snapped. 'Do you know how many civilian management staff this force has?'

'No, sir. Sorry, sir. I just assumed.' Weekes's voice was surprisingly soft; his accent was Scottish, but with a hint of his mother's influence.

'You're brought here with no notice,' McGuire growled, leaning his massive forearms on the edge of the desk, 'no indication of what it's about, but your assumption seems to be that you're in the shit. That, of itself, tells me a hell of a lot about you, Constable. You can stand easy . . .' he paused as Weekes relaxed his stance '. . . but not too easy. You've upset my colleague and me, and that's never a good thing to do.'

'Sorry, sir: beg your pardon, sir. How have I upset you?'

'By not fucking knowing us! For your enlightenment, I'm DCS McGuire, the head of CID, and this charmer on my right is Detective Superintendent McIlhenney, known occasionally to our friends as the Glimmer Twins, and to our rapidly dwindling body of enemies as the Bad News Bears. For better or worse, we're two of the most recognisable officers on this force. You're standing there with five years' service, and you don't know us?'

'Sorry, sir. Now you say it, I . . .'

'Bullshit! What's your station inspector's name?' McGuire asked.

'Chippy . . . Sorry, sir, Inspector Grade.'

'Name and rank of your divisional commander?'

'Eh . . .'

'Failed that one. Who's the chief constable?'

'Mr Proud.'

'Sir James to you. Deputy chief?'

'Mr Skinner.'

'ACC?'

'Eh . . .'

'Exactly. You're not interested in the force, Weekes. You're interested in the uniform. You like the job security, and the promise of an early pension. Most of all, though, you like the power it gives you. It lets you throw your weight about, scare the wee neds in the town centres, slap the odd law student around.' The constable's eyes narrowed. 'You don't think that's been forgotten, do you?' the chief superintendent challenged.

'No proceedings were taken, sir.' The response was mumbled.

'None were,' said McIlhenney, 'but only because the divisional commander whose name you don't even know wrote a letter of apology to the kid's parents . . . lucky for you they weren't lawyers themselves . . . blaming your recklessness on the stress that beat officers suffer on the job.'

'I didn't know that, sir.'

'No, you thought you'd got off with a telling-off from Inspector Varley, and that's all you cared about. You probably thought that the transfer to South Queensferry was a bonus. It wasn't. It was what they do with an officer whose attitude might lead to him picking on the wrong ned and getting a blade stuck in him. Have you ever done any firearms training, Weekes?' The change of subject was so swift that the man blinked, and his mouth fell open.

'Yes, sir,' he said, when he had recovered himself. 'Three years ago I applied for armed-response duty. I was tried out, but I didn't get in.'

McIlhenney knew from the file that he had been a good shot, but had fallen short in the rigorous psychological assessment given to potential members of the armed unit.

Curiosity seemed to embolden Weekes. 'Why do you ask, sir?'

'Just wondering, that's all.'

McGuire checked his watch. 'Congratulations,' he said. 'You've just broken the record.'

'What record, sir?'

'You've been in this room for five minutes without asking what you're here for. The previous best was four and a half. But you don't need to ask, Theo, do you? You bloody know why you're here.'

The man stuck his chest out, his first show of defiance. 'No, sir. Sir, I'd like a Police Federation rep present.'

'You'd what?' McIlhenney exploded. 'It's not a Fed rep you need, it's a lawyer . . . but you're not having one of them either, not yet at any rate. You're here for questioning in a murder investigation, Weekes, not for backchatting a sergeant.'

'A murder investigation?' the constable exclaimed.

'Sugar Dean. You were engaged to her, until you dumped her, two years ago. True?'

Weekes's gaze dropped to the floor; he nodded.

'Have you been locked in the bog for the last twenty-four hours, maybe missed the TV news, not seen a paper?'

'No, sir.'

'Did you have your eyes closed when you walked into your station this morning, past the poster with your ex's face plastered all over it?'

'No, sir.'

'Then why have you failed in your duty as a police officer by not volunteering the fact of your relationship with a murder victim to the officers handling the inquiry into her death?'

Weekes's shoulders quivered in what might have been a shrug. 'Don't know, sir.'

'Look at us when you're insulting us,' McGuire ordered, 'not at your feet.'

The command was obeyed. 'I never insulted you, sir.'

'Of course you did. You insulted our intelligence.'

'Are you two picking on me because I'm black?' the man exclaimed.

McGuire stared at him, in genuine astonishment. 'Are we what? Constable, you've just insulted us again. We're questioning you about what appears to us to be a serious failure on your part in your duty as a police officer. Your skin tone has nothing to do with it. You could be purple and it would make no difference to us. Is that understood?'

He nodded. 'Yes, sir. I apologise.'

'Fine, as long as we're clear about that. Now, please answer Superintendent McIlhenney's question.'

'I never thought it was important, sir. That's the truth.'

McGuire sighed. 'He's done it again, Neil, and you know how much I hate it when suspects take the piss.'

'I hoped nobody would find out,' Weekes blurted out. 'Okay?'

'Okay?' McGuire gasped. 'Of course it's not fucking okay! Why did you want to keep your broken engagement to a murder victim a secret? How did you ever think you could? Did you not think that her parents would tell us about you?'

'I hoped they'd forgotten about me by now.'

'Oh, no, Weekes. From what the investigating officers tell me, John Dean is not going to forget you in a hurry. Come on; for the last time, why were you so shy about being engaged to Sugar? I promise you, you're not leaving this room without telling us the truth.'

Weekes looked the chief superintendent in the eye, and became a believer. 'I'm engaged again,' he said tamely.

'We know that. Her name's Mae Grey and she's a constable, stationed at Livingston. I don't see your problem. Did you tell her you're a virgin? Or were you worried that she might think you're a bad bet, having chucked one fiancée already?'

'I never chucked Sugar. She chucked me.'

'Why did she let her parents think it was the other way around?' asked McIlhenney.

'I suppose she didnae want to tell them the truth.'

'And what was that?' McGuire asked impatiently.

'We had problems.'

'Christ, I feel like a fucking dentist here, drawing wisdom teeth. What sort of problems?'

'Sexual problems.'

'Elaborate,' said McIlhenney, 'or we really will start pulling your teeth out.'

'I gave her a dose. The clap. Gonorrhoea. Ken?'

'Yes, Weekes, we may be senior officers but we know what the clap is. But I've got a problem with that. There's no record of it in her medical history.'

'She didn't go to her own doctor, so there wouldn't be. She went to a clinic: we both did.'

'Okay. This infection, where did you pick it up?'

'Off a bird I was with.'

'Name?'

'Christ, sir, I dinnae ken.'

'Casual sex, indeed. As in "Good morning and what's your name again?" Were you on duty when this encounter took place?'

'Do I have to answer that?' The constable looked at McIlhenney hopefully.

'Oh, do you ever!' the superintendent told him.

He nodded.

'Say it!'

'Yes, sir, I was on duty.'

'So who was the woman?'

'Inspector Varley's wife.'

'Aw, Jesus.' McGuire groaned. 'If you think you'll get us to back off by telling us a story like that . . .'

'It's true, sir, honest. I had to pick the inspector up from home once. I thought she gave me the eye then, but I wasn't sure. Then a week later I was on patrol in the shopping centre in Livingston and I saw her with a load of parcels. She said that he had the car so I ran her home, tae save her the taxi fare, ken. Ah'd no sooner dumped her bags in the kitchen than she grabbed me by the ba's.'

'Did you threaten to charge her with assault, as you should have?' the head of CID asked.

'No.'

'You gave her one on the kitchen table instead?'

'Well, it was upstairs, but aye.'

'And you're sure that Mrs Varley was the source of your later infection?'

'It couldn't have been anybody else.'

'Did it ever occur to you that Sugar might have given it to you rather than the other way around?'

'No, Sugar wasn't like that. Besides,' he added, 'I had the symptoms before Sugar and I actually did the business ourselves.'

'You incredible bastard.' McGuire sighed.

'I never kent what it was, though. At that stage it was a bit sore when I had a pish, that's all. It was after that the discharge started.'

McIlhenney leaned forward. 'How much of the truth did you tell Sugar?'

'All of it.'

'So she knew that Inspector Varley's wife puts it about?'

'I told her that. I said I couldnae help it. I said I was feart she'd tell him it was me that made the move. It did no good, though. She broke it off.'

'I'll tell you something now, Weekes,' said the superintendent, sincerely. 'If I ever find a bloke like you around my daughter, I'll fucking rip it off.'

'When was the last time you saw Sugar Dean?' asked McGuire.

'Two months ago.'

'You did? Where?'

'At the Gyle. I asked her to meet me there, so I could tell her about me and Mae getting married.'

'How did she react?'

'She said she was pleased for me and wished me all the best. She seemed really happy for me.'

'When you saw her did you refer to the break-up of your relationship?'

'I might have mentioned it, sir.'

'Did you ask her to promise to keep the truth to herself?'

'No, sir, I didn't, honest.'

'Were you worried that she might not?'

Weekes shifted his stance; his cap slipped from under his arm and fell to the floor. 'Ah've been worried about that for the last two years, sir,' he replied.

'Do you remember Stacey Gavin?' McIlhenney fired the question at him.

He frowned. 'Who?'

'Do better.'

The constable wrinkled his brow as if to give the impression of thought. 'Was she the lass that was murdered in South Queensferry?'

'That's the girl. Were you on duty that day?'

'Yes, sir.'

'Were you at the scene?'

Weekes shook his head. 'No, sir, I was baby-sitting a probationer that week, so the desk sergeant sent Taffy Jones and Meg Ritchie.'

'Did you talk to them afterwards?'

'I might have. They got the piss taken out of them when it turned out to be a murder. They came back saying it was an overdose.'

'But that's all?'

'Yes, sir.'

McIlhenney leaned back, handing the floor to McGuire. 'Back to attention, Weekes,' said the head of CID. 'I'm advising you that I'm recommending that the chief constable issues a formal reprimand to you because of your failure to offer information immediately on your relationship with Sugar Dean. That was a clear dereliction of duty, whatever the reason. I'm ordering you now to rectify that omission by going to the investigation team, and making a formal statement to Detective Inspector Stallings, who's in charge. If she should ask you for details of your break-up, you may tell her for the record that you decided you didn't want to marry her after all. That's what her family believe, and it's fine with me.' He stood, for the first time since Weekes had entered the room. 'Now get the fuck out of my sight, and don't even dream of ever applying for CID.'

The two colleagues watched the door as it closed behind him. 'Do you believe him?' the superintendent asked.

'Dunno,' McGuire admitted. 'You?'

'I'm not ruling him out. I'm going to check Jock Varley's record, to see if he had any sick leave a couple of years back.'

'Do that, and go further. Tell Shannon to do a Special Branch vetting job on Varley; I want access to his medical records, and his wife's. Plus, get her to check all the places in our area that offer advice on sexual matters. She's to look for records of Sugar and the shit that just left here, and also to see if the Varleys were treated anywhere too.' He looked at McIlhenney once more. 'Could he have done it?'

'You heard him, Mario. He's been worried for two years that she might spill the beans. Maybe he decided to make sure she didn't, and set her up to look like Stacey Gavin as cover.'

'Is he that clever?'

'Desperate people do desperate things. Let's see if we can find out where he was when Sugar died. We didn't put that to him, but I'll make sure Stallings does, just to keep him on edge. If he satisfies her, fair enough; if not, we look further. Meanwhile, I'm going to have a talk with PC Mae Grey. Maybe the lass needs to know what she's marrying.'

Twenty-eight

'Thank God for satellite navigation,' said Aileen, as they passed the sign that advised them they were entering the town of Collioure. 'That was quite complicated after we left the motorway.'

'No, it wasn't,' Bob protested. 'I'm a police officer: I know how to follow traffic signs.'

'Then why did you have the system installed in the car?'

'I didn't; Alex did, so she can go exploring when she's out here. She uses the Spanish place more than I do now. She grabs cheap weekend flights whenever she can.'

'Alone?'

'I never ask. We had this deal, before Sarah, in her final school years, and when she was starting university. Information like that was never sought by either of us, only volunteered, if we chose.'

Aileen smiled. 'And did you always stick to that?'

'Sure, but she always told me what she was up to.'

'Did you always approve of her boyfriends?' she asked, teasing.

'Sure, once I'd had them checked out.'

'What? You had your daughter's teenage boyfriends vetted?'

'Too bloody right. So would you, in my situation.'

'Did you ever veto anyone?'

Bob frowned. 'There was one guy, when she was nineteen, who gave her trouble, very bad trouble.'

'What did you do with him?'

He gave a quick, awkward smile. 'I killed him. What else would a caring father do? Then there was Andy, of course,' he said, moving on. 'Now, I did not see that one coming. Christ, I even asked him once to chum her to a university dance, when she was stuck for a date. Alex has always been smarter than me; it took me a while to work out that she was only stuck because she wanted me to ask him to chum her!'

'How did you handle it when you found out about them?'

'Hasn't Alex told you?'

'Yes,' she admitted, 'but I want to hear your version.'

'Very badly, I confess. I blew up at them both, told Andy he'd betrayed my trust. He transferred out of CID for a while, into uniform. Everybody thought I'd pushed him, but I didn't. I wanted to keep him in post regardless, but he went to the chief and asked for a move.'

'How did you get over it?'

'Common sense kicked in. One day, I realised that my daughter had grown up. I worked out something else too: that if I was from another culture, one in which arranged marriages were the norm, Andy was probably the guy I'd have picked for her. So I was happy, and when they got engaged, I was well on-side.' He sighed. 'Then it all went pear-shaped.'

'She got pregnant?'

'She told you that too? Yes, she did, and had an abortion, without ever telling Andy about the kid. He's Catholic, quietly devout, for all that he can be a tough boy when he has to. He took it very badly.'

'I can understand that, but . . .'

'There was more, though, that maybe she didn't tell you. Alex had a fling with a young guy, a cousin of her pal. The wee bastard got himself lifted on some drug-related thing, and he gave her as his alibi for the time in question. Very messy, and for Andy, very embarrassing. Not terminal, though, he'd have got over that: but the abortion, no.'

'And you,' Aileen asked, 'how did you feel about it?'

'I don't know, to be honest. She was wrong on two counts . . . no, three. She shouldn't have allowed herself to get pregnant in the first place if she had any doubt about it. Also, she should have told him about it, and let him state his case at the very least. Plus, she was in a relationship that was supposed to be monogamous, so she shouldn't have been shagging the boy. Mind you,' he added, 'that's the one I'm least able to criticise her about. There were times when I wasn't a great role model for her. Bottom line, though, she's my kid and I will always support her, right or wrong. That outweighs any disappointment I might have felt.'

'Disappointment that they didn't marry?'

'No, at the way she hurt Andy. That their engagement broke up? No. The truth was she was bored, or she wouldn't have slept with the boy. The truth was she was more committed to her career than to getting married. The truth was, she was way too young to have been thinking about it.'

'But now she isn't too young any more. Her career is well on track, and before you know it she's going to be a partner in that firm of hers. Do you suppose she ever thinks about Andy?'

'You think she might be carrying a torch?' he asked. 'Is that your impression, from talking to her?'

'She hasn't said anything. But the way she spoke about him, when she did, there's a fondness there, still. Not a torch, perhaps, but a small candle at least.'

'If that's so, I hope it burns out of its own accord. Andy's happily married now, with a growing family.'

'He never looks back?'

'No. There was a time when he was a serial womaniser, before Alex, and then again, as a reaction, I suppose, to what happened. But then he and Karen . . . found each other, I suppose. They're a nice couple, and he won't let anyone come between them. Plus, I like to think that my daughter wouldn't . . .'

'In three hundred yards, turn right!' The firm voice of the navigation system interrupted him.

'Wouldn't dream of even trying,' he murmured, as he obeyed.

'You have reached your destination.'

He looked along the road into which they had turned and saw, twenty yards ahead, a sign that read 'Gendarmerie'.

'Okay,' said Bob, 'this is where we split. You take the car and explore the town, if you're happy doing that. I'll call your mobile when I'm done and you can tell me where to meet you.'

'Fine by me,' Aileen replied. 'I'll probably have lunch first, unless you want me to wait for you.'

'No, you do that. I can grab something later.'

He held the door open as she slid behind the wheel and drew the seat a little further forward, then waved her off as she turned and headed back to the junction. Only when she was out of sight did he turn and walk into the gendarmerie station.

Skinner had been in local police offices in seven countries, on three continents, and found them more or less interchangeable: busy, untidy, poorly furnished, and marked by the underlying body odour of those who worked there. The Collioure version was an exception to his rule of thumb. There were freshly cut flowers in the reception area, and a modern air-conditioning unit was going full blast, a blessed relief from the heat of the day outside.

'Oui, monsieur?' the desk officer greeted him.

'Bonsoir,' he replied. 'Je suis Monsieur Skinner, d'Edimbourg, ici pour Lieutenant Cerdan.' The words felt thick on his tongue. He wondered how far his limited French would carry him. Every sentence had to be thought out carefully before it was uttered: he knew that conversation would be very difficult.

He sighed inwardly with relief when a voice behind him said, in clear, confident English, 'Good day, sir, and welcome to Collioure. I am Lieutenant Jérôme Cerdan.' He turned, to see a slightly built man with dark hair and a small moustache, dressed, almost identically to him, in a white short-sleeved shirt and lightweight tan trousers. The two shook hands. 'I am told you are here to find a young Englishman,' the French officer continued.

'That's right: a lad called Davis Colledge. I'm grateful for your help.'

'No, it's you who have done me a favour: I am based in Perpignan, but on days as hot as this I take every opportunity to come to the coast.'

Skinner smiled. 'Glad to be of service. Have you been told why I need to speak to the boy?'

'His lady friend is dead, yes? Murdered?'

'Yes, in Edinburgh, almost two weeks ago. We have no reason to regard the boy as a suspect, but we need to interview him.'

'And there is a delicacy, yes?'

'His father is a public figure. As far as I'm concerned that doesn't win him any favours, but if our press found out about his involvement, they'd give him a hard time. We don't have the privacy laws that you do in France.'

'I understand, sir. You have an address for him?'

'Yes; three Passage Jules Ferry, studio apartment.'

'Then we will go there at once. It's not far, but a local officer will take us.'

Cerdan led the way through the station, past a row of cells, of which three seemed to be occupied, to a courtyard at the rear, where a uniformed corporal waited beside a police car. He saluted as they approached, then opened the front passenger door for the lieutenant, and the rear for Skinner.

Rather than take the busy main thoroughfare, the driver showed his local knowledge by picking his way through a maze of back-streets, deserted but for parked cars, all with French registrations, and most of them covered with dust. As Cerdan had said, it was a short journey, less than five minutes, until they took a turn and the sea-front opened out before them, a tight bay bounded on the right by a tall domed tower, and on the left by a pier, leading to a rocky outcrop, on which stood a stone shelter, topped by a bell, and beside it, a life-sized figure of Christ on the cross.

The corporal pulled up at the roadside, on a red line that could have meant only one thing, and spoke quietly to the officer.

'He says we have to walk from here,' Cerdan explained. 'These are old streets and only for pedestrians and cyclists.'

They stepped out of the car's chilled air into the blazing afternoon heat, the corporal leading the way. He took them along the beach-front past a crowded restaurant, two art galleries, a busy *crêperie* and, improbably, an ancient Fiat Abarth motor-car that had been converted into a soft drinks bar, until they reached a street that was little more than a wide alley. They had gone no more than a hundred yards when he turned right into a cul-de-sac that was even narrower.

'Ici,' he announced.

There were no shops or bars in the passage, only a dozen or so houses. Number three was half-way along and beside it a blue door, bearing the word 'Studio'. There was no sign of a lock, only a handle. Without bothering to knock, Cerdan seized and turned it, revealing a stone stairway behind that appeared to lead up to the roof. They climbed until they reached a landing, barely large enough for the three men, with a second door, this one brown, with a mortise lock, and a Yale, for extra security. Skinner rapped on it firmly and waited. He knocked again, harder this time, and called out, 'Davis. Davis Colledge. Open up, please. I'm a police officer from Scotland.'

The corporal reached out and tried the handle, but the door was secure.

'Bugger,' Skinner muttered. 'He's probably gone out for lunch. I guess we might have to hang around and wait for him, Lieutenant.'

'Maybe,' Cerdan replied, 'but let's ask first.' He spoke to the corporal, who nodded, and trotted back down the stairway.

He was gone for several minutes: Skinner filled them by asking the Frenchman about his career, about the structure of the gendarmerie, and about its interface with its parallel force the Police Nationale, the Sûreté of Simenon's Maigret. Much of it he knew already from the research he had done in preparing his paper for Aileen, but he found it interesting to have the perspective of a serving officer in one of the forces. 'It's all right,' the lieutenant said finally, 'as long as we take care

135

not to become involved together. That can lead to arguments over . . .' He paused. 'I don't know the word.'

'Jurisdiction?'

'That is it. Do you have such problems in Scotland, sir? I understand that you have a different way?'

'Yes, but it's relatively simple. We're organised on a territorial basis; there's the boundary line and we don't cross it, operationally, other than in hot pursuit. There is a national body tackling serious crime, but that co-operates with forces like mine.'

The noise of footsteps on the stairway announced the corporal's return. He was smiling and holding a key-ring, breathing slightly hard as he reported to his officer.

'Some good news,' Cerdan announced. 'Madame Marnie, the lady in the house below, is the owner of the studio. She has given us keys. But now, not so good. The young man is not here. He left early this morning.'

'He's gone back to Britain?'

'It seems not. He told her that, since he was alone, he was going to see some more of the coast. He asked her also that if his friend should arrive she should tell her that he would be back in a few days.'

'A few days,' Skinner muttered.

'I can find him,' the lieutenant offered. 'I can put out an order to all the stations in the region to look out for him. We can find out if he uses a credit card.'

'We can, but then we'll have started a manhunt. We'll have made it look as if he's a murder suspect, and I don't want that. Let's take a look. Maybe there's another way I can play this.'

The Frenchman nodded, took the keys from the corporal and unlocked the door, then held it open for Skinner. He stepped inside.

'The studio' was exactly that, a big living area, with a kitchen in a corner to the left, a double bed against the wall on the right and a sofa and armchair in the middle. In the furthest part of the room a door lay ajar, revealing a basin and mirror. Two wider doors, half glazed, lit the apartment; they opened out on to a roof terrace.

The place was a mess. The bed was unmade, and the area was littered with pizza boxes . . . Skinner counted four . . . beer cans . . . Davis Colledge appeared to be a Kronenbourg drinker . . . and discarded wine bottles. But all that was incidental.

In the middle of the room there stood an easel, supporting a large canvas. The picture seemed to be complete: it was a woodland scene and in the centre was a female nude, slim, fair-skinned and dark-haired, with heavy, brown-nippled breasts. In the background, to the left, a young man stood, observing her. Skinner moved closer. The male figure was also naked, with a shock of fair hair and an erect penis. It was a beautiful piece of work, spoiled by only one thing; the woman's face had been obliterated, wiped out by a great black smudge that gave the painting an air of menace. Skinner moved closer, examining its detail. The female form had a small pink scar on the right side of the abdomen. He made a mental note of that, then looked at the self-portrait of Davis Colledge. As he studied it, he whistled. The young man's eyes were vivid, and his mouth was a slash across his face. He held something in his hand. Unmistakably, it was a gun.

Skinner reached into his trouser pocket and produced a small digital camera. Using its LCD screen to frame the image, he photographed the picture.

'Lieutenant,' he said quietly. 'I'm going to leave my business card and a note for Davis, if he comes back here, asking him to call me as soon as he finds it. But I hope it doesn't get to that stage. I've changed my mind about your looking for him. I think you should. If this picture represents his state of mind, then he is a very troubled young man.'

Twenty-nine

'What the hell is this?' asked PC Theo Weekes. 'Why couldn't I have given you my statement at the mobile HQ? What's wi' dragging me down to Torphichen Place?'

'Shut it, Constable,' said DS Jack McGurk. 'You're in no position to complain. You've kept us waiting for information we should have had yesterday.'

'And much good will it do you. I know fuck all about this. I went out with Sugar a couple of years ago, and now she's dead. That's a pity; I'm really sorry. But I had nothing to do with it.'

'Whoever said you had?'

'You're treating me like a suspect,' the constable snapped, as the door opened.

'Not yet,' said DI Becky Stallings, as she stepped into the interview room. 'We're treating you like a witness for now. You've made a voluntary statement and that's good, but there are some questions we'd like to ask you.'

She reached for the tape-recorder on the table, then paused, her hand hovering above it. 'Before I switch this on, I want you to know something. Mr McIlhenney called me, so I'm aware of the story you told him, about why you and Miss Dean split up. That's being checked out separately, but at this stage it's not going on the record.'

'Did those two no' believe me?'

'Don't be dense, Weekes. You spin them a story about your station inspector's wife giving you the clap and you think they're going to take it at face value? But even if it's true, it may not be relevant to this inquiry: so what I'm saying to you, and what I believe Mr McGuire said to you also, is that I don't want any reference to it while this tape is running. Understood?'

'Fine by me. Can we get on wi' it? I was due off shift half an hour ago.'

'In that case, let's be brief,' said Stallings, coolly. She switched on the twin-deck recorder, announced the venue, date and time and identified the three people in the room.

Jack McGurk took over. 'Constable Weekes, you've given us a voluntary statement about your former relationship with the murder victim. In it, you said that it terminated because you had second thoughts about marrying her. Why did you have your first thoughts?'

'Eh?'

'Why did you ask her to marry you in the first place?'

The constable pursed his lips as he considered the question. 'Dinnae ken. I suppose I liked her.'

'You liked her? Is that your criterion for a wife?'

'Eh?'

'Criterion. Singular of criteria. Is that all you need to marry someone, that you like them?'

'It's a start. From what I've heard your wife disnae like you much.'

McGurk stiffened: his eyes hardened as they locked on to Weekes. Stallings leaned forward as if to intervene, but he held up a hand. 'I'm impressed, Constable,' he said, 'not by you, but by the power of the police-force grapevine. Mind you it's not always accurate. My wife and I are separated, but that doesn't mean she doesn't like me. As it happens, we're very fond of each other. No, more than that; we love each other, only not enough. We have a problem living together, and we can't get over it. Did you love Sugar?'

'Ah suppose.'

'You're as certain as that? She must really have swept you off your feet.'

'Well, like I said, Ah liked her. We got on.'

'After your split, did you keep in touch?'

'I called her a couple of times.'

'Why?'

'Ah dinnae ken. Just to see how she was doing, I suppose.'

'And with whom?' asked Stallings.

'What do you mean?'

'Did you want to know how she was getting on without you? Whether there was a new man in her life?'

'Dunno. Maybe.'

'Did you ever ask her?'

'Ah suppose I must have.'

'And was there?'

'Not that she told me.'

'When did you meet?' the inspector probed.

'About four years ago.'

'Where?'

'The Tap o' Lauriston.'

'The top of where?'

Weekes looked at her scornfully, as he repeated the name. 'It's a pub,' he replied. 'Up near the art school.'

'How did that come about?'

'There was a wee bit of bother up there: outside, like. I was stationed here then, and my mate and I went to sort it out. Sugar was there, trapped in the doorway by the rammy. It was controlled quick enough, but even after the van had taken the hooligans away, she was scared to walk across the Meadows. She was living in a flat then, up Warrender place. It was a wild night; lots of drunks about and such. So my mate and I, we ran her home. He drove, and Sugar and I got talking. When we got there, I walked her up the stairs and we made a date.'

'And you went on from there?'

'Aye, the usual thing, Ah saw her a couple of times a week, depending on my shift pattern. I was moved out to Livingston not long after that, but we still kept on.'

'Where did you live then?' asked McGurk.

'Gorgie.'

'With your parents?'

Weekes scowled at him. 'With my wife.'

'I see.' The sergeant smiled. 'Did you like her?'

'Of course.'

'Then why were you going out with Sugar?'

'I liked her too.'

'When did you and your wife split up?'

'We were divorced two years ago.'

'Why?'

Weekes glared across the table. 'What the fuck's that got to do wi' you, Sergeant?'

'Constable, you're on tape,' Stallings reminded him.

He ignored her. 'Well?' he demanded.

'That's interesting, Theo,' McGurk replied calmly. 'You were quick to take a crack at my marriage, yet you go all prickly when I ask about yours. Why did your wife divorce you?'

'She didn't. We just agreed.'

'Then who left who?'

'Ah moved out; got a wee house out East Craigs way.'

'When?'

'Three years ago.'

'But according to your personnel file, you were living with your wife in Caledonian Crescent until two years ago.'

'I never got round to telling them until then.'

'But all of us have to be contactable all the time, for emergencies. You must know that.'

'It took me a while to get the phone into ma new place.'

The sergeant frowned. 'Let's imagine that you're under oath. You're not, but humour me. If you were, would you have perjured yourself just now with that answer?'

'Eh?'

'Don't get coy on us, Weekes, and don't lie to us either. You've already had one formal reprimand today. Where you live is cabled. You have a choice of two telephone providers, fighting with each other to get you on line, without any waiting time. So let me ask you again. Why did it take you so long to report your change of address?'

The constable sighed. 'Because I was still at Gorgie most of the time. Okay?'

'No, it isn't, but let's go on. What you're saying is that while you were going out with Sugar Dean, you were still living with your wife.'

'On and off.'

'Enough!' Stallings shouted. She leaned forward and slapped the table. 'Don't bloody prevaricate with us, Constable. When you were dating Sugar, you were two-timing your wife. Yes or no?'

'I suppose so.'

'Yes or fucking no?'

'Yes, then.'

'At last. What's her name, by the way, this wife, or ex, of yours?'

'Lisanne.'

'Did Sugar know about Lisanne?'

'No.'

'Not at all? Never?'

'No.'

'When you started going out, where did she think you lived?'

'I told her I lived at home, that was all.'

'You lied to her.'

'Not exactly.'

Stallings whistled. 'It's men like you that make women like me glad we're still single. At what point did you and Sugar begin a sexual relationship?'

'Not until after I got my house; after we got engaged.'

'And when was that?'

'About two and a half years ago.'

'Are you telling us,' McGurk asked, 'that you asked her to marry you so you could get your leg over? Because that's how it's beginning to sound.'

'Don't be daft.'

'Whose idea was the divorce? Yours or Lisanne's? Which one of you was first to suggest it?'

'Me,' Weekes murmured.

'Louder for the tape, please.'

'Me!'

'How did you put it?'

'I said our marriage was goin' stale, and that I thought we needed space between us.'

'When?'

'Before I got the house.'

'But you didn't move out for a year?'

'Not finally, no.'

'When did you last sleep with Lisanne?' asked Stallings, sharply.

'About three weeks ago.'

'Jeez. Where?'

'Gorgie.'

'How often do you go there?'

'Quite a lot.'

'You say Sugar never knew about Lisanne. Did Lisanne ever know about her?'

Weekes shook his head.

'It's easy for a cop to cover his tracks, isn't it, when he's got a bit on the side?'

'I suppose,' the constable grunted.

'Trust me, I'm a woman, it is. When did you first go out with Mae Grey?'

'About two and a half years ago.'

'Around the time you became engaged to Sugar?'

'Yes. She was my neighbour at work. We went out sometimes after a shift.'

'Do you have a sexual relationship with Mae?'

'Of course. She's my fiancée.'

'When did that begin?'

'Two and a half years ago. The first time I took her back to ma place.'

Stallings leaned back in her seat, appraising the man on the other side of the table. 'How many other women do you have on the go, Theo?'

'Just Mae,' he replied.

'And Lisanne.'

'She's a pal.'

'So you help her out? She can't be going short, though: single woman, good job. She works in a bank, doesn't she? She must be getting as much as she likes.'

The constable's mouth seemed to tighten. 'She's not like that,' he snapped. 'She doesn't go wi' other blokes.'

'How would you know?'

'Because Ah do.'

'Would it upset you if she did? You divorced her, remember.'

'Aye, but . . .'

'Aye, but you don't see it that way,' McGurk intervened. 'Isn't that the truth of it? You talked her into a phoney divorce to give you a free hand with Sugar, and Mae. You signed a declaration that you'd been living apart for two years, when in fact you hadn't. I know all about Scots divorce law, Theo, for personal reasons. If we chose, I reckon we could do you for that. So let's get to it. You like women, don't you?'

'Yes.'

'Sure, you've got Mae, and Lisanne, and how many others?'

'There's a girl in Queensferry I see now and again.'

'And you're possessive about them, aren't you? The idea of Lisanne with another guy wound you up a minute ago. She's still the one, isn't she, out of the three or four or however many it really is?'

'We're divorced.'

'Sure but you keep an eye on her, don't you? I'll bet you sit outside her place without her knowing it, looking for the bedroom light going on when it shouldn't, looking for shadows on the blinds. I'll bet you do.'

'You speaking from experience, McGurk?' Weekes snarled.

'You're fucking right I am! Yes, I did that, at first, till I got used to the fact that Mary and I really had split up. So you can't lie to me, pal; I can see right into you. I can even tell that part of you wants to see the light go on, to see the curtains pulled a second before it goes out, not after. I bet you get a hard-on, sitting there in your car, waiting for that to happen, so that you can go in there and batter the shite out the guy.'

'Fuck you!' he yelled.

'Yeah. That's how you feel, isn't it? Lisanne's yours, and whether you're porking Mae or not, keeping up the pretence that you might marry her, Lisanne will always be yours. Come on, you bastard, admit it. That's how you think!'

'Okay! Clever cunt! Okay!'

'And it was the same with Sugar, wasn't it? When you and she split up, that really was it, Theo. You were never getting in there again, but the idea of someone else shafting her, that did your head in. That's why you kept calling her. That's why you followed her. I'll bet you went fucking crazy when you saw her with the boy. Didn't you, Theo? You went fucking apeshit, didn't you?' McGurk was on his feet as he roared the question at him.

'Too fucking right!' Weekes screamed. 'He's only a fucking schoolie! Only a kid! And they were holding fucking hands; in the fucking street!'

The sergeant smiled as he settled his long frame back on to his hard steel chair. 'Thanks, pal. You want to sharpen up your act; you are way too easy.' He looked sideways at Stallings. 'Sorry about the language, Becky,' he said.

'That's okay, Jack. I know, it's a boy thing: it's the same in London.' She drew herself forward an inch or two, until she could lean her forearms comfortably on the table, and looked at Weekes. He was breathing hard; his expression suggested that he knew something bad had just happened, something he could not quite pin down. 'Yes, Constable,' she began, 'thank you for being so frank. Let's move on . . . or, rather, let's go back. Back to the Friday before last, in fact. I'd like you to tell me where you were at around eight thirty that morning.'

The man's anger had dispersed like steam, condensed and settled on his face in rivulets of sweat. 'In my house,' he replied.

'With which member of your harem?'

'I was on ma own.'

'Oh dear,' said the inspector. 'That is unfortunate.'

Thirty

'And you are?' asked Michael Colledge. 'A detective constable, my researcher said.'

'Not quite,' Bob Skinner replied. 'He misheard me. Deputy chief constable, in fact, but rank's irrelevant here.'

'What's wrong?' the MP exclaimed. 'Has something happened to Dave?'

'No. To the best of my knowledge your son's fine.'

'Come on,' said Colledge, 'deputy chief constables don't call to tell one one's won the lottery.'

'Maybe not, but we delegate the bad-news calls whenever we can. This isn't one of those. I'm calling from Collioure.'

'I thought I heard seagulls in the background. Now I really am confused. A deputy chief constable's gone looking for my son; I didn't realise I was that important.'

You're not, chum. My girlfriend outranks you by quite a bit. Skinner held back the retort, but only at the last second. 'Circumstances, that's all. I happened to be in the region, and so my colleagues asked me to visit Davis and break the news to him about his friend's death.'

'And did you? Is he with you?'

'No, I'm afraid not. I found his apartment, no problem, with the help of the local police, but he's not there. His landlady says that he's gone off for a few days, touring.'

'God.' Colledge sighed. 'He's a sod, but at least he's all right. Thanks for taking the trouble, Mr Skinner: I'm sorry your courtesy's been

147

wasted on him. I'm sure he'll phone me, sooner or later. When he does I'll tell him to get in touch with your officers, as they asked.'

'I don't think we can be as informal as that,' the Scot replied. 'This isn't a minor offence we're looking into: it's a murder investigation. Your son's a close friend of the victim. He may have information that we need, so we can't just wait for him to turn up. Bottom line is, I've asked the French police to find him.'

'Are you saying that you've put an APB out for my son?' There was a change in the MP's tone.

'Nothing as heavy as that, but they're keeping an eye out for him. When they find him he won't be apprehended, but they'll make sure that he gets in touch with us. And with you, of course,' Skinner added. 'If he gets back to Collioure before they do, I've left a note for him.' He chose not to add that Madame Marnie, the landlady, had promised to call the gendarmerie as soon as he returned.

'You've been in his digs? Did you have a warrant?'

The DCC bridled. 'We had the permission of the owner. Is that enough for you?'

'Of course, I'm sorry. Stupid question. What's the place like?'

'It's fine. Not a hovel by any means. He's comfortable, and the set-up's ideal for the work he went out there to do.' He paused. 'Tell me about your son, Mr Colledge. What sort of a guy is he?'

'What do you mean?'

'He's a dedicated artist, I know that, but does he have any other interests?'

'Of course. He's a normal chap in that respect. He got his school colours in rugby: played in the centre in the first fifteen. He plays a pretty decent squash game: left me behind when he was fourteen, and I'm not bad. He was a sergeant in the school's army cadet force. That's how he met Sugar in fact: the force is a joint effort with Mary Erskine. He was along there one day and they got talking. Someone had told her he was a very talented painter.' Colledge chuckled. 'Oh, yes, one other thing: he's a Chelsea supporter.'

'What did the cadet force involve?'

'Kids playing soldiers, really. But no, that's unfair: its purpose is to give them a basic military training, to give them a taste of army discipline and of the reality of service life. If a lad wants to get into Sandhurst, does no harm to be able to include that in his application.'

'They don't use real bullets, though?' The enquiry sounded casual.

'Sometimes, but only on a military range, under army supervision. As a matter of fact, Dave's a pretty good shot. He showed me one of the targets they let him keep.'

'How's he going to react,' asked Skinner, 'when he finds out that Sugar's dead?'

'He's going to be devastated.'

'I'm sure, but how will that express itself? Is he a volatile lad? Will he be numb, will he be tearful, or will he be angry? If you feel it would help, I don't mind coming back up here, when he does show up.' Since seeing the painting, it had been his intention to return, if and when the French police found Davis Colledge.

'That's good of you, Mr Skinner. If you did that, it might help him deal with it. Dave's a good lad, nice boy, but he could handle the news in any one of the ways you've described. You used the word "volatile". I confess that description's been applied to me a few times, and he is my son.'

'Okay, Mr Colledge. I'll take that on. For now we have to wait for the French to trace him, or for him to show up of his own accord. So long for now. I'll be in touch.'

He flipped his mobile closed. 'Sorry again,' he said. 'I'd hoped that this would be a quick job, a day trip, interview the boy, send him home to his folks and that would be that.'

'It's not your fault,' said Aileen. 'But look on the bright side. The lad will probably turn up before you've finished your lunch.'

'I don't think that's going to happen.' He told her about the painting, and about Michael Colledge's assessment of his son.

'Are you telling me that Davis has suddenly become a suspect?'

'Not suddenly; he was never entirely discounted. He always needed to be interviewed, to be eliminated. But now, having looked through that window into his state of mind, I'd say he's moved up the pecking order. The look on his face in the painting, the gun in his hand: I want to get hold of this boy, soon as I can.'

'They're bound to find him.'

'No,' said Bob, firmly. 'If the kid wants to disappear, he's got a fair chance of staying hidden. You know what worries me most? He left his phone behind him; we found it in the apartment, with the charger.'

'Maybe he just forgot it.'

'He didn't forget anything else. There were no other personal effects left there, but the damn mobile was right in the middle of the table. He's got a return air ticket, but there was no sign of it. If he's going away for a few days, why bother taking it? It's no good to anybody else. No, I don't think he wants to be found. I bet that he's used his plastic again, to pull as much cash as he can. I told Neil to find out. If he has, that'll be a sure sign he's done a runner.'

'When do you step up the hunt?'

'I won't take that decision. It's for the guys on the ground, but my guess would be a couple of days.' He took a sip of his mineral water and looked across at her. 'Have you ever met his dad?'

Aileen nodded. 'I have, as a matter of fact. I was down in London last year, at a parliamentary reception, and I was introduced to him by the then Defence Secretary.'

'Did you form any impression,' he grinned, 'or did your natural antipathy to Tories get in the way?'

'Hey, I'm broad-minded: I like quite a few Tories. I even suspect I'm sleeping with one.'

'Most people would agree with you about that, but you'd all be wrong.'

'You're just saying that to keep me in your bed. But, please, tell me you're not a Liberal.'

'No danger of that. But what about Colledge?'

'He'd never be one of the Tories I like. He's a smooth wee chap on the outside, but there was something about him that I didn't take to, something bubbling under the surface. If that lot do get in next time and he's in the cabinet, I reckon his civil servants will be in for a hard time. But, please, don't let that cloud your view of his son.'

'I'm not. I'm just indulging in a wild flight of fantasy. The night before she was killed, eighteen-year-old Davis introduced twenty-six-year-old Sugar to Mum and Dad across the dinner table, and told them that they were off to France for a month in a one-bed apartment. Now, I don't believe for one moment that Mr Colledge was as relaxed about the relationship as he made out when DI Stallings spoke to him.'

'Maybe it was entirely innocent. You told me that Sugar assured her head teacher that she'd done nothing wrong.'

'The boy wasn't really her pupil,' Bob pointed out. 'He was at another school, remember, even if they are both Merchant Company jobs: separate staffs, separate head teachers. Plus, see that neat wee appendix scar you've got?'

'What about it?'

'Sugar had one too, and it's in the painting.'

'Mmm. A bit of a giveaway, I admit. Okay, they may have been having it off. So?'

'So I don't reckon Dad would fancy that. He was a big-bucks lawyer before he became an MP, and his father before him was an Old Bailey judge. You've met him, now use your instinct and tell me what he felt inside when his son told him he'd fallen for an artist eight years older than him and that he was going to make painting his career.'

Aileen steepled her hands, brushing her lips with her fingertips. 'I don't think he'd be happy,' she admitted. 'So what's your wild flight of fancy?'

'I find myself wondering how unhappy he was. After all, he was still in Edinburgh when the girl was killed.'

'But he's the shadow Defence Secretary!'

Bob grinned. 'So?'

Thirty-one

'I hope you don't mind me coming down here, Becky,' said Neil McIlhenney, 'but after big McGurk's bravura performance this afternoon, it seemed best to me that we should work in tandem.'

'No, sir,' Stallings assured him. 'I don't mind at all. Why should I?'

'It would be understandable if you did. Your first major inquiry in Edinburgh as senior investigating officer and the brass muscles in. I'd probably be pissed off myself. It's just that having pulled PC Grey in for interview I don't think I can chuck her across to somebody else. I want you to sit in, though.'

'I understand.'

'Where are we with Weekes?'

'He's admitted to stalking Sugar Dean since she binned him, and to seeing her with Davis Colledge, but he's sticking to his story that he was at home when she was killed.'

'Are you buying that?'

'I'm not taking his word for it. I've taken a DNA sample from him, for comparison with the various traces that were found at the site. The way things stand, at the moment, he's our number-one suspect.'

'Having listened to your tape, I can't argue with that. I hope it never has to be played in court, though: Jack got a bit personal when he was going for him.'

'Yes, he did,' Stallings agreed. 'Is his marriage really bust?'

'I hope not, but this is the second time that he and Mary have separated. It started to creak when he was posted down to the Borders.

I thought the move back to Edinburgh had sorted it out, but apparently not. Back to Weekes, though. I've done some very confidential checking. He and Sugar were both prescribed antibiotics two years ago by a doctor in a private clinic in Edinburgh. Not long after that, Jock Varley had a couple of weeks on the sick. No medical certificate was ever submitted, but he and his wife were both treated at the genito-urinary unit . . . or the cock doctor's, as my dear old dad used to call it.'

'Will we have to talk to Varley about that?'

'Not unless we've got no choice. Where is Casanova now?'

'I've kept him here. He agreed to stay, but only because he knew he didn't have any option. I want a warrant to search his home, and his locker, looking for a firearm and for anything else that might connect him to the crime scene. Do you agree?'

'Of course,' said McIlhenney. 'We've got to do it, and it had better be formal. Get Jack on to it, right away. We've probably got grounds for searching the ex-wife's place too, since he's admitted to going there.'

'And what about PC Grey's?'

'Let's leave that until we've spoken to her. Before we do that, there's something else you should know. Remember I told you I'd take care of contacting Davis Colledge?'

'Yes.'

'Well, I did. I sent a special representative up there to liaise with the French police and pay him a visit. The lad wasn't at his digs: he left Collioure yesterday, telling his landlady he was going touring for a few days. But he left some stuff behind, stuff that bothers my man.'

'Are you saying we should be giving the kid more priority?' asked Stallings.

'That's what I'm being told, so we'd better. The French police are looking for him in all the coastal resorts: that's where he said he was going. We need to help them by running a plastic chase.'

'I'll put Sauce on to it right away, and Jack on to those warrants, before I have Grey brought up from the front office.'

McIlhenney smiled. 'Don't have her brought. You go and get her, and when you do, make sure you walk her past the room where Weekes is waiting, and that the door's open, enough for them to see each other.'

'But not talk?'

'Hell, no.'

Stallings left.

The superintendent looked around her office, wondering how she had managed to cope with the change from London. One thing struck him: she had the neatest detective's desk that he had ever seen. The live files, on which she was working, were all stacked in a tray. There were no notes scattered about on scraps of paper, just a single pad, with a pen alongside it. Her computer keyboard was slid away out of sight. This was a person whose working life was meticulously organised. He made a mental note to find out, subtly, from Ray Wilding whether she was a slob at home.

She returned after a few minutes, followed by a woman in uniform. 'Detective Superintendent McIlhenney,' she announced, 'this is PC Grey.' The newcomer looked as if the summer had passed her by: her face matched her name, and she seemed to be shivering slightly as she took a seat, facing the detectives across the desk. They looked at her, neither speaking.

'What have I done?' she asked, at last, tremulously.

A friendly smile spread across McIlhenney's face. 'I don't know, Mae,' he replied. 'What have you done?'

'Nothing that I know of.'

'Good for you.' He laughed. 'I've done plenty that I know of, and wouldn't want to talk about. Don't worry yourself: it's not you that's under the spotlight. Take your hat off, put yourself at your ease.' He paused as she took him up on the invitation, revealing blonde hair, pulled back behind her head. He glanced at her left hand as it lay on her lap. There was a ring on her third finger, with a chip of something that might have been diamond. 'Can you remember where you were the Friday morning before last, between seven and nine?' he continued.

As the constable searched her memory, a little colour began to return to her face. 'Yes,' she replied. 'Most of the time I was filling in for the lollipop man at the primary near the station; he'd called in sick and they needed someone to see the kids across the road.' She frowned. 'But nothing happened. I mean, there were no incidents or anything.'

'I know; that's not why we want to talk to you.'

'Is it about Theo?' she blurted out. 'I saw him in a waiting room when I was brought up here.'

'You and he are engaged, aren't you?'

'Yes, sort of.'

'Sort of?' The superintendent chuckled. 'That's a bit like being sort of pregnant, isn't it? Not that I'm implying anything,' he added.

PC Grey smiled, briefly. 'Well yes, we're definitely engaged.' She paused. 'And I'm definitely not pregnant.'

'First things first, eh?' said Stallings. 'Have the two of you set a date yet?'

'No, not yet. There's plenty of time for that.'

'Is that what you both think?'

The constable looked at her a little quizzically. 'Well, yes, I suppose so.'

'How long have you been engaged?'

'Officially?'

'There's no other way in my book.'

'Nearly two years: since three months after we started seeing each other.'

'That's a long time, by current standards. But I don't blame you, not rushing into things, especially since he must have been on the rebound when you met.'

'On the rebound? No, his marriage was over well before we got together. I'd have been wary otherwise.'

'Does he ever talk about his ex?'

'Now and again. He says she was a cow and he doesn't know why he ever married her.'

'He's well out of it, then. But, actually, I wasn't talking about her. I meant he was on the rebound from Sugar.'

'Who?'

McIlhenney studied her face: she seemed genuinely bewildered. 'DI Stallings meant Sugar Dean,' he said. 'He was engaged to her before you.'

'Sugar Dean?' Grey repeated. 'The girl that was murdered. Her whose picture's all over our station?'

'That's the girl.'

'Theo was engaged to her?'

'He never told you?'

She bit her lip, and shook her head.

'Maybe you just didn't realise they were engaged,' Stallings suggested gently. 'Maybe he just didn't make himself clear.'

'No. I never heard of Sugar Dean until last night, on the news on Talk 107.'

'Did he ever mention anyone else, other than Lisanne, his ex-wife?'

'No.'

The inspector frowned. 'I'm sorry to have to ask you this, Mae, but when did you and Theo first have sex?'

She glanced at McIlhenney: he was staring at a point on the wall. 'More or less as soon as we started going together.'

'Were you seeing anyone else at the time?'

'You mean was I sleeping with anyone else?'

'Yes, I do.'

'No, and I hadn't been for some time.'

'This is where it gets even more delicate. About two years ago, maybe just before you were engaged, did you contract an infection?'

'I had the flu.'

'I didn't mean that kind of infection.'

The constable stared at her; then her face reddened. 'No!' she protested. 'Certainly not!'

'Thank God for that. But Theo did: he told us so and we've confirmed it. That was why his engagement to Sugar ended.'

'You mean the bitch gave it to him?'

'No. Other way around.'

The woman seemed to rock back in her seat, stunned by the news. 'The bastard,' she hissed. 'Wait till I see him!' She thought for a few moments. 'Of course,' she went on, 'it was unlikely that I'd get it, because we always use rubbers. Theo's always on at me to go on the pill, but I won't. I don't fancy the health risks.'

'I can understand that,' said Stallings.

'This disease: did Theo say where he got it?'

'I think that's something you have to ask him.'

'Right now, I'm not sure I want to ask him anything.'

'Do you find him possessive?' the inspector asked.

'What do you mean?'

'Jealous.'

'No, but he's got no cause to be. Mind you, he's always asking about the job, who I've been working with and such. There was one time I was out on patrol in Livingston and I saw him. I asked if he was following me, and he laughed.'

'How's he been lately, Mae?' McIlhenney asked. 'His usual self?'

'Randy as ever.'

'I know your listed address is your folks' place, but do you actually live with Theo? No comeback if you do, you can be frank with us.'

'No,' she replied. 'I've suggested it a couple of times, but he's always said it's better to wait until we're married.'

'Do you have a key to his house?'

'No, and now I can understand why. You asked how he's been. Normally Theo's easy-going, as long as I don't put pressure on him . . . he's not a guy you nag . . . but about three weeks ago I was at his place, and I could tell there was something wrong. Eventually I asked him.

At first he said it was nothing, but I could see it wasn't. So I asked him again, and he said, "She's a fuckin' bitch and I could kill her." I don't know what Lisanne had done, but it had really got to him.'

'We don't think it was Lisanne, Mae. According to his statement, they're still on intimate terms. We think it was Sugar.'

'And you think . . .' the woman gasped.

'Let's just say that we're looking into the possibility,' Stallings told her. 'That's all for now, Mae.' She took a card from her pocket and slid it across the desk. 'We'll contact you if we need to speak to you again. If anything else occurs to you, at any time, that's my mobile number. Don't hesitate to use it.'

Thirty-two

'Where are we? We're just crossing the border at a place called Cerbère. Aileen's driving, to the car's great relief. We've been up in France and now we're taking the long twisty way back.'

'Day-tripping?' said Andy Martin. 'That's not like you. I thought you hardly went the length of yourself when you went on holiday.'

'This was a special case; just doing a favour for our friends Mario and Neil.'

'What the . . . ? You're a workaholic, man.'

'No, I'm not, honest,' Skinner assured him. 'My sabbatical's cured me of that. It was something that needed doing and the easiest way was for me to do it. Now listen, this call's costing me a bomb: you'll have heard from Jimmy by now, yes?'

'Yes. A few hours back.'

'And you agreed to what he asked?'

'He talked me into it.'

'That's good; I need the best for this.'

'I'm not sure you do. It's cut and dried. I interview people, with Mackenzie alongside me as back-up. I've checked that it's okay to use him, and it is, since he was off sick when all this stuff happened, and not involved in any of it.'

'Do it formally, on tape.'

Martin laughed. 'Of course I will; it'd be fucking "Tea and biscuits, how're you doing?" otherwise. But I know most of the people in the

Crown Office, apart from this guy Dowley. They're all sound.'

'You start with that bastard. He's the reason for all this fuss. Plus, he pissed off Jimmy and tried to bully Neil.'

'Silly man, twice. But, Bob, I don't have to point out to you, do I, that this is an independent inquiry?'

'Sorry, you're right,' Skinner conceded. 'You'll have to interview me before it's done.'

'Not if I find a leak first. How do you rate my chances?'

'What did Muhammad Ali say? "Slim and none, and Slim's on vacation." There probably isn't a leak. This may not be a copycat at all, whatever the Glimmer Twins think. There are two suspects directly linked to the Dean girl. We've got the likelier one in our hands and we're looking for the other.'

'Then why do you need to haul me down from Dundee?'

'Because I want you to exceed your brief. Fulfil it, yes, but while you're at it, I'd like you to review the whole story, everything that led up to the row with the Crown Agent. Are you up for that?'

'From the beginning?'

'Yes, the Ballester murders, Stevie Steele's death, right through to the Sugar Dean case. I want you to look at it all, to see if anything strikes you that we haven't hit on. That's the real reason I want you in Edinburgh. I could handle Dowley myself, but I don't want to do that. He's done me a favour: he's given me the chance to bring you on board. I want you to do what you do best: I want you to think outside the box.'

Martin chuckled. 'Just like old times?'

'Just like old times,' said Skinner. 'I've missed you, son.'

'Okay. I'll do it. Will anyone else have to know?'

'Mario. And if you tell him, his blood brother had better be in the picture as well. But that's all. Mackenzie's in on the leak inquiry, but not this.'

'Fine. I'll be there tomorrow.'

'That's good. I've fixed it for you to use my office till I get back next Monday.' Skinner paused. 'Hey, did Jimmy tell you anything else?'

'He told me he's leaving next month. Decision time, Bob. Are you going for it?'

'Decision made. Answer, yes.'

'In that case, you should know I won't be getting in your way.'

'That's entirely your decision. I'll understand if you do apply.'

'That won't happen.'

'In that case, if I'm appointed . . .'

'Let's cross that one when we get there. How does Aileen feel about it?'

'The fact that I'm doing it should tell you that. We've got a deal. I apply for the job, she marries me.'

'She's a brave woman.' Martin chuckled.

'She is that. See you.' He ended the call, and looked across with a smile of satisfaction. 'Done,' he said quietly.

'What do you think he's going to find?' Aileen asked.

'We'll see; maybe zilch. Tell you one thing, though: if it's there, Andy will turn it up.' He flipped the phone open and scrolled through the address book. 'Now let's see what I can dig out myself.' He dialled a number and put the phone to his ear. A female voice answered, cautiously.

'Dennis.'

'Amanda, it's Bob Skinner.'

'Hello, Bob,' said the acting director of MI5. 'Are you in London?'

'No, I'm not. As of a couple of minutes ago, I'm in Spain.'

'Too bad, I reckon you owe me dinner.'

'You're right. I'll tell you what, start a tab and I'll square you up next time we meet.'

'What does that mean?'

'Someone in my set-up is doing a bit of freelance work, trying to get an angle on Dražen Boras. She might need a couple of doors opened.'

'Freelance work? Don't you have confidence in your Northumbrian colleagues' ability to find him?'

'Not a lot, no. They don't have this person's motivation.'

'Who is it?'

'Maggie Steele.'

'Jesus, Bob, the victim's widow?'

'Are you shocked?'

'You're taking a chance.'

'No, it's purely a desk job. But if she does come up with any leads, she may need help in checking them out.'

'Sounds to me like you really need a contact in MI6.'

'I don't think our interests coincide. From what you told me, they might not want Boras traced.'

'True. Very well, if she needs our assistance, tell her to ask for Adrian St John. He's in our counter-terrorist unit, but he's best placed to help. I'll brief him.'

'Thanks.' He paused.

'There's more?' Amanda Dennis chuckled.

'One more thing.'

'Your tab's getting longer by the minute.'

'Remember in the bad old days in Ireland, people who were considered targets were issued with firearms for personal protection? I haven't come up against it for a while, but in this new high-alert era, I wondered if it still happens, say, with someone who might not qualify for full-scale protection-squad cover.'

'It's possible. Do you have anyone in mind?'

'Let's keep it broad and say politicians.'

'You don't want to give me a name?'

Skinner sighed. 'Shadow Defence.'

'Him? Wouldn't be surprised; he's abrasive and high profile, bloody well asking for it. He's also Jewish, although he says he's non-practising; that makes him an even more inviting target for Islamic terrorists. I'll find out. Call me back in a couple of hours.'

'Will do.'

'By the way, Bob,' said Dennis, 'I'm rather partial to a place called Passione.'

Thirty-three

Sauce Haddock stuck his head round the inspector's door. He nodded to McIlhenney. 'Sorry to interrupt, sir.'

'Don't be,' said Stallings. 'What have you got?'

'A result from Davis Colledge's bank, ma'am. His debit card was used again yesterday morning, in Collioure, at the same ATM he used on Saturday. He pulled another three hundred euros. But there's more. He used it again today, in Perpignan, at a terminal in the railway station: another three hundred.'

'He's drawn nine hundred euros since last weekend? What the hell's he doing?'

'Good question,' the superintendent murmured. 'And here's another. What's he doing in Perpignan? According to his landlady, he set off to explore the coast. Perpignan's inland.'

'If he was at the railway station, he's catching a train. Maybe he meant the Mediterranean coast as a whole, not just the local area. Maybe something got lost in translation.'

'Maybe, maybe. But I don't like it. We need to find this boy, yet it's as if he's out to make sure we don't.' He looked at Haddock, still in the doorway. 'Thanks, Sauce,' he said. 'That was quick work.'

'I've still got to check his credit card, sir.'

'You do that. See if he's used it for anything that might give us a clue as to where he's headed.'

'Very good, sir.'

Stallings smiled as the door closed on the constable. 'It's a long time since I've seen enthusiasm like that in a young DC,' she said.

'Me too,' McIlhenney agreed. 'You might be calling him "sir" before you retire. He's quite a contrast with PC Weekes. What are you going to do about him?'

'What do you want me to do?'

'It's your decision. I might have taken part in the Grey interview, but you're still the SIO.'

'I want to hold him overnight; would you have a problem with that?'

The superintendent smiled. 'Christ, Becky, why do I have to say it twice? You're running this investigation. You want to hold him, you hold him. You've got grounds. He's uttered threats against the victim and he can't offer us an alibi for the time of the murder. On top of that he has a pattern of obsessive, controlling behaviour towards women. Has he asked for a lawyer yet?'

'No.'

'You might want to make sure he's given the opportunity. Otherwise, bang him up, and I'll have the press office say that someone's helping with our enquiries. He'll need to be formally suspended, but I'll take care of that.' He paused. 'When are you going to talk to him again?'

'Not until the searches are complete, and maybe not even till I get the DNA result. I want to talk to his ex-wife first: Jack and I are taking the search team up to her place. We'll go in first to explain what's happened; it'll be kinder that way.'

'Safer too. If PC Grey's anything to go by, this woman may know little or nothing about Weekes's other life. The last thing we need is to be heavy-handed with her and send her running to the press.'

Thirty-four

'Wasn't that an interesting drive home?' Bob asked, with a slightly mischievous look on his face.

'Interesting?' Aileen exclaimed, unbuttoning her shirt as she spoke. 'It had so many twists and turns I'm still dizzy. Mind you, the view across the bay from the far side was worth the effort. It's left me parched, though. Do we have any beer in the fridge?'

'Always, love,' he replied, 'always. You go and have a swim and I'll fetch us some.'

She was in the pool when he returned from the kitchen, with two bottles of Coronita, uncapped. 'Hey,' he laughed, as he lowered himself on to its edge, 'what's this with you and swimming in the buff?'

'I like to,' she called back. 'Always have. It's okay. None of the houses around us can see into the garden.'

'That's true.' He pointed upwards. 'But there's all sorts of traffic in the air around here, light aircraft and helicopters. I wouldn't put it past some of our sleazier tabloids to try for some candid-camera shots of the First Minister, off duty. I've had experience of the paparazzi; I don't want to see you embarrassed.'

She winked at him as she pulled herself out of the water and sat by his side. 'Who says I'd be embarrassed?' she teased. 'I'm proud of my body.'

'I'm proud of your body too,' he replied, 'but I don't want to share it with a few million readers.'

'Don't worry. It's all yours.' She prised one of the beers from his hand and took a long slug from the neck. 'Jeez, I needed that. It's been a long day already, and there's still some to go.'

He bumped her, shoulder to shoulder. 'Then maybe we should have a siesta to get ready for the rest of it.'

He felt her wet arm slide under his shirt and up his back. 'That, my boy, is not a bad idea, not a bad idea at all . . . as long as it involves a couple of hours' sleep.'

'Yes, that too.'

She swung herself round and sprang lithely to her feet. Bob was in the act of following her when his mobile sounded in his breast pocket. He flipped it open. 'Yes?'

'Bob, it's Amanda. Can you speak?'

'Yes,' he replied, gazing at Aileen's slim back as she ran indoors, 'we're back home.'

'Fine. The answer to your question is yes. That gentleman was issued with a side-arm by the protection squad, and with a supply of ammunition. He's been schooled on the Metropolitan Police firing range.'

'Did you find out anything about the weapon?'

'Nine-millimetre Beretta Storm, seventeen-shot capacity.'

'A proper gun, then.'

'Oh, yes. It will do the job. Exactly what job do you think it might have done?'

'Someone put a bullet in the back of his son's girlfriend's head a couple of weeks ago.'

'Good heavens! Is he a possibility?'

'Only in my book so far. There are other people above him on the list.'

'Have someone send me a detailed image of the bullet taken from the woman . . . assuming you found it. These pistols are all test-fired before issue.'

'Will do. Right now. Thanks, Amanda.'

'No problem. I find myself hoping that we get a match. I know people who do not want to see Mr Colledge become a member of Her Majesty's Government. As a matter of fact, I'm one of them. There's been talk that after the next election he might become my boss. I wouldn't like that.'

Thirty-five

'I'm Detective Inspector Rebecca Stallings, Mrs Weekes, and this is DS Jack McGurk. Do you think we might come in? We'd like to talk to you about your former husband.'

The woman seemed to slump in the doorway of the tenement flat. 'What's wrong?' she asked urgently. 'What's happened to him?'

'Nothing,' McGurk assured her. 'He's fine. It's just something that's come up at work.'

Lisanne Weekes sighed. 'He's not in bother, is he? He hasn't been on the take, has he?'

'Not as far as we know. It would be much better if you let us in, though, rather than talk on the stairhead.'

'Sure,' she replied, stepping aside to allow them to enter. 'Living room's straight ahead. I'm sorry about the mess. I'm not long in from work so the place is as I left it this morning . . . a pure tip.'

'I know you work in a bank, but what do you do there?' asked Stallings.

She slipped off a lightweight blue jacket, part of a suit that the detectives recognised as a uniform. 'I'm a mortgage adviser.' She was a tall woman, big-breasted, narrow-waisted, physically similar to Mae Grey, but dark-haired rather than blonde.

'Sit down,' she said, dropping into a chair herself. 'So, what do you want to ask me about Theo?'

'Do you see much of him?'

She nodded. 'Quite a bit. Truth is, we get on better now than when we were married.'

'In what way?'

'All the fun with none of the hassle, I suppose. I don't have to worry about where he is any more, but I know he'll always come back here.'

'And he does?'

She looked at McGurk as if his question had annoyed her. 'Yes, and what's wrong with that? Being divorced doesn't mean never seeing each other again.'

'Granted. How long were you separated before your divorce came through?'

'I honestly can't remember. Our difficulties started not long after we were married. It was the hours he was working: add on his playtime and it was pretty difficult.'

'Playtime?'

'He likes a pint, likes to go out with the boys.'

'And the girls?' McGurk suggested.

'Not as far as I know; but then I never ask. As far as I'm concerned we have an open relationship.'

'And as far as Theo's concerned?'

She winced slightly. 'I don't see other guys, so that's irrelevant.'

'But if you did?' McGurk probed. 'Are you sure it wouldn't be relevant then? Are you telling me you've never dated another man since you and PC Weekes were divorced?'

She sighed. 'There was this bloke, once, right after the divorce. I admit I was a bit angry with Theo then, and I decided that I'd get on with my life and sod him if he didn't like it. So I went out with Byron, a man I work with. We went for a meal, then to the Omni centre, and afterwards he brought me home. I invited him up for coffee.'

'Coffee?'

'Maybe more. We were necking a bit and it was heading that way, when the doorbell went. I opened the door and it was Theo. He barged past me, said, "Who the fuck are you?" to Byron and thumped him.'

'He beat him up?' Stallings exclaimed. 'A serving police officer?'

'Not exactly. Byron's huge, bigger than Theo: he nutted him, laid him out. I made him leave before things got worse.'

'Who, Theo?'

'No, I chucked Byron out. Theo wound up staying the night.' She looked at the other woman. 'He's my weak spot.'

The inspector gave her the understanding she sought. 'You are not alone,' she said, with a smile. 'So you and Theo, divorce or no divorce, you still see each other?'

'On and off . . . on mostly.'

'Where?'

'Usually he comes here. I've been to his place, but usually, he comes to me, or we go away somewhere for a weekend when his shifts allow it.'

'Does he ever leave stuff here?'

'He has a wardrobe, if that's what you mean.'

'No, not clothes; personal items.'

'He might. I never look. Has he been stealing? Is that it?'

'No, Mrs Weekes,' said McGurk. 'That's not it. We'll get to the problem in a bit. When did you see him last?'

'Monday night. We got a takeaway, and he stayed over.'

'And before that?'

'A couple of weeks ago, a Friday night.'

'How was he, those times? His usual self?'

'He was maybe a bit quieter than normal on Monday. The time before that he got drunk: that's unusual for him.'

Stallings sighed inwardly. She had taken to the woman, and was not looking forward to what was about to happen. 'Lisanne,' she began, 'have you ever heard of Sugar Dean?'

Mrs Weekes thought for a moment or two. 'The name's familiar,' she replied, 'but I can't place her.'

'What about a woman called Mae Grey: Police Constable Mae Grey?'

'Never. Why?'

'Because Theo Weekes has been engaged to both of them since your divorce.'

'What?'

'I'm afraid so. His relationship with Sugar Dean ended two years ago, but he's been going out with PC Grey since before that time.'

The woman's mouth tightened; then she shrugged. 'He's a free man,' she declared. 'He's got the right. He was probably getting back at me for Byron.'

'He's never said anything about other women?'

'Not a word.'

'And you've seen each other regularly since he moved out.'

'There was a time, year before last, it would be, when I didn't see him for a couple of months, but apart from that, yes.'

'Did you really want to divorce him?'

'What do you think? But after what you've told me, maybe I should be glad I did.'

'Does Theo have a temper?'

'Not with me. The Byron incident, though, that was pretty fierce.' She paused. 'Has he assaulted a prisoner, is that what it is?'

'No, it's not. Lisanne,' said Stallings, 'Sugar Dean's name was familiar to you because it's been all over the press for the last day or so. She was murdered, shot dead, twelve days ago, on a Friday morning. Her body was discovered on Monday. Those are the two days when you last saw Theo. And yet he told us that he hadn't seen you for three weeks.'

'Oh, my,' the other woman gasped. She sat forward in her chair, and grasped her knees. 'Do you think he did it? No, no, not Theo, surely not.'

'He's admitted to stalking her,' the inspector told her. 'He also made

172

a threatening statement against her to a third party. At the moment, we're carrying out certain tests that may tell us if he was at the murder scene. We're also searching his locker at the station in South Queensferry, and his flat. We need to search here too, I'm afraid. We have a warrant to do so, but we're hoping that you'll allow us.'

'Just his wardrobe?'

'No; the whole place, I'm afraid. Something could have been hidden without you being aware of it. I have to ask you this: Theo hasn't given you anything to keep for him, has he?'

'No, he hasn't.'

'Can you remember back to the Friday? Specifically, the clothes he was wearing?'

'Yes, tan jacket, blue shirt and jeans. I washed the shirt for him and put it in his drawer, but the other stuff must be hanging in the wardrobe. When he left next day he was wearing a dark blue top and chinos. I'd just bought them for him in John Lewis.'

'Good. Thanks.'

'When do you want to do this?' she asked.

'It has to be now,' Stallings replied. 'We have a team of officers waiting out in the street. We'll be as quick, as neat and as discreet as we can, I promise you.'

'What are you looking for?'

'Primarily, a gun: but generally, anything that shouldn't be there.'

'A gun! My God, this is unreal.'

'I'll bet. Before we start, do you know of anything in the flat that isn't yours?'

'There's some shaving stuff in the bathroom, and a toothbrush, but other than that, no. Everything that's his should be in his wardrobe and in the bottom drawer of the chest alongside it.'

'Nothing is locked away?'

'No.'

'That's helpful.'

'Can I stay while you do it?'

'You might find it distressing. We'll be very thorough.'

'Then let's get it over with,' said Mrs Weekes. 'Once you're finished,' she continued, 'can you do something for me?'

'Sure, if it's appropriate. What is it?'

'If I box up his stuff, all the things you don't need, will you take it away with you and give it to him, or dump it at his place, or in the first skip you find in the street? After tonight, I don't want anything of him in this house, ever again.'

'We'll handle that for you,' McGurk told her. 'Have you got somewhere to go while the team does its work? We'll be a few hours.'

She sighed despondently. 'Not really, no.'

'Maybe we can help with that too,' said Stallings. 'Jack, I'll stay here while the search is under way. Would you like to take Mrs Weekes for something to eat? Cooking here's going to be impossible. Is that all right with you, Lisanne?'

A small, sad smile crossed the woman's face. 'It's the best offer I'm going to get tonight, that's for sure. If it's all right with you, Sergeant Jack, it's okay with me.'

Thirty-six

'Thanks, boss. Sorry, thanks, Bob,' said Maggie Steele. 'That contact may well come in useful. I have a feeling that I'm about to run into a brick wall. I've been digging into Dražen's company. He's no longer part of it: his shares have been sold to a Bermuda trust.'

'What about his co-directors and senior colleagues?'

'I've spent most of the day digging into their backgrounds. Leaving aside his mum, who's taken over as chair of the company, there are only two of any consequence. Fishheads is a very tight operation: there's no excess baggage at the top level. The CEO is an accountant named Godric Hawker. He was originally recruited as finance director, from one of the major accountancy firms, to impress the City, it's said.'

'Any connection with your man before that?'

'None that I can see. I did find out something interesting about him, though, from a friend of a friend who did some asking around for me. Hawker jumped at the chance to join Fishheads because its headquarters are in London. He has a severe flying phobia; that meant that his promotion prospects with an international accountancy practice were a bit limited. It also means that if Dražen were to contact his old associates, Hawker would hardly jump on a plane to go and meet him.'

'That's assuming Dražen's not hiding somewhere in Britain.'

'He isn't,' Maggie replied. 'On the day the Met raided his apartment his father's company jet logged a flight plan for Iceland. There's no record of it ever landing there. Three days later it flew into our air

175

space from the US and landed back at its home airfield. It was flown by Davor Boras's driver, David Barnes. The day before that, Barnes was a passenger on the morning flight from Heathrow to Dulles International, in Washington.'

Skinner laughed. 'Maggie, my girl, you really are good. Dražen flew the plane across the Atlantic, his friends in the intelligence community helped him disappear, and his dad sent his minder and pilot to fly the thing back.'

'Why would anybody help him?'

'For services rendered, and maybe still to come. What about the other business associate?'

'He's very interesting. His name's Ifan Richards; he's the public face of the company in the City. Age twenty-nine, a year older than Dražen, son of a Welsh printing millionaire. They were at Charterhouse, and they both attended Harvard Business School. Ifan majored in management sciences, and Dražen did international business. They were both on the students' council board in their final year. Dražen was a vice-president and Richards was the communications director. Both graduated *summa cum laude* on the same day. Ifan was recruited by IBM in London, and was there until he joined Dražen in the start-up of Fishheads dot com.'

'Dražen's best mate, from the sound of it,' said Skinner. 'What's his personal background? Gay? Mind you, Dražen's hetero: we found that out from Amy Noone.'

'He's still single, but he has a girlfriend called Chandler Lockett, who was a member of a girlie band when they were fashionable. Nowadays she's mostly seen with him on the pages of *Hello!* magazine and the like.'

'Legends in the surgery waiting room?'

'And the hairdresser's.'

'So? What's your thinking?'

'If anyone's going to lead us to Dražen, it'll be Ifan.'

'Not his mother?'

'I'm going to assume she wouldn't put him at risk. We know for sure his father won't. Anyway, Sanda's a figurehead in the business. I wouldn't be surprised if she was replaced as chair pretty soon by the non-exec that the LTN Trust put on the board.'

'Who's he?'

'Nobody I've ever heard of. His name's Ignacio Riesgo.'

'What? Spell the surname.'

'R-I-E-S-G-O.'

Skinner's laugh took her by surprise. 'He wouldn't,' he said. 'Yes, he bloody would!'

'What are you on about?' asked Maggie, puzzled by his reaction.

'His name. Riesgo, translated, means "risk" in English. You're telling me that Dražen's replacement on the board of the company he founded is called "I. Risk". He's pulled another one, the cheeky bastard. You find Ignacio, and you've found Dražen.'

'But his shares have been sold. I checked with the company registrar: his signature is on the transfer document.'

'Transfer being the key word. They've been moved into a trust, not sold to an individual. Mags, I don't know anything about this LTN operation, but if the L doesn't stand for "Langley" I'll bet you it should. This will be a CIA front. I wanted to tell you this face to face, but Davor Boras has been enabling operations in the Balkans for years, and latterly his son's been involved too. These guys have a stack of Brownie points with the Americans; now some of them have been cashed in.'

'Maybe, but if I can find him . . .'

'There will be one significant problem with that.'

'What?'

'Three of our people have met Dražen. Mario, and the two DCs down in Leith, Tarvil Singh and Griff Montell. But that was weeks, months ago. I'm pretty sure that by now they could all sit in the same room as the guy and not know him, at least until he spoke. He'll have had cosmetic surgery, his hair colour and style will be different, he'll be bearded and he'll probably have been to fucking Specsavers. We're going to need his DNA to identify him for sure.'

'If that's what it takes,' said Maggie, grimly, 'I'll take a blood sample myself.'

'You've got to find him first. That may be impossible. Right now, I agree, it looks as if your best route is through Richards, but that won't be easy. He's part of an international trading company, and if the CEO won't fly, he must be all over the place on business. He'll have dozens of opportunities to make contact with Dražen in the course of a year. Best thing to do is have a talk with our friend Adrian; see if he can help.'

'First thing tomorrow. Thanks again, Bob, for all this. You're only indulging me, I know, but I appreciate it. You've no idea how much it helps.'

'Indulging you? I'm bloody well not. You've only been on this for a couple of days, and look at the results you've got already.'

'The next part's going to be the hardest, though,' she said. 'But I promise not to disturb your holiday again. Say sorry to Aileen for me, please.'

'I will. She's upstairs just now, refreshed after a siesta and getting ready to hit the town.'

'Sounds good. How's it going anyway? Are you having a quiet time, apart from me, that is?'

She heard him chuckle. 'Quiet time? You ask your ex and his mate how quiet it's been.'

Thirty-seven

'From where you're sat, Jack,' Lisanne Weekes asked, 'do I look like a fool?'

'No. You look to me like someone who's guilty of nothing worse than trust, and that isn't a crime in my book. It's a virtue, even though it can get you hurt.'

'Like when it's given to the wrong person, you mean?'

'Yes.'

'See?' She smiled at him wistfully. 'You do think I'm an idiot.'

'I don't, honestly. I don't think that Mae Grey's an idiot either, and from what I've heard of Sugar Dean, I don't believe that she was. You're good women, all of you, who happened to fall for a bad man. In my job, I've met a hundred people like you ... not all of them women, I have to say.'

They were in an Asian restaurant, near Haymarket, not far from McGurk's office. It had not been one of its busiest nights: as their coffee arrived they were the only customers left, although the sergeant expected that there would be a late rush as the pubs began to empty.

'Are you a good person?'

He looked at her across the table. 'What do you reckon?'

'I reckon you are, otherwise I wouldn't be here. But there you are, I've never met you before in my life and I trust you to keep me company while your people tear my home apart.'

'And put it back together again.'

'I'm sure they will, as best they can, but I'll still know they've been

179

there, touching my stuff. I'm sure I'll feel terrible about it tomorrow. Right now, it's all a blur: I don't really think I believe it yet.'

'I'm sorry. Truly, I am. It's not a job that Becky and I enjoyed.'

'You did it very well, though. You were very kind, both of you. You've been kind here too. I was expecting the interrogation to go on, but we've talked about football, films, the Royal Family; anything but Theo bloody Weekes.'

'We've asked you all we need to ask you,' said McGurk. 'You can interrogate me now, if you like.'

'About him? No, he's a rat: I don't want to know any more about him. He and I have been cruising along for too long. Like I said, he's been my weakness. I don't think I've ever stopped to ask myself whether I love him, but sitting here now, I know that I don't. We were young when we met, barely out of school. One thing just followed another, until we wound up married, just before he gave up his garage job and joined the police.' She stopped abruptly. 'You're holding him overnight,' she said, 'but will he be out tomorrow?'

'Maybe. I can't say.'

'If you do have to let him go, will you tell him to stay away from me?'

'I can pass that on.'

'But can you make him?'

'I can't order him not to go near you. But if he does, and he persists, you should phone me or Becky and make a complaint. His feet won't touch the ground then. Mind you, even if he is cleared and released, his police career will still be hanging by a thread. If he's got any thought of staying on the force, he'll listen when he's warned to leave you alone.'

'Is there anything you haven't told me about him?'

'Yes, but you probably don't want to hear it.'

'You're bloody wrong: I do.'

'Sure?'

'Sure.'

'Sugar chucked him because he gave her gonorrhoea.'

Lisanne threw back her head. 'The bastard,' she hissed. 'The dirty bastard.'

'You told us about that time a couple of years ago when he didn't see you for a bit? It was probably because he was being treated.'

'I'm surprised he didn't accuse me of giving it to him.'

McGurk frowned. 'All other things aside, he'd know you didn't have the opportunity. Remember Byron? Weekes was stalking you, Lisanne: all the time, you, and Sugar, and Mae.'

'He's nuts.'

'Whether he is or not, his return to the job will depend on a psychologist's report.'

She shuddered. 'That's enough. Not only do I never want to see him again, I don't want to hear any more about him. Change the subject. Let's talk about you instead. Are you married? I guess not, since you were free to take me out.'

'Separated,' he told her.

'Do you stalk your ex?' She put her hand to her mouth, as if to stop the question, but it had escaped. 'God, I'm sorry, that was terrible.'

He grinned. 'Yes, but in the circumstances, understandable. I admit that I had a problem for a couple of months; I went through the jealous phase, and I did watch the house once or twice after I moved out. But we're fine now. The job's been our main problem. Mary's never liked it. Eventually she gave me an ultimatum.'

'And you chose the police?'

'I'm afraid so. Still think I'm a good person?'

'I think you're an honest one. I think Mary's dead wrong, expecting you to give up a career you love. If you did that you'd never look at her in the same way again . . . at least, I wouldn't in your shoes.'

'That's what I've tried to tell her, but without success. She's tried support groups for officers' wives, we've tried marriage-guidance counselling . . . disastrously, for the counsellor turned out to have a police record and took her side . . . but nothing's helped. I reckon we're at the end of the road now.'

'And you don't sleep with her any more?'

'No.'

'Wise man. If you're ever tempted, look at me and the bother that got me into.'

They were still laughing when his mobile sounded. It was Stallings.

'That's us done, Jack,' she said. 'You can bring her home now. No firearm. Nothing at all, in fact, but we've bagged the jacket and jeans Lisanne told us about for further examination.'

'And the rest?'

'Bin-bags. I'll have someone dump them in Weekes's place tomorrow.'

'Okay. See you in the morning, unless you want me back at the office.'

'Hell, no! I'm off home to debrief Detective Sergeant Wilding. Good night.'

'Cheers.' He switched off the Samsung and slipped it back into his pocket, then waved to a waiter for the bill. 'That's it,' he said. 'We're out of your life.'

He paid by card and kept the receipt. 'Theo knew about Mary and me,' he told her, as they left the restaurant. 'I used to be the deputy chief's exec, and his marriage broke up at the same time as mine. "The curse of the command corridor," they called it. It was the talk of the force for a while, went all the way round the gossip circuit.'

'Were they saying you had a thing going?' Lisanne laughed.

'You've never met the deputy chief. Anyone whispering that even in jest would be singing soprano for the rest of his short, sad life.'

The drive back to her flat took less than five minutes. 'I'll walk you up,' said McGurk. 'I need to reassure myself that they haven't left a mess.'

They climbed to the second floor of the old sandstone building. It had been renovated, like most of the property in the area, and the stairwell was brightly lit, and carpeted. The front door was larger than usual, but the six-foot-eight-inch sergeant still had to watch his head as he stepped inside.

He stood in the hallway as Lisanne moved from room to room; when she reappeared she was smiling. 'It's tidier than I left it,' she told him, 'and I'm not kidding.'

'That's good. I must get them in to do my place.' He turned and ducked under the door. 'Good night, then.'

'Jack.'

He paused.

'Would you think I was pushy if I asked if I could see you again?' she asked.

He frowned, until his eyes gave him away. 'I was going to give it a couple of days,' he replied, 'then call you. What are you doing on Friday night?'

'Whatever you like.'

'A meal and a couple of pubs? Pick you up about seven?'

'Sounds good. See you then.'

He was half-way downstairs when she called after him: 'Hang on!'

They met on the first-floor landing. 'There's something else,' she said, removing, as she spoke, the necklace charm he had been admiring all evening. It was silver, like its chain, but he had been unable to see what it was meant to be. 'I forgot I had this on. Would you put it with the rest of Theo's stuff? He gave it to me that last Friday he was here. I want no part of it now.'

'No problem.' He held out his hand and she dropped it on to his palm. He looked at it in the bright light of the stairwell and felt his heart jump. The charm was small, about half the normal size, but it was, unmistakably, a representation of a cube of sugar.

Thirty-eight

'You're looking good,' said Andy Martin.

'But different, sir, yes?'

'That can't be denied. The uniform suits you, though.'

'Thank you, sir.' Chief Inspector David Mackenzie snapped his heels together and gave a small mock bow. 'It's taken some getting used to, I admit, but the alternative was losing it, leaving the force altogether, and I didn't need that. I may have said so, when I was at my blackest, but the job's important to me.'

The two men had met before, on a drugs operation in Edinburgh. It had been successful, but it had started a chain of events that had proved disastrous for Mackenzie, plunging him into depression and a bout of near-alcoholism.

'I'm different in a few ways,' he said. 'For a start, nobody calls me Bandit any more. That persona's gone for good: when it came to the test, I didn't have the nuts to live up to it.'

'That's not what I've heard. It was a bad scene, and you went into it.'

'Then froze solid, sir. You can't do that: if you do, you're putting the lives of colleagues in danger.'

'That's true,' Martin conceded, 'but, David, you didn't go to work that morning expecting to go into armed action. You weren't part of a specialist unit, you just happened to be there at the time. I was told that you volunteered, and that once you were in you went as far as you could. That's all any of us can do. You're a damn good officer, and I'm happy to be working with you.'

'It's good of you to say so, sir.'

'Ask around and you'll find that I never say things I don't mean. Now, let's get on with this task. You know what I've been asked to do?'

'Yes, sir. The chief constable gave me a full briefing.'

'Good. Before we get started, though, that's five "sirs" in as many minutes. I've never been one for formality, among senior officers at any rate, so when it's just you and me, it's Andy. Fair enough?'

Mackenzie nodded.

Martin moved behind Bob Skinner's desk, settled into his chair, and glanced out of the window, across to the deserted Broughton High School, its pupils turned loose to holiday with their parents, or to roam the city's streets. 'Right,' he continued. 'I've been doing some thinking about this overnight and I've decided how I want to proceed. The investigation shouldn't take more than a couple of days, but for its purpose I must be formal, from start to finish. I'm going to be interviewing people I know, guys I used to go to the pub with when I was here. So we'll do it in uniform, both of us, and we'll record every word said.' He smiled. 'From what I've been told, that's going to cause the Crown Agent a lot of grief, but I haven't been brought down here to massage his ego.'

'How do you want to begin?' asked Mackenzie.

'I'm going to spend this morning reading the files relating to all the investigations, including the Sugar Dean inquiry. While I'm doing that I want you to speak to DCS McGuire and Detective Superintendent McIlhenney and have them help you compile a list of all the people in this force who had access to those details of the Ballester murders that were kept from the media. Before that, though, I want you to phone the Crown Agent and have him do the same thing, list the people in his office that we need to interview. That's where we'll begin, this afternoon. And I want Joe Dowley himself to be our first appointment. There's something about his whole attitude that I don't understand, and I'm going to find out what it is.'

Thirty-nine

Becky Stallings glanced at her watch as McGurk stepped into the incident room, transferred from the golf club to divisional headquarters at Torphichen Place.

'Sorry, boss,' he said. 'I had a call to make before I came in.'

'Ah,' said the inspector. 'I was beginning to think you'd had an unexpectedly late night.'

He smiled ingenuously. 'Don't know what you mean.'

'Nice meal?'

'Yes, it was. I kept the receipt, though.'

'God!' Stallings gasped. 'I put you in the way of a date with a nice girl and you want to put in on exes. You Scots guys, you're amazing.'

'That's often said, Becky. Any developments?'

She nodded. 'Some. The boys at the lab have been putting in overtime. They found a hair on Weekes's jacket that's a match for the victim.'

'Have you charged him yet?'

'It's not as easy as that. That jacket's three years old. Sauce checked the bar code with River Island and they confirmed it. He could have picked up that sample a while ago, so it doesn't help us place him at the crime scene.'

'What about the DNA traces that were found there? Does he match any of them?'

'No, that's a blank.'

'So what's our next move?'

186

'We're going to re-interview him, but he's got a solicitor on the case now, and she's insisting on being present. Her name's Frances Birtles. Do you know her?'

'Frankie Birtles? Also known as Frankie Bristles. Oh, yes, we all know her. She's a hard case.'

'I was afraid of that. That's how she struck me, and it's why I'm not getting excited about the jacket. We could try and bluff him, hit him with it, hard, but we wouldn't get far: she'd be on to us straight away.'

'We could lean on his behaviour,' McGurk suggested, 'his admission of stalking Lisanne and Sugar, and the threat Mae heard him make. Female lawyer: even Frankie might not be too impressed by that.'

'He's already backed off that. His brief's already told me that any statements made at his first interview were under duress and are withdrawn.'

'Duress, my arse.' The sergeant laughed.

'She's saying more than that, though. She's claiming he felt under career pressure, and that he was telling us what he thought we wanted to hear, to protect his job. No, Jack, we'll interview him, but then we'll have to turn him loose, maybe even return him to duty if she pushes it.'

'I don't think that's going to happen.' McGurk was still smiling.

'What's with you?' said Stallings. 'You didn't score, did you?'

'In a manner of speaking.' He reached into his pocket, took out a small, clear evidence capsule and laid it on the inspector's desk. 'Lisanne gave me that last night,' he said. 'It was a present from Theo, on the day that Sugar was murdered. I've just been to see John Dean. He confirmed that his daughter had an identical necklace to that one. It was a Christmas present from Weekes, when they were going out. She liked it: after they broke up it was the only thing from their relationship that she kept. She wore it all the time, and she had it on the last time her father saw her, when she left for work on the day she was murdered.'

Stallings stared up at him, her mouth slightly agape. 'Jack,' she murmured, 'you have made my morning. Let's go and talk to PC Weekes.'

'And will we do his lawyer the courtesy of telling her what we've got?'

'Nah, I'm out of courtesy. She can find out at the same time as he does. Come on. They're both waiting for us in the interview room. The custody officer told me that Weekes is in a foul mood after his night in the cells. Let's go and make it worse.'

She led the way downstairs, to the interview room at the back of the building.

Theo Weekes was seated at the table, beside a fair-haired woman, power-dressed in a pin-striped trouser suit. He glared up at the two detectives as they entered: his eyes were bloodshot and the dark outline of an incipient beard covered his chin.

'You're fucked,' he said, glaring directly at McGurk, ignoring Stallings. 'This is going all the way when I get out of here. The Federation's going to crap all over you, pal, and so am I.'

'If that was a threat,' the sergeant replied, 'I would think better of it, if I were you. Remember Byron? I'm even bigger than him, so Lisanne tells me.' Weekes started out of his chair, but his solicitor seized his arm in a surprisingly strong grip. 'Morning, Frankie,' he continued. 'Long time no see. What do you think of your client so far?'

'I think he's standing up to his ordeal very well, Jack,' the lawyer said. 'I know what's going on here. You've got another dead artist on your hands, and you're desperate for a quick result, so desperate you're prepared to throw one of your own to the lions.'

'Trust us,' McGurk told her, 'we didn't throw this guy anywhere. He jumped into the den, aided only by his blind stupidity.'

'Let's get on with it.' Stallings switched on the tape, as she and the sergeant took their seats. 'It's nine twenty, this is interview room two in the police office at Torphichen Place, I am Detective Inspector Rebecca Stallings, accompanied by DS Jack McGurk, and we are about to interview Police Constable Theodore Weekes, represented by Ms Frances Birtles.'

'Fine,' said Birtles, 'that's the formalities over. Now maybe you'd tell us for the record why a serving police officer with an exemplary record has been held overnight in these atrocious conditions.'

'Because he's a murder suspect,' the inspector snapped, 'and before we go any further, let me tell you something. I'm new to this force, so I don't know your ways, but this is my interview, this is my nick, and we're playing by my rules. Those say that you're here to advise your client, and that's all. That means that I ask the questions and he answers them.'

'I'm answering fuck all,' Weekes growled.

'Okay.' She glanced to her left. 'Jack, charge him.'

'Hey, wait a minute!' Birtles exclaimed.

Stallings shrugged her shoulders and began to rise. 'That's what's going to happen anyway. I'm not going to waste time on him.'

'My client will be co-operative. Won't you, Theo?'

As Weekes nodded, fear replaced ebullience in his eyes.

'On that basis,' the inspector went on, 'I'll tell you what we've got. Last night we recovered clothing from the home of PC Weekes's ex-wife. This included a canvas jacket, which, we believe, he was wearing when he arrived there on the day of Sugar Dean's murder. From that jacket we recovered hair samples that match the victim's. You don't deny you were wearing the jacket that day, do you, Theo?'

'No, but . . .' Frankie Birtles laid a hand on his arm, then leaned close to him and whispered. He nodded again.

'My client points out,' she said, 'that he owned the jacket in question during his admitted relationship with the victim, and that he had not worn it regularly since. Is that the extent of your forensic evidence?'

'I'm afraid so.'

'Then will you please stop auditioning for the role of Widow Twanky, cancel this pantomime, and let my client return to his duty as a police officer?'

'We would do,' McGurk drawled amiably, 'if it wasn't for this.' He took the necklace, in its packet, from his pocket and held it up between two fingers. 'Sugar Dean's father identified it this morning as his daughter's. It was the one thing she ever had from your client that she valued, and she was wearing it when she died. Later that day, Theo gave it to his ex-wife, as a present.' He paused. 'And by the way, Frankie: wrong pantomime. From where I'm sitting, Becky's Cinderella, and you are most definitely one of the Ugly Sisters.' He switched his gaze to Weekes. 'Okay, Buttons,' he said, 'talk your way out of this one.'

The effect was dramatic. The man slumped back in his chair, his eyes fixed on the tiny trinket. His eyes filled with tears and, slowly, they began to run down his face.

'Can I have a minute alone with my client?' Birtles asked quietly.

'You can have all the time you like,' Stallings told her. 'It gets deadly serious from here on in. We don't have the gun, but with that thing there, I don't reckon we need it. Let us know when you're ready, but be in no doubt about this. When we come back in here, we won't accept anything less than a full and truthful account of what happened that morning.'

Forty

Since stopping work in the second half of her pregnancy, Maggie Steele had come to realise that many of the things she had taken for granted in her youth, in the days before she left for work early and returned late, had gone for good.

The one that annoyed her most was the unpredictability of the postal delivery service. Once she had been able to count on her mail being in the hall before breakfast. Latterly she had become used to finding it waiting for her in the evening. This was unacceptable, since she was used to an ordered life, to a daily timetable in which specific things happened at specific times. Thus she found it frustrating that her mail seemed to arrive at the whim of the postman or postwoman who happened to be on duty on any given day.

That morning she was lucky. It was five to ten, and she was loading the washing-machine, when she heard the thud of envelopes and packages from the entrance hall below, and the rattle of the closing letterbox flap. She threw in a detergent capsule, started her chosen cycle, then rushed downstairs.

When she carried the delivery into the kitchen, she saw that most of it was unsolicited, from computer companies, supermarkets and someone offering to cut the cost of her home insurance in half. Apart from those, there was a phone bill, a letter confirming her next dental appointment, and a large packet, with her address handwritten on the front and the logo of Levene and Company on the back. She tossed the rest on to a work surface and tore it open.

191

The annual report and accounts of Fishheads.com plc had been published almost four months earlier, when Dražen Boras, under his business pseudonym, David Barnes, had still been running the company, and when Stevie, her husband, the man he killed, had still been alive. For a few seconds, that thought overwhelmed her, but she pushed it away and focused on the document.

It was a thick, glossy publication, undoubtedly produced by a high-powered design house, with the aim of making a statement of success to shareholders, to bankers and to the financial world in general. She scanned the index. The accounts were of no interest to her, and so she went straight to the section headed 'Directors' Report'.

The text was sketchy, giving only headline descriptions of the company's activities throughout the year. She guessed that the consultancy that had drafted it had taken the annual press release output and edited it into a single story. Most of the space was filled with photographs of the directors, out and about, at business meetings in Europe and further afield, in Asia and the United States . . . or, rather, of two of the directors. Most of the captions began 'Chairman David Barnes and director Ifan Richards . . .' The few in which Godric Hawker was seen were set in the firm's London head office, confirming Maggie's information that the finance director was the corporate equivalent of the footballer, Dennis Bergkamp, who never flew during the last ten years of his career. The counterpoint to this seemed to be that Barnes/Boras and Richards never seemed to travel separately.

She scanned the photographs minutely, using a magnifying-glass at times, trying to uncover anything that would take her search forward, without the vaguest notion of what that might be. Finally, she gave up. She pushed the report to one side, and thought, *That was then. So what about now? Richards must be lonely.*

'Up-to-date information,' she exclaimed suddenly, so firmly that it startled Stephanie in her carry-cot. 'Aw, baby, I'm sorry,' she said, picking up the infant and soothing her before her cries reached their full impressive volume.

'Does she need feeding again?' asked Bet, slouching into the kitchen, dressed in slippers and a knee-length T-shirt.

'No, it was my fault.' She looked at her sister. There were circles under her eyes, and she looked hung-over. 'Did you creep out last night? Have you been off clubbing again?'

'Are you nagging?'

'No, my dear; what you put into your body . . . or who, for that matter . . . is up to you. I'm just concerned, that's all.'

'Sorry. No, I wasn't on the batter. I had a sleepless night, that's all, coming to a decision. Margaret,' she continued, 'once you're a bit further into your treatment, do you think you'd be up to looking after me for a couple of weeks? I've been thinking about this consultant of yours, and the pre-emptive strike he wants to do on me. I'm going to talk to him, and if he persuades me, I'm going to go for it.'

Maggie placed Stephanie, restored to her slumber, back in the carry-cot. 'I can't tell you how happy that makes me,' she said. 'I trust Mr Ronald absolutely: so should you.'

'Okay. I'll call him once I've had a shower and some breakfast.' She shuffled back into the hall.

Her sister was smiling as she picked up the phone and dialled.

'*Scotsman* business,' a familiar voice replied. Even in mid-morning it sounded tired.

'Mo,' she said, 'it's Maggie. Thanks for that contact you gave me the other day. It worked out well. Now I'm shamelessly in the market for another favour.'

'If I can, I will. But I might ask for one in return this time.'

'Likewise. If I can, I will.'

'You go first.'

'Okay. Do you ever receive press releases from Fishheads dot com?'

'All the bloody time. It's a very talkative company.'

'And photographs?'

'Yes. They like to show us what they're up to as well as tell us.

They're not hard copy, you understand. Everything comes in electronically, these days.'

'What do you do with them?'

'Run the ones that are worth it: file them all for reference.'

'Can I see them? All of them for the last three months.'

'No problem. Do you have broadband? If not, I'll print and post them.'

'I'm on line.' She recited her e-mail address.

'Fine,' said Goode. 'I'll do it after the morning news conference. Now my turn. The truth is, it's not for me; it's for a pal on the *Evening News* crime desk. He needs something for the next edition. Do you know about the Sugar Dean murder inquiry?'

'Probably less than your mate. I'm not as clued up on CID as I used to be.'

'Shit.' The journalist sighed. 'Maggie, I'm sorry. It was bloody tactless of me to ask you a question like that.'

'It's all right, Mo,' she assured him. 'I meant, being on the uniform side, that's all. I wasn't talking about Stevie. What is it?'

'They've had a guy in the nick overnight. The press office has said that much, but they won't give us the sniff of a name. However, there's a rumour going round that it's a cop. If that's true, could you give me the nod?'

'Let me make a call. I'll get back to you.'

'Thanks. Appreciated, even if you can't help at the end of the day.'

She hung up and dialled Mario McGuire's land line, hoping he was at his desk.

He was. 'Hey, Blondie,' he said, as he answered. 'How's your project getting on?'

'Better than I could ever imagine. I think, or at least big Bob thinks, that I've found Dražen's new identity.' She told him about Ignacio Riesgo, the man of mystery.

'That would fit the pattern,' he said emphatically. 'There's an arrogance about the Borases, father and son, that beggars belief. So you're chuffed with yourself, and quite right too. Is that why you're calling, to show me you're still a better detective than me?'

'Nice of you to admit it,' she replied cheerfully, 'but no.' She told him about Mo Goode's favour, and heard him moan.

'Bloody hell, Mags. They need you back there if Torphichen Place is going to be as fucking porous as that. We've got Andy Martin down here doing one leak inquiry as it is; I might have to start him on another.'

'It's not good, I'll grant you, but I take it from what you're saying that it's true.'

'Yes. The guy's name's Theo Weekes.'

'I remember him. He was at Torphichen a few years back, wasn't he? Big, good-looking lad. Fancied himself with the women.'

'That's him: and you've got him spot on. He's in deep shit. They've placed him at the murder scene. They haven't found the weapon, but they've got the jacket and jeans he was wearing; the lab's giving them the full treatment, trying to find gunshot residue. Even if they don't, he's not going to walk from it.'

'But?'

'But nothing.'

'Sure? You don't sound a hundred per cent.'

'Och, I am. It's just . . . The girl was shot with a silenced nine-millimetre pistol. When the hell's a balloon like Weekes going to get his hands on one of them?'

'Firearms amnesty,' she suggested. 'It could have been surrendered, then spirited away as a souvenir. It's happened before, in other forces.'

'Yes, that may well be it. Mags, I don't mind giving the News a steer on this. If they use the phrase "believed to be a policeman", we won't deny it, but we can't confirm or give them a name until he's appeared in court.'

'And he will?'

'Oh, yes, one way or another, he will.'

Forty-one

'Interview resumed at ten forty-four a.m.,' said Becky Stallings. 'Same four people present. Ms Birtles,' she asked, 'does your client wish to make a statement?'

'Yes,' the lawyer replied, 'his position is . . .'

The DI held up a hand. 'No, not you. He's going to speak for himself or we're going to charge him right now. PC Weekes.'

The prisoner was ashen-faced: his body odour filled the room, but the detectives were used to that experience. He mumbled a few barely audible words.

'Loud and clear, please, for the tape,' McGurk reminded him.

'Ah never killed her,' Weekes repeated. 'I was there but it wasn't me.'

'A bad boy done it and ran away?' said the sergeant, caustically. 'That's the oldest defence in the book.'

The other man glared at him. 'That's what happened.'

'So who did kill Sugar?'

'I don't know. She was dead when I found her, but there was nobody else there.'

'So you admit going after her.'

'No. I waited for her. I knew the way she went to work.'

'How come?' asked Stallings.

'I'd watched her before, leaving her house in the morning, heading for the woods. I went there on my own one day and found out where the path led to. So that day I went in from the other end and waited for her.'

196

'To kill her.'

'No! Tae talk to her. To ask her what the fuck she was doing wi' the boy, making a fool of herself.'

'Nobody else saw it that way. His parents were happy enough to let them go to France together.' Stallings paused then frowned at him. 'That wasn't news to you, Weekes, was it? You knew about that, didn't you?'

'No.'

'I think you did. Let me put something to you. Your meeting with Sugar in the Gyle centre, the one you told Mr McGuire and Mr McIlhenney about. I don't think you arranged that at all, as you said you did.' She kept her eyes fixed on his, leaning closer. 'I think you were following Sugar, but you made a mistake, as you did with Mae Grey once, and she saw you. So you had to front it up. You had to talk to her. And I think that when you did, she told you that she had a new boyfriend and that she was going to France with him at the end of the term. That's what happened, wasn't it?'

'No,' he muttered.

'Yes,' she countered firmly. 'This is not the time to be lying to us. I'm right; that's what happened. And after it, you kept on following her, until you saw Davis Colledge. Come on. It's the truth, isn't it?'

'Okay, okay, okay, it's the truth. But I still didn't kill her.'

'So, tell us, what happened?'

Weekes drew a deep breath, trying to compose himself. 'I waited for her, like I said. But she never came. I waited until after she should have reached where I was, but she never came. So I started to walk the other way, towards where she should have been coming from, along the path. And then I found her.'

'But she was hidden away in a copse,' McGurk told him. 'You couldn't have found her there.'

'I never. I found her lying just off the path.'

'Describe her.'

'She was on her back, looking up at the trees, with her hands by her

side. Her dress was all spread out . . . it was long, no' one of her minis
. . . like she'd lain doon. She was almost smiling, ken. I never knew she
was dead. I thought she was . . .' He gulped. 'For a minute I thought
she'd seen me and was lying there waiting for me. I said, "What's the
game, Sugar?" but she never moved. Then I thought she must be ill,
have fainted or something. I knelt beside her, and put my hand behind
her head, to lift her up. And then I felt the blood, and looked in her
eyes, and I could see that she wasn't playing at anything.'

'And at that point, PC Weekes,' said Stallings, 'you did what any
serving officer would do, on or off duty, you got your mobile out and
called for back-up. Only you didn't. You left her there. Or, rather,
having killed her, you hid her body and left her there.'

'I never killed her!' Weekes's voice rose to a scream. Frankie Birtles
grabbed his arm once more, and held it until he was calm. But she said
nothing, simply waited until he was ready to take up his story once more.

'I panicked,' he said. 'There was I and there was Sugar, dead. If I'd
called it in, the whole thing would have come out, about me and her,
and about me and Varley's wife. Mae would have found out, Lisanne
would have found out, and I'd have been booted off the force. So I hid
her, okay? I dragged her into the bushes, I arranged her nice like,
smoothed her hair, closed her eyes, and then I got the fuck out of
there.'

'And kept quiet as a mouse, even after her body was found?'

Weekes nodded.

'An audible reply, please,' Stallings snapped.

'Yes.'

'But the necklet, Theo,' McGurk said. 'Why the hell did you take
the necklet?'

'To remind me of her. I gave it to her, after all.'

'So why did you give it to Lisanne?'

'So it wouldnae just be stuck away in one of my drawers, so I'd see
it all the time on her, and so that when I looked at Lisanne I'd think of
Sugar as well.'

The sergeant whistled. 'Weekes, you are one sick man.'

'So that's your client's story, is it?' Stallings asked Birtles.

'Yes,' she confirmed, 'and he's going to be sticking to it. So charge him with murder, if you think you've got the evidence, which I for one doubt, or release him.'

'I don't need to charge him with murder,' the inspector replied. 'Not yet. I'm going to charge him with everything he's admitted in this room. We'll begin with attempting to pervert the course of justice, and leaving the scene of a crime, add in concealing a body, and round it off with theft. That's more than enough to hold him overnight, pending a court appearance. Who knows what else we'll have on him by then?'

Forty-two

Aileen walked in from the terrace to the living area, towelling herself off after a swim in the pool. Bob smiled when he saw that she was wearing a bikini. 'Want a coffee?' he asked.

'Let's go out for one.'

'That's what I meant.'

'Then wait a minute till I put some clothes on and dry my hair. Where will we go? Into the old town?'

He wrinkled his nose. 'Nah, it was crawling with people when I went down for the croissants and papers, and that was just after nine. Let's walk along to the Hostal Empuries.'

'Is that the place right on the beach? The one we can see from the terrace?'

'That's the one.'

'Yes, I fancy that. I won't be a minute.' She ran off towards the stairs.

Bob glanced down at his shirt and saw patches of sweat under the arms. Heading off after Aileen, he started to unbutton it, tossing it into the laundry basket as he reached the bedroom. Looking for a fresh replacement, he took a cream-coloured T-shirt from his drawer and slipped it on. The letters 'FBI' were emblazoned on the front and back in big black letters. It looked like one of a few million sold on souvenir stalls across America, but his was different, a gift from the deputy director at the end of a visit to Quantico. He grinned at himself in the mirror, remembering the trip.

The sound of a hairdryer came from the bathroom. Idly, Bob picked up a pair of binoculars that had been left on the dressing-table and stepped out on to the sun terrace. He put the glasses to his eyes, and focused on the Hostal Empuries, which lay across the bay. He could see people on the terrace, but several empty tables also. He hoped that one would still be free when he and Aileen arrived.

He tracked down to the small curving bay, with its mushroom-shaped parasols and blue sun-loungers; it was packed, thronged with sun-worshippers of all ages, shapes and sizes. He made a mental note not to join them. He swung the binoculars to the right, following the line of the path that led to L'Escala, and then picking up the sea, as it washed gently up on to the rocks. A woman lay there, on a gentle slope away from the rest of the sunbathers; she was on her back, arms by her sides, wearing only a pair of black pants. Bob guessed that she was local, someone who knew where the quiet spots were, even in summer. He moved on, and was scanning the larger beach that led up to the road when he felt a hand tug his elbow gently.

'I'm ready.'

He turned. Aileen was dressed in blue shorts and a matching shirt, tied below the third button, to leave her midriff exposed. She smiled at his T-shirt. 'You look like my bodyguard.'

'I am your bodyguard, love, duly authorised by the Mossos d'Esquadra, the Catalan police force, to carry a firearm for your protection while we're in this country.'

The smile became a frown. 'Are you serious?'

He nodded. 'Oh, yes.'

'You don't have a gun, though.'

'They offered me one.'

'You didn't take it, did you?'

'No. If I had we'd have argued about it.'

'Yes, we would, sure as hell. I don't need an armed guard, not even you.'

'My darling, you're a head of government. If you didn't live with me, you'd have full-time protection officers.'

'No, I bloody wouldn't. I don't believe in them. Look at that man Colledge, carrying a gun. A fat lot of good that'll do him against a suicide bomber.'

'They tend not to go after individuals ... No, but a man with a knife, that's different. If someone gets close enough to you with a blade, a gun's pretty much useless. You haven't got room to get it out.'

'So what do you do?'

'You die, or you take it off him, if you're good enough.'

'You are good enough, aren't you?' she asked.

'Oh, yes.'

'Speaking of Colledge, any news of his son?'

'Yes, I called Edinburgh while you were swimming. He's pulled another six hundred euros from his bank account.'

'What does that tell you?'

Bob wrinkled his nose. 'It tells me that he's running around with quite a bit of cash for an eighteen-year-old on a painting holiday. But what does it suggest to me? That's the real question. He's a bright lad, so he probably knows that plastic leaves a trail. Maybe he doesn't want anyone to know where he is. His last withdrawal was made at Perpignan railway station: that's on the main line. It goes everywhere.'

'Maybe somebody will remember him buying a ticket.'

'I phoned my friend Cerdan and asked him to check, but it's a big place. They have thousands of travellers every day, and at this time of year half of them will be backpackers from northern Europe buying their tickets in very bad French. Anyway, finding the boy may have dropped a point or two in the importance stakes. We've got a guy in custody and it's looking bad for him. He's one of us, unfortunately.'

'A police officer?'

'I'm afraid so. But don't let's dwell on it, or my morning will be blighted.'

Aileen frowned. 'Maybe it will be anyway. I haven't finished with this protection stuff. Until now I've written it off as one of your jokes. Do you have a gun in the house in Gullane?'

'No. I won't, with the kids there, but you're protected in other ways. There are sensors all around the place that tell me if anything heavier than a cat comes anywhere near.'

'But it's only me,' she protested. 'I'm nothing. And it's only Scotland: we're only a devolved assembly.'

'Government,' he corrected her. 'And you are its leader. That makes you my responsibility, professionally as well as personally, and I will look after you as well as I can . . . without a firearm.'

'I've got faith in you.'

'Let's hope it's justified,' he said. 'But enough of the heavy stuff: let's be on our way.'

They left the house and took the footpath that led down to the entrance to the beach road and to the one-armed headless statue, erected to mark the 1992 Barcelona Olympics. The walk to the hotel took less than ten minutes even at a gentle pace. When they arrived, all but one of the terrace tables were occupied. Bob took the steps two at a time, and sat down, just beating a German couple to the prize. He glanced at his watch as the waiter approached. 'Will we make it lunch, rather than a coffee break?' he asked.

Aileen nodded. 'Might as well.'

They ordered a selection of tapas from the menu, with two beers. The young waiter was attentive. When Bob complimented him on his English, he replied that his father was British, his mother Catalan. They ate slowly, watching the holiday-makers on the beach below. 'I wish we could stay here,' said Aileen, as she finished the last of the *patatas bravas*.

'Nothing's impossible,' Bob replied. 'In a few years I hit fifty, and I can retire on a decent pension. If the electorate decides in its wisdom to get rid of you at the same time, we could move out here, put the kids in one of the English schools . . .'

She stared at him. 'Would you do that?'

'My love, if that's what you wanted; I'm told the schools are pretty good.'

'Not that good, though. Your ex-wife would go crackers if you even suggested it. And you'd go crackers too, after a few months out here. The last thing I want to do is cage you, or even get in the way of your career. Let's just leave all that as a distant dream.'

'Speaking of my career,' he said, 'we still haven't discussed that report I prepared for you. Have you read it yet?'

'Of course I have. Three times. It makes perfect sense, especially when you look at the examples you quoted. Given the size of Scotland, a single police force would work very well. And, as you say, Britain as a whole is almost unique in not having a national police force as such.'

'Could you get a Bill to set one up through the Parliament?'

'I reckon so. If I read them right, our coalition partners would support it, and maybe the Tories as well.'

'Will you try?' he asked.

'That depends on one thing.'

'What's that?'

'Your approval. The document sets out the case for amalgamation of the existing forces, but that's all I asked you to do. It doesn't have any recommendations. You haven't told me what you think of the idea.'

Bob slid his Ray-Bans down his nose and fixed his eyes on her. 'I'm a cop; I do what I'm asked or ordered.'

She raised an eyebrow. 'You're also my closest and most trusted adviser, so cut the crap.'

'Okay, if you insist. I've consulted one or two people close to me in drawing it up, but the paper you have is the only copy. Burn it, shred it, chuck it in the sea, whatever; but don't let anyone else see it.'

'You think it's a bad idea?'

'No, no. I think it's a terrible idea. The structure we have at the moment is in the public interest because it makes it difficult for badly intentioned politicians to put improper pressure on the police. Your predecessor wanted to control us; if he'd just had one guy to lean on it would have been much easier for him.'

'But,' she countered, 'the paper's very specific about the machinery for the appointment of the commissioner and senior officers. It would leave it all in the hands of the local authorities, and that's how it would be enacted. That's what the Bill would say.'

'Sure,' he said, 'that's how it would be set up. But suppose you lot get the boot at the next election and the SNP get in? Or suppose the hairy-backs on your extreme left gain a significant number of seats and decide that they want control? There would be nothing to stop them changing the rules, if they had the votes in Parliament to do it.'

'I could fix it for Westminster to veto it if they tried.'

Bob snorted. 'The way the polls are looking for your party, you won't be able to fix anything down there after the next general election. No, you asked for my advice and you've got it, as firmly as I can express it. The present system works, and the crime figures prove it. So since it ain't broke . . .'

'What if I went ahead anyway?' she asked. 'What would you do?'

'If I had to, I'd lead the opposition, and I'd mobilise the chiefs' association to speak out against it. I wouldn't seek any post in the new force; in fact, I'd leave the service the day it was set up.'

To his surprise, she laughed softly. 'How did I know that was what you'd say? Lover, I've got a confession to make: I've never had any thought of amalgamating the police forces. I feel exactly the same way you do about the notion.'

'Then why the hell . . .'

'. . . did I ask you to undertake the study? For your sake, to give you something to focus on, and to bring you out of yourself. Bob, after that business up at St Andrews, you were a psychological mess. Jimmy Proud told me that if you hadn't agreed to go on sabbatical he'd have ordered you. He and I dreamed up the idea of the study between us.'

'So you and my chief constable were plotting behind my back,' he said heavily.

'I'm afraid so.'

'In that case . . . thanks.' Suddenly, his grin reflected the brightness of the day. 'You were right: I really was in a fucking mess. But your wee scheme worked. It took me out of all that shit, out of my brooding self.'

'When Stevie Steele died,' Aileen confessed, 'I was afraid you'd sink back into your depression.'

Bob shook his head. 'No. If anything, that had the opposite effect. When something like that happens, it makes you want to be twice the cop, to honour the memory, so to speak. I'm ready to roll now and, for all our fantasy a few minutes ago, I'm itching to get back into action.' He glanced at their empty glasses. 'Want another beer?'

'No, thanks. We've probably outstayed our welcome at this table. Let's move on, and give somebody else the chance to eat.' She waved to their waiter, who read the gesture correctly and brought the bill.

Instead of heading back to town, they carried on along the beachside walkway. After a few minutes they reached an entrance. 'Are these the ruins you told me about?' asked Aileen.

'That's right. That pile of rocks on the other side of the fence was the first Greek colony on the Iberian peninsula; it goes back over two and a half thousand years. They called it Emporion ... means "market". There were people here before the Greeks; there was the indigenous population, and Etruscans, Phoenicians, maybe even Persians, visited and left traces. The Romans showed up eventually, and built their own town. For a wee while, this was the most important place in Spain. Want to go in?'

'Of course.'

They spent two hours exploring the carefully excavated streets and buildings, tracing the city from its founding years through to its expansion under the Romans. Finally, Aileen cried, 'Enough! I'm historied out!'

They made their way home on the Carrilet, a tractor-drawn train that provided the town's main public transport during the summer. It dropped them at the top of L'Escala's main street, leaving them with one last, uphill walk to the villa. 'Swim,' Bob gasped, as the door closed behind them, jogging upstairs to change into his trunks.

In the bedroom, he heard a splash. Aileen's voice drifted up from the pool. 'It's okay,' she called out. 'There are no helicopters up there.'

He smiled, and picked up the binoculars he had discarded earlier to retrace their journey. He found the ruins, or those he could see through the trees, then tracked back along the line of the walkway to the hotel, and beyond.

The sun-worshipper was still on the rocks. 'You must be fried, lady,' he murmured. 'You've been there for hours.'

In another micro-second, he would have moved on, had something not held his attention . . . or, rather, the absence of something, the absence of anything. 'Where are her clothes?' he whispered. 'Where's her water bottle? She can't have lain there all that time without drinking.'

The glasses had a zoom facility. He slid it to the maximum, and focused as sharply as he could, watching the woman for long seconds that turned into minutes. He looked for signs of movement, but she lay still, unnaturally still, terminally still.

He was frowning as he stripped off the bathing trunks he had only just donned, exchanging them for running shorts. Quickly, he pulled his FBI T-shirt back over his head, then rescued his trainers from the back of his wardrobe. Aileen was still in the pool as he stepped out on to the terrace. 'Changed my mind,' he told her. 'I'm going for a jog.' He headed for the door, picking up his mobile on the way.

He was an experienced all-terrain runner, used to uneven surfaces on his routes around Gullane, and so he took the steps down to the roadway in his stride, keeping his knees very slightly bent to maintain his balance. He picked up pace as the ground levelled out; as he ran past the one-armed statue he glanced across the bay, and saw that the woman was still there, her pose unaltered. He sprinted around the curve in the road, feeling the sweat begin to pour from him as he cruised past walkers, holding his line and forcing two oncoming cyclists to alter theirs.

It took him only two minutes to reach the start of the path that led to the rocks. It was rough, and he had to drop his pace, picking his way carefully to avoid slipping and plunging into the sea. At first, he passed one or two people, escapees from the throng on the beach, but soon, as the ground became so rough and uneven that he had to slow to walking pace, there was no-one.

He passed the woman by. She was hidden from his view by a spur of rock, and it was not until the Hostal Empuries came into sight that he realised he had missed her. He retraced his steps until he discovered where he had gone wrong, until he stood, looking down at her from only a few yards away. Her face was calm, composed, peaceful. She was naked; the black garment he had assumed he saw through the binoculars was, in reality, a thick pubic triangle.

'*Hola*,' he called out. 'Hello. *Bonjour*.'

There was no movement.

'*Esta bien?*' he asked, 'Are you okay?', guessing the answer and fearing it.

He approached the woman and knelt beside her on her hard rock bed. He reached out and touched her shoulder. Her skin was hot, from the sun, and yet there was an underlying coldness also. He put two fingers against her neck and pressed, searching for a pulse that he knew, within himself, he would not find.

Moving to a sitting position, he reached into his pocket and took out his mobile, then found its stored phone numbers. He scrolled through until he found the entry that read 'Mossos d'Esquadra' and pressed the call button.

Forty-three

'Realistically,' Neil McIlhenney asked, 'what do we have?'

'We've got him for everything he's already been charged with,' said Stallings, leaning back in her chair with her feet on her desk. 'He's admitted to all of it in his signed statement.'

'Which can be withdrawn at any time.'

'He can try, sir, but the sugar-cube necklet does him. He took it off the girl's body and gave it to his ex-wife. I'll grant you that I'd have been happier if the lab had found gunshot residue on his clothes, but even without that, and without the weapon, the evidence against him is so strong that I want to do him for murder. Think about it. We don't even need to prove that he shot her: a jury might find that by moving the body he made himself an accessory.'

'Maybe in England, Becky,' the superintendent chuckled, 'but on this side of the border we have a third possible verdict, "not proven". In this case, your jury might well decide to hide behind that.'

'What's the difference between that and "not guilty"?'

'For the accused, there is none in practical terms. He's acquitted of the charge, once and for all. For the jury? I've never been on one, so I can't say for sure, but most people reckon that it gives them the chance of saying to the guy in the dock, "We reckon you're guilty, but we needed more proof." I can't give you any better explanation than that, but it's been around for a long time, and it was a cop-out in capital cases when at least eight out of the fifteen couldn't bring themselves to send someone to be hanged.'

'Fifteen?'

McIlhenney nodded. 'We have a fifteen-person jury, and eight–seven is an acceptable verdict. If you want to press on with a murder charge, do that, but ultimately it's a Crown Office decision and they'll have all these things in mind. However, as you say, we have him by the short and curlies on a charge of perverting the course of justice. In theory, he could get life for that; he won't but if I was in his shoes I'd plead guilty in the hope that my counsel would offer enough in mitigation to talk the judge out of an exemplary sentence.'

'He'll go to jail, though?'

Seated beside her, Jack McGurk snorted. 'Too bloody right he will. This is a murder inquiry, and he's a police officer: if he gets less than five years, he'll be lucky.'

'And if he's guilty of that murder, he'll be even luckier. He and his solicitor had time to concoct that story between them.'

'You've met too many bent lawyers in London, Becky,' said the sergeant. 'Frankie Bristles may be a police witness's worst nightmare, but she's an officer of the Court and one of the highest legal-aid earners in Scotland. I might not like her very much, but I don't have any doubts about her integrity. If Weekes made up that story, then he did it himself.'

'If?' Stallings exclaimed. 'Jack, are you saying you think he was telling the truth?'

The superintendent intervened: 'No, I think he's saying we can't disprove it categorically. If Weekes is charged with murder, that's what he'll come out with in the witness box. Unless we can find the gun and put it in his hand, through a witness or through forensics, then at least eight of those fifteen people I mentioned earlier will see that hole in our case, and he'll get off through the bastard verdict, as "not proven" was described by none other than Sir Walter Scott.'

'Who's he? A famous Scots lawyer?'

McIlhenney looked at her, shook his head sadly, and continued: 'On Monday, our first reaction was that we were looking at a copycat.

The defence will suggest that we still are, and who knows? They might be right.' He frowned. 'You can forget the accessory idea, by the way. You'd need to establish a link with someone else to make that stick. In this one, he either did it or he didn't.'

'So what do you want me to do, sir?' Stallings asked.

'I want you to make a choice,' McIlhenney replied. 'You can go downstairs and lay the murder on him right now, or you can go and see the procurator fiscal and ask for his opinion. As I said, at the end of the day it's the Crown Office that does the prosecuting, not us.'

'That would be the sensible thing to do, wouldn't it?' the inspector mused.

'Pragmatic.'

'Then that's what I'll do. I'll go up to Chambers Street this afternoon.'

'No,' said the superintendent, quickly. 'Leave it until tomorrow morning. Gregor Broughton's due back then; he's got the soundest hands in that place. I wouldn't trust anything to that new assistant of his. Be in his office as soon as he's hung up his jacket, and tell him where we've got to. Before Weekes goes into court for his first formal hearing, Gregor can decide whether to proceed with the murder charge, and whether to oppose the bail application that Ms Birtles will undoubtedly make.'

Forty-four

'What made you come to this place?' the officer asked, in clear English. He wore three chevrons on his epaulettes, which told Skinner that he was dealing with a sub-inspector, a rank in the Mossos d'Esquadra that had no direct equivalent in Scotland.

He pointed back towards the town. 'I have a house over there. Earlier today, I happened to look at this area through my binoculars and noticed the woman. A few hours later, I looked again. I saw that she was still here, and that she didn't appear to have moved.'

'You were watching her, señor?' The policeman's left eyebrow rose; so did Skinner's hackles.

'I was observing the scene, sonny. It's a habit of mine; it comes with my profession.'

'And what is that?'

'I'm a police officer, in Edinburgh. In your ranking structure I'm a *comisario*. What's your name, Sub-inspector? Como te llamas?'

'Torres.' Caution crept into his voice; Skinner guessed that he might be remembering hearing of a senior Scottish policeman who was in town.

'Well, Señor Torres, I suggest that you stop playing the boy detective and get your arse into action. This lady is dead. That's not in doubt; I've seen more dead people than you have officers in your local station, and I'm telling you she is. You need to find out how and why. You may have been the first available English-speaking officer to respond to my phone call, but now it's time for you to follow proper procedures. You

212

need to get a medic here, and you need to call in your specialist colleagues. Then you need to position your corporal colleague to prevent any curious people making their way down here to see what's happening.'

Sub-inspector Torres came approximately to attention and saluted. 'Yes, Comisario.' He reached for the radio on his belt, then hesitated. 'What should I say? She died of the heat, yes? Too long in the sun?'

Skinner sighed; clearly, Torres had spent much of his career in the administrative section of the Catalan force. 'If she did,' he said, 'she committed suicide. And in twenty-five years' police experience, I've never heard of anyone setting out to kill themselves by UV radiation. Look at her, man! She has no water. She has no sun-cream. She has no shade. She has no towel. Last, but not least, she has no clothes. That tells you what, Señor Torres?'

The sub-inspector shrugged, in a way that very few people can, other than Catalans.

'It should tell you,' Skinner continued patiently, 'either that the seagulls have stolen everything she had, that she threw her kit into the sea, that she walked here naked and unburdened, or that somebody walked with her or followed her here, and took everything away after she was dead, after he had killed her.' He looked at the man intently. 'You understand what I'm saying?'

'Sí, Comisario,' Torres murmured.

'Then get on your radio, and tell your criminal division they're needed here.'

As the sub-inspector did as he had been ordered, Skinner stared down at the woman's body. With his instructions being relayed, his thoughts returned to other images he had seen, photographs taken in other places, and the uncanny similarity to his own discovery.

He knelt beside the body once more, but this time he rolled the dead woman on to her side. It was difficult, as rigor mortis was advanced, even in the heat, but he had the strength to turn her and then to hold her in position with one hand, as he lifted the hair from the back of her neck with the other . . . and looked at the impossible.

There, just above the hairline, in the centre of a patch of encrusted blood, was a single small entry wound.

He laid the body of the murder victim back as he had found her, then sat on the rocks. 'Oh, shit,' he whispered softly to himself, allowing all the implications of his find to flood into his mind.

Forty-five

'I'd hoped for an earlier appointment,' said Deputy Chief Constable Andy Martin, stone-faced. 'It's gone three thirty.'

The Crown Agent peered at him over a pair of half-moon spectacles. 'You're damn lucky I'm seeing you at all,' he snapped. 'This business has grown legs: it's a damn nonsense. I tell you, Martin, the Lord Advocate agreed to co-operate with this against my advice. It's a reflection on this office, and it's a waste of my valuable time.'

'I'd be grateful if you'd repeat that for the tape, Mr Dowley, once Chief Inspector Mackenzie sets it up.'

'Tape? What bloody tape?'

'This is a formal interview. It will be recorded.'

'Oh, really! This is too much. I'm Her Majesty's Agent, man. You wouldn't treat the Lord Advocate like this, or the Lord President.'

Martin remained impassive, as Mackenzie produced a portable mini-disk recorder from his briefcase and laid it on Dowley's coffee-table. 'The Lord Advocate has agreed to be interviewed,' he said, 'if it proves necessary. As for the Lord President, if Sir James Proud asked me to rake through his dustbin, I'd do it.' Uninvited, he settled into a chair, and stared hard at his host until he followed suit. In his mind's eye, he saw McGuire and McIlhenney, in similar circumstances, making barbed comments about the absence of coffee and biscuits.

He had done his homework in advance of the encounter, and was familiar with the man's background. He had been in the Crown Office for over twenty years, having joined as an assistant fiscal after a short,

215

unremarkable career in private practice, and had worked his way quietly through the ranks. His appointment as Crown Agent had come in the new age of openness and public accountability ushered in by the Scottish Executive. It had been a surprise, as few senior figures in the legal establishment had ever heard of Joe Dowley, but he had wasted no time in making his mark.

Looking at him, Martin saw a small man, with red cheeks that spoke of excitability and perhaps a touch of hypertension, and hair that seemed to fly backwards from a high forehead. In spite of the warmth of the summer day, he wore a three-piece suit with a watch-chain falling from one lapel of his jacket into its breast pocket, and a small circular gold badge on the other.

'Shall we begin, Mr Dowley?' he said. 'For the record I am DCC Andrew Martin of Tayside Police, accompanied by Chief Inspector David Mackenzie, from Fettes, and we are with Mr Joseph Dowley, Crown Agent, in his office.'

'An intrusion which I protest,' the civil servant responded. 'I maintain that this is an entirely unnecessary procedure. It's a charade. I'm told that your colleagues already have a man in custody for this latest crime, and that the press are saying he's a police officer. That makes this discussion irrelevant.'

'Nobody's told us to stop, Mr Dowley, and I'm pretty sure that Sir James would have if the issue had been resolved. As for your opinion, you're entitled to express it, but don't expect me to agree with you. I don't play charades. I wouldn't have agreed to undertake this task if I hadn't believed it to be appropriate. I'd remind you also that it was set in motion by the chief constable, not a man given to flights of fancy, although you seem to be questioning that.'

For the first time, Dowley's face took on a look of something other than aggression. 'No, no,' he said hurriedly. 'I don't doubt Sir James's integrity, only his judgement, in this one instance.'

'I don't see how you can,' Martin replied. 'If my information is correct, he didn't set this ball rolling. You did.'

'How?'

'By refusing to allow your staff to co-operate with a murder inquiry.'

'This office instigates murder inquiries.'

David Mackenzie's laugh took Dowley by surprise. The Crown Agent glared at the chief inspector. 'What's so damn funny?' he barked, taking the offensive once more.

'I always thought that murder inquiries were instigated by murderers,' Mackenzie replied. 'And here I've been wrong all along. God knows how I got so far in the polis.'

'Don't be flippant, man! This is a serious matter.'

'That's funny. A minute ago you were calling it a charade.'

'I mean, you fool, that it's serious that you're here wasting my time. Martin,' he snapped, 'I'm putting a stop to this right now. Switch off your machine and leave this office.'

'If I do that,' said the deputy chief constable, 'I'm taking you with me, back to Fettes, where you'll be interviewed under caution with a view to a possible charge. I remind you that I'm operating under the authority of the Lord Advocate, your boss, with the approval of his boss, and you know who she is. So unless you want to find your glittering career hitting the buffers at high speed, you will answer every question I put to you, here and now. If you like, before we go any further, you can make a couple of phone calls; ask people who know me, then tell me whether they think I'm kidding.'

In the silence that followed, Dowley and Martin stared at each other across the coffee-table, until finally the Crown Agent broke the impasse. 'Let's get it over with,' he murmured.

'That's better,' said the police officer. 'Now, will you please tell us who in this office was privy to the contents of the report into the Ballester murders?'

'Joanna Lock, the assistant fiscal, Gregor Broughton, the area fiscal, and myself.'

'Who prepared the report?'

'Primarily Mr Broughton.'

'It was based on what, exactly?'

'On the papers passed to him by Chief Superintendent McGuire, at Fettes, following the death in England of Daniel Ballester, the principal suspect, indeed the only suspect, for all four killings.'

'And its conclusion?'

'That although Ballester's death was the subject of an inquiry by the Northumbria police force, and by the coroner, there was no doubt that he was responsible for the deaths of Gavin, Boras, Paul and Noone, the four victims.'

'On what basis?'

'Motive and opportunity, backed up by the fact that the murder weapon, a Sig Sauer pistol, and several items belonging to the three female victims were found hidden on his property.'

'What was the recommendation?'

'That all four cases should be closed.'

'Without any public process? You could have held fatal accident inquiries into each case.'

'I could, at considerable expense, and not just to the Crown Office either. Ballester's estate would have been entitled to representation, and we'd have had to allow counsel for each victim's family. What would its purpose have been? An FAI can't make findings of guilt against individuals, dead or alive, yet a media circus would have grown around it. So it was decided that it should all be put away in a box. I still stand by that.'

'Did the final report contain details of each killing?'

'Oh, yes,' said Dowley. 'It was extremely thorough. It was, in effect, the case for the prosecution, had Ballester still been alive and in custody.'

'Surely someone else saw it. A typist, for example.'

'No. Gregor and Ms Lock drafted the document themselves, on their computers.'

'What about the senior Advocate Depute, the Solicitor General, or the Lord Advocate himself? Who made the determination you've just described?'

'I did.'

'Four murders, and you signed them off personally?'

'It's within my authority.'

'So we're only looking at three people in this building who knew exactly how the three women were killed?'

'Yes.'

'Then Sugar Dean turns up, murdered in exactly the same way. Surely you can see the grounds for concern?'

'Of course, but no fault lies here. Ten times that number of people within the police service must have been privy to the same facts.'

'Not quite that many. No more than a dozen, actually. But we'll be interviewing them all, don't you worry.'

'Including Sir James?' Dowley sneered.

'He was our first, while we were waiting for you to fit us in. ACC Mackie was second. I'm going to be thorough; if I think I need to put someone on oath, I will. You, for a start, if you don't give me a convincing answer to my last questions.' Martin's green eyes locked on to the Crown Agent once more. 'Have you ever discussed these matters with anyone outside the immediate circle of knowledge?'

'No! Of course not.'

As he replied, Martin thought he detected a very slight flicker in the man's eyes. 'Never?' he asked again.

'No.' Dowley's gaze moved to the window.

'Would you like me to put that to your wife?' Suddenly he focused on the badge on the Crown Agent's lapel, and felt a flash of inspiration. 'Or your fellow Rotarians?'

'For God's sake!' the man shouted. 'Of course there's pillow talk! And you don't seriously think that Blackford Rotary Club is a hotbed of serial killers.'

Martin allowed silence to fill the room, never taking his eyes from Dowley. When he was ready, he shifted in his chair slightly. 'Did you tell the whole Rotary Club?' he asked quietly.

'I made a few remarks one night,' the Crown Agent blustered. 'At a meeting, when it was my turn to discuss my still fairly new job. I quoted examples of things I did, and I may have mentioned the Ballester case.'

'You may have, or you did?'

'I did.'

'What did you say?'

'I can't remember.'

'Mr Dowley,' said Martin, quietly but with menace, 'if you prevaricate just one more time, I'll take you out the front door of this building in handcuffs.'

'Damn you, man: I told them how the three killings were tied together.'

'You told them that the three women were shot in the back of the head at close range?'

'I may have.'

'I'll take that to mean you did. Mr Dowley, who's the secretary of your Rotary branch? I'll need to report this to the investigating officers in the Sugar Dean case. They, in turn, may have to interview every member of your club.'

'You can't be serious.'

'Never more so, sir. Never more so.'

Forty-six

Neil McIlhenney had been in the act of reaching for the phone when it had rung, beating him to the punch.

'Yes,' he answered, pressing the instrument to his ear for at least the twenty-fifth time that day. He almost added, 'Becky,' assuming that it would be another report on the Dean murder inquiry, and on the preparation for Weekes's court appearance the following morning.

'Neil?' The voice was male, and very familiar. It was also on edge. 'It's Bob. I'm glad I caught you; I need someone to talk to. You will never guess in one thousand years of trying where I am.'

'You're at a crime scene,' McIlhenney replied, without a pause for thought.

'How the hell did you know that?'

'Call it intuition. Or call it knowing the difference between you calling me on something job-related and to tell me you've just broken par round the pitch and putt.'

'Clever bastard. Now describe it to me.'

The superintendent frowned. 'This has nothing to do with Aileen, has it?'

'No. She doesn't even know about it yet. She won't be best pleased either, when she finds out that I'm involved in another murder investigation.'

McIlhenney gasped. 'Only you,' he said. 'Only you could go on holiday and stumble across something like that. Can you tell me about it? Are you able to, where you are? I can hear all sorts of noise in the background.'

'That's the sea. I'm on a rocky outcrop, facing my house. The Mossos d'Esquadra CID officers are on their way here from Girona. I'll have to wait and give them a statement. But that doesn't stop me talking to you.'

'Who's the victim?'

'We don't know yet. None of the officers who've got here so far recognises her.'

'Her?'

'Yes. She's maybe around thirty, Spanish, I'd guess, from her hair colouring, skin tone and general appearance, but there's nothing here to back that up. There are no clothes, no personal belongings at the scene.'

'So it looks like she was killed somewhere else and dumped there?'

'That may very well be so; but either way she must have been put here when there was nobody else around. She's been lying in the sun all day, and she could have been here overnight, unnoticed until I spotted her. There's a medical examiner here, and if my limited Spanish lets me understand him right, he's saying that he's not even going to guess at time of death. The sun's been blazing down all day, so the rocks are fucking hot. It's like she's been lying in a pizza oven all this time.'

'You mean she's covered in anchovies?'

'Jesus, Neil, spare me the crime-scene humour. The one thing I do know is what killed her, because I've had a look for myself.'

Call it a premonition, call it a second flash of intuition, but a wave of certainty seemed to wash over McIlhenney as he sat there. He was a thousand miles away from Skinner, but it was as if he had been teleported to his side in an instant, and could see the victim. He knew how the body was lying, he could picture the peaceful expression on her face. 'A single wound to the back of the head,' he said. 'Small-calibre weapon.'

'I can't vouch for the calibre,' the deputy chief constable replied, 'but there's no exit wound. It's even possible that this could be a knife wound, but you get the picture. It looks as if she never knew what hit her.'

'So what are you saying to me?' the detective superintendent asked.

'You know what I'm saying. I'm not familiar with the Gavin and Boras crime scenes, or the third girl, Amy Noone. I wasn't involved in those inquiries, only in the aftermath because of Stevie's death, but from the way they've been described to me, this one's identical.'

McIlhenney sat silent for a while, thinking about what he should do next. In normal circumstances, there would have been no doubt, but the shock of the news that Skinner had just imparted made him hold back. Finally, he decided. 'Boss,' he said, 'I'm going to have to talk to Mario. How long will you be there?'

'As long as I have to. I'm sort of in charge here at the moment. None of the attending officers has encountered anything like this before, so I've been advising them. The team that's on the way is being led by your equivalent. Once they get here and I've spoken to them, I'll head back home. Let's say I'll be there in an hour. Meantime, I'd like you to email me the crime-scene photographs from the Ballester killings and from Sugar Dean.'

'Okay, I'll arrange that. Meantime, boss, if you can take a photo of your scene as it is, even if it's only with your mobile, I'd like to see that too.'

Forty-seven

For most of the afternoon, Maggie pushed Dražen Boras to the back of her mind and caught up on the domestic tasks that had been sidelined by her pet project, and on spending quiet quality time with her daughter. As she did so, her sister worked on the desktop computer, using the software that was at the heart of the graphic-design business she had built up in Australia, and was attempting to sustain at very long distance.

As she folded the last ironed garment she thought about Bet's decision. It was both brave and sensible, and might well prove to be a positive spin-off from her own illness. Having undergone the same procedure she knew that it would be no picnic for her, but at least she would not be going into surgery in the immediate aftermath of childbirth.

She stored her laundered clothes in the drawers where they were kept and returned to the computer room. 'How are you doing?' she asked.

'Almost done,' her sister replied. 'The client will find the finished product waiting for him when he comes in tomorrow morning, which will be about eleven p.m. our time.'

'How much are you losing by being here?' Maggie asked.

'Less than you think. I have a core group of loyal customers who pay most of my bills without the need for constant face-to-face meetings. I told them I'd be out of Australia for at least six months, and they were all fine with it. Mind you,' she continued, 'while I've been here I've shown my work to a few Edinburgh design agencies, and to companies; the feedback's been pretty positive.'

'Are you telling me you're thinking about staying?'

'It's crossed my mind. You and Stephanie are the only family I have, Sis. I dunno, though. I might find the winter a bit hard to take; that's one reason why I left in the first place.' She pushed the chair back from the desk and stood, stretching her long back. 'You want your machine back?'

'If you're sure you're done. I need to check my email.'

'Yeah, that's me finished; you go ahead. I'll make supper tonight. What do you fancy?' She clicked the mouse to send her document, then exited her program.

'Whatever you fancy cooking. It's been a few days since my last treatment, so my appetite's back to normal.'

'You've asked for it,' said Bet, ominously, heading for the kitchen.

As she left, Maggie settled down at the computer, and clicked on the icon that led to her mailbox. As he had promised, there was a message from Maurice Goode: she went to it, downloaded the attachment to her 'received files' folder, then opened it.

She found a series of dated documents, each headed 'A word from Fishheads.com' with a series number. There were twenty in all, stretching back over a nine-month period. The most recent was the announcement she had already seen, of the board changes and the transfer of Dražen's shareholding.

She returned to Goode's covering message and read:

Hi, Maggie. These are the most recent releases from your friends. Let me know if you'd like to go further back. As you can see, their PR consultants are persistent bastards. They must be impressing the City though, for the shares are flying, despite the founder having bailed out of the business and buggered off to parts unknown to enjoy the serious millions he must have got for his stake. If you're thinking of this as an investment, I wouldn't put you off. Mind you, Davor Boras's company, Continental IT, might be an even better bet, in view of never-ending speculation that he's about to sell out to American interests. Knowing how devious Davor is, the market reckons that this talk might be a ploy to start a bidding war.

'Mo,' Maggie whispered, 'the only thing I would invest in the Boras family is the time it's going to take me to find Dražen and see him put away.'

She returned to the press releases and opened them one by one. Most of them were bland, announcements of quarterly, half-yearly and annual profit figures. The others dealt with business development across Europe and around the world, and invariably were accompanied by photographs.

Two were expanded versions of stories she had read in the annual report, four others dealt with supply deals struck with major companies, one referred to an international congress in Las Vegas, 'attended by David Barnes and Ifan Richards', with a photograph of the pair in front of the black edifice of the Wynn resort, the newest and biggest on the Strip, and another spoke of a 'successful trip' to South Africa by Richards, shown in Cape Town, casually dressed, with Table Mountain in the background. Since David/Dražen's disappearance, there had been only two: the board announcement and a release built around a sales drive on the US eastern seaboard, as part of what was referred to as 'Fishheads' American invasion'.

'And what does all that tell you, Maggie?' she asked herself aloud. 'Damn all, so far,' she replied, 'but there's something there, I know it.'

Forty-eight

'Andy, how did you know to go for Dowley?' asked David Mackenzie, as they walked out of the Crown Office into Chambers Street.

'It was something I learned from Bob Skinner,' Martin told him. 'The two you look at first are the one who shouts loudest and the one who says the least.'

'So who's the other one?'

'Joanna Lock, I reckon. What did you think of her?'

The chief inspector smiled. 'It's been a long time since I saw a person watch her back so carefully. She's got her career all mapped out, and nothing's going to sidetrack her.'

'I agree. I don't see her jeopardising it by talking out of turn.'

'Is that us done here?'

'There's still Gregor Broughton.'

'Of course. His secretary said she'd call to tell me when he can see us. Are we going to take that? Shouldn't we be telling him?'

'Hell, no. Gregor's an old pal; he won't mess us about. He's also, David, one of the most discreet men I've ever met. Everybody expected that he'd be the new Crown Agent when the job fell vacant, but he didn't apply; his wife's a judge and he said that he wouldn't have felt comfortable.'

'So tomorrow we start interviewing our own guys?'

'Yes,' said Martin. 'And that's where it could get a wee bit sticky. Mario McGuire had a word with me this morning, off the record.

Maybe I shouldn't have allowed it, but I did, on the basis that he wouldn't be saying anything he wasn't prepared to put on tape. He told me that on the day of the second murder he and Neil discussed the details with Lou and Paula across the dinner-table. What Mario wanted to know was whether, when this was disclosed formally, we'd want to interview the girls too.'

'What did you tell him?'

'That I'd think about it. I have done, and I've come to the conclusion that I'll accept written declarations from each of them that they haven't spoken to anyone else about what they were told. The final report will mention it, but won't comment critically unless . . . and God forbid . . . either of the pair confesses that they did blab about it to a mate. If police officers can't let off steam to a spouse or partner when they really need to, the job'll become intolerable, or their marriage will suffer. I've done it; truth is, I do it all the bloody time, and I know for a fact that Bob Skinner has.'

'Yes, but your wife was a cop, wasn't she? And his ex was a pathologist.'

'So what? Most of the time you're not looking for expert analysis. You want a shoulder to cry on, somebody there who understands why the anger is coming off you in waves, or why your hands won't stop shaking while you're having your dinner. Police wives are unpaid counsellors. Are you telling me that you don't confide in yours?'

Mackenzie frowned, as they slid into Martin's car. 'I won't tell you that I haven't,' he said, 'but the one time when I really should have talked to Cheryl, I wound up having serious discussions with Mr Miller Draft and Mr Vodka and Tonic instead, and nearly fucked my career. When I took on this new job, I did a hand-over with big McGurk, who did part of it before me. His marriage is tits up: I got the impression that often he wanted to talk to his wife, but that she didn't want to listen.'

'Or wasn't able to,' Martin suggested. 'It can be rough, and some partners can't handle it. I'm not just talking about the aftermath of armed situations, or child murders and so on. The people on the traffic cars see some fucking awful stuff, on a regular basis; they take all that home with them too. When Karen and I were married, and I was still down here, she set up a support group for officers' wives who were having trouble dealing with their husband's job. By God, it took off . . . Mary McGurk was a member . . . and before she knew it she had more clients than she could handle on her own, including quite a few husbands. She does the same thing up in Tayside.'

'What happened to her group in Edinburgh when she left?'

'It's still there. She recruited helpers, and handed it on to them. Lady Proud's the leader now, Sheila Mackie's involved, and so is Jen Regan, George's wife.'

'Maybe Cheryl should volunteer.'

'Maybe she should.'

Mackenzie was thoughtful as the car headed into the traffic. 'Andy,' he asked, after they had made the turn on to the North Bridge, 'where's this going to lead?'

'It may go nowhere if the fiscal decides that he has evidence enough to convict the current suspect on the Dean case, because the copycat theory will be stopped in its tracks. On the other hand if the inquiry stays open it may lead to new avenues for the investigators. Our brief from Proud Jimmy is to uncover possible leaks of information. We've just hit the bull's eye with our first dart, and I suppose that raises a new question. If it comes to it, who investigates all the Rotarians who heard Dowley shoot his mouth off? Is it us, or is it Becky Stallings and her people?'

'Logic says it's them.'

Martin smiled. 'In this situation, I'm not sure that logic applies.'

Forty-nine

Bob Skinner's Spanish was better than he was prepared to admit, but not up to a professional situation, so he was more than pleased that Intendant Josefina Cortes, the Mossos d'Esquadra's chief regional criminal investigator, had spent, as she was quick to tell him, two years on an exchange programme with the Los Angeles Police Department, and did not require him to put it to the test.

She was in uniform when she arrived at the crime scene, the insignia on her shoulders leaving no-one in any doubt as to who was the ranking officer. Her manner underlined the fact. She was in her mid-thirties, sharp and authoritative, and in no way subservient to Skinner, although she had been briefed on his background before her arrival.

'You have an eye for detail,' she asked, 'or just a good memory? You look at this woman twice, hours apart, and know something is wrong. Did you not think that they might have been two different people?'

'You reckon?' he replied. 'Two identically undressed women sunbathing on the same hidden spot on the same day? That would mean that someone killed the victim in broad daylight, in the middle of the day, in full view of anyone who happened to be watching from L'Escala, then bundled up her clothes and possessions and took them away.'

Cortes smiled. 'You have a point, Comisario.'

'Yes, but now you have me kicking myself that I didn't catch on first time to what had happened.'

'Would it have made any difference if you had?'

'Of course. It would have meant that the person who did this would have been four hours closer to us.'

'Us? You are not in Scotland now, señor. You are only a witness in this thing.'

Skinner snorted. 'Only a witness? Rephrase that: I'm the only witness. This guy is good.'

'You speak as if you have knowledge of him.'

'I wish I did. This is a very surreal situation, Intendant.'

'Surreal? I don't see anything surreal about it. I see a dead woman with a bullet in her head, according to my medico. As soon as I find out who she is, I will look for a husband or a boyfriend, or maybe the wife of someone else's husband or boyfriend.'

'And maybe you'll get lucky. I really hope you do. But if you're wrong, we'll have a really worrying situation . . . and don't correct me this time, for I'm saying "we" deliberately. In recent months, we've had four murders in Scotland that are practically identical to this one.'

'Maybe,' said Cortes, unconvinced, 'but in Los Angeles in two years we had fifty homicides where the body looked like this, gunshot to the head.'

'Edinburgh ain't Los Angeles, señora. Our homicides were very specific. The first three cases have been closed, as the only suspect is dead, but two weeks ago there was a fourth killing, so similar to the others that my people in Scotland are concerned that somebody is imitating him.'

'Yes, but that's in Scotland.'

'Indeed, but yesterday I was in France trying to help my colleagues by tracking down the boyfriend of the most recent victim. He's supposed to be on holiday in Collioure, but he isn't. He's gone missing, last heard of at the train station in Perpignan. He could be anywhere. He could be here.'

'What is his name?'

'Davis Colledge. He's eighteen years old.'

'Why would he do this?'

Skinner looked at her. 'Come on,' he said. 'You know sometimes that's the last question to be answered. There are people who say that there's no such thing as a motiveless crime. I'm not one of them.' He smiled, and flexed his shoulders: his FBI shirt was sweat-soaked, uncomfortable against his skin. 'I agree with you on at least one thing, though. Our . . .' He paused. 'Sorry, your first priority is to identify this woman. Whoever killed her did his best to make that difficult.' He glanced across at the small forensic team that Cortes had brought with her. 'Is that a Polaroid your guy has?'

Her eyes followed his. 'Yes.'

'Then ask him to take a snap of the woman: full face, close up.'

Cortes called across to the technician, who did as she ordered, then waited for the image to develop, shielding it from the sun with his hand. When it was ready, he brought it across.

'Good,' said Skinner. 'Now, can I make a suggestion?'

'Please.'

'Let's say this woman has been here before. Did she come for a swim off the rocks? Or just to take the sun in the morning before it got too high? She isn't too heavily tanned; that suggests that she took some care of her skin. When she was finished, did she go home?'

'Or maybe did she go for a coffee?' the *intendant* murmured.

'Exactly.'

'Let's check the *hostal*,' she said, then glanced up at Skinner. 'Would you like to come?'

'I'd appreciate the professional courtesy,' he replied.

A rough path led from the rocky outcrop towards the beach, and Hostal Empuries. At its end they had to climb a small fence, before reaching the walkway that Skinner and Aileen had taken that morning. He checked his stride, allowing Intendant Cortes to lead the way towards the building. Afternoon was edging into evening, but the small bay was still thronged with sunbathers and swimmers. Heads turned as they passed; eyes followed the uniform.

The same young waiter, half Catalan, half British, who had served them earlier was still on duty, near the top of the steps as they reached the terrace. He frowned, but approached them. 'Hello again,' he said, in English. 'Is there a problem?'

Skinner realised that the crime scene was so far off the track that not even a rumour of the incident had spread to the beach. 'Not for you,' the Scot told him. 'The officer has a photograph she'd like you to look at, to see if you can identify the person in it. I warn you, though: it's not too pleasant.'

His frown deepened. He took the Polaroid from Cortes and looked at it. As he did so, his eyes widened and his mouth dropped open. 'Fuck!' he whispered. 'Is she . . .' Skinner nodded. 'Ah, *madre!*' he cried, distressed.

'You know her?' Cortes demanded.

'It's Nada,' he replied. 'Nada Sebastian. She comes here a lot, most mornings, when the weather's fine.'

'Nada?'

'Short for Nadine.'

'Is she local?' Skinner asked.

'She lives in Bellcaire. Her studio's there.'

'Her studio?'

'Yes. She's an artist.'

Fifty

'I shouldn't be doing this,' he said quietly, sipping the cold beer in his hand. 'I've got to interview you guys formally tomorrow. I should steer clear of you till then.'

'Andy,' Mario McGuire replied, lounging behind his desk, 'if it makes you uncomfortable, drink up and bugger off. But we're not going to ask you anything about your investigation, I promise.'

'I know, or I wouldn't be here. What the hell? I've done a few thousand things in my life that I shouldn't have, so what's one more? Anyway, it was purely a social invitation, you said.'

'That's right,' Neil McIlhenney confirmed. 'How's life in Tayside?' He paused. 'Here, that was a right shambles in the High Court in Dundee yesterday, was it not? Everybody there to begin the trial except the prisoner. Who is he anyway, this Grandpa McCullough? Sounds like the senior citizen from hell.'

'He would be, if he was a senior citizen, but he's still a few years short of that. He got the name because he became a grandfather when he was thirty-six. His daughter got pregnant when she was fifteen: she kept it a secret from him until it was too late for her to have a termination. The dad was one John McCreath, aged twenty-three, local playboy, but married with a kid. Not long after the news broke, he was found in a lock-up in Arbroath. I won't tell you what Grandpa did to him: it would put you off your dinner. That was twenty-two years ago; silence prevailed, he got away with it, and nobody's laid a glove on him since then, until now.'

'How did you nail him?'

'We didn't, not really: McCreath's son did. They moved to Aberdeen after it all happened, she remarried and the boy, James, took his stepfather's name, Dickson. He grew up wide, and got involved in a drug deal with Grandpa. He set him up, then shopped him to us. We got him stone cold: as soon as he was in custody, McCreath's widow and her sister came forward and gave evidence about the night John was taken away by Grandpa and his team. We picked up the two guys who were with him. One hasn't said a word, but the other turned out to have terminal cancer; his priest persuaded him to make a dying declaration before a sheriff about the killing. Since then, the trick's been to make sure the surviving witnesses, the women, stay that way.' Martin smiled. 'You guys, you laugh at Tayside . . .'

'We don't!' McGuire protested.

'You bloody do; you think it's a backwater, and that all the locals are either clods or sheep-shaggers. It's not. It's a more varied society than this one, and its subculture is more serious and better organised than yours.'

'That's because Bob Skinner, and guys like the three of us, got rid of most of ours.'

'Maybe, but Grandpa McCullough is right up with the likes of Tony Manson and Jackie Charles in terms of violence and ruthlessness: maybe even ahead of them. If you looked at those guys closely, you might have found a redeeming feature. Grandpa doesn't have one. He's like a stick of rock with the word "evil" going all the way through.'

'But even he fell to the might of a graduate of the Edinburgh school,' said McIlhenney, grinning.

'He hasn't fallen yet,' Martin countered tersely. 'I won't be happy until the jury comes in and says, "Guilty," and the judge gives him a minimum of thirty years . . . as she will when she reads the autopsy report. Even then, we'll have to hide the witnesses, maybe abroad.'

'What about the kid?' asked McGuire.

'James Dickson? He's in limbo. Like I said, he was wide, but he got revenge for his dad by grassing Grandpa. If he'd just killed him . . . You know the code, that would have been understood, admired even, but instead he shopped him. He's got no friends anywhere. The wild side will shun him, and we don't like him much either. He'll go as far away as his mum. After that, it's up to him.'

'That's too bad for him, Andy, but I didn't mean him. I was talking about Grandpa's grandchild.'

'Granddaughter. Cameron McCullough; christened so, believe it or not, after Grandpa. That's his real name.'

'That's okay these days. There's Cameron Diaz: she's a girl.'

'This one's twenty-one now.'

'I'd worked that out. How does she feel about Grandpa killing her dad?'

'She's twenty-one, and she drives a Mercedes SLK. I'd say she's come to terms with it.'

McIlhenney shook his head. 'Lovely family. But at least they're simple and uncomplicated. You know what they are; you know what you're dealing with.'

'That sounds a bit ominous.'

'It is. Just before you came along, we had a video conference through the computer with the big man, out in Spain. He wasn't alone; he had a local detective with him, a woman, high-ranking.'

Martin grunted. 'And there you were, telling me that this was only a social gathering.'

'See, you top brass,' said McGuire, 'you're too smart for the likes of us. The fact is, we lied . . . not that we wouldn't be asking you for a beer anyway, while you're here. The boss told us to bring you in on it.'

'So what was this video conference about?'

'This,' McIlhenney replied, handing him two sheets of photo-quality paper. 'Those were taken with a Polaroid and scanned into Bob's system, but they're clear enough. It happened in L'Escala this morning: he found her.'

Martin studied them one by one. The first showed a naked woman, lying serenely in the sun. She looked for all the world as if she was asleep, but he guessed that she would never waken again. The second was a close-up shot of the back of her head; it was darker, but as he peered at it he saw, in the parting of her hair, a small wound. 'What the hell does this mean?' he whispered.

'It means that our copycat theory is right back in place, but that he's moved abroad. The dead woman, Nadine Sebastian, was an artist.'

'And what about Weekes, the cop that your team has banged up, ready for court tomorrow? Last I heard you were ready to charge him with murder.'

'Not quite,' said McGuire. 'We were leaving that up to Gregor Broughton. In fact, we still are.'

'Have you told the defence about this?'

'Not yet. That can keep.'

'You'll have to disclose at some point.'

'Maybe, but not now. The bastard can sweat it out for a while longer. We've got him on other charges.'

'But you've got no direct evidence of murder?'

'We've got him at the scene, and we've got him concealing the crime for ten whole days while the poor girl decomposed. And we've got him nicking a trophy from the body. A smoking gun in his hand? No, we don't have that.'

'He's saying he found her?'

'Maybe he did at that.'

'Still,' Martin muttered, 'you're right. Fuck him. Let him spend a sleepless night on a hard bed in the Torphichen Place cells. He deserves it. Who's his agent?'

'Frankie Birtles.'

'Miss Bristles, is it? We don't owe her any favours either.'

'I don't think she's bothered,' said McIlhenney. 'According to Becky Stallings, by the time Weekes had finished dictating his statement, she was looking at him like he was something nasty she'd just found in her boyfriend's underpants.'

Martin held up the images, gazing at them. 'So where do you go with this?' he asked.

'We're sending all the forensics on the Dean case to the Spanish for comparison.'

'How much do you have?'

'Not a hell of a lot. We've got the bullet and various foreign DNA samples from the victim's clothing. Most of them are animal, but five of them are human. One sample turned out to be from Lord Archibald.'

'The ex-Lord Advocate? Used to be Archie Nelson?'

'He found the body,' McIlhenney told him. 'I'm sorry about that. I'd have liked him on the bench when Weekes goes to the High Court.'

'I can guess why. What about the other samples?'

'One was from her dad, one from her mum. The other two, we haven't identified.'

'Weekes?'

'Hers was on his jacket. They reckon he must have pulled some hairs out when he took the necklace she was wearing.'

'So, where are you now?' Martin asked.

'Like I said, the copycat notion is back in play, but with a twist. Davis Colledge, the boyfriend, has gone walkabout in the South of France, not too hellish far from L'Escala where that girl was killed.'

'Indeed?' he mused. 'I'm down here investigating a potential leak of information from the Ballester investigation to a second murderer, who's imitating his style of killing.' He smiled. 'But if that has happened, how would such a leak get to the kid, if he's a suspect?'

'Andy,' said McGuire, 'he's our only viable suspect. He was close to the dead girl, and he's geographically placed to have killed the Spanish victim, another artist, as Neil said. Plus he's one himself, a painter.'

'How would he know about the newest one, Sebastian?'

'I knew you'd ask me that, so before you came along I Googled her name on my computer and up she popped. She's got a website, in Spanish, Catalan, French and English. She was thirty-two years old, with a studio in a town called Bellcaire, and a gallery to display her works, mainly painting, but some sculpture, all of it with a Christian theme. It says that her philosophy is "to create a universe of simplicity and impressive impact", and the stuff it displays is fucking good . . . to my reasonably educated eye at least: my mum's a bit of a painter, remember. She's exhibited in Barcelona, Paris, Leipzig, New York, and . . . wait for it . . . last year, at the Edinburgh International Festival.'

'Okay, that's two ways he could have known about her.' Martin paused. 'As for knowing about the Ballester killings, the question I asked a minute ago was a wee bit rhetorical. For your ears only, I've found the leak . . . or, rather, a leak, for there could still be more than one. That unpleasant wee man Joe Dowley couldn't resist bragging about the investigation to his pals at the Rotary. The branch secretary's getting me a list of attendees on the night in question.'

'You'll pass it to us when you get it?' McIlhenney asked. 'Do that and I'll put the team on to finding a lead from there to young Colledge.'

'I can't, Neil. It could put the finger on Dowley publicly, and I'm not ready for that. Mackenzie will check every name on the list. If he can make a connection, he'll pass it on. Fair enough?'

The big superintendent shrugged. 'You're the ranking officer here, not me. But I can live with that.'

'Thanks. You said the boy's AWOL. What's being done to find him?'

'What was a fairly casual look-around's being turned into a full-scale alert. His picture's being circulated everywhere by the police in Spain and by the gendarmes in France.'

'National publicity?'

'Not yet: airports and railway stations.'

'The boy's only eighteen,' Martin pointed out.

'He's got a complicated background, and he's firearms trained, thanks to the school cadet force.'

'Is he indeed? I can see why you've stepped up your interest. Mind you,' he raised an eyebrow, 'there's something you're overlooking.

Davis Colledge isn't the only person who was in the area where each of these murders were committed. There's one other.'

McGuire frowned. 'Who?'

'Bob.'

'Fuck! You're having no more beer.'

'Hey, come on. I'm a police officer, and more than that: I might wear a uniform now but, like you guys, I'm a detective at heart. All I'm doing is stating pure facts. Bob was in the Edinburgh area on the day that Sugar Dean was killed, and now you tell me that this later murder happened right on his doorstep. You don't have a fucking clue where young Colledge was this morning. On the basis of what I've just said, who's the likelier suspect?'

McIlhenney pushed himself out of his chair. 'Andy!' he growled.

Martin held up a hand. 'Calm down, bear. He's my best pal too, remember. But Señora Plod, over in Spain, she doesn't know him at all. Now that she knows all about the Edinburgh murder, don't be surprised if she gets professionally curious. If that happens . . . who's Bob got with him over there?'

'Yes,' McGuire murmured, 'all true. Maybe he should get out of Dodge.'

'Don't get that carried away. Bob will protect Aileen from any embarrassment, don't worry about that. Interesting, though, I had a call from him yesterday about my inquiry after I'd agreed to do it. It'll come as no surprise that the thing was his idea. But it was strange: he asked me to think outside the box about the whole situation.'

'What did he mean by that?'

'I've no idea, but I suppose that's why he told you to brief me on this.'

'You will talk to him, won't you?'

Martin's green eyes flashed. 'Too bloody right I will,' he said.

Fifty-one

'Margaret,' said Bet, severely, frowning across the supper-table, 'you have to ease up. I don't know what it is you're up to just now, but whatever it is, it's taking over your life. You were on that computer for three hours, almost non-stop, apart from changing Steph. You barely spoke to me all the way through that sensational meal I conjured up out of nothing, and now you say you have to go back to it.'

'I won't be long,' Maggie pleaded. 'It's some research I'm doing, that's all, work-related; I'm keeping my hand in, so I'll be ready when it's time to go back.'

Her sister sighed. 'You haven't changed a damn bit, you know. You were always a workaholic. Do I have to remind you that you're recovering from a life-threatening illness, not to mention the birth of a child?'

'No, you do not! Chemotherapy is not like a dose of antibiotics. But, as my boss is fond of saying, your birth certificate doesn't come with warranties or guarantees in small print on the back. Nothing is certain. The consultant could be wrong. The disease could recur. That's why I have to do this thing now.'

'Does it have to do with Stevie?' Bet asked suddenly, taking Maggie by surprise.

'What makes you think that?'

'I can't see you getting so obsessive about anything else.'

'Okay, you're right.'

'I know I am. You always did get defensive when I'm right. Go on, then, get back to it if you must, but please, just another half-hour. It's a lovely evening, and I'd really like to spend some of it sitting in the garden with my sister, my niece, and a nice glass of Aussie Chardonnay.'

Maggie smiled. 'That doesn't sound like a bad proposition,' she conceded. 'Okay, half an hour it is. Let me help you tidy up first, though.'

She rose and started to clear the table, but Bet waved her away. 'No! I'll do it. Away you go and get it over with. Half an hour and the clock's ticking now.'

She left the kitchen and returned to the computer; she had left it switched on and the screensaver was running. Stevie's face filled the monitor. She had taken the photograph on his digital camera the day after they were married, on their brief winter honeymoon in Morocco. She smiled at him, then whispered, 'See you later, love,' as she clicked the mouse and the image disappeared, replaced by the folder of Fishheads press releases.

Bet had been right: she had spent too long at the task. She was tired, frustrated and had nowhere else to go. She was reduced to doing the same thing over and over again, looking for something that, in all probability, was not there.

She went back into the folder and opened the penultimate press release; it was only a week old and told the story of Ifan Richards's visit to the eastern United States, during which he had had meetings in Atlanta, Georgia, in Charlotte, North Carolina, and in Columbia, South Carolina. She opened the accompanying photograph and studied it for the fourth or fifth time: Richards, dressed in jeans and a polo shirt, flanked by the president and vice-president of the Columbia Chamber of Commerce. She peered at his image, trying to read the logo on his shirt, guessing that it was the Fishheads corporate image, but frustrated by its size.

'Wait a minute,' she murmured. 'Brainwave.'

She went through each release in turn; where there was an attached illustration she copied it into her 'My Pictures' folder, in a new sub-folder, christened 'fish'. When she was finished she ran all the photographs full-size as a slide show.

The executives of Fishheads were not men for formal dress. Even Godric Hawker, the new CEO, eschewed a tie. Ifan Richards wore either polos or, as in the case of the Las Vegas shot with Dražen Boras, T-shirts. Maggie froze the image of the two men, in front of the Wynn Resort, and studied it. They wore identical garments, each with a logo. It was blurred, but to her eye it seemed similar to the one in the South Carolina photograph. She ended the slide show, then double-clicked on the thumbnail file to open it in the picture viewer, where she would be able to enlarge it.

She hit the 'zoom' icon once, twice, again and again. Fourth time lucky: the lettering resolved itself into 'Margaritaville, Las Vegas'.

She closed the image, opened the Columbia picture in the viewer and repeated the process. The insignia on Richards's shirt read 'Margaritaville, Myrtle Beach'.

Something clicked at the back of her mind. She picked up the file that Mario had sent her, the one that he and Bob Skinner had put together to establish Dražen Boras as Stevie's killer. There was a photograph, taken from a CCTV camera, of the jacket he had been wearing when he had arrived in Edinburgh, at the Leith Police office. It had been enlarged already, for the print: across the back of the garment were emblazoned the words 'Margaritaville, Jamaica'.

She tore through the slide show again, checking for more instances, and struck gold. In the enlarged version of the Cape Town shot, Richards was seen to wear a pale blue polo, all the way from 'Margaritaville, Key West'.

'Whatever the hell Margaritaville is,' Maggie murmured, 'these boys are big fans.'

Fifty-two

It was Aileen who answered the call. 'Hello, Andy,' she said warmly. 'I'm sorry about the poisoned chalice you've been handed. If my Lord Advocate had a bit more steel about him, it wouldn't have been necessary.'

'Don't worry about it,' he told her. 'It's on the way to being sorted.'

'Ooh! That sounds as if it could mean trouble for someone.'

'Private embarrassment, maybe. Mind you, that assumes that the geezer in question is capable of feeling embarrassed for longer than it takes him to straighten his tie.' He could hear mellow music in the background. 'What's that?' he asked.

'Melissa Etheridge. I put it on to help Bob chill out.'

'He's moved on. It used to take half a dozen beers and a couple of Del Amitri albums.'

'Don't worry, he's working on the beers. He even took one into the shower with him, as soon as the Cortes woman left. You've spoken to the boys, have you?'

'Yes. They've brought me up to speed. This must have been a hell of a shock for you. You okay?'

'Me? I'm fine. Shocked, yes, and sad about the poor woman, but I learned a long time ago that life isn't for the squeamish.' She paused. 'Here's Bob.'

Martin waited as she handed the phone over. 'You a fucking magnet?' he said, as Skinner came on the line.

'Hush now, boy. That's exactly how I feel. It's as if somebody's taking the piss, Andy, right on my own doorstep. And when I told them what's been happening in Scotland! The fucking thing's following me around, man. Eventually I had to stop being diplomatic, and pull rank, hard, with the investigating officer, Intendant Cortes. I'm glad I'm Comisario Skinner, and not a civilian, or she'd still be putting the fucking thumbscrews on me.'

'Have they made any headway so far?'

'No danger. They're going to have to put out an appeal for witnesses, but even that's not going to be easy. It's not just a matter of putting something in the press and on telly. I'll guarantee you that, right now, at least half the people in this town don't speak Spanish, far less read it. They'll have to put up posters in English, French and German, maybe even Russian.'

'What about the woman's background? Is there anybody there?'

'Hah!' Skinner grunted. 'Know what her day job was before she became a full-time painter? The lad who identified her was friendly with her; he told us. She was a nun. She studied art in the convent; when it became clear that she had a real talent, she decided that the way she could use it best was by devoting it to God. That meant leaving her convent, to be free to travel, but she gives most of the money she makes from her work to her order. So nobody's looking for a jilted boyfriend.'

'Who are they looking for?'

'After what I told them they're looking for Davis Colledge, as a first step. I called his father, and told him what had happened. He still hasn't heard from the boy, or so he said.'

'Do you fancy him for it?' asked Martin.

'He's a possible for Sugar Dean, and Collioure's a short hop from here, so he can't be ignored. But then there's the copycat thing. Sugar's body was moved, but this one looks like a carbon copy of the Ballester jobs. How would Davis know how they were done? How would anybody know?'

'I may have a lead on that.' He told his friend about his interrogation of Dowley.

'It was him?' Skinner exclaimed. 'All that fuss was to cover his own indiscretion?'

'That's not what he says, but it's a fair conclusion.'

'Are you going to copy your report to the Lord Advocate? We might be able to get rid of the bastard.'

'No,' said Martin, firmly. 'I report to Jimmy, that's all.'

'In that case I may do something about it . . . once I've cleaned up my own mess.'

'You're finished in Spain, though, aren't you?'

'Cortes has promised to brief me regularly on her investigation but, yes, I hope we are. We're due to fly home on Saturday. Unless the Colledge lad shows up, of course.' He sighed. 'But there's something I've got to do in Scotland, pal.'

'What's that?'

'I have to give a formal statement to Neil. I remembered something this morning, when I was down town getting the bread and the *Daily Telegraph*. Guess where I was on the morning of Sugar Dean's murder? Murrayfield fucking Golf Club, that's where, as a guest at a Criminal Justice golf outing, organised by the Law Society. The courts weren't sitting that day, so they invited people from all sides of the system; lawyers, judges, cops, the lot.

'But know what, Andy?' Skinner sighed wearily. 'Maybe these murders aren't following me around. Maybe I'm following them.'

Fifty-three

Mario McGuire looked at what had been a bottle of Budweiser. 'If I have another one of these,' he said, 'I'm going to have to get a taxi home.'

'Go ahead,' McIlhenney told him. 'I'll give you a lift.'

The head of CID tugged his fridge door open and took out a replacement. 'You want another Irn Bru?'

'Hell, no. If I have another of those I'll start to rust.' The detective smiled. 'Who'd have thought it a few years back? I never turned down a pint. Now here I am even saying no to the fizzy stuff.'

'And looking a hell of a lot better for it,' McGuire pointed out.

'Maybe. Feeling better, that's for sure.'

'How's my godson?'

'Louis is absolutely ace, top notch; three months old and growing as fast as a briar rose.'

'And his mum?'

'She's magic too. I don't think anyone could look any happier than she does.'

'What about her career? When's she planning to revive it?'

'I don't think she is, not the way it was. When we got married, the idea was that she'd take a few years off to try for a family. Well, we've managed that, and she says she's still not feeling any itches. Someone rang her last week and asked if she'd be interested in joining the board of the Scottish National Theatre. She's thinking about that, and she's also mentioned the possibility of directing, on the stage again, in

Scotland, but that's it. She says she doesn't want to be Judi Dench, graduating into playing Queen Victoria in her dotage.'

'Jesus, she's nowhere near that.'

'She's over forty, the point at which most of the lead roles start to dry up for a woman. I think I'd like to see her direct. I have a feeling she'd be brilliant at it. Even watching a play on telly with her is an experience, the way she analyses the whole thing afterwards ... sometimes before it's finished, if she doesn't fancy it.'

'Tell me about it.' McGuire chuckled. 'Paula talks her way through most of the stuff we watch.'

'And you love it.'

'I sure do. Living together's something we should have done a long time ago.'

'Come on, now, you can't write off your marriage to Maggie just like that.'

'I can, you know. At the end of the day neither of us got anything out of it. The sex wasn't much good either.'

'That's too much information, mate.'

'It's true, though. You and I both know why that was: that bastard of a father of hers and everything. I wasn't the right man to help her over it, and that's all there is to it. I'm really happy she found Stevie, even if it wasn't for long.'

'Yeah.' McIlhenney sighed. 'Poor lad. He died by mistake, but the effect's the same. The bloody affair won't go away either.'

'What?'

'Dead artists. Copycats. I've got a bad feeling about this latest one, out in Spain.'

'Why? If the big man hadn't tripped over the corpse, we'd never have heard about it. The woman was robbed, remember; it was probably a mugging gone wrong. Have you any idea what the crime rate's like in Spain? They have all those fucking police forces and none of them knows what the others are up to.'

'A bit like us, eh?'

'Not at all. We don't overlap jurisdiction.'

'Side issue. Like I said, I'm not happy; you can't brush off the consistencies between the Spanish killing and ours.'

'Neil, we're getting excited about young Colledge, but is Weekes in the clear for the Sugar Dean job? No. Becky's meeting Gregor in the morning. He may well decide to do him for that, and he may well get a result. That man Broughton could get Mary fucking Poppins convicted for flying without a pilot's licence.'

'And Frankie Bristles could get her off on appeal. No, I have a bad feeling, and it doesn't involve either Colledge or Weekes.' He glanced at the wall clock: it showed almost seven. 'Now drink up; it's time I took you home.'

Fifty-four

'This place is your retreat, isn't it?' said Aileen. Her elbows were on the table, wrists pressed together, her hands enclosing a large, elegant goblet. He watched the red wine swirl slowly with her gentle movement.

'Yes,' he admitted, 'that's a perfect description. I've been coming to La Clota for twenty years, since my Alex was a kid. The Pallares family know me, they treat me like one of them, and they look after me in all sorts of ways.'

'They look after you?'

'Sure. They know when I don't want to be disturbed and they arrange it so that I won't be. You're part of it now; their protective parasol shields you too. They know the job you have back in Scotland, and that you and I value our privacy while we're here. Look at the table John kept for us, at the back of the terrace, so that nobody walks past us on their way in or out. You're facing the entrance: a lot of people have glanced our way in the time we've been here, but nobody's come across. Tell me if I'm wrong.'

'No, you're spot on.'

'There's an army of Brits here now, and a lot of Scots among them. If we were closer to the door, our evening wouldn't have been our own. John and his folks understand that, and they make sure it doesn't happen.'

As Bob spoke a figure appeared at his shoulder. He glanced up and smiled. 'This is the patriarch,' he said 'Don Carles, John's dad. How're you doing, my friend? Pull a chair over and have a glass of fizzy water.'

'I'm okay,' the restaurateur replied, accepting both invitations. 'Everything ticking over. I am so pleased to meet your lovely lady, and to see you both so happy. And your daughter? How is she? A big-shot lawyer in Edinburgh now, they tell me.'

'Not quite big-shot, not yet at any rate, but she's doing well.'

'No boyfriend just now? That's what she tell me last time she was here.'

'She goes out with the guy next door sometimes. He's one of mine, a cop, which sort of guarantees good behaviour. He's a decent lad, but more a minder than a boyfriend, I'd say.'

'And the kids? The little ones?'

'With their mother in America. That's good too: I couldn't spend all the summer holiday with them, but she can.'

'I pleased it work out for you.' He looked at Aileen. 'It's funny, we both have kids called Alex, but mine is a son.' Carles Pallares paused, and a small frown wrinkled his permatanned features. 'Hey, Bob,' he murmured. 'What's this story I hear, about the dead girl?'

'It's a true story, mate. I found her.'

'So I hear, at the bar inside, from Gary and Dilwyn. She die of the sun?'

'Is that what they're saying?'

'Sí.'

'Then let them till they find out different. She was shot. She's from Bellcaire; her name was Nada Sebastian.'

The frown deepened. 'Sister Nadine? Oh, my God. She had an *exposicio* in the town hall in March. Every picture she sell, she give one third of the money to the church in L'Escala. She's been here too, you know.'

'Well, I'm sorry, friend, but she won't be here again.'

'Carles!' The call came from a tall blonde woman in the doorway.

'Kathleen wants me,' said her husband. 'She call, I go. I'll tell her later about Nadine. She'll be upset. See you later.'

'I see what you mean, about being part of the family,' Aileen murmured, as he left.

'We're all like that,' Bob told her, 'all the long-term visitors. It's not just me. *La familia* La Clota is big, and multi-national. Maybe I should stop sitting with my back to the rest of them, now we're finished eating. Bunk over and I'll come round.'

He was sliding his seat alongside hers, when his Spanish mobile sounded. 'Bugger,' he murmured, as he picked it up from the table and flipped it open.

'Comisario Skinner?' a female voice asked.

'Yes, Intendant. What can I do for you?'

'Something has happened that you should know about. I just heard from my colleagues in the Guardia Civil. The young man Colledge bought a ticket on the Transavia flight from Girona to Rotterdam this afternoon.'

'They intercepted him? Excellent.'

Cortes drew a deep breath. 'No,' she said. 'By the time they got round to alerting the airlines, it had departed. Worse than that, it had landed in Holland. He's been there for hours.'

'You've checked that he actually caught it?'

'Yes. His name was confirmed on the passenger list. I apologise, Comisario, this is not good. I will have someone's *cojones* for this.'

'One for yourself and one for me,' Skinner growled. 'Thanks for alerting me. I'll advise my people in Scotland.'

'Balls-up?' Aileen asked, as he closed the phone.

'Ripped off, if Cortes is as good as her word. Inter-agency co-operation's been less than perfect. The kid's been in Spain all right, but now he's left the country. I'll have to call Neil.'

She watched him as he punched in McIlhenney's home number, then listened as the call was connected, and as he briefed the superintendent on the news from Cortes.

'Where can he go from Rotterdam?' he said to the phone. 'Anywhere he bloody likes: Holland's a major European travel hub.

I'm not going to tell you what to do, because you know.' Pause. 'No, you advise the father. I've had it for now. We've got a holiday to finish. I don't expect to hear from anybody until Sunday, earliest, by which time we'll be back home. Cheers, Neil; best of luck.'

'Do you think that'll hold?' Aileen asked, as he finished. Her smile drove the scowl from his face.

'Bloody well better,' he chuckled, 'but I don't hold out any real hope.'

'Do you want to change the flight?' she asked. 'Go back tomorrow instead?'

He shook his head. 'No, my love. I have very firm plans for tomorrow. None of them involves travel, and all of them involve you.'

Fifty-five

'Thank Christ for a pause button,' Mario McGuire exclaimed, as the phone rang for the second time in ten minutes, 'or this DVD would be a total waste of time.'

'Stop moaning.' Paula Viareggio laughed. 'You must know *Pirates of the Caribbean* off by heart now. I'm beginning to think of you as an outsize Johnny Depp.'

'Sorry, I can't do the accent.' He glanced at the caller number on the handset. 'Hello, Mags,' he said. 'Are you and McIlhenney conspiring to ruin my evening?'

'I'm sorry, Mario.' She sighed. 'I forgot the time.'

Her crestfallen tone made him feel instant guilt. 'It's okay. I didn't mean it, honest. What can I do for you?'

'Probably nothing. I wanted to share something with you, that's all.'

'Then share away. I'm listening.'

'I think I've found a route to Dražen Boras.'

'You've what? Explain!'

'Have you ever heard of Margaritaville?'

'Jimmy Buffett's greatest hit. He's a country singer. Wrote a couple of books as well.'

'He's more than that, and so's Margaritaville. It's been turned into a franchise, a chain of bar restaurants in hip places, like Jamaica, Las Vegas, Florida and so on. Remember the jacket Boras wore when he came to Edinburgh, the day you saw him down in Leith?'

'Margaritaville,' said McGuire. 'You're right.'

'That was the Jamaican one,' she told him. 'He's also been to the Las Vegas version; there's a Fishheads press release all about his trip, and a photo to prove it. His pal Ifan Richards was there as well, according to a shirt he was wearing in a shot taken a few months ago in Cape Town. He's also been to the Margaritaville in Key West.'

'They seem to be big fans of Mr Buffett.'

'Very much so. Ifan Richards was in Columbia, South Carolina, on Wednesday last week, and guess where he bought the shirt he was wearing in the pic that his PR firm circulated last Friday? Margaritaville, Myrtle Beach: South Carolina.'

'That's bloody good, Mags,' Mario conceded. 'But we can't stake out every one of these places indefinitely in the hope that Boras drops in for a beer, and nobody else will do it for us.'

'We don't have to,' Maggie retorted. 'On Monday, the document recording the sale, or transfer, of his share-holding in Fishheads was lodged with the company's registrar in London, in accordance with company law. It was dated the previous Tuesday, the day before his mate showed up in Columbia wearing the Myrtle Beach shirt . . . and Dražen's signature was on it.'

'It could have been couriered to him from anywhere.'

'It could,' she admitted. 'But I don't think it was. Do you? You're the one who spoke of the Boras arrogance. Don't you think that he'd show up with his new identity and his old signature to meet his mate?'

'I'll give you that,' he murmured. 'Go on. What's the next stage?'

'We don't waste time looking for Dražen,' she said. 'We concentrate on his mate instead. And we don't write off Davor; we keep tabs on him too. We track every flight booking Richards makes, and every flight plan that's filed for Davor's private jet. If either of them heads for a place that has a Margaritaville, then so do we, and we check out the local hotels for a booking in the name of Ignacio Riesgo.'

'That's bordering on the brilliant, Mags, but . . . forgive me for saying this . . . "we" aren't looking for Dražen. Stevie was murdered in Northumbria: it's their investigation.'

'And they're stuck!' she snapped. 'They could have done this, if they'd been willing or able, but they've got nowhere. Their thinking doesn't extend beyond the River Tees.'

'But how are you going to do all of this keeping tabs?'

'I've got a contact, through Bob. His name's Adrian St John.'

'Thames House?' asked Mario, taken by surprise.

'Yes.'

'I've met him. In that case, you've got a chance. Those people probably know my shoe size. What happens when he gets a hit?'

'I get on a plane.'

'Mags!'

'Just kidding,' she said quickly. 'When that happens I talk to you and Bob. Hopefully you can go to the Met, and ask them to arrange for the co-operation of the local agency, whatever that is.'

'That's a sound idea. Listen, kid, if we get that far, and I can swing it, I'll get on that plane myself. Seeing Dražen in the dock has been your dream up to now, but I'm starting to buy into it.'

Fifty-six

Although Detective Inspector Becky Stallings was the senior police officer present in the elegant office, she felt at a disadvantage. She was the only person there who had not met Gregor Broughton, the area procurator fiscal. She looked at him, and saw a bulky man with a face that told of younger days spent in the front row of many a rugby scrum.

He seemed to sense her hesitancy, as she took her place at his conference table. 'First time in the Crown Office?' he asked her, with a reassuring smile.

She nodded.

'First major case in Scotland?'

'That too,' she confessed, although she guessed that he had known already.

'Don't worry about it. The principles are exactly the same on this side of the border, but we're better. The chain's shorter, and you get to deal with me directly, round a table like this one, instead of sending your report up the line and waiting for some character in the Crown Prosecution Service to decide whether or not you've got a ninety per cent chance of getting a conviction.'

'I know that scenario,' said Stallings. 'I've had a few sent back marked "no pro", I don't mind telling you.'

'Well, not here,' said Broughton, cheerfully. 'Here you're dealing with real lawyers, experienced prosecutors, not some kid straight out of university who's never been in a courtroom in his life. We're braver, too. We're not worried about percentages. A fiscal has one benchmark.

Can I sell this to at least eight out of fifteen jurors?' He glanced at McGurk. 'What do you think, Jack? Can I convict Weekes of murder?'

The sergeant was impassive. 'That's the question we came to ask you, sir.'

'Hah!' the fiscal laughed. 'It's well seen you've spent some time in my friend Bob's office. He's shown you the ropes, all right.' He looked to his left, where Weekes's solicitor sat. 'Well, Frankie,' he asked, 'how did you draw this one?'

'He asked for me, Gregor,' she replied. 'I must have been doing something right these past few years.'

'Your television advertising can't do you any harm either. "Been arrested? Then call Frances Birtles." Not too subtle, but effective, no doubt about that. Even a cop knew your number off by heart when he found himself in trouble.' His smile vanished. 'So?' he asked abruptly.

Birtles had played the game many times before. 'So what?' she retorted.

'I've read the papers in the case, and I've listened to the tapes. Your boy is teetering on the edge of the precipice. The jury at his trial will know he's a police officer: that's not going to win him sympathy, however clever you are at empanelling them. There's enough there for me to ask them for a murder conviction. If I do that will you plead him guilty?'

'It would be my client's decision, Gregor. You know that. Plus, if I retain counsel, his or her view would have to be taken on board too.'

'Frankie,' said Broughton, 'you've got rights of audience in the High Court. You can appear for Weekes yourself, and we both know you like the limelight that an acquittal brings. We both know also that you've got a bloody good record of "not guilty" and "not proven" verdicts, precisely because you have a talent for reading the evidence and then reading the jury's collective mind. If you bring in an advocate to defend this guy on a murder charge, you're as good as telling me you think he's guilty. Come on. Are you going to plead him, and save us the cost of a trial?'

Birtles shook her head. 'On a murder charge, no . . . and I'll defend him myself.'

'Now we're getting somewhere. And on the other charges?'

'On those I'll be offering mitigation.'

'What does that mean?' asked Stallings.

'It means,' Broughton told her, 'that Frankie knows when she's on a loser.'

'If I do that,' the lawyer continued, 'what's the deal?'

'I won't ask the judge for more than five.' The fiscal frowned again. 'But we're not there yet. I'm not afraid to face you in court on the murder charge.'

McGurk looked at Stallings, and nodded.

'Before we go there,' the inspector said, 'we have some new information. I'm sorry you haven't had advance sight of this, Mr Broughton, but we didn't hear of it ourselves until this morning.' She opened her case and took out a slim folder from which she extracted a print, an image of a woman, lying on a rock. 'Her name's Nadine Sebastian, she was an artist, and she was shot dead yesterday morning in Spain, within sight of DCC Skinner's house there. He saw the body from his terrace and alerted the local police.'

As the fiscal studied the photograph, Stallings handed him another, showing the bullet wound. 'It's almost a perfect match for Dean, isn't it?' he murmured, then passed the sheets to Birtles. 'Curious.'

'That's an understatement,' the lawyer declared, after a few seconds. 'You can't nail my client for this one, and the similarity is striking. Has there been an arrest in Spain?'

'No. But . . . Remember Davis Colledge, Sugar Dean's *protégé* slash boyfriend?'

'Yes. The one you haven't interviewed yet.'

'We know he was in the area at the time of this incident, and we know that he caught a flight to Holland not long afterwards.'

'Do you know where he is now?' Broughton asked.

'I'm afraid not. We've advised Customs to be on the lookout for him, obviously. We don't think he caught a connecting flight out of Rotterdam, or Schiphol, but to be honest we can't be sure.'

'Have you checked with his parents? His father's an MP, as I recall from your report.'

'He was contacted yesterday,' said McGurk, 'and again this morning. Mr Colledge is still saying he hasn't seen or heard from him since he left for France almost two weeks ago.'

'But he will. Sooner or later he'll show up at the family home, wide-eyed and innocent, and probably pleading ignorance of Miss Dean's death.' He turned back to Birtles. 'Frankie, this changes things. The Spanish incident may have no connection to the Dean case, but until this young man is found and eliminated as a suspect, it would be unwise of me to proceed with a murder charge against your client. I'm still going to do him for attempting to pervert and the lesser charges, make no mistake about that, but anything more serious is on hold, without prejudice. We'll stick him up before the sheriff as planned this morning, for the remand hearing.'

'I'll ask for bail,' Birtles told him.

'I imagine you will. I'm not of a mind to oppose it, unless the police have a strong view that I should. Inspector?'

Stallings shook her head. 'No, sir,' she said, 'we won't ask for a remand in custody. However ...' she paused for emphasis '... I do want, as a condition of bail, that Weekes be forbidden from contacting or approaching his former wife, Lisanne Weekes, and his by now, I reckon, ex-girlfriend, PC Mae Grey. It's possible that both these women may be witnesses against him.'

'Frankie?'

'I've got no problem with that.'

'In that case,' Broughton announced, 'I'll see you in court in about an hour. Now, if you'll excuse us, I'd like a further word with the officers.'

Birtles smiled, going from severe to attractive in an instant. 'I'm sure you would,' she said, sliding her papers into a black leather document holder, and heading for the door.

The fiscal watched her leave. 'The lad,' he began, as the door closed. 'What do we know about his movements on the morning of the Sugar Dean murder? We know where PC Weekes was, but what about him?'

'He was a boarder at the school,' McGurk replied. 'The problem is that by the time the body was found, it had broken up and the other pupils were scattered to the four winds. We've been as thorough as we could: we located his dormitory warden and interviewed her. She says that he came in for breakfast at nine sharp. They were given a lie-in that morning as it was the last day of the session. She hadn't seen him before that, though. She gave us the names of some of his pals; since he left his digs in France we've been contacting as many as we can find, but they've all been pretty vague. What we have been told, though, more than once, is that Davis is a very fit lad, and that he often got up early and went for a run.'

'So it's possible that he ran up to the golf course, intercepted the victim and shot her, then got back in time for a late bowl of All Bran?'

'All other things being equal; for example, him having access to a firearm, yes.'

'So why wasn't he taken seriously as a suspect from the start? Because of his dad?'

'Because there was no reason to, Mr Broughton,' said the sergeant. 'The victim's parents spoke well of him. The night before the murder he took her to meet his folks, and they all got on. The day after, they were supposed to be meeting up in France for what was shaping up as a pretty intimate holiday. Where does any of that put him in the frame?'

The fiscal nodded. 'Well put, Jack. You're right: I accept that. And then, of course, PC Weekes lumbered on to the scene and offered himself up as the perpetrator.' He looked at Stallings. 'Be in no doubt, Inspector, regardless of what's happened elsewhere, I still fancy him.

But before I lay it all on him, we must pursue the Colledge alternative. Do all you can to find him. When you do, I want him brought back up to Edinburgh for questioning. There will be no cosy chat in Mummy and Daddy's drawing room, with them eyeballing the proceedings. I need you to interview him in the same room and under the same conditions as Weekes, and I want you to go just as hard at him as you did on the tapes I heard this morning. Squeeze him and see what pops out. Don't worry about comeback from the Shadow Defence Secretary. I'll deal with any flak from that quarter.' He winked. 'You never heard anything like that from the Crown Prosecution Service, did you?'

She returned his smile. 'Sir,' she said, 'I never even got to talk to them.'

Fifty-seven

'Can it be done?' Adrian St John repeated. 'Yes, Chief Superintendent, it can be done. It's an unusual request to be coming directly from a Scottish police force, rather than through Special Branch at the Yard, but we can access that information.'

'That's good,' said Maggie Steele.

'We can do it, but . . . You understand that I'll need to take it up the line for authorisation. I know I was told to co-operate with you, but this is a bit special.'

'Adrian, I don't care if you clear it with the Prime Minister, as long as it gets done.'

'I won't have to go that high.' He laughed. 'Top floor will do.'

'How long will that take?'

'If I'm lucky, two minutes.'

'And if you're not?'

'If I'm not, I'll come back to you . . . or that someone up the line will.'

'Let's hope it doesn't come to that.'

'If I'm asked why you need this information, what should I say?'

'That the people under surveillance may be attempting to contact a fugitive from justice.'

'That isn't normally our concern.'

'Come on, now,' said Maggie, sharply. 'We're all playing for the same team.'

'Yes, but . . .' he paused '. . . if you want to continue with the

263

sporting analogy, we all have different roles. You're a striker, whereas I'm one of those unsung chaps labouring away in mid-field.'

'In that case, think of it this way. The boys at the back have let a goal in. I'm after the equaliser.'

'Indeed? Let me ask you something. Should this task you've asked me to undertake lead to me slipping you a scoring opportunity, how do you propose to convert it?'

'Like any good striker. I'll improvise.'

'That may be more difficult than you think. Are you aware of the terms of the new extradition treaty between the US and Britain?'

'Not really: I've never had occasion to use it.'

'Think yourself lucky. It's a one-way street. It means that the Americans can have anyone they ask for without presenting any sort of a meaningful case against them, whereas we still have to show solid evidence of guilt. In this case, since the man you're after has disappeared, your greatest difficulty . . . should, by some miracle, you make an arrest . . . may be in proving that the man you've caught is who you say he is.'

'Adrian,' she asked, 'how do you know who I'm after?'

'I had dealings with your colleagues a few months ago,' he told her. 'On that occasion they were tracing Boras junior. My guess is that you still are.'

'You're too clever for your own good.'

'That has been said, Chief Superintendent. That's why I've been running my own checks on the logged movements of Davor Boras's plane ever since his son disappeared. If anyone's made contact, it isn't him. The thing hasn't left its hangar since it returned from its unauthorised journey to the USA.'

Fifty-eight

'Your Scottish courts don't waste any time,' said Becky Stallings. 'That can't have taken more than a couple of minutes. I'd have had to write off the best part of a day for this in London.'

She glanced from the gateway to Edinburgh Sheriff Court back towards its doorway.

'It's a cost thing,' McGurk replied. 'You know how we Jocks are when it comes to watching the pennies. The Scottish Courts Administration lays down the limits: ninety seconds maximum for a first appearance, twenty minutes for a guilty plea, mitigation speech and sentence, one week for a murder trial, two for fraud.'

The inspector gasped. 'You're kidding,' she exclaimed.

'Sure, but I had you for a second or two, admit it.'

'You bastard. Somewhere along the line you're going to suffer for that.'

'It'll be worth it. Forget golf: taking the piss out of the English is our real national sport. Hasn't Ray taught you that yet?'

Stallings let a half-smile cross her face. 'Our relationship is still too new for DS Wilding to be taking chances.'

'Jeez. It must be the real thing if that one's minding his manners.'

'You've worked with him?'

'For a bit, back in Dan Pringle's time.'

'Dan Pringle?'

'My old boss, latterly head of CID. He retired last year. He didn't have blue-eyed boys, but . . . let's just say that Ray and I got on pretty well with him. Old-fashioned cop.'

'What's he doing now?'

'Drinking.'

'Shame. I've seen that before, though, an old-timer retiring, then discovering he doesn't have a life.'

McGurk shook his head. 'It's not that with Dan. He lost his daughter, and it crushed him.'

'Poor guy. You must find the new regime different.'

'What does Ray say?'

'We've never discussed it. He's never mentioned Dan Pringle.'

'We tend not to. But you're wrong about Mario McGuire, and Neil McIlhenney for that matter. The Glimmer Twins might seem a bit flash . . . no, scratch that, they are a bit flash, especially Mario . . . but below all that, they're bedrock. You can trust them.'

'That's good to know. The Met's full of flash guys too, but they tend to be scrambling up the ladder as fast as they can, without caring whose fingers they step on.'

'Glad to be out of it?'

'Are you asking me if Ray was just an excuse?'

'Hell, no!'

'I'd forgive you if you did, but the answer would be no. Private life first, job second; I've always managed to stick to that.'

'Maybe I should have too.'

Stallings gasped. 'Oh, God, Jack. Don't take that personally; I wasn't thinking.'

'That's okay, boss. I tried it your way, but that didn't work either.' He looked at his watch, then back towards the court building. 'They're taking time turning Weekes loose,' he said. 'Bail formalities, I suppose. Either that or Frankie's got another case in court and he's waiting for her to chum him out of the building.' He pointed towards the throng of press and television cameras waiting in Chambers Street. 'He won't fancy running that gauntlet.'

'Is there a back door? Maybe he's used that.'

'No, they won't let him. He'll be coming this way.'

'Are you sure?'

'Put it this way: if he doesn't, some uniforms in there will be looking for a place to hide.'

'You fixed it?'

McGurk nodded. 'This guy's getting no job-related favours. Every other punter comes out the front door: so does he. Besides . . .' As he spoke, the door opened and Frankie Birtles stepped out, followed by her client. As he stepped into the summer sunshine Weekes looked out into the street; a look of panic crossed his face as the camera-bearing horde sprang into life and surged towards the entrance. He started to remove his jacket, to cover his face, the sergeant guessed, as he stepped back through the gate, into the court precincts, out of bounds to the media.

'A word before you go, Theo,' he said, taking Weekes by the arm and drawing him to one side. 'We'll see him into a taxi, Frankie,' he called to the solicitor.

'No,' she replied. 'My car's across the road. I need him back at my office.' She stood, waiting, prepared to allow the detective privacy.

'What is it, you great long cunt?' Weekes hissed at him.

'I love you too, arsehole,' McGurk growled. 'Here it is. I want to make sure you understand what your lawyer agreed to in there,' he said. 'Especially the bit about not approaching potential witnesses. I think you'll find that PC Grey will arrest you herself if you go anywhere near her, and the girl you mentioned in South Queensferry thinks you're a dick anyway. But if I hear of you hassling Lisanne, whether it's by phoning her, texting her, sending her emails, whatever, your flat feet won't touch the ground. You'll be back in front of the sheriff and banged up on remand. On top of that, I have friends in Saughton Prison. No protective segregation for you, pal: you'll be on open association with the other inmates from day one, never able to eat without somebody gobbing in your food, never able to take a

267

shower without the fear that you might be gang-banged. With me?'

Weekes's eyes flashed in a last show of bravado, but only for a second or two. He mumbled something that might have been 'Fuck off', then headed towards Birtles, and the cameras, pulling his jacket up and over his head.

'Nice one, Theo,' McGurk called after him. 'Do that and you'll really look guilty. Tell him, Frankie.'

The solicitor whispered in her charge's ear. He stopped and glowered at her, but slipped his jacket back on, then followed her out into the street, under the implacable gaze of two dozen lenses as they followed him all the way to her black Mercedes.

Fifty-nine

'But apart from that, Mrs Lincoln,' said Bob, 'how did you enjoy the play?'

Aileen lifted her head from the sun-lounger; her pale blue eyes stared blankly at him. 'Eh?' And then his meaning dawned on her. She pushed herself up on her forearms, until her nipples were just clear of the towel on which she lay; the midday sun glistened on the sheen of perspiration that it had brought to her back, her buttocks, her long legs. 'Apart from the abortive trip to France to interview a witness . . . which wasn't too bad . . . and you finding a body across the bay . . . which was . . . I've had a lovely time.' She smiled, then blew away a strand of blonde hair that had found its way into the corner of her mouth. 'As a matter of fact I'm still having it. I could easily stand this for another week or so.'

'Me too,' he conceded. 'But you've got a country to run and I've got a job to get back to. Maybe we can fit in a week with the kids during the school half-term in October. Sarah and I are agreed that it's too short for them to go to America.'

'You miss them, don't you?'

'Of course I do, love, but that's the way it has to be.'

'Not necessarily. I know couples who stay together for the sake of their children, and nothing else. If you went to America and said to Sarah, "Come back and let's give it another go, for Mark, James Andrew and Seonaid," don't you think she might?'

'No, not for a second. She might say, "You stay here and we'll give it a go," but that's not going to happen either.'

'What makes you so sure?'

'We've been over this. She doesn't love me, and I don't love her. I love you, and that's it.'

'But didn't you once?'

'Maybe, but I'm not so sure of that any more. If I did, if we did, at some point it just stopped. There's no way back, even if you and her new boyfriend weren't factors.'

The killer blue eyes widened. 'Sarah has a new man? How did you find that out?'

'There are no secrets between the Jazzer and his dad. He told me.'

Aileen laughed. 'Will I remember that?'

'Cuts both ways. When I tell him we're getting married, his mum will be the next to know.'

'You've got something to do before that happens.'

'Yes,' he said firmly, 'and I will, if I don't get arrested first. It's fucking weird, Aileen, the way that these killings all manage to have links to me. If I was running this thing on the ground, I'd be my own chief suspect.'

'Just as well you're not. You're so bloody conscientious, you'd lock yourself up.' Her laugh faded as she saw his expression. 'What is it?' she asked.

His frown deepened, highlighting the scar above the bridge of his nose. 'Grave-walking. Do you ever have thoughts that cross your mind so fast you can't catch them?'

'No, but I reckon I know several opposition politicians who do.' Her smile restored his. 'And you don't have to lock yourself up,' she added. 'I'm your alibi for the latest murder.'

'Honey-child,' he told her, 'just about the time Nada Sebastian was killed, I got out of bed, went downstairs, swam for about twenty minutes, dried myself off and got back into bed. That's the first you knew of it, isn't it?'

She looked at him, as if his eyes would tell her whether he was serious.

'Isn't it?' he repeated.

'Yes.'

'Yes indeed. I've never told you this before, but you could sleep for Scotland. So you're a lousy alibi.'

'I could lie.'

'Thanks, but you'd make an even worse liar.'

'No worse than you, I'm happy to say.' She rolled off the lounger, and on to his, on to him, along his length, her arms on his chest, her palms on his shoulders. 'That's how I'll know,' she murmured, gazing down at him, 'if the moment comes when you stop loving me.'

'It won't,' he promised, sliding his hands down her back, cupping them around her firm buttocks and pressing her into him. 'You're different. You fill me up. You make me truly happy. You make me believe I could achieve anything ... even filling Proud Jimmy's uniform.'

'Then go get it.' She lowered her lips to his. 'Speaking of filling up,' she murmured, as the kiss ended, 'how about ...'

From the other side of the house, they heard the door chime. 'How about we just ignore that?' he suggested.

'Second that.'

They heard the sound again, and again and a fourth time. 'Bugger.' He sighed. 'It's the police. Can't be anyone else, not as persistent as that.'

'Whoever it is,' said Aileen, 'you'd better cover the bulge in those trunks.'

'And you'd better hide upstairs.'

'Sounds like a deal to me.'

He picked up his towelling robe and put it on, knotting its cord firmly, then walked to the door, just as its warning chimed for a fifth time. He twisted the handle and jerked it open. Intendant Josefina Cortes stood there, cool in her uniform shirt, a yellow folder in her hand. 'Bon dia, Comisario,' she said, in Catalan.

'And a good day to you too.' He held the door wider for her to enter. 'What do you have to tell me? Have you made an arrest?'

'No,' she replied. 'Have you?'

'You may not have noticed,' he said, 'but I'm off duty. My people don't report to me every step of the way. Last I heard we had a guy in court this morning on holding charges relating to the Edinburgh murder, but we're still looking for young Colledge.'

Cortes's expression frosted over. 'You did not tell me yesterday about this other man.'

'True, because he may not have done it. So? What brings you here?'

She waved the folder she was carrying. 'I have the autopsy report. I thought you might like to see it.'

'I appreciate that,' said Skinner, 'but to be honest, I don't really fancy looking at photographs of brain tissue and extracted organs. Summarise it for me. Shot dead, yes?'

'Yes, as we knew already. The pathologist believes she died at around seven thirty in the morning. We talked to her neighbours in Bellcaire. One of them told us that she liked to sketch very early, and to take photographs of the sea and the town with the sun low in the sky. She had a digital camera, a very good one, the man said. We found several images on her computer to bear out his story.'

'No camera, no sketchbook, no clothes: the killer took the lot.'

'We found her clothes,' Cortes told him. 'They were in one of the *basuras*, the public rubbish bins, in the street that goes behind the beach nearest the town. We're looking for traces of the criminal on them, but . . . it was a mess in there.'

'Nothing else?'

'No.'

'So he has the camera and the pad.'

'It seems so.'

'If there is no connection with the Edinburgh murder . . . that is, if it wasn't the Colledge lad who did it . . . you're back to it being an opportunist killing. In that case the killer might try to sell the camera.'

'We are looking for that all across the region. We recovered the serial number from the studio in Bellcaire.'

'What about the bullet? Did you recover that?'

'Sí. As you suspected it was small calibre. We're not sure, but our scientific people think it may have been fired from a modified starting pistol, or a replica firearm.'

'Which might imply a degree of skill on the killer's part?'

'Exactly.'

'That gives me something to go on. I'll ask my team to check up on what the boy did at his school. We know already that he was in the CCF.'

'What is that?'

'Military cadets.'

'You did not tell me that either.'

'True. Forgive me, Intendant, but if you had caught up with Davis Colledge in Spain, I didn't want your people shooting first, then checking to see if he was armed.' He saw outrage rise in her eyes, and forestalled it. 'And don't tell me that only happens in London.'

'Maybe not,' she admitted.

He turned back towards the open door, a hint that her visit was over. 'Thanks for that information. I'll call my officers straight away, and tell them about the camera too. Who knows? When they find the kid, he might just have it.'

'Merci,' she said. 'You'll keep me informed when you return to Scotland?'

'Yes. You'll get me there as of tomorrow evening.' He opened a drawer in a hall table, and took out a card. 'These are my business numbers. Mobile's usually best.'

He closed the door as she left, and went straight to the phone. McIlhenney was away from his office, but his number was on voicemail. He left brief instructions to check on Colledge's metal-working capability, then hung up.

Aileen looked at him as he hung his robe behind the door of the

273

en-suite bathroom. 'I see you're not in the mood any more.' She chuckled.

'I wouldn't say that, but there's no time to do you justice, First Minister. Get yourself ready; we're out of here. One last surprise: I've booked us a room in the Hotel Arts in Barcelona, and arranged a lift down there. Our pick-up comes in an hour and a half. It's the last night of our holiday and we will spend it where no bastard can find us.'

Sixty

'I appreciate your finding the time to come to see me, Gregor,' said Andy Martin, reclining in Bob Skinner's comfortable chair.

'No problem. I always like seeing what life is like at the sharp end of the criminal justice system.' He stopped. 'How's the family?' he asked.

'My girls? They're great, and they'll be having company soon. Yours?'

'Ranald and Fergus? Aged twelve and nine now, and they're growing frighteningly large. As for Phil, she's taken to her new job with a vengeance . . . Nice phrase for a judge, don't you think?'

'I couldn't top it.'

'And how about you, my friend? I hear you've been up to Chambers Street.'

'Yes,' Martin chuckled, 'and I'm not sure I'll be welcome there again.'

The fiscal smiled across the desk. 'He didn't go into the detail of your conversation, but I don't think you're the Crown Agent's favourite person right now.' He winked. 'That's no bad thing, but watch out that he doesn't try to bite back at some time in the future.'

'He hasn't got the fucking teeth for that. He may not have much of a future either, not in his present job, at any rate. I've had DCI Mackenzie go through the list of people at the Rotary meeting where he shot his mouth off about the Ballester killings. One of them is the principal maths teacher at Stewart's-Melville school. Mackenzie had a

275

quiet chat with him at home, about an hour ago. He admitted talking about it in the staff room, so the genie's well out the bottle, and your boss is entirely to blame.'

'What have you done about it?'

'For now, I've passed the information to DI Stallings. It establishes the possibility that this missing youngster, Colledge, was familiar with Ballester's methodology. For later, I'll be reporting to the chief constable that I'm as satisfied as I can be that information did leak and that Dowley is the only source. You were my last interview: I'll be writing everything up this afternoon.'

'What do you reckon Sir James will do?'

'Can't say for certain, but I suspect he'll pass my findings to the Lord Advocate. It'll serve the guy right if he does. If he'd kept his head down and his mouth shut when your assistant went running to him, none of this would be happening.'

'Maybe not,' Broughton agreed, 'but any potential case against Davis Colledge would be missing a vital element: possible knowledge of the previous murders.'

'Cases,' said Martin.

'Of course, the Spanish incident: Ms Stallings briefed me about that. In the process she prevented me from going ahead and charging the man Weekes with the Dean murder . . . for now at any rate. Very strange circumstances, Andy, if you're not a believer in the power of coincidence: that the Spanish murder should happen on Bob Skinner's doorstep.' He paused. 'Only it's not so strange. If the young man Colledge did leave Collioure to explore the coast, as he seems to have told his landlady, that would take him quite naturally through L'Escala, as I understand the geography.'

'That's right. I've been there.'

'About Dowley,' said Broughton. 'Any chance you could persuade the chief not to take it any further? To be honest, it would suit me if he stayed in post. As you know, the deputy Crown Agent is staring retirement in the face. If Joe went I'd come under renewed pressure from colleagues to apply for the job, and I'd really rather not. I don't mind stepping into the deputy's shoes, but with Phil on the Supreme Court bench, the top job would be too high profile for me.'

'On the other hand, a big chunk of the police service would like a change,' Martin pointed out. 'Dowley isn't popular. The promotion's gone to his head.'

'I can control him, Andy, especially if I become his deputy. This embarrassment is bound to bring him down a peg or two. Let me work on him, and I'll make him manageable. I've seen a couple of Crown Agents come and go in my time.'

'If that's how you feel. We owe you a couple, Gregor. I'll try to talk Jimmy and Bob out of going for his throat.'

'Bob?'

'Of course. Dowley crossed one of his guys; demanded that he be disciplined. You do that at your peril.'

Broughton laughed. 'I'll remember that. Be seeing you.' He headed for the door, then stopped, admiring one of the works of art that decorated the walls of the absent deputy chief constable's office. 'Nice picture. The Crown Office has works on loan from the Scottish Arts Council. I wonder if that's one of theirs.'

'No. That's one of Bob's own. He has more pictures than he has wall space at home, so he brings one or two in here.'

As the fiscal closed the door behind him, Martin stepped closer to the painting, studying it. He had been glancing at it for much of a day and a half, aware of it, without paying it too much attention. It was an oil on canvas, around two feet square in a blue wooden frame, a coastal scene. In the background the sun was rising out of the sea, giving its waters a reddish tinge. To the left of the picture were distant hills, to the right a rugged, castellated building, and in the foreground, on a beach, a small female figure kneeling as if in prayer.

His eye moved to the signature: it was a single word, and it could have been either forename or family appellation. 'Sebastian'.

Sixty-one

'You know, Jack, I'd forgotten that you could have nights like this, on the town, just hanging out. Theo's idea of a fun evening usually involved the Odeon, then Ben and Jerry's.'

'I know what you mean. Mary and I got out the habit too. Mostly my fault, I think; most evenings I'd have a pint or two with Dan Pringle after work and fall asleep in the armchair after dinner. I don't blame her for chucking me.'

'Don't be too hard on yourself,' she said. 'It's a two-way street. If she'd been that keen herself she'd have dug you in the ribs. The truth of it is, I settled for what I had with Theo. He's a good-looking guy . . . I have to give him that . . . and he made me believe that what we had going was best for both of us, him with his place and me with mine. That's how good a con-man he is. I see now it was never "mine", always ours.' Her face twisted with the bitter recollection. 'What a swine he is!' she hissed. 'He took that neck charm off a dead girl and gave it to me.' She looked up at him. 'He really did that? You're not making it up?'

'Lisanne, I couldn't make that up. That's what he did, all right. We have his signed statement admitting it.'

'And he'll go to jail, for sure?'

'One hundred per cent sure. How do you feel about that?'

She stared at the array of bottles lined up behind the bar, or perhaps she stared at nothing at all. 'Who'll decide where he goes?' she asked.

'The system will. It'll depend on how long he gets; if it's more than four years he could go to Shotts, or maybe Kilmarnock, for the first part of his sentence.'

'Could you fix it for it to be somewhere really nasty?'

Jack caught her eye in the mirror behind the Rose and Crown bar. 'It's the jail, kid; wherever he goes it's not going to be nice. And with him being a cop . . . Need I say more?'

'Good. Let's see if he likes it up the . . .' She stopped herself in mid-sentence. 'Sorry: I nearly said something awful there. We'd got through a meal and a couple of drinks without talking about him. Subject closed for the rest of the evening, I promise.'

He put a finger on her chin and turned her face towards his. 'Get it out your system if you need to.'

'I have done.' She smiled. 'The thing that amazes me, Sergeant McGurk, is that here I am out with another plod. Does that show a lack of imagination, or what?'

'I'd like to think it shows good taste.'

'I'll accept that analysis for now.' She finished her drink. 'Here, let me get them in.'

'Okay,' he agreed, 'but not here. It's beginning to fill up.'

'Let's go to Kay's, in Jamaica Street. It's nice, and a bit off pitch: I've been a couple of times with my work crowd.'

'Take me there.'

They left Rose Street behind and headed north, crossing Queen Street, then turning into India Street, off Heriot Row. Kay's was half-way down, a few yards into Jamaica Street; as Lisanne had promised, it was busy, but not thronged. 'Pint of heavy and a vodka tonic,' she called to the barman, from the doorway. Some of the drinkers looked round, appraising the six-foot-eight-inch detective for a second or two before returning to their conversations.

'Jack!' The call came from the far end of the bar. He waved in response.

'Who's that?' Lisanne asked, glancing along at the dark-haired woman, as she picked up their drinks and handed the beer to McGurk.

'The deputy chief constable's daughter,' he told her, 'Alex Skinner: with, if I am not mistaken, Detective Constable Griffin Montell.'

'He's brave, isn't he?'

'So they say. But I reckon he's a handbag.'

'What's a handbag?'

'My worldly wise female cousin tells me that it's a bloke you're not really serious about, there to keep the wolves at bay.' He took a mouthful from his glass. 'I'd better go and say hello.'

'Want me to stay here, in case of awkward questions?'

'Hell, no. Come on.' The customers parted for them as he eased his way along the bar. 'Alex. Griff. This your local?'

'One of them,' Alex replied. 'It's a bit of a lawyers' pub.'

'It'll suit you, then. This is Lisanne.' He slipped an arm around her shoulders, drawing her into the circle.

'Pleased to meet you,' said Montell. 'Are you two an item?' he asked, with a wicked grin.

'That remains to be seen,' she told him. 'First date.'

'What do you think of the sarge so far?'

'I'm impressed.'

'That's good to hear.' He glanced up at McGurk. 'You've had a busy week.'

'Yes,' he agreed, 'but let's not talk shop in front of the ladies.'

'Come on, man, Alex is practically one of us. The guy you had in court this morning, are you doing him for the murder?'

Alex leaned forward on her bar stool and jabbed him forcefully in the chest. 'Montell,' she said, 'is there any part of "Shut the fuck up" that you don't get? Lisanne doesn't want to hear this, and I'll get it soon enough from my old man.'

'It doesn't bother me,' Lisanne told her. 'I don't think he did it. Theo's a shit, but he isn't a murderer.'

'Inside knowledge?'

'I was married to him. Jack and I met when he and his boss came to turn my flat inside out. Finally, the bastard did me a bit of good.' She smiled up at McGurk, and slid her arm around his waist. 'There you are, it's all out in the open now, so you needn't make both of us feel awkward any longer.'

'Witness-protection programme?' asked Alex, mischievously.

'I couldn't have put it better,' the sergeant told her. 'Hey,' he added casually, 'have you heard from your father lately?'

'No, I haven't. He and Aileen have been looking forward to a holiday together. I haven't been calling him, and his silence tells me that it's gone well. You can brace yourself, though, he's due back tomorrow afternoon.'

'I'm not his exec any more, remember?'

'Maybe not,' she laughed, 'but if Mr Weekes isn't your man, and you haven't made another arrest by Monday, I reckon you'll be seeing him pretty soon afterwards . . . maybe even before. Damn it,' she said, 'you boys have got me at it now.' She finished her drink. 'Let's go, Griff, our taxi should be outside by now. Office summer party,' she explained. 'Late-night do. Enjoy the rest of yours.'

McGurk watched them all the way to the door, then turned back to Lisanne. 'You're cool,' he told her. 'Amazingly so, in fact.'

'I didn't embarrass you, did I?'

'No way. The look on Montell's face was worth the price of admission. The news would have got out anyway; he works with my boss's other half.'

He finished his beer, as she finished her vodka. 'Want another?' he asked.

'No, I've had enough.'

'Let's get you home, then.'

They hailed a taxi out in India Street, as it dropped a fare at one of the grey sandstone terraced houses that McGurk knew would command up to and beyond a million in Edinburgh's twenty-first-century housing market. They sat in the back, silent most of the way to Gorgie, responding occasionally to the driver's monologue. The cab was about to turn into Caledonian Crescent, when the detective

ordered the driver to stop. 'Let us out here,' he said. 'That'll be fine.'
He paid the man through the divider window and joined Lisanne on
the rough, uneven pavement.

'Why did we stop here?' she asked.

'Call me paranoid. Tell me I've been in the police too long, but . . .'
His eyes tracked along the line of parked cars: with a combination of
effective street lighting and high-summer gloaming, he could see them
all clearly, all shining, all empty, save for one, facing the flow of traffic
as it sat opposite the doorway that led to Lisanne's apartment. 'Look,'
he murmured.

'Jesus,' she whispered.

'Wait here,' McGurk told her, 'behind this bin. Stay out of sight
until I call you.'

As if it might make him seem smaller, he hunched his shoulders as
he walked towards the vehicle, casually at first then picking up his
pace. The driver's door was beside the pavement. Without a word, he
pulled it open, reached inside and hauled the occupant from his seat,
lifting him off his feet in the same movement and throwing him across
the bonnet.

Theo Weekes snarled as he launched himself at the giant detective,
only to realise, when a huge fist hit him between the eyes, that he had
taken on more than he could handle. His legs buckled, but McGurk
caught him before he could fall, propping him against the side of the
car.

'What the fuck are you doing here?' he moaned.

'Keeping a promise. You're going to jail, you bastard.'

'Aw, McGurk, no. Gie's a break. I won't do it again, I promise.'

'Give me one good reason why I should.'

Weekes stared up at him for what seemed like a minute. 'I can't,' he
sighed, at last.

'Okay,' the sergeant said. 'One more chance: let me down and
you're in for the hammering of a lifetime . . . and then Saughton
Prison. Go home, and stay there. There'll be a police car driving past

your place at least every hour from now on. If I hear you're missing, I'll go looking for you myself, and this will be the first place I'll try. Now, fuck off.'

He stood back, allowing the man to slide behind the steering-wheel. He watched him as he started the engine and drove off, as he took the next turn and disappeared, then waited for a few more seconds before calling out to Lisanne.

'I had a feeling he'd try that,' he told her, as she rejoined him.

'Will he be back?' she asked, as they crossed the roadway to her door.

'Not unless he wants his shiny white teeth in a brown-paper bag. I think I put the fear of God into him this time. Still, if you're not comfortable here, is there anywhere else you could go?'

She turned to face him. 'Thanks, Jack, but I'm not letting him drive me out of my home.' She slid her fingers under the lapels of his jacket. 'Mind you,' she murmured, 'I'd feel a lot safer if you came upstairs with me.'

'For coffee?'

Lisanne smiled. 'Eventually,' she replied, 'if you absolutely insist.'

Sixty-two

The aircraft came in from the east, and Bob Skinner knew that he was home again. The day was fine, the skies were clear and the sun was high in the sky, lending an unaccustomed sparkle to the grey waters of the Firth of Forth. He leaned forward in seat 1B, drinking in the cityscape as the pilot banked to the left.

Aileen pointed through the small window. He followed the direction of her finger to a broad building on the crest of a rise, not far from Arthur's Seat, and below it, to the boat-shaped structure of the Scottish Parliament's controversial home.

'The centres of power,' she said. 'It hardly seems real. It looks like Toytown from up here.'

'It is bloody Toytown,' Bob murmured, 'only the games are for real: half a million people laughing or crying, shopping or stealing, fighting or fucking. That's life, honey. But you're at the top of the pyramid.' He leaned closer to her, his voice becoming a whisper. 'Have I told you lately that it's a privilege to be sleeping with you?'

She laid her forehead against his and smiled. 'No,' she replied, 'but you should. Not many people have, and I'm thirty-seven years old. I'll bet you've had a woman for every year of your life.'

He started to count on his fingers; at nine he clenched his fists. 'Divide by five and you'd be close.'

'Those are just the ones you remember.'

'No, I've got a flawless memory when it comes to nooky. I was widowed for about fifteen years, and in that time I had three relationships.'

'With anyone I've met?'

'Not as far as I know. One was with a divorcée in Gullane; she moved south ten years ago. One was with a television presenter who hit the big-time and settled in London. One was with a very nice lady who decided to marry somebody else, and got it right too.'

She laid a hand on his heart. 'Were you wounded, my darling?'

'I didn't have any right to be. I never asked her.'

'That wasn't my question.'

'Bloody politicians,' he grumbled. 'Too sharp for your own good. I suppose I was, at the time, but I got over it.'

'That's comforting to know.'

He blew softly in her ear, making her shiver. 'Worry not. I keep on telling you: no ghosts in our bed.'

She leaned against him as the Boeing came in to land, squeezing his hand hard in the second before the wheels hit the Tarmac. 'I don't have a fear of flying,' she had told him, in the VIP lounge before the outward journey. 'I don't like it, that's all.'

'In my book,' he had told her, 'anyone who says that he enjoys the experience is either a fool or a liar.'

When he had booked the flights, Bob had not asked for special treatment, but the airline, spotting the First Minister's name on the passenger list, had provided it nonetheless. They were fast-tracked off the plane and through immigration control; even so, by the time they reached the baggage hall their suitcase was waiting for them.

'Are you just a wee bit embarrassed?' Aileen asked, as they walked through the blue channel.

'Not in the slightest. You'll never get used to who you are, will you?'

'That's just it. I'm plain Aileen de Marco from Glasgow.'

'That was then, honey: this is now. I'll tell you one thing, though.'

'What's that?'

He glanced sideways, looking her up and down, taking in her sleeveless white shirt, short white skirt and sandals. 'There isn't another head of government on this blessed planet with legs like those.'

As they strode through International Arrivals, two uniformed officers, each armed with a Heckler & Koch carbine, gave them looks of appraisal, then, recognising Skinner, took their hands from their shoulder-slung weapons and snapped off salutes. 'Afternoon, sir,' said one, a sergeant.

The deputy chief constable paused. 'Afternoon, Eck. Has Scotland changed since we've been away?'

'It's been unnaturally warm, sir. Must be something in this global warming, after all. I wish we could take off this body armour on days like this.'

'Feel free,' Skinner replied. 'But before you do, write letters to your widows, just in case, and leave them with my office.'

'It must be tough for them,' said Aileen, as they walked on. 'Could we do something to help?'

'Gimme the budget and I'll buy lighter protective gear.' He laughed. 'Listen to us. Our feet are barely on the ground and we're back to work already.'

As they turned into the airport concourse, Skinner expected to see Alex waiting for them. Instead, Neil McIlhenney stood there, casual in light cotton trousers and a pale yellow shirt. 'Welcome back,' he said. 'Good to see you, First Minister.'

'And you, Neil,' she replied. 'How's the baby?'

'Brilliant.'

'Where's my kid?' asked Skinner. 'She was supposed to be doing the taxi run. Is she okay?'

'She's fine. You know it was her office piss-up last night?'

'First I've heard of it.'

'She probably didn't like to tell you. They were spending the profits on a big do at the Dome. She mentioned it when I spoke to her the other day, and I offered to sub for her.'

'Bleary-eyed job, was it?'

'Four a.m., she reckoned.'

'That firm makes too much money.'

McIlhenney led the way outside: his car was parked next to the doorway, being frowned upon by a bearded traffic warden with an evil eye.

'You shouldna' be doing this, ken,' he grumbled. 'Polis or no polis.'

'We've had this conversation, pal,' the detective told him. 'Now bugger off before I arrange for you to be transferred to checking tax discs in Muirhouse.' He opened the back door for Aileen, as Bob heaved the case into the boot.

'This is good of you,' the DCC said. 'It's Saturday, after all.'

'No problem. We're having a barbie later; Louise and Lauren are getting ready for it, and Spencer's looking after his kid brother.'

'How is your daughter? I haven't seen her for a while.'

'Growing. Difficult stage. Puberty and such. Missing her mum, even though she and Lou get on great.'

'I've been there with Alex, remember. Don't worry, it's like shedding a chrysalis. She'll be a butterfly any day now.' He buckled his seat-belt and glanced over his shoulder. 'Permission to talk shop, ma'am?' he asked.

'If I have permission to sleep,' Aileen answered.

Skinner stayed silent as McIlhenney manoeuvred the vehicle into the constant traffic and made his way through the series of roundabouts and junctions that led to the main road. 'How's Stallings?' he asked, once they were on course for Gullane.

'She's brilliant. She's a real acquisition. It's no wonder the Met were sticky about approving her transfer. Jack McGurk's coming into his own as well; they make a really good team. Mario and I have both been impressed by the way they've handled the Dean investigation.'

'We still haven't charged anyone, though.'

'There's Weekes. We've got him.'

'But not for the murder.'

'Not yet. The fiscal felt he couldn't do that, given the lack of hard evidence. We've done him for perverting justice.'

'Where is he now? On remand in Saughton?'

'No. Frankie Birtles asked for bail. We agreed, with the usual conditions.'

'You can prove he was at the scene, can't you?'

'Yes, and he admits it. But that's as far as it goes. He says he didn't kill her and as yet we've got no hard evidence that says he did. When we heard about the Spanish incident . . .'

'I might argue that the fiscal could have ignored that, since it was a thousand miles out of his jurisdiction.'

'But could you really, and expect him to agree with you?'

Skinner shook his head. 'Not really. That reminds me, did you get my message, the one I left yesterday?'

'Yes, and acted on it. Becky spoke to one of the guys in the local army-cadet training team. He told her that the kids are made familiar with firearms, as part of their training. They're taught to dismantle them, then reassemble them from their component parts. Davis Colledge was very good at it, apparently. As for converting a starting pistol, the soldier told her that any idiot could do that.'

'And this boy is not an idiot.' The DCC frowned. 'Neil, on that subject, there's something I have to tell you.'

'About being at Murrayfield Golf Club when Sugar was killed? Andy gave me a heads-up on that. What time did you get there?'

'About eight o'clock. Had coffee and a couple of bacon rolls, hit some practice balls then teed off at ten past nine.'

'And you didn't see anything out of the ordinary?'

'Neil!'

'Sorry. I suppose you'd better dictate something and give it to Stallings to put in the murder book, just for the record. But . . . if you were there, how come your name didn't show up when we checked the names of the people who played that morning?'

'Block booking. It wouldn't show. In theory it leaves a bit of a hole in your witness list, but I reckon the Law Society will vouch for everyone who was there.'

'Yes, I suppose . . .' He broke off in mid-sentence as his mobile sounded. 'Yes?' he said.

A new voice came from the car's small Bluetooth speaker. 'Superintendent McIlhenney?'

'It better be.'

'It's DC Haddock here, sir. I'm in the office and I've just had a call from the uniform people out in West Edinburgh. There's trouble at Weekes's place.'

'What sort of trouble, Sauce?'

'They didn't say, sir. Just that there's been an incident. I called DI Stallings at home, sir. She and DS Wilding are heading out there, but she asked me to let you know.'

'Thanks, lad. Keep me informed.'

McIlhenney pressed a button to kill the call, then glanced at Skinner. 'Weekes lives up at South Bughtlin Road,' he said. 'That's only a couple of miles from here. Want to take a look?'

The DCC glanced over his shoulder. Aileen was sound asleep. 'On balance,' he said, 'I rather think not.'

Sixty-three

Theo Weekes was in the doorway of his terraced house when Stallings drew up outside. He was wearing a vest and boxer shorts, and his brown skin was blotched with sweat; a line of blood ran down his left cheek, from the corner of his eye. A uniformed woman constable stood in his way, blocking the path, although he towered over her. A police traffic car was parked on the other side of the street; there was a figure in the back, his face buried in his hands, and a second officer, a portly, middle-aged sergeant, stood by the driver's door. Apart from the small gathering, South Bughtlin Road was quiet, with only two neighbours curious enough to stand and watch the scene.

'Wait in the car if you want,' the inspector told Detective Sergeant Ray Wilding.

'Not on your life,' said her partner. 'The guy looks as if he could be ready for trouble. If he kicks off, two women and the fat boy might not be enough.'

'Okay, but just back me up. Don't get involved unless I ask you to.'

She led the way to Weekes's door. 'Inside,' she snapped at him.

'No' while he's still here.' The reply was a snarl.

'You do what I tell you, Theo,' said Stallings, evenly, 'or you're on your way to the cells and I'm on my way to the sheriff to have your bail revoked.'

He glared down at her. 'It might be worth it,' he muttered.

Wilding took half a pace forward. 'I hear you're tough with women,'

290

he said. 'You threaten my girlfriend, and I'll fucking bury you, right in your own front garden. Now get inside, like she says.'

The man looked at him, weighing him up. For a moment, it seemed that he might take the reckless course, until inherent cowardice asserted itself. He shrank into himself, turned and stepped back into his hallway. The two detectives followed him. 'Sorry, love,' the sergeant whispered to Stallings. 'I couldn't take the chance of him taking a swing at you.'

'I wish he had,' she whispered, turning her right arm to show him the extendable baton she had hidden there. 'I'd have had his nuts for paperweights. I'm good with this thing,' she smiled, 'and don't you forget it.'

She turned to Weekes. 'The call I had said that the traffic car drove by as you were thumping a bloke in the street. Let's have your story, but it had better be good, otherwise I'll let them outside charge you with assault and hold you for court on Monday morning.'

'What was I supposed to do?' he protested. 'The bell rang, Ah opened the door and he hit me.' He pointed to his eye. 'Look! I'm fuckin' bleeding.'

'How many times?'

'What?'

'How many times did he hit you?'

'Just the once.'

Stallings pointed to a dark, circular bruise in the middle of his forehead. 'Then where did you get that?' she asked.

'That was . . .' For a second Weekes's eyes flashed, but he stopped himself short. 'That was something else.'

'Tell me about it.'

'Ask McGurk,' he growled.

'I will, Theo, don't you worry. But let's get back to this situation. You opened the door and this man stuck one on you. Did he say anything first, or did he get straight down to business?'

'Don't remember.'

'Please. You might be a shit but you're not an idiot. Did he say anything?'

Weekes sighed impatiently. 'He said something about needing to talk to me. I told him I wasn't interested. Told him to go away. That was when he hit me.'

'As a result of which, you, a police officer trained to restrain and control, laid into him with both fists, until you were restrained yourself by the two officers in the traffic car. Suppose they hadn't turned up when they did?'

'I'd have let him go.'

'Maybe,' said the inspector, 'but in what condition? Look at me, Theo, not at the carpet.' She waited until his eyes met hers. 'That's better. I have one more question, and you'd better give me the right answer. Do you want to make a complaint of assault against the man in the car?'

Weekes held his breath for a second or two. 'No,' he replied.

'That's what I wanted to hear; best if this doesn't go any further, most of all for you. Do you want medical attention for that cut?'

'No. It's nothing, just a nick.'

'If you're sure. Tell me, are your parents still around, or do you have any other family where you could go for a while?'

'Nah. Ma mother moved back to Barbados after my dad died. I've got a sister, but she's in Canada. Anyway, I'm no' leaving here, and you cannae force me either.'

'I'm not trying to. I thought it might be better for you, that's all.'

'Kind of you,' he sneered. 'You really are looking after me, you and McGurk.'

'You'd better believe it. Word to the wise, though. I noticed a spyglass in your front door. Maybe you should use it next time the bell rings. We're off now. Keep your head down.'

'House arrest, is it? Can I no' even go for a pint?'

'Don't be silly. If you know somewhere that'll serve you, carry on. All I'm saying is that you can't afford any more disturbances.' She glanced at Wilding. 'Come on, Ray. We're done here.'

Outside in the street, she stopped on the pavement. 'What did you think of him?' she asked.

'I've met him before,' Wilding told her. 'I was a DC at Torphichen and he was a rookie. Cocky bastard; he thought he was a hard man, but the rest of us had him down as a poser. I doubt if he killed your girl. I don't see him having the bottle.'

'That's my reading too.' She put a hand on his shoulder. 'Wait here for a minute, love. I need to speak to the man in the car before we go.' She trotted across the street and slipped into the back seat of the patrol vehicle.

'John,' she began, 'how are you?'

Sugar Dean's father turned towards her. His left cheek was swollen and there was a red smear under his nose. 'I'm fine, Inspector,' he replied. 'Humiliated, but unhurt. I just wish I'd . . .'

'What? Left him a bloody heap on his doorstep?'

'Something like that.'

'He's thirty years younger than you.'

'I keep myself fit. Fifty-eight's not old, you know. I've never been a fighting man, you understand, but I'd hoped that when it really mattered I'd have been up to the task. We're all Lennox Lewis in our imagination.'

'Was that why you came here, to give him a thumping?'

'No, it really wasn't. I wanted to talk to him, to ask him what had happened with my daughter.'

'John, the fiscal may still charge this man with her murder.'

Dean stared at her. 'Do you know, that thought never occurred to me? I saw what was in the press, and I wanted to ask him about it, about what had happened to Sugar. That was what I said to him when he opened the door. I asked if I could come in for a chat. I told him I needed to talk about my daughter, about her death. Did he tell you what he said?'

'He told us his story.'

'Did he tell you that he said to me that Sugar had got him into enough fucking trouble and that he wasn't fucking interested in talking about, and here I quote directly, "the cock-sucking little bitch"? That's when the red mist came down. That's when I hit him.'

'I don't blame you,' Stallings murmured sincerely. 'Trouble is, it was still the wrong thing to do. Mind you, John,' she continued, 'Weekes doesn't want to make a complaint against you, but on the basis of what the uniformed officers actually saw, that is, several unanswered blows, they could charge him with assault and breach of the peace.'

'Would it help Sugar?' he asked rhetorically. 'Ask them not to.'

'I will, but in return, I'll ask you to do something for me. Stay away from this man. I've seen too many fathers like you in my career, and I'll tell you something, with authority. He has no sort of comfort to offer you.'

'I'll do my best,' said Dean, 'but the thing that scares me most is this: I never thought I'd find myself wanting to see someone dead.'

Sixty-four

'So, son, what did you think of your first baseball game?'

Even with the jerkiness of the web-cam image, James Andrew Skinner could be seen to give serious thought to the question. 'It's all right, Dad,' he replied, when he was ready. 'But it goes on for a long time, and sometimes it's . . . slow.'

'Did you understand what was happening?'

'Yes, that's easy. We play it at school sometimes, only we call it rounders. It's a girls' game, really.'

'Did you tell Armando that?'

'Yes. He laughed.'

'I'm not surprised. Have you decided which team you support?'

'Yes, the Red Sox. They're from Boston,' he added.

'Not the Yankees?'

'No. Everybody was supporting them; the Red Sox didn't have anybody supporting them so I did.'

'That was pretty good of you.'

'Armando says he's going to take me to Boston to see a home game.'

'What about Mark?'

'I don't like baseball,' said Bob's older son. 'I'd sooner watch paint dry.'

'And did you tell Armando that?'

'No. That wouldn't have been polite. I told Mum I didn't want to go again, and she explained to him. He's going to take me to the Metropolitan Museum instead.'

'What about Seonaid? Where's he going to take her?'

'Me, me, me!' squealed the youngest of the three children on the monitor screen.

'That's your theme song, lass.' Her father chuckled.

'He and Mum are taking all of us to the children's zoo in Central Park.'

'And we're going to ride in a horse and carriage,' James Andrew added.

'Indeed? When you do, look out for the bucket.'

'What bucket?'

'The one tied under the horse's tail.'

'Why do they tie a bucket under the horse's tail?'

'You'll find out.'

'Pops!' said a voice from behind him. 'What the hell are you telling him?'

'Alex!' Jazz yelled, as she pulled over another seat and took her place in front of the camera.

Although she spoiled her young siblings in equal measure, there was a bond between James Andrew and his adult half-sister that touched their father every time he saw them together. 'You lot catch up,' he said. 'I'll speak to you in a couple of days.' He ruffled Alex's hair as he stood. She smiled and slapped his hand away.

Aileen was waiting in the kitchen. 'They're late,' she said.

Bob glanced at his watch; it showed one forty. 'Only ten minutes; you know what the by-pass can be like. Is Alexis on her own?' he asked. 'Or is her companion lurking somewhere?'

'No, she's alone. And that's what he is, you know, a companion, nothing more. He's beefcake, that's all, like the boy in that old Diet Coke ad.'

'Beefcake.' He laughed. 'There's a term from the past. How do you categorise me?'

'You, my darling, are the thinking woman's hunk. Alex is too bright for DC Montell. He may have his uses, but she's a woman who needs intellectual stimulation as well.'

As she spoke, a buzzer sounded. Bob stepped across to a small video screen set in the wall, near the kitchen door, and pressed a button below it. Through the window, Aileen saw the heavy wooden gate at the end of the driveway swing open on its pivot. Tyres crunched on the gravel as a metallic blue Ford Mondeo approached the house. It drew to a halt beside Alex's sports car and Andy Martin stepped out.

'Hey there,' his host greeted him from the doorway. 'Where are your girls?'

'I'm sorry, Bob. Karen chucked her breakfast; the morning sickness is tough on her. She sends her apologies, but she didn't fancy a long drive. The wee one can get a bit fractious in the car, so we decided it was best if she stayed at home too.' He nodded to Aileen as she appeared from the hall. 'Afternoon, First Minister,' he said. 'You both look the better for your holiday.'

'Just as well,' she replied, 'for the big blue boxes have started to arrive. I had my first delivery this morning.'

'Is that your car?' Martin looked wistfully at the sleek two-seater. 'My days for those are over . . . for the foreseeable future at any rate.'

'No, mine's a conventional saloon, and it's in the garage alongside Bob's. That's . . .'

'Mine,' said Alex, from the doorway. 'Hi, Andy.' She came forward and kissed him on the cheek, then patted the lapel of his navy blue blazer. 'You're looking very distinguished. What happened to the old leather jacket?'

'It got ripped. It was never the same after the repair. Still in the wardrobe, though.'

'Come on in,' said Bob. 'Alex, you're staying for lunch?'

'I don't want to impose,' his daughter protested. 'I drove down to say hello, that's all . . . and to apologise for fielding a substitute yesterday.'

'Neil told me why. No problem, it gave us a chance to catch up. And now, DCC Martin, you and I can do the same. Let's go round to the front. We can talk while I fire up the barbie.' He led the way through the house, to a paved patio area, where a big gas barbecue stood on a complicated stand, with towels and utensils hanging from it. 'There's a wee fridge in the garden room,' he said. 'Grab a Corona for me and whatever you want for yourself; there's soft in there as well.'

Andy nodded and followed his friend's instructions, returning with an opened bottle and a can of Red Bull. They toasted each other as Bob pressed the barbecue's ignition button. 'In case you're wondering,' he said, 'I didn't plan on Alex being here. She just turned up, and she didn't know you were coming either.'

'How is she?' The question sounded casual.

'My kid? She's fine; loading up on experience in that firm of hers. Associate at twenty-six; that's pretty good, puts her on the fast track for a partnership.'

'No surprise, but how is she?'

Bob stopped adjusting the barbecue and frowned. 'Personally? She's enjoying life. She had a crisis a few months back, which you know about, but she was over that in a couple of days, although it was a big help to have the boy Montell living next door with his sister. She's playing the field; no serious attachments, or so I'm told. If you're asking me whether she still has any regrets about you two breaking up, I'm not going to hazard a guess. You'll need to ask her yourself. As far as I'm concerned, the most important thing is that you don't. You're married with one and a half kids, son. You can't be thinking like that.'

'I'm not,' Andy exclaimed quickly. 'I've got everything I've ever wanted. A wife I love, a daughter I worship and another on the way. No, my life is set in stone. But, if I'm being honest, I'll admit that I regret the way it ended between Alex and me. When she did what she did, I acted like a total prig. I got on my religious high horse, and yet I've never been a model Catholic, Bob. You know that better than anyone. I went to confession afterwards and my parish priest gave me a real tongue-lashing. He told me I should spend a few years in a seminary before rushing to moral judgement. I just didn't want to face the truth: Alex didn't want to marry me. I rushed her into an engagement that she wasn't ready for.'

'I can't disagree with that,' Bob said. 'And now you're going to ask me why I didn't say anything at the time.'

Andy grinned. 'Maybe.'

'It's a simple answer. You were both adults with freedom of choice, and I didn't have the right to interfere with that, or even try. Was I happy when you broke up? Yes, although I didn't like to see you both getting hurt in the process. I wasn't especially pleased that my grandchild had been aborted, but that was an emotional reaction. If I'd known she was pregnant, I wouldn't have tried to talk her out of a termination. Maybe she should have told you about it, probably she should have. And yet I can see why she chose not to.'

'Why?'

'So she couldn't be pressured into a decision that would have changed her life.' Bob sighed. 'But enough of that. Have you finished your report for Jimmy?'

'Yes. And a copy for you in your in-tray stamped "Secret". There was a leak; its name was Joe Dowley. He talked too much at a Rotary meeting. And that's all. There were no others.'

'Does it lead anywhere?'

'Right into Davis Colledge's school.'

'Oh dear. This young man's turning into a serious possibility.'

'Why would he kill his girlfriend?'

'We'll need to ask him that when he surfaces.'

'And the other one?'

'That's a much trickier question. I know that the time-line fits, but there are other considerations. Did he just happen upon Nada Sebastian, or did he know about her and follow her from Bellcaire on her morning journey to the rocks at Empuries? And there's the big coincidence, the one that would have any objective investigator shouting, "Wait a minute!" The fact that she died within sight of my house.'

'And the fact that you were at Murrayfield Golf Club when Sugar Dean died.'

'At which precise time I was away on the practice ground hitting golf balls, on my own, while all the other guys were laying into the bacon rolls.'

'But it gets worse,' said Martin. 'Then there's the pictures. One of Sugar Dean's works is hanging at Fettes . . .'

'In the conference room. I know about that.'

'. . . and there's a seascape hanging in your office, one of your own. An original by Sebastian, signed.'

Skinner gasped. 'You're joking. That surreal thing? It's one of hers?'

'There's no forename. I suppose it could be "Sebastian Somebody", but the way things are going . . .'

'It's her, all right.' He sighed. 'I bought it in the Galeria Mestral in L'Escala three years ago. The lady there told me it was by a local artist who was beginning to do well. I brought it home, but I couldn't find the right place for it in the house, so I took it into the office. It's been there ever since. I'd forgotten the artist's name until you mentioned it. At the time I assumed it was a bloke. Andy, this is getting well beyond a fucking joke.'

'It is. There's something I've got to say, and you probably don't want to hear it. Maybe I should wait till after lunch.'

'No. I can guess what it is. You're going to come back to that objective investigator I mentioned a while back, and you're going to say that the time may have come to bring him in, since officers under my command are engaged in an international investigation in which much of the fucking evidence points at me!'

Martin nodded. 'That's more or less it. It's a bizarre situation, I know. Why would you suddenly decide to copycat Ballester?'

'Why indeed? But let's focus on what you're saying. I got you involved in this situation, Andy, because I knew that your leak investigation would spill over. I've been twitchy from the moment I heard about the Dean murder. That's why I wanted you down here, and that's why I asked you to think outside the box. Now you're involved, and you know what you know, you have a duty as a serving officer to bring it to the attention of my chief constable. However, there is a need for discretion. Any public scandal involving me would wash all over Aileen, and I'm not having that. There will be an objective investigator from an outside force, and that will be you. I had this conversation with Jimmy Proud two hours ago, and he agrees. Your secondment from Tayside is extended as of now. Mario, Neil, the whole team, all report to you.'

'Bob, we've been friends for ever.'

'Andy, every senior officer in Scotland is either a friend of mine or an enemy. If Jimmy brings in somebody else, it will draw attention, and Aileen gets sucked into the whirlpool. The media would make it bloody near impossible for her to stay in office, at least until I'm exonerated. If it's not you, then whoever it is will have a choice to make, whether to lock me up, or to have me conduct my own investigation on the outside. I leave you to imagine what sort of mayhem I'll cause if that happens.'

'Jimmy's agreed?'

'Yes, and he's spoken to Graham Morton, told him he'd like you to look at another situation for him. Graham's released you for another week, initially. Greatorix will stand in for you. You are it. Don't worry: I won't be in your hair. Technically, my sabbatical has another week to run.'

'Ah, Jesus. In that case, let's get something out of the way.'

'No.'

'You want to do it formally?'

'Yes, we have to, but I'm saying, no, I didn't do it. I didn't know Sugar Dean or Nadine Sebastian, I had no reason to harm either of them, and I didn't, any more than I committed any of the four murders attributed to Daniel Ballester.'

'Thankfully that case is closed.'

Skinner smiled. 'Yes, it is, isn't it? But let's go back to thinking outside the box. What if you're not looking for a copycat at all? What if Ballester was innocent?'

Martin was staring at his friend, wide-eyed and open-mouthed, as Aileen and Alex appeared from the garden room, carrying a tray of steaks and burgers, a salad bowl, and four baked potatoes in foil wrappers.

'But of course,' said Bob, 'for the duration of this lunch at least, all that's between you and me.'

Sixty-five

'Did you have to hit him, Jack?' Stallings asked.

'Either that or he hit me. Given the choice . . .'

'Fair enough. There was a moment yesterday when I thought he was ready to have a go at me.'

'Where?' McGurk looked puzzled.

'At his house. There was a disturbance. Sugar's dad paid him a visit and they wound up having a fight. Two uniforms in a patrol car saw it and broke it up; they called it in and Sauce phoned me at home. Funny place for a traffic car to show up.'

'That's down to me. When I chased him from Lisanne's on Friday night I warned him that we'd be keeping a regular eye on him. If young Haddock had given me the word, I'd probably have had him lifted.'

'It wasn't as easy as that. John Dean threw the first punch. Mind you, after he told me what the charmer said about his daughter, Ray had to stop me going back into the house to beat the crap out of him myself.'

The sergeant threw her a small smile across his desk in the CID room. Torphichen Place was quiet, in Sunday mode. 'He is a pig, isn't he?' he murmured. 'Except . . . Lisanne says that his other side does appeal to the ladies. She fell for it for a few years. He has a way of making them believe that what he's telling them really is what's best for them.'

'Did he see her with you on Friday?'

'I don't think so. I made her stay out of sight while I sorted him out.'

'Still, he must have worked out what had brought you there.'

'I doubt it. I reckon that, for all the stalking, his ego's so big that it just wouldn't occur to him . . . and Lisanne agrees with me.'

Stallings chuckled. 'And you're so big he wouldn't do anything about it even if it did. What's his timetable with the court?'

'There'll be a Sheriff Court pleading diet . . . hearing, in other words . . . in a few weeks when the indictment will be read out. By that time Frankie will have done a deal with Gregor Broughton to drop the minor charges in exchange for a guilty plea. She might try to talk him into a charge of simply attempting to defeat the ends of justice, and he might go along with it, since we weren't very far into our investigation.'

'Will it make much difference?'

'I don't think so: the sheriff's powers are limited, so he'll send him to the High Court for sentencing. When the judge hears that the body lay undiscovered for ten days, and adds that Weekes was a cop, he'll hammer him.'

'That assumes that he hasn't been charged with murder by then.'

'Come on, Becky. We know there's no chance of that.'

'Doesn't it also assume that we haven't charged anyone else? Wouldn't the Weekes hearing be delayed in case it was prejudicial?'

'That shouldn't make any difference. The judge would impose restrictions on what the press could report about the case, but he'd still put the hammer on Theo.'

The inspector sighed. 'It's a bugger, Jack,' she said. 'When we got into him on Wednesday, and then when you came in with that necklet the next morning, I thought, "Great, my first big inquiry in Scotland and we've wrapped it up in three days." Now it's Sunday, we're sitting having a case conference, the murder's still unsolved, there are new complications, and we have no positive leads to go on.'

'It's depressing, I'll grant you,' McGurk agreed. 'But don't take it personally; nobody's going to blame you. As for me, I'm not bothered about complications. I look at that image on the wall over there . . .'

He pointed at a large print of Davis Colledge's defaced picture, which Skinner had emailed from Spain. Stallings had cut a square from an adhesive label and pasted it over the young artist's erection. '. . . and I see an angry young man. Why was he angry? That's what I want to know. He's my top priority. I want to speak to him.'

'Yeah, you're right. There is that avenue. We won't be talking to him today, though, so let's rescue what's left of our weekend.'

'Sounds good to me. What have you and Ray got planned?'

'We're going to get our bikes out and cycle to the Northern Bar for a couple. You?'

'Nothing in particular,' he replied noncommittally.

They walked through the moribund station and out through the back door. McGurk was lowering himself into his car when he heard the inspector's mobile sound. He waved to her as he started his engine . . . but stopped when he saw the look on her face as she stared at him. He lowered the window. 'What?' he called.

'That was Mae Grey,' she told him. 'She's at Weekes's place, and she sounds in a right two and eight. We need to get there straight away.'

Sixty-six

'They're taking a while,' said Andy to Alex, as they stood at the foot of the garden looking out across the Firth of Forth. 'How long does it take to load a dishwasher?'

'They may be doing them by hand,' she replied. 'Or Aileen may have opened one of her blue boxes and Dad's helping her. Or they may be having sex . . . less likely during a lunch party, I'll grant you, but us youngsters often underestimate the middle-aged libido. If you want my best guess, though, they've made themselves scarce so that I can ask you how you're getting on.'

He smiled. 'In that case, I'm fine, thanks. You know Karen's pregnant again?'

'No, Pops never said. You're good at that, eh?'

'Nice one, Alex. I fed you that one, didn't I?'

She winced. 'Sorry, that just slipped out. I wasn't chucking harpoons, honest. I am very happy for you and Karen. Your wee girl's lovely too. My dad sent me a picture in an email. I'm really pleased it's all come together for you.'

'So pleased you've never spoken to me since the day we split up?'

'What was there to say? Each one of us would have been expecting the word "sorry" to come up, but you wouldn't have heard it from me.'

'I might have said it, though.'

'But would you have meant it?'

'Yes,' he said, 'for expecting too much of you. I should have seen that we were rushing things.'

'We weren't rushing things, Andy. You were. I was happy to be just you and me, but you wanted the whole deal right away, wife and two point four kids.'

'But you did get pregnant.'

'Yes, silly me.'

'Don't be flip about it, Alex.'

'I'm not. Do you know what hurt me the most back then? When I told you about it, that I'd had an abortion . . . a word I couldn't even say for a while afterwards . . . you went berserk. For a split second I actually thought you were going to kill me. You didn't say anything rational. You called me a murderer and said you could never forgive me.'

'Yes,' he began, 'but . . .'

'But nothing, Andy. That's what happened. Now ask yourself this. You know how I feel about my kid brother. I love him in a way I'd never imagined I could since the day he was born. How easy do you think it was for me to decide to terminate my pregnancy when all the time I was thinking about him? I hated myself for it. It's the most selfish thing I've ever done in my life, but I saw it as essential, not just for me, for us. And the worst of it is that every single day since it happened, I've regretted it,' she prodded herself hard with her index finger, between her breasts, 'right in here.'

She turned to face him, and he saw hot tears in her eyes. 'You couldn't forgive me?' she said. 'Well, fuck you, Andy. I had my own wee Jazz growing in me, and I was wicked enough to have him killed. The forgiveness I need, I'll never have: and it's not yours, sunshine, it's my own, and most of all it's his.'

There was a gate in the garden wall, a few feet in front of them. Alex dashed towards it, opened it and ran off down the grassy hill towards the sea.

Andy stood his ground, wanting to go after her, but fearing the consequences if he did. He watched her as she moved through the busy car park, and as she disappeared down the path that led to the sea.

'Hi,' said a heavy voice behind him.

'That, Bob,' he replied, without turning, 'was not one of your brightest ideas.'

Sixty-seven

Theo Weekes's car was in the driveway of his house. A second vehicle, an elderly Nissan Micra, was parked behind, its tail imposing on the pavement by a few inches. PC Mae Grey was sitting in the passenger seat, her eyes wide in her pale face, unaware of the two detectives as they approached.

McGurk crouched beside her open window, his right knee cracking as he did so. 'Tell me,' he murmured.

'He's in there,' she replied slowly. 'In the hall.'

Stallings led the way up the path. The front door was very slightly ajar, but even before she pushed it she could smell what lay behind: a mix of urine and something else, something slightly sweet.

A stairway ran from the hall to the upper floor of the house. Theo Weekes's body lay in the space beside it, on its side, right arm extended, fingers pointing towards them in the doorway. The carpet beneath him, a dirty cream when the inspector had seen it twenty-four hours earlier, had turned deep, dark crimson. The walls on either side were streaked with blood. She stepped inside carefully, hearing a soft thump behind her as McGurk forgot to duck beneath the lintel. 'Jack,' she said, 'go and ask her if she rang anybody else. If not, call the cavalry. And stay with her until they arrive.'

'She didn't do it. If she had she'd be covered in blood and there would be a trail out to her car. Besides, you can tell he's been dead for a while.'

'Don't jump to conclusions, big boy. She could have been here twice.'

The detective sergeant whistled. 'With a mind like yours, Wilding'd better behave himself.'

'He knows that.'

As McGurk ducked back outside, Stallings stepped into the living room, on her left, then went to a second door that led to the rear of the hall and the kitchen area. It was closed. When she opened it, she saw that it, too, was splattered with Weekes's blood. Not wanting to contaminate the scene any more than she could help, she grasped the door-frame on either side then leaned out as far as she could over the body. The man had died in the clothes he had worn when she had seen him last, but his vest was torn in many places, and his boxer shorts had been pulled down below his buttocks, perhaps, she thought, as he had tried to crawl away from his attacker.

As she looked closer, she could see stab wounds and slashes everywhere: on his back, arms, abdomen, side, face, and across his neck where, she suspected, the jugular had been severed. His mouth hung open. He had been stabbed in the cheek and through the left eye. She reached with her right hand and touched his left hip, one of the few parts of the body neither marked by a wound nor stained with blood. It was colder to the touch than the door-jamb had been.

Stallings pulled herself upright, and stepped back into the living room. She realised that she was trembling, and that her stomach was starting to churn. She went quickly to the exit, and stepped, with as much dignity as she could muster, back into the street.

Mae Grey was standing beside McGurk, leaning against her car as if for support, drawing heavily on a cigarette and staring ahead, at nothing at all. The inspector looked her up and down, from head to foot, and saw that her flat canvas shoes, which had been pale blue, now sported dark blotches.

'Calls made?' she asked the sergeant.

'She didn't,' he replied. 'I did. There's a full uniform team on its way, plus scene-of-crime. I rang the boss too.'

'McIlhenney?'

'Yes. He's coming too. I suspect we may see a few more big chiefs. Weekes was still on the payroll, after all, even if he was more than a wee bit tarnished.'

She turned to the woman. 'Are you ready to talk about it, Mae?'

'No,' she whispered. 'But I never will be, so . . .'

'Why did you come here?'

'I'd left some stuff: a few CDs, some clothes. Plus, I wanted to shove his engagement ring up his arse.'

'Maybe we should stop there,' said Stallings, quietly.

'It's all right, ma'am, I didn't.' Her face twisted savagely. 'If there is anything up there, it wasn't me that put it there.'

'I thought you told us you didn't have a key?'

'I don't.'

'So how did you get in?'

'Back door: there's a path three doors up that takes you there. When I got no reply to the bell, I thought he might be sitting out in the back garden. We did that sometimes. But he wasn't. The kitchen door was open. I went inside and I found him . . . like that.'

'Did you touch anything?'

'No. I stepped into the hall, though; just in case he was still alive. But then I felt the carpet all sticky with his blood and I realised he couldn't be. I lost it a bit and I just ran straight out the front door. I nearly peed myself. I couldn't go back inside, so I squatted down between the two cars and did it there.' McGurk glanced to his right and saw a damp line leading from the driveway across the pavement to a roadside drain. 'When I could get my breath back properly, I found your card and rang you on my mobile.'

'He's been dead for quite some time,' Stallings told her. 'I'm going to ask you this informally; one way or the other I have to. Have you been here before in the last twenty-four hours?'

'What do you mean?'

'Exactly what I've just asked you.'

'No, I haven't,' Grey protested.

'If you have . . . We've had cars doing regular drive-bys of this place. If you have, there's a pretty good chance you'll have been seen by one of them, if not by some of the neighbours.'

'Ma'am, you can ask me informally, formally, any way you like. You can give me a fucking lie detector. I'll tell you the same thing every time. I haven't been here since last weekend. That was the last time I saw Theo.'

'Very good,' said the inspector. 'Let's leave it for now, but you'll need to give us it formally for the record.'

'Of course,' said the constable, beginning to recover her self-control. 'Can I do it soon? I'm on night shift.'

McGurk smiled. 'We can get you the night off, Mae.'

'So I can spend it staring at the ceiling and thinking about that in there? Thanks, Sarge, but I'd rather work.'

'Okay. Look, you know what to do. Give us a statement: type it up, print it and sign it. If we need to interview you after we've seen that, we'll get in touch. On that basis, you can go for now. You'll need to leave us your shoes, though.'

'But I told you exactly what happened. Do you still not believe me?'

'It's not that. They might have picked up something other than Theo's blood, a trace left by whoever did for him.'

'Yes, I see.' She opened her car door, sat in the passenger seat and removed her shoes, then handed them to McGurk, who took them carefully from her, suspending them from a single finger on each hand.

'Thanks,' he said. 'On your way.'

The detectives watched her as she reversed out into South Bughtlin Road and drove off, slowly and carefully, past an ever-growing number of neighbours who had emerged from their homes, realising that something was happening beyond the Sunday norm.

'I hope I was right to do that,' McGurk murmured.

'It was my decision as much as yours. I'd have said if I disagreed. She's given us her story, now she's best off out of it. She's not on my list of suspects.'

'So who is?'

'Who isn't? Anybody who ever met that charmer in there. Realistically, John Dean's got to be at the top, though.'

'Agreed, because he and Weekes had a fight yesterday.'

'And because he told me that he wanted to see him dead, when I spoke to him afterwards.'

'He said that?'

Stallings nodded.

'And then came right back and did it?' McGurk queried. 'How likely is that?'

'Confession first, crime second? I wouldn't rule it out. Maybe he felt it was something he had to do.'

'And maybe not. If that was the case, wouldn't he have called us as soon as he did it?'

'If it's not him, we have to move on to Lisanne.'

'Lisanne didn't do it.'

'I'd expect you to say that; you're seeing her socially. You realise that means you can't have anything to do with any part of the investigation that involves her?'

'Sure, boss, but how long's he been dead?'

'He's cold and he's stiff. Several hours. Maybe since yesterday.'

'Then I repeat, Lisanne didn't do it. I didn't just drop her off on Friday: I stayed the night, and I was there all morning. About midday, she drove me to my place. I changed clothes and we went to the Botanics for the afternoon, then did an early movie and back to mine. We were there until this afternoon, when I came into the office to meet you and she went home.'

'Lucky for her you were available and horny.'

McGurk shot her an uncharacteristically hostile look. 'If you doubt

313

me, you can send a SOCO to my place to go over the sheets.'

'Hey, calm down, Jack. That'll only happen if they find her DNA in the house.'

'They probably will: she's been there a couple of times, remember. If they find her prints in blood on the handle of a knife, that's another matter, but they won't.'

'Fair enough,' Stallings declared. 'Whatever, I'm the one who breaks the news to her, once we're set up here. Is the mobile police station on its way?'

'Yes. I'm beginning to think we should put bunks in it.' As he spoke, a blue people-carrier swung into South Bughtlin Road and headed towards them. 'That looks like DI Dorward and his team.'

'Good. I was beginning to feel lonely. We should get organised ourselves. Door-to-door interviews first.' She looked at the houses on either side of the one in which the body lay. 'Unless things have changed since yesterday, these are unoccupied.'

'I'd guessed as much,' McGurk agreed. 'Since we've been here there hasn't been as much as a twitching curtain either side. I don't imagine that Weekes died quietly. If they'd been occupied, somebody would have been bound to hear something.' He looked along the street. 'It's a shame this neighbourhood's so quiet. It would have made life easier if there was a closed-circuit camera here.'

'It would. Mind you, the closed-circuit coverage is quite extensive in Edinburgh. Find out where the nearest cameras are and arrange to review their footage for the last couple of days. See if anything or anyone jumps out at you.' Stallings broke off as a red-haired man approached in a crime-scene tunic. 'DI Dorward,' she said. 'Sorry about your Sunday.'

The newcomer shrugged. 'What's new? Weekends are our busy time.' He took Mae Grey's shoes from McGurk's extended fingers and passed them to an assistant. 'Thanks, big man. Whose are these?'

'The woman who found the body.'

'Have you been inside?'

'I only stood in the doorway. DI Stallings has, though.'

Dorward turned back to her. 'Yours too, please. There are some disposables in our van that you can have.' He watched as the inspector slipped her shoes off. 'Now there's a shapely ankle,' he said cheerfully. 'Right,' he called to his team. 'You know what to do. I want the house taped off, front and back. Any sign of the doc?'

'Just coming, Arthur,' a female voice called from the roadway. Beyond her, Stallings saw DC Haddock emerging from a Mini.

'Jack,' she announced, 'I'm going to take young Sauce and call on Lisanne. It's best she hears about it sooner than later. You get things under way here when the HQ van arrives.'

'Yes, boss,' McGurk replied. 'But, Becky . . .'

'Sure.' She grinned. 'Don't worry, I'll tell her that you'd have come but I wouldn't let you.'

Sixty-eight

The tide was on its way out, and so Bob knew where he would find her. He walked down towards the beach, but rather than follow the main path from the car park, he took another track, one that headed westward and had been cut to allow a gentler descent for the horses which were exercised there.

Once, when Alex was a child, eight, as he recalled, she had broken a house rule, and she and her father had argued. Since she had inherited much of his nature it had ended with her stalking through the front door, declaring that she was running away from home. He had followed her at a distance as she had headed up Goose Green, through the narrow alley that divided the villas along Marine Parade, then across the bents and down to the sand. He had followed, never letting her out of his sight, and she had marched on, never once looking back.

When he had caught up with her, she had been sitting on a low flat red rock, a few yards below the high-water mark. 'Is this it, then?' he had asked. 'The place you've run away to?'

She had looked up at him, and wrinkled her nose. 'Yes,' she had announced, with the kind of dignity that only a child can affect. 'This is my huffy rock.'

She was there again. She said nothing as he sat down beside her, as he had done almost twenty years before, and slid his arm around her. 'Andy thinks I set the two of you up,' he told her, 'but, honest, baby, I didn't. The dishwasher was full and just finishing its cycle, so we did the lunch things by hand, then we emptied it, stacked everything away and tidied up the kitchen.'

'Whatever,' she murmured, 'it had its effect. Did he tell you? Everything I said, everything I yelled at him?'

'All of it. I have to say,' Bob chuckled, 'you chose your moment. When we were outside, Andy and I, he was beating himself up about the two of you, and the way he acted back then. No wonder he thinks I turned you loose on him.'

'Oh, God, I'm sorry, Pops.'

'Don't be. It needed to happen, for your sake, and maybe even for his. I'm to blame too.'

'What do you mean? How can you be?'

'For not getting involved at the time, for not being a proper dad and letting you soak my shoulder. You and Andy did nothing but shout at each other when you should have been talking. But he wasn't rational, and I don't suppose you were either. You should have been able to talk to me, but I wasn't around for you.'

'Yes, you were, and so was Sarah. I chose not to talk to you, that's all.'

'You chose to bottle all that up inside you, and get on with your life?'

'Yes.'

'For how long now, going on four years?'

'Yes, and you want to know why? Because the more I thought about it, the more ashamed of myself I became. Pops, I came off the pill for one month because Andy kept going on about having kids, and in that time I got pregnant.'

'And you took a decision for good and valid reasons. It's all right, love.' He gave her a one-armed hug.

'But it's not,' she cried, with a desperation that cut into him. 'It was expedient, it was cowardly, and I'm ashamed of being the kind of person who could do something like that.'

Bob took his arm from around her waist and clasped his hands together, his elbows on his knees. 'Your mother had two miscarriages,' he said. 'One when we were engaged, just before we were married, and another a year after you were born. It happened while she was at work, and she was whipped into hospital for an emergency D and C. Except that wasn't true: she never went to work that day. She went straight to Roodlands and had an abortion.'

Alex stared at him. 'How did you find out?'

'I'm a detective, kid. I took her head teacher a box of chocolates to thank her for her help. She was in on it; she said, "Don't mention it," and thanked me for the chocs, but there was something in her eye, and I read it. I made some personal enquiries and found out the truth. Scared the crap out of a gynaecologist in the process.'

'God, Pops. How did she justify it to you?'

'She didn't, because I said nothing about it. The gynae bloke was shitless because I told him what I'd do to him if she ever found out from him that I knew. I loved your mum, Alexis; if she felt that's what she had to do, it was all right with me, even if it hurt me like a broken bone. I'm sure she pined for that kid, though, and so did I, for a long while, even after Myra was dead.'

'How did you get over it? God, did you get over it?'

'I told your Granddad Skinner. He said, "That's too bad, son, but it's history. Now treat the child like all the others that are gone and get on with your life." And that's what I did. I put it in my mental box of cherished things and got on with my life.'

She squeezed his arm. 'Your what?'

'My mental box of cherished things. Your past selves are in there, as a baby, then as a kid. So's your mum, and your grandparents. Sarah, from the early days when things were okay with us: she's there too. And even a couple of others that I've never told you about, and won't, for now at any rate. You, they, are all in there, and every so often, when I'm alone, I open the lid and put myself inside for a while. Then I close it again. That's what you have to do. Define that box in your head and put the kid you never had in there. Then go forward. You can do that because essentially you're me, even if I can't read you all the time.'

'If you have that box, what do you do with the demons?' she asked.

'They're in another one. It's locked up tight, and I've hidden the key, even from myself.' He stood and held out his hand for her to pull herself to her feet.

They walked back up the bridle path and across the bents, the rough, rising ground beyond the shore, until they reached the garden gate. Andy and Aileen were waiting for them in the garden. 'Sorry, Andy,' said Alex, awkwardly, as she approached him.

He shrugged and smiled. 'All the better for the telling,' he replied. He looked at Bob. 'I believe you now. Aileen told me what kept you.'

'Don't make disbelieving me a habit, for Christ's sake,' said his friend, heavily.

'There was a phone call,' Aileen told him. 'Neil. He asked if you'd call him back on his mobile as soon as you got in.'

'Sounds like the sort of call you don't want on a Sunday . . . but Neil wouldn't do it if he didn't have to.' He took out his phone and strolled across to the corner of the garden, calling up McIlhenney's number as he went. 'What's up?' he asked, as they were connected.

'Somebody's put paid to Theo Weekes. In his house. With what looks like a very big, very sharp knife, only Arthur's people can't find it at the scene.'

'Which of his surviving women did that?'

'Neither. PC Grey found the body. When he was killed, about six last night, the pathologist reckons, his ex-wife was with Jack McGurk. And please, don't give me the witness-protection joke again: I've heard it four times so far this afternoon.'

Skinner beckoned to Martin. 'I won't,' he promised McIlhenney. 'I won't give you anything. I want you to tell all this to Andy. He'll be looking into something beyond the leak inquiry, and this is too close to it to be treated separately.' He handed the phone to his friend and walked away, back to Aileen and Alex.

Sixty-nine

'This thing you're doing, Andy,' said Neil McIlhenney, standing outside Theo Weekes's house, in the evening sunshine that baked South Bughtlin Road. 'It makes my flesh creep. I can't lose the thought that if it was anyone else we'd have had him in for serious questioning, or the Spanish would have if they'd known all the facts about the Dean murder, and especially about the picture connection to the second one.'

'That's why he wants me involved.'

'What do you mean?'

'He knows me, and he knows that if the evidence becomes overwhelming, I might have to lock him up. He'd rather it was me than anybody else.'

'Come on, you're not seriously suggesting that Bob's in the frame for these killings, are you?'

'He's suggesting it himself. At least, he's pointing out the obvious, that there's a chain of circumstantial evidence connecting him to the victims, not just these two but the Ballester victims as well.'

'But those cases are closed. We know Ballester did it.'

'As you say,' Martin concurred, 'those cases are closed.' He glanced along the road to where the press corps was mustered behind a barrier. 'But maybe they shouldn't be.'

'Stop it, for fuck's sake!' McIlhenney protested. 'You're suggesting that our deputy chief, never mind that he's a friend of both of us, might have gone on a killing spree.'

'No, I'm not, Neil. But that's what the circumstances are suggesting. Among the six victims, there are four artists. Bob owns work by three of them and he's in close proximity to a piece by the fourth, in his office. Three of the victims died on his doorstep, two in Gullane and one in Spain. He was at the scene of a fourth death and within reachable distance of the other two. He doesn't have a cast-iron alibi for any of them: I know this because he volunteered it, but you've been there while it all happened. You must have put the same facts together for yourself.'

'I have,' the superintendent admitted. 'Of course I have.'

'Then you've been ignoring something he's taught us: never back off from thinking the unthinkable.'

'No, I haven't. I've thought it, and I'm sure that Mario has too. But neither of us believes it.'

'Neither do I, but I'll continue to look at the evidence, as he wants me to do. And there is something else, something you know about. Last year, before any of this started, Bob was involved in that major incident at St Andrews. So were you. The situation was resolved successfully, but there were deaths.'

'Yeah,' McIlhenney murmured. 'Something happened that night, Andy. I was there, I saw the bodies, and I maybe even accounted for one of them, but there was something else that was never talked about afterwards. One of the dead: he was never identified.'

'I know who he was,' said Martin. He paused, looking the superintendent in the eye. 'Neil, you know that the big guy isn't conventionally religious, but he has a couple of confessors. I'm one, and Jim Gainer, the Archbishop, is the other. He told me everything about that night: Jim probably knows too, but neither of us can talk about it. Suffice to say that it was bad. It hit him very hard: it would probably have broken anyone else, but not him. However, if other investigators came into this thing and looked at the total picture, it might be hard to persuade them that it didn't knock him off the rails. He's vulnerable, Neil, and he knows it. What he's really asked me to do here is clear him.'

'On the face of it, there's only one way to do that: find our killer.'

'Maybe not: confirming Ballester's guilt would help. It would keep the copycat theory firmly in play. And it would put Davis Colledge back in the spotlight.'

'He's never been out of it, Andy. We just can't find the wee bastard, that's all. We lost his trail in Holland.'

'He'll turn up. Meanwhile, brief me on what we've got here.'

'We've got a situation, DCC Martin. This man Weekes spent the last few days of his life drawing trouble like a turd draws flies. On Friday evening, Jack McGurk found him parked outside his ex-wife's house, in breach of his bail conditions. Weekes threw a punch, but big Jack whacked him. He let him off, sent him on his way, with a heavy warning not to come back. He also arranged for frequent drive-pasts of this place, just to keep an eye on him.'

'Was McGurk with the ex-wife?'

'They'd been out on a date. They're two single people, so why not? I have no problem with it professionally, and in practical terms it's helped her by removing her as a suspect. Jack's finished up here, and he was keen to get off to see her, so I've let him go.'

'Fair enough. Back to the story.'

'Yes. Yesterday afternoon Weekes had a visitor: John Dean, Sugar's dad. His story is that Weekes insulted his daughter and they came to blows. One of the drive-by cars broke it up. Stallings was called; she acted as peacemaker. No charges, no arrests. Incidentally both of those officers, she and Jack, are now feeling a bit of guilt, thinking that if either of them had taken a harder line and had him locked up, when they could have, he'd still be alive. I've pointed out that Frankie Birtles would probably have had him released inside an hour, but it's still niggling at them.'

'I'll have a word with them, if you think it'll help.'

'It might. Anyway, that brings us to today, when PC Grey, the victim's by now former fiancée, arrived to collect some personal possessions and, in her words, to shove his engagement ring up his arse. She found said arse sticking up in the air in the hall, having been as dead as the rest of him since last night. Incidentally, now that the time of death's more or less confirmed she's also well alibied, since she and her mother were on their way home from shopping, and she has time-stamped till receipts to prove it. Dorward's team are still working inside, lifting prints and DNA traces, but they haven't found anything that looks remotely like the murder weapon. The pathologist believes that to be a large, broad-bladed knife of the sort carried by hunters or, more likely, scuba-divers, with a cutting edge on one side and serrations on the other. As you'll have seen, we've got uniforms searching the surrounding area, but so far, nothing. On top of that, Jack McGurk's found a closed-circuit camera. It belongs to the local supermarket and it covers its car park and the bus terminal for this area. He's had a quick look at the footage for late yesterday afternoon. The only thing it told him is that there were a lot of people around; no familiar faces, though.'

'Did the doc offer any theories on the attacker?'

'Physically strong, she said, and almost certainly male, from the degree of force used. The attack was savage and sustained. The blood trail begins in the kitchen. The first blows were delivered there, before Weekes either staggered or crawled out into the hall, with his attacker following him, hacking and stabbing away at him. The doc counted twenty-seven penetrating wounds and six slashes, but she reckoned that he was finally killed by a deep cut to the neck that severed the jugular and the carotid. Some of the wounds, including one to an eye, might have been *post mortem.*'

'Speaking of which, who's doing it?' asked Martin.

'Old Joe; Professor Hutchinson. He's still around, and still the best there is, especially now that Sarah's gone.'

'Undoubtedly. What about the man Dean? Has he been interviewed yet?'

'Becky went to see him: there was nobody home. He and his wife left last night for their place up north. He called in to see his neighbour at about five thirty to let her know they were off, and she saw them drive away about fifteen minutes later.'

Martin frowned. 'So far, Neil, you've done a hell of a good job of eliminating suspects. As far as I can see, all the runners were withdrawn before the tape went up.'

'All the obvious ones, yes, but then someone else turned up at the starting gate. Our door-to-door questioning turned up two neighbours who mentioned seeing a car parked outside yesterday evening; definitely after five, they both said. It was a dark blue Volvo and they noticed it because it was parked across Weekes's drive, blocking the exit.'

'Number?'

'Neither of them could tell us, but Stallings checked with the traffic department. It was noted by a patrol car at five forty. Just for fun, they ran a number check. Guess who popped out? Do you remember Jock Varley, a uniformed inspector?'

'The name's familiar.'

'Have you read the Sugar Dean file, including Weekes's formal statement?'

'Jesus, yes!' Martin exclaimed. 'He claimed that Varley's wife gave him a sexually transmitted disease.'

'That's right. And our investigation found evidence to support that.'

'What have you done about it?'

'I've sent Stallings and young DC Haddock to pick Varley up from his home and take him to Fettes. Mario and I will handle the interview. Do you want to sit in?'

'Thanks, but no thanks,' said Martin. 'I can listen to the tape, if I need to. I've got to get back to Perth. When I tell Karen I'm going to be out of town for another week, she's not going to be best pleased. I don't want to stoke her fire any more than I have to.'

Seventy

'Will she be all right?' Aileen asked, as they watched the gate close behind Alex's car.

'She'll probably be in a better state than she was when she arrived,' Bob replied. 'If I didn't think so, I'd have insisted that she stay the night. She got something off her chest that's been festering for too long. I suspect its intensity surprised even her. I don't recall my daughter ever getting so emotional.'

'Does she have any surviving grandparents? I know your folks are dead, but what about her mum's?'

'No, they're gone too,' he told her, as they walked through to the garden room. 'I never really got to know Myra's dad, but I confess that I miss her mother more than I miss my own. Which reminds me, lady: when do I get to meet my new prospective in-laws?'

'When they get back from my dad's retirement trip, in a month or so.' She laughed. 'And when I'm sure that my mother will behave herself. She's only ten years older than you, she's pretty attractive and she's a hell of a flirt.'

'Does your dad play golf?'

'He's a member of Royal Troon; handicap eleven, last I heard, so you'll be giving him shots.'

'With pleasure. He can bring his clubs when they come to visit us.'

'No, dear, you can take yours. Custom dictates that you call on him to ask for my hand, doesn't it?'

'Maybe he'll tell me I'm not having it.'

'You've got all the rest, so it won't matter much. What's a hand, anyway? But worry not, he approves of you. He knows you by reputation, and he's a big fan.'

'What's he like . . . off the course, that is?'

'I doubt if he votes for me.'

'I'll bet he does. If my daughter told me she was standing for the Raving Loonies at the next election I'd vote for her.'

'You would too! My mum votes Labour; I know that for sure.' She paused. 'Bob, changing the subject, that chat you and Andy had, indeed Andy's visit itself, what was that about?'

'I need his help, love. It's these killings: the pointers to me are beyond coincidence. Somebody's trying to set me up, and the way things are going he's succeeding. I'm trying to head it off before it all gets beyond control and sucks you in, and Andy's my best hope.'

'Can't you do it yourself? You're usually your own best hope.'

'How can I investigate myself?'

'Point taken.' Aileen frowned, and bit her lip. 'Bob,' she said, 'last Thursday morning, when the Sebastian woman was shot, I was swimming alongside you at the time. Don't you remember?'

'No, because you weren't. The pool's not that big; I'd have noticed. You were upstairs all the time, sound asleep.'

'Don't you remember?' she repeated.

'Aileen,' he sighed, 'I love you and I wouldn't let you do that, even if I was in the dock. Don't even hint at it again, please.'

'Bob, who would want to set you up?'

'I can think of a few hundred people.' He grimaced as the phone rang. He reached out and picked it up, answering by reciting his number.

'Bob,' a female voice said.

'That's me. Amanda, this is a surprise.'

'You're back in harness,' she replied, 'so you're the man I speak to in your place.'

'That's not quite the case, but fire away.'

'First, the markings on the bullet your people sent me. The gun that fired it has no criminal history. It's not on IBIS and I've even had my people check with the American Bureau of Alcohol, Tobacco, and Firearms. The most positive information I have for you is that it's likely to be an expensive weapon. The bullet that killed your victim was relatively unmarked. The traces that we find are made by imperfections in the barrel, and there are fewer of these found in high-quality guns than in mass-produced.'

'Sugar Dean won't have cared how much the damn thing cost,' Skinner muttered.

'No, but it probably made a difference to her killer. This is someone who knows firearms, I'd say. It's also unlikely that the weapon was the kind a criminal can buy, or even rent, in the back room of a pub. One other thing. I can't tell you which gun fired your bullet, but I can tell you which ones didn't. It wasn't a firearm used or issued by any police force, by this department or by the protection squad. That, I am glad to say, takes the Shadow Defence Secretary out of the equation. That would have been nasty all round.'

'Unlikely too,' Skinner conceded. 'I never really fancied him, but I did wonder if young Dave might have borrowed Daddy's gun when he wasn't looking.'

'Evidently not.'

'It was just a thought. Is that it?'

'Not quite. My boy Adrian . . . you met him, remember? . . . was quite taken by Mrs Steele and her quest when he contacted her, so much so that he's been doing a little digging, with the help of a friend in the FBI. He got him to run a passport check with hotels in the area of Myrtle Beach, South Carolina, last week. He discovered that among the guests last Tuesday night were Mr Ifan Richards, UK citizen, and Señor Ignacio Riesgo, a Panamanian national, according to his passport. Bob, to get a Panamanian passport, all you need to do is open a big enough bank account there, over a minimum five-year term. A hundred and twenty-five thousand US dollars will do it.'

'The way things are going up here, I may bear that in mind.'

'What?'

'Nothing; only joking.'

'Whatever. That wasn't Adrian's only success. He's discovered that Davor Boras is on the move on Tuesday. He's filed a flight plan for his aircraft.'

'Where's he going?'

'Gatwick to Nice, returning Thursday.'

'Two nights. Where's he staying?'

'Adrian's looking into that.'

'You'll let me know, as soon as you get a hit?'

'Of course.'

'Not Maggie, you understand. She's taken this as far as I'm going to let her.'

'Understood. One way or another I'll be in touch.'

As he hung up, he saw that Aileen was staring at him. 'She'll let you know?' she exclaimed. 'I thought you were hands-off for the next week.'

He chuckled. 'I seem to remember you telling me over dinner, just a few nights ago, that it was okay to be hands-on.'

Seventy-one

Inspector John Varley had been plucked from his garden. He was wearing a check shirt with rolled-up sleeves, tan shorts and a pair of ancient trainers that might once have been white. His grey-streaked hair was ruffled and stubble showed on his chin, accentuating his dark moustache. He sat at a small table, his big fists clenched and tense. A dirty bandage was wound round his left hand, strapping the middle fingers together. He glared at McGuire and McIlhenney as they stepped into the interview room at the back of the force headquarters building, and as the uniformed officer who had been guarding him stepped out.

'You two,' he said, as McIlhenney switched on a twin-deck recorder and spoke into its microphone. 'I might have known.'

'You're in a bad place, Jock,' the head of CID told him. 'You should be pleased that it's us who've come to interview you and not some young DS, eager to make a name for himself. We're deferring to your rank by taking this on ourselves.'

'You're deferring to my rank? This is a fucking insult, sir, if you don't mind my saying so. You send a woman I've never met to my house, and a boy straight from the playground, and they tell me to get straight into their car, without a word to my wife or anybody else. She won't be happy, I'll tell you.'

'Bluster won't work, Inspector,' said McIlhenney, evenly. 'My wife isn't happy either.' He jerked a thumb in McGuire's direction. 'And as for his partner . . . his tea will be in the dog when he gets home, I promise you. What happened to your hand?' he asked.

Varley held up his left fist. 'This? I broke my ring finger a couple of weeks ago. They splinted it to the one next to it.'

'How did you do that?'

'I slipped on wet tiles at home, and caught it on the edge of the kitchen table.'

'That was a bit careless. Did you have something on your mind at the time?'

Varley stared at the superintendent. 'No, why should I? It was a pure accident.'

'What did you have on your mind yesterday?'

He turned to McGuire. 'What?'

'You heard. What were you thinking of yesterday, about twenty-four hours ago?'

'Is that what this is about?' the inspector exclaimed. 'Aw, Jesus.'

'Did you think you wouldn't be seen, Jock? We were watching the house.'

'Aw, for fuck's sake! I should have . . .'

'Guessed? Yes, you bloody should. Weekes was on bail on the strict condition that he stay away from potential witnesses. One of them's an officer at your station. Of course we'd look after her. So tell me, for the record, why did you go there?'

'Because I found out about that bastard and my Ella,' he snarled, 'about him having sex with her.'

'That bastard being Theo Weekes?'

'Of course.'

'Jock, that happened two years ago.'

'Maybe, but I only found out about it on Friday.'

'How?'

'I've got a contact.'

'What do you mean, a contact?'

'In the force. That's how I found out.'

'What?'

'That you'd been checking on Weekes's medical history and on Ella's and mine. At the VD clinic.'

'So you found out that Weekes had caught a disease from your wife? But I suppose you assumed it was the other way round, that he'd given it to her.'

Varley gazed at a point in the corner of the room. 'No,' he said. 'That's not how it was. It started with me. I had a . . . a . . . I don't know what to call it, not a relationship or anything.'

'Try sex,' McIlhenney murmured. 'You had sex with somebody, casual sex.'

'That'll do. I drink in a hotel, not far from the house. There was a woman there one night, a resident; she chatted me up in the bar and made me an offer. I took her up on it. Unfortunately, one of Ella's pals was there, at the back of the bar. She saw me, I never saw her. About a week later, the bitch shopped me. Ella did a ballistic act, threatened to leave me. I got down on my knees, almost literally, and said I was sorry. It was just afterwards Weekes saw her in the Almondale Centre, laden down with bags, and offered her a lift home. He came on to her in the kitchen, after he'd carried the bags in, and, well, recent history and all, she took him on. At that point, we didn't know about the disease. It can take a while for the symptoms to show.'

'Ella didn't tell you about Weekes at that time?'

'No. I'd never have found out if the shite hadn't mentioned her by name when you two interviewed him. That's what made me angry, that he named her. God, I'm not mad with Ella. I've no right.'

'He was being questioned in a murder inquiry, Jock,' McGuire pointed out.

'He didn't have to name her. His medical record was there: it wouldn't have hindered the investigation if he'd kept her out of it.'

'True, but he volunteered her identity, under very little pressure.'

'Who's your contact in the force, Inspector?' asked McIlhenney.

'I'm not telling you. I'm not Theo Weekes. That can stay confidential.'

'Unfortunately, Jock,' said the head of CID, 'it's not that simple. Weekes's allegations about your wife were checked out by Special Branch, under cover of a vetting operation. Your wife's name doesn't appear anywhere in the murder book; the investigating officers used discretion. So your contact has to be in SB, and I can't allow that. I will find out; so save a lot of grief and tell us.' He reached across and switched off the tape. 'Just us, for now.'

Varley sighed. 'Oh, bugger. It's Alice Cowan, DI Shannon's assistant. She's my niece; she wanted to warn me that it might all come out in court.'

'Damn it,' McIlhenney growled. 'Alice is a bloody good officer, but she can't stay in SB now.'

'No,' said McGuire, 'but after she's had her arse kicked she'll be an asset somewhere else. We'll deal with it quietly.' He switched the recorder on. 'Back to business, Jock. So yesterday evening, blazing mad, you went to see Weekes. Tell us about it.'

'What's to tell? I rang his doorbell, and I got no answer. So I thumped the door, just about hard enough to knock it down, and eventually he opened it. He must have looked through the spyglass, for he knew who it was straight away.'

'What happened next? Describe it in detail.'

'I shoved him back into the hall. He knew what I was there for. He held up his hands and asked me, begged me almost, to hold on.'

'But you didn't.'

'Like fuck I did. I ripped right into him and I didn't stop until I'd got my message across. Then I just turned around and left him there. I know, I shouldn't have, but you must know what it's like when the red mist comes down.'

McGuire leaned back in his seat. 'There's red mist, Jock . . . and then there's total complete loss of control. What did you do with the knife?'

Varley stared back at him. His mouth fell open as if a string had been cut. 'Knife? What fucking knife?'

'The knife you ripped him with.'

'What? What the fuck is this?'

'Jock, as soon as this interview is over, Neil's going to front a press conference at which we're going to confirm to the press that Theo Weekes was found dead in his home this afternoon, and that we're treating his death as murder. He's also going to say that a man is helping with our enquiries, that man being you.'

'Sir,' the inspector said earnestly, 'I never touched him. When I said that I ripped into him, I meant verbally. I told him that I knew about him and Ella, and that the jail was the best place for him. But apart from shoving him back into the hall, I never laid a finger on him.'

'Jock, you were there at the time Weekes was murdered. And by your own admission you were angry with him.'

'I'm a serving police officer, man!'

'So you will co-operate with our investigation. Yes?'

Varley nodded. 'Yes,' he said.

'At any time yesterday did you go into Weekes's kitchen?'

'No, only the hall.'

'Could you see into the kitchen?'

'Yes, but I wasn't looking there.'

'How did you leave?'

'The same way I went in. And I closed the door behind me.'

'Could the back door have been open?'

'It could, but I can't say that it was.'

'Okay. Jock, you'll be held here while a search of your home is carried out, under warrant. We're also taking your car for forensic examination. Once that's complete, we'll talk again. I hope to God that we don't find any corroborating evidence, but if we turn up that knife, or bloodstains on your clothing and in your car, you know what we'll have to do.'

The man sat there, stunned. 'Yes,' he whispered. 'I know. But I promise, you won't have to.'

Seventy-two

Karen Martin looked at her husband, sitting in his armchair with his lap-top computer open on a low table in front of him. 'Andy,' she said, 'your eyes aren't getting any younger. Give those contact lenses a break, will you?'

'I'm sorry, love,' he replied, folding the monitor down. 'You've been putting up with a lot from me these past few days. I know I'm pushing my luck.'

'It's not that. I'm one hundred per cent behind you on this thing that Bob's asked you to undertake. But you're beginning to show signs of DUOA syndrome. You've been home for two hours and, apart from saying goodnight to Danielle, you've been on that thing all that time. For the last half-hour all I've been hearing are tuts and sighs. You're beat, man.'

'I'm beginning to get cross-eyed,' Andy admitted. 'And, by the way, what's DUOA syndrome?'

'Disappearing Up Own Arse. You're going round in ever-decreasing circles.'

'That's what happens when you try to find something that's probably not there, but you want it to be.'

'What's that?'

'Daniel Ballester, the man who's been credited officially with the murders earlier this year of the artists Stacey Gavin and Zrinka Boras, and of two potential witnesses.'

'The man who owned the house where Stevie Steele died?'

'Yes. He was murdered there himself by Dražen Boras, Zrinka's brother, in revenge. Stevie was killed by a booby-trap meant to take out the only two guys who could link Boras and his father with the location.'

'So what are you after?'

'Anything that undermines the case against Ballester. I'm damned if I can see it, though.'

'Maybe you're losing your touch.' She held out a hand. 'Let me see it. I used to be a cop once upon a time, remember? Put your headphones on, listen to some music, and let me see if I can crack it.'

He reached out and gave her the computer. 'Go on, then. If you get a result I might even let you rejoin the force.'

'Not in my darkest moment would I do that,' said Karen, sincerely.

Andy did as he was told. He selected a John Coltrane CD from his collection, fed it into the deck and slipped on his headphones. He leaned back in his chair, and allowed the music to envelop him, watching Karen as she worked, letting his mind drift . . .

His eyes glazed as he drifted towards sleep: the figure at the dining-table became blurred, and seemed to take on a different form, taller, slimmer, darker, full-breasted rather than massive, a body he knew as well as his own, someone for whom he had once burned, someone he used to call 'Lexy', but only, as his mind heard her say, in her laughing voice, when they were naked.

'Hey,' Karen called, attracting his attention through the sound of Coltrane's mellow sax, jerking him out of slumber. 'Is it that good?'

'Sorry?'

'The music. You were grinning there as if it's really hitting the spot.'

' "Central Park West",' he replied, the headphones making him unaware that he was shouting. 'One of his finest.'

'You bugger.' She laughed. 'I was expecting you to say you were thinking about me.'

She turned back to the lap-top and focused on it once more, with

Andy watching her more closely, until gradually the pace of the day began to catch up with him again.

He had no idea how long he had been asleep when she called to him again, but the CD had played itself out, and his ears were clammy from the pressure of the headphones. 'Andy, wake up,' she said, as she took them from his head, leaning forward, her formidable bosom close to his face.

He blinked and straightened himself in the chair. 'Sorry, love,' he said. 'You done? I reckon I might as well go to bed. Are you coming?'

'Eventually, but I want you to look at this first.' The lap-top was still open on the table.

'You'll need to read it to me,' he told her. 'I don't think my eyes can focus on that screen any more.'

'They will when you see this.'

Instantly, she had his attention. 'What are you looking at?' he asked.

'The post-mortem report on Daniel Ballester.'

'I've looked at it. Death by strangulation, due to hanging with a ligature: no sign of a struggle, but two small marks on the body are consistent with his being subdued by a powerful stun gun.'

'That's right, but remember this. The autopsy was performed in Northumbria, where he died. They were looking at him then as a suicide victim, not as a perpetrator.'

'True.'

'So they didn't attach any significance to this, and because there was so much evidence found at the site to confirm Ballester's guilt, the investigating officers overlooked it too. There's a sub-section of the report that contains general information on the man's medical condition. He was a big strong guy, with excellent cardio-vascular fitness, but . . . it says that tissue testing, backed up by an indicator in his cornea, showed that he was suffering from Wilson's disease, and that it was almost certainly undetected.'

'What the hell is Wilson's disease?'

'It's an inherited disorder, in which the copper levels in the body get out of control. When I was in my teens, one of my neighbours developed it; they caught it in time, and she was okay, but it can be fatal. I remember it because my dad made a bad-taste joke about it. He said that back in the sixties and seventies the whole bloody country had Wilson's disease. The thing is, I remember the poor woman's symptoms, and I've just done some research on the Internet to confirm them. They included very shaky hands, really strong tremors; that was how they got on to it in the first place.'

'Go on,' said Andy, his green eyes shining.

'You can see what I'm leading up to. Ballester's supposed to have shot four people. Up close, maybe he could have done that. But there was a fifth victim: Stacey Gavin's dog, Rusty. That was shot at a distance, while it was running away from the killer. By a man who'd have been struggling to hold the gun steady? I don't see that. Bottom line, I think you should get somebody else to look at that PM report, but if I'm right, Ballester's not your man.'

Seventy-three

Bob Skinner was up and running, in the truest sense. The day on which he had planned to be back at work had dawned, but he found himself still in exile, banished by a set of circumstances stranger than any he had ever experienced. He had never been one to lie and brood, and so, when Aileen's alarm had sounded at seven fifteen, he had risen with her, donned shorts, a sweatshirt and trainers and had set out to work off his frustrations, as far as he could.

His route took him down the hill into Gullane, then westward out of the village, following the Edinburgh road for the best part of two miles until he reached the solid pedestrian bridge that led across the Peffer Burn into the nature reserve. Tranter's Bridge, the locals called it, after the beloved author and historian who had crossed it every day until the end of his long life, plotting his latest work as he walked, and making notes that would be turned in time into chapters.

As he ran across the wooden structure it occurred to Skinner that in a way he was following in Tranter's footsteps, literally and metaphorically, picking his way through a story as strange and even as fascinating as his had been, if more brutal than most of them. But that was where the similarity ended, for this was a mystery in which he was entangled, right at its very heart, and for the author it was no fantasy, but a deadly reality. Not far from the path that he trod, a woman had died, killed in a way that was almost ritualistic, as if she had been offered up as a sacrifice. There had been two others, and they had all been photographed in death, their images found on Daniel Ballester's computer.

Had Ballester killed them, as he had believed, with all of his colleagues? If that was the case, had someone else out there happened upon the pattern and decided to carry it on, putting him in the frame in the process? Or was it all mere circumstance? Had Nada Sebastian been the victim of a particularly ruthless mugger, after all? There were enough of them around: the opening of eastern Europe's borders had been marked in Spain by an increase in petty crime and roadside prostitution. Had Theo Weekes, obsessively possessive with his women, killed Sugar Dean after all, in his acknowledged rage over her relationship with Davis Colledge? The only certainty in all of that was that Theo Weekes would be admitting nothing more.

On the other hand, he reasoned, as he ran round the outer reaches of Gullane Golf Club's three courses, if he, McGuire, McIlhenney, Stevie Steele and everyone else involved in the investigation had been wrong about Ballester, if he was not the murderer of Stacey, Zrinka and the others, then they had been cleverly deceived. The evidence against him, the murder weapon, pictures and other trophies taken from the victims, had been found at his cottage. The photographs of the victims had been found in files on his computer. If he had not been guilty, he had been not only murdered but framed as a murderer. And who could have done that? Who had known of Ballester's hideaway?

Only one man: the man who, they knew beyond doubt, had killed Ballester in a fake suicide and had set the trap that had caught Steele. 'Dražen,' Skinner said. 'Dražen fucking Boras,' he shouted, as he pounded towards the high sand dunes that guarded the beach beyond.

Ballester had been a campaigning journalist, out to make a name for himself. He had been digging ruthlessly into the Boras empire, even cultivating Zrinka as a route to its secrets. Dražen and his father, Davor, had every reason to eliminate him. But that would mean, Skinner reasoned as he ran . . . that Dražen had killed his own sister. 'In that family,' he said aloud, to the morning breeze, 'who knows?'

He sprinted on, legs pumping hard as he climbed a grass-topped sand-hill, his stride lengthening as he plunged down the other side on to the curving beach, which stretched eastward for more than half a mile. It was isolated and deserted, as he had expected: the tide was less than full, and so he ran below the high-water mark for a better footing.

He was half-way along when his mobile rang in the pocket of his shorts and his hands-free headset buzzed in his ear. He reached up and pressed the receive button, slowing as he did so. 'Yes,' he said, breathing heavily.

'Jesus, Bob, have I interrupted something?' Amanda Dennis exclaimed.

'Nothing involving anyone else,' he replied, 'or otherwise embarrassing. I'm on the beach, trying to put myself in a decent mood for the rest of the day. Are you in Thames House already?'

'The state never sleeps, my boy. But the truth is, I don't like the London rush-hour. There's been a development; one of Adrian's feelers has had a response. Continental IT, Davor Boras's company, has made a booking for two nights, Tuesday and Wednesday, in the Hôtel de Paris, Monaco.'

'Very interesting.'

'There's an "and" that will make it even more so. They've booked not just one suite, but two, one of them with two bedrooms. No names provided, but you might surmise from it that Davor and his wife no longer sleep together and will be using the larger, and I'm sure you being you will make a wildly optimistic guess about the occupancy of the other.'

'Amanda,' said Skinner, 'you're a treasure beyond price.'

'You'd better believe it.'

'You know what? I've got some time on my hands this week, and my partner's gone back to running the nation. I think I might just fly south for a couple of days.'

Seventy-four

Lisanne was ready for work, ready to face the day, and whatever it held, and so was Jack McGurk. She took hold of his lapels, pulled him downwards to her and kissed him. 'Thanks,' she whispered.

'What for?'

'For being there for me when my life got turned on its head,' she replied. 'And especially for letting me stay here last night. I know he turned out to be a scumbag, but I was married to him, and I cared for him. He didn't deserve to die, and certainly not like that.'

'Nobody does, love.'

'Whoever killed him does,' she said bitterly. 'Well, thanks anyway.'

'Don't be daft. It's a funny thing . . . ill wind, I suppose . . . but a part of me will always be grateful to Theo. If it wasn't for him, I'd never have met you.'

Lisanne smiled. 'It's not such a big city, and you are a very large and visible guy. Maybe we'd have met anyway.'

'Around the singles bars? Through the *Scotsman* dating service? I don't know if I'd have gone down either of those routes.'

'Me neither: I'd be too scared.'

'Once bitten?'

She poked him in the chest. 'Depends who's biting me. No, I'm a very cautious person by nature.'

'I suppose I am too.'

'So why did we hit it off the way we did?'

'Possibly because we've both been through similar marriage

experiences.' He grinned. 'Or maybe the first time we met we had a shared inclination to rip each other's clothes off.'

'Could be.' She looked in the mirror, and adjusted the cravat that was part of her bank uniform. 'So where do we go from here, Jack? Is it "That was very nice. I'll see you around," or . . .'

'Is that what you want?'

'No. Until last night when I heard about Theo, that was the nicest weekend I've ever had in my life. I don't want it to stop.'

'Me neither. Do you want to come back here tonight?'

'It's tempting, but I don't think so. The longer I stay away from my place, the weirder it'll be when I go back there. See you later in the week, though?'

'How about Wednesday?'

'That'll do. Come to mine, about six, or whenever you can.'

'Six should be fine, as long as the inquiry doesn't go pear-shaped.' He paused. 'Which reminds me. There's something I need to ask you about Theo. His police personnel file still has you down as next of kin, but you're not any more.'

'No,' she said. 'That would be his mother, Minnie. She went back to the West Indies. She lives in Bridgetown, in Barbados.'

'Right. We'll need to contact her.'

'I've got an address for her, back at the flat. Her maiden name was Walcott, if that's any help.'

'The High Commission should be able to find her with that information. I'll call you tonight for the address, if I have to.' He slapped his forehead theatrically. 'What am I saying? I'll call you tonight anyway.'

'You'd better, my man. I'm not a girl to be fucked and chucked, you know.' The smile left her lips as quickly as it had appeared. 'Jack, this man the radio said was assisting with your enquiries: that was Inspector Varley, was it?'

'I guess so. Did you ever meet him?'

'Once, at a station do with Theo: he seemed like a nice guy.'

'They say he is, those who work with him. But I've known a few nice guys who are doing long prison sentences now.'

'I hope it isn't him. Theo messed his life up enough. I really don't want it to be him who killed him.'

'You and an entire police force, my dear,' said McGurk, sincerely.

Seventy-five

'If I hadn't been a police officer, would you have released me last night?' asked Inspector Varley.

'No, Jock,' said Detective Chief Superintendent Mario McGuire, solemnly. 'It wouldn't have made a blind bit of difference. The search of your house, your car and your office didn't yield any results, but you don't have to be a cop to know not to take a murder weapon home. Given twenty-four hours, you'd expect most people to do a pretty good job of destroying incriminating clothing too. I'd still have waited for the post-mortem report, and for the completion of testing of foreign DNA traces found on Weekes's body. As a matter of fact, those tests are still under way.'

'So I'm stuck here, a . . . a . . .' He stopped, lost for words.

'A victim of your own lack of caution might be a good way to put it,' Neil McIlhenney suggested. 'But you're not stuck here any longer, Inspector. We're releasing you.'

'What's made you see the light?'

'Professor Hutchinson, the pathologist who did the autopsy. He's completed his report, and we've just finished reading it. Old Joe doesn't prevaricate: when he gives you an opinion, it's one that he's prepared to defend in the witness box, under any level of hostile questioning. He says for sure that most of the wounds on the body could only have been inflicted by a left-handed man, including the one that ripped his neck open and put an end to him. I've just spoken to the doctor at the Western General who treated you when you broke your finger. He told me that it'll be another week or so before you can as much as pick your nose with your left paw. So you're no longer a suspect. You're free to go: we'll get a car to take you home.'

Varley leaned back and let out a huge sigh.

'Jock,' said McGuire, 'I hope you understand that the two of us are as relieved by this outcome as you are. Also, I'll admit that while we might have gone on about you being reckless when you went bombing after Weekes, neither one of us would have done any different in the same circumstances. Truth is, I wouldn't have been as restrained as you, and I say that from experience. When I was married, a toe-rag cut my wife when she went to arrest him, slashed her arm. Nuff said. No hard feelings, I hope.'

The inspector shook his head. 'None, sir. Now it's sorted and I can look at it a wee bit less nervously, you did what you had to, both of you.'

'Thanks for that. Jock, now that you're no longer a suspect, you've become a witness. The PM report puts time of death more or less when you were there, so there's a chance that you might actually have seen the killer, either hanging about or on his way there, as you were leaving. Think back; can you help us?'

'To tell you the truth,' said Varley, 'when I left there, all I saw was red. The Auchendinny Ladies' Flute Band could have been marching naked down the street and it wouldn't have registered. One thing, though. Last night you asked me about the back door: I've been thinking about that, and I'm pretty sure now that it was open.'

'So it's possible that while you were giving Theo the heavy message, his attacker could have been waiting at the rear of the house?'

'Entirely. Have you got any other suspects in the queue?'

'None of the obvious ones,' McIlhenney told him. 'The next stage will be to interview his work colleagues and friends.'

'You can cut that in half,' the inspector replied. 'From what I remember of PC Weekes when he was at Livingston, he didn't have any friends. He was a real outsider. Maybe it had something to do with his colour, but I don't really think so. I reckon it was just the way he was.'

Seventy-six

'If you're going to do that, Bob, won't you need support?' Aileen asked. 'Do we have an embassy there?'

He was barefoot, but otherwise still in his running gear, glistening from his exercise as they stood in the hall. 'No,' he replied, 'but there's an honorary consul, a government-appointed back-watcher. I've already spoken to him and told him I'm coming on to his patch, and that I want to see him as soon as possible.'

'But what can you do on your own?'

'I won't be alone. I'm taking somebody with me. I've just spoken to Ruth, my secretary, and told her to get us both on to this afternoon's Globespan flight from Edinburgh to Nice. I'm sorry about the short notice, love, but I only got this information this morning.'

'Where are you going to stay?'

'There's a hotel called the Columbus next to the helipad. I've asked her to book us in there. I'm sorry to leave you on your own for the next few nights, but this is something I have to do.'

'I know you have, for Maggie's sake . . . just as long as it isn't her you're taking with you.'

He laughed. 'Worry not. But this isn't just about Maggie. Part of it's about me as well, especially after the phone call I've just had from Andy. He, or rather his talented ex-cop wife, has come up with a theory. He'll need to take medical advice to confirm it, but if it stands up, it changes everything. It makes this trip I'm taking all the more important.'

347

'Then off you go, my sweaty old darling, and get yourself ready for it. Tell me the whole story as soon as you can, but I can't keep my driver waiting any longer. Don't worry about me being here alone. I'll probably stay at the residence while you're away. Yes,' she said firmly, 'I'll do that and I'll invite Alex for dinner one evening, just to make sure she's all right after her emotional explosion yesterday.'

'Good idea. With all that happened, we never got round to telling her she's going to have a new stepmother. You can let her in on the secret.'

She gasped. 'Sometimes you live in your own wee world. That is down to you and nobody else. See you soon.' She kissed him and walked out to the government car that waited for her in the drive.

Left alone, he trotted upstairs to his bathroom, where he stripped off his T-shirt and shorts and stepped into the shower. He set the temperature at cool and the control to power jet, then allowed the water to pound him, turning slowly as it massaged his body. He was smiling, fuelled by the thought that he was about to become a participant in events, rather than the mere spectator he had been for most of the previous week, and more.

He stayed under the spray for almost ten minutes, then towelled himself vigorously until he was almost dry. He was in the middle of shaving, thinking of how much he would miss Aileen for the next few days, when his mobile sounded on the surface beside the inset basin. He scowled at it, but laid down his razor, picked it up and said, 'Yes?'

'Is that Mr Skinner?' a voice enquired, a young voice, a voice he did not know.

'Yes, it is. Who is this, and how did you get this number?' he asked, ready to savage the caller if he was yet another salesman trying to induce him to switch networks.

'You left it for me. My name is Davis Colledge.'

Skinner's back straightened involuntarily, causing the towel to slip from round his waist and fall to the floor. 'Davis?' he repeated. 'Where are you?'

'I'm in Collioure,' the young man told him. 'I've just got back from a trip and I found your card and your note waiting for me. What is it? Is this about Sugar?'

'Why did you go away?'

'I was angry with her. She stood me up. She was supposed to join me but she never turned up. She switched off her mobile. And I couldn't get an answer from her parents' place. Finally I decided that I'd bugger off out of there, so that if she did arrive, eventually, she could have some of what I'd been through. That's why I left my mobile behind, so she'd know she couldn't find me, and that she'd just have to sit and wait for me for a change. And that's why I painted her face out of that picture you must have seen if you were here. It was me saying, "Fuck you," to her.'

'Not the most mature reaction,' said Skinner, 'but never mind. What made you think she would stand you up?'

'She'd said she would sleep with me when we got to France. I knew that was her way of backing out, and I was right. She's still not here.'

'Backing out? I've seen your painting, son. You got her appendix scar right.'

'She posed for me back in Edinburgh, but that was all. She was my girlfriend, but she said she couldn't have sex with me until I'd left school.'

'Where did you go when you left Collioure?'

'Listen,' the youth interrupted, 'can I ask you something?'

'Not yet,' said Skinner sternly. 'You'll answer my questions first.'

'I hitch-hiked down into Spain and then I got a flight to Holland.'

'Where did you go in Spain?'

'Girona. That's where I got the plane.'

'Did you go anywhere near a place called L'Escala?'

'Where? No. Never heard of it.'

'Why did you go to Holland?'

'I decided to go to Amsterdam; there are plenty of women there.'

'From what I remember, most of them are old enough to be your mother.'

'They're clean, though. My dad told me.'

Skinner filed that statement away. 'So,' he said, 'you went to Holland to get laid. Then what?'

'Then I came back down here, and Sugar's still not here. But what's all this about, sir? Why were you here looking for me?'

'Sugar's not coming, son. Sugar's dead. Her body was found last Monday in Edinburgh. It happened on her way to school, on the last day of term.'

There was silence, then the sound of sobbing. 'She's dead?' Davis Colledge said indistinctly, through his tears. 'How?' he asked. 'Was it an accident?'

'No, she was shot. We're treating it as murder.'

'Who did it? Who'd want to hurt Sugar?'

'You've just told me you did.'

'But I was angry with her,' he protested, 'and I wouldn't hurt her like that. Have you? Have you caught anybody?'

'Not yet. We're hoping you can help us with that. We'll need to interview you, Davis, about Sugar, about the nature of your relationship and about anyone she might have mentioned, anyone who might have had a grudge against her.'

'Yes, sir, of course. But I can't think of anyone.'

'You haven't had time to think at all.'

'What will I do?' the young man asked.

'First, I want you to call your father. Then you need to go to the local gendarmerie and tell them that you've returned. They'll take you to Perpignan airport and put you on the first plane home. My people will contact your dad and arrange for him to meet your plane, and bring you up to Edinburgh to see them. Do you understand all that?'

'Yes, sir. Mr Skinner, this is all a joke, isn't it?'

'Am I laughing?'

Skinner ended the call. He stepped into the bedroom, and searched through his data organiser for the number of Lieutenant Cerdan. Happily, he was in his office. 'Lieutenant,' he said, 'the boy has surfaced. He's back at the studio and he's just rung me. I told him to report to your local office, but to be on the safe side, I think you should go to him now.'

'I agree, sir,' the Frenchman replied. 'We do not want to have to chase him all over again. I will send my men at once.'

'Thanks. Once you've done that, I'd be grateful if you could spare some more resources in Collioure. There's something I'd like checked out.'

Two minutes later, the conversation over, he returned to his interrupted shave, starting again from scratch on the side of his face that was still rough. Once again, his mind wandered as he gazed into the mirror, as he thought of his situation, the morning's development and the stalemate he was trying to break.

As he did, a slow smile spread across the face he could see in the glass.

He finished, still beaming, then rubbed his jaw and top lip with the baby lotion that he always used, to Aileen's great amusement, as after-shave balm. That done, he dressed casually for a journey then packed a small suitcase with clothes sufficient for three days.

Only when that was done did he pick up his mobile once more and ring McIlhenney. When they were connected, he told him about his surprise call, and asked him to contact Michael Colledge as soon as possible.

'Will do,' said the detective superintendent. 'And I'll brief the team. Anything else, boss?'

'As a matter of fact,' Skinner replied, 'there is. I've just had a weird idea. It's complicated, and you'll need to move very fast, but if you can put all the pieces together, this is what I'd like you to do.'

Seventy-seven

'Any news of Inspector Varley?' asked Jack McGurk, as Becky Stallings stepped out of her cubicle and into the CID general office in Torphichen Place.

'He's in the clear,' she told him.

The detective sergeant's eyebrows rose. 'Is he indeed? I shouldn't admit it, but while most of me is pleased to hear that, there's a small piece that's saying, "Bugger it, there goes our speedy clear-up." I must admit, I thought he was four square in the frame for it. What was his story?'

'He went along to tear a strip off Weekes for naming his wife, nothing more. When he left, he was alive.'

'Run that past me again, boss. He knew about Weekes spilling the beans about his wife?'

'I asked the same question. Superintendent McIlhenney was less than forthcoming about it. He told me, very politely, not to take it any further.'

'Somebody's in the shit, then.'

'I imagine so. Any unexpected personnel moves should give us a clue. Meanwhile . . .'

'Excuse me, ma'am,' Sauce Haddock called from across the room. 'I've just taken a call from Gayfield Square. They've got something there they think might interest us.'

'What?'

'A pale blue T-shirt. It was handed in by a cleansing worker. He found it stuffed in a dustbin in George Street when he was emptying it.'

'And?'

'And it's got blood all over it. Could be it's related to another incident, but the Gayfield people don't have anything on their books that fits the bill.'

'Is there a bar code on it?'

'No. All the labels have been cut off.'

'Call them back. Tell them to bag it and . . .' She stopped when she saw the detective constable nod.

'I have done, ma'am. It's on its way to the lab for analysis.'

Seventy-eight

She stared at them resentfully. 'This isn't fair,' Detective Constable Alice Cowan declared. 'I've been in my job for a while now, long enough to have worked for both of you. Doesn't that count for anything?'

'In this situation,' DCS Mario McGuire told her, 'fairness takes a back seat. We like you, Alice, both of us; we know you're a good officer. But there can't be any second chances in Special Branch.'

'Forgive me, sir, but does SB report to you? As I understand it DI Shannon's immediate line manager is the deputy chief constable.'

'Like Mr McGuire said,' Neil McIlhenney replied, 'you're good; you've got the reporting chain right. But give us a bit of credit too; DCC Skinner's been consulted about this, and he's delegated authority to act. Sure, you can ask for a personal hearing with him when he comes back, but whose carpet would you rather be on, Detective Constable, this one or his?'

McGuire smiled. 'Trust us, Alice, that's a no-brainer. Be honest with yourself: you can see the situation. You passed on sensitive information about an inquiry to somebody who was one of its subjects. It was your uncle, sure, he's a serving police officer, sure. You weren't to know that he'd do something reckless and inappropriate with that knowledge and land the pair of you in deep shit. But none of that is a mitigating factor, given the sensitivity of what your department does on a day-to-day basis. You've got to be moved out of there, and that's that. No appeal.'

The sturdy woman's eyes misted over; she chewed a corner of her bottom lip. 'I'm sorry,' she said quietly. 'I should have known better. What happens to me?'

'In career terms, nothing,' the head of CID told her. 'Do you think we're complete bastards? As you said, you've been in that job for a while. It was time for you to be moved out anyway. Officially that's what's going to happen; a routine move. You're going to be replaced by DC Tarvil Singh, from the Leith office. That's where you're going; it'll be a straight swap.'

Cowan brightened up almost instantly. 'Will that be working for DI Pye?' she asked.

'Yes,' said McGuire, 'and DS Wilding. But first, there's something else we'd like you to consider. It's a sensitive task; you should take that as a sign of our continuing faith in you. Although you'll be under observation all the time, there will be a degree of personal risk, so it would be entirely voluntary. If you turn it down, there will be no blame, no pointing fingers.'

The detective constable looked up at him, clear-eyed once again. 'Tell me about it,' she said.

'I've got a plane to catch,' he replied, rising from his chair, 'but it's Mr McIlhenney's operation. I'll leave him to run you through it.'

Seventy-nine

'That's us.' Becky Stallings looked at her watch. 'We're twenty-four hours into the Theo Weekes homicide investigation. One week since the Sugar Dean murder. And what have we achieved?'

'That depends on how you want to look at it,' her sergeant answered. 'We've eliminated all the immediate potential suspects; now we can concentrate on the rest.'

'Jack,' she said, 'we haven't worked together long, but already I know what I like about you. You don't seem to buy negativity. You're like those Man U supporters who used to sing "Always Look on the Bright Side of Life" to the opposition supporters, as their team was being thumped.'

'You're not a Red, are you?' he asked her.

'Hell, no! I'm an East End girl, a Hammer through and through. That's why I've got a tendency towards the pessimistic. The way I see it, "the rest" of the suspects means the whole bloody world. It was bad enough running one investigation into the buffers, but two! "Stallings by name, stalling by nature," my male colleagues in London used to say, whenever I got into a bind. It'll be spreading up here soon.'

'Not around me it won't. You're a bloody good detective, boss. But you're wrong in your analysis, as far as the Weekes investigation goes at any rate: it's much narrower than that. We're looking for a male; that takes half the population out of the frame. Kick out the elderly and children, and that knocks it down to a quarter. We're looking for someone who's powerful, and able to overcome a big man like Theo.

That's us down to about five per cent. Finally, we're looking for a left-hander. So we're not trawling through the entire population: less than one in a hundred fit all those criteria. Now, this wasn't a random killing: the guy was sought out and executed. If we take what we know and look at every person who knew the victim, his killer should be staring us in the face.'

'You know what that means, don't you?' Stallings asked.

'I'm afraid so. It's more bad news for the police force. We'll have to interview every officer who's ever worked with Weekes, or even been in the same station.'

'No, Jack, not all of them, just the southpaws.'

'True. But I don't suppose that detail's on the HR files, is it?'

'There was nothing about it on my transfer form.'

'Excuse me, ma'am.' Stallings and McGurk both turned and looked across at DC Haddock.

'Yes, Sauce?'

'I heard what you and the sarge were saying,' he began. 'Isn't it possible that whoever killed PC Weekes might have had a heavy-duty grudge against him, without actually knowing him all that well, at least?'

'Anybody in mind?'

'Well, we know it wasn't Sugar Dean's dad, but what about PC Grey? Does she have a father, and is he left-handed? And then there's the ex-wife. Are her parents still alive and well?'

'That's a good point, Sauce, but we weren't actually going to confine the trawl to police officers, were we, Jack?'

Silence.

'Jack?' she repeated.

Still there was no response. McGurk was somewhere else, staring at the wall.

Eighty

Lena McElhone, the First Minister's private secretary, was happy again. During her boss's absence on holiday, the deputy First Minister had been in charge of Scottish affairs, and Lena did not trust him to find his way to the toilet unaided, much less to take important decisions.

Consequently, she had hidden the more important submissions and correspondence from him, even though several were stamped 'Urgent' in red, risking complaints about delay from people who were considerably senior to her in the civil-service hierarchy, but fielding them firmly when they arose.

Although Aileen had noted that her blue box was full to overflowing when it was delivered to Gullane at the weekend, she had not been surprised. The deputy First Minister was a political necessity, forced upon her by the electorate, but she and Lena were agreed that he should never be allowed to do any damage.

She had worked all morning in her St Andrews House office to clear the backlog, sending back the red-letter submissions, with decisions rendered, and had spent much of the afternoon in a catch-up meeting with the Permanent Secretary, her most senior civil servant, but eventually she was finished. She pressed a button on her desk console; less than a minute later the massive door opened and Lena stepped into the room, a folder in her arms.

'More?' she complained.

'Diary stuff, First Minister, that's all. The usual raft of official invitations to events.'

'Such as?'

'Hibernian Football Club want you to unfurl the league championship flag at the start of the new season.'

'No danger. I'd upset half my voters.'

'I thought you'd say that. Delegate to the sports minister?'

'Yes.'

'I thought you'd say that too, so I warned him. Next, there's an invitation from Scottish Opera to a performance of *Tristan and Isolde*. That's in October, in the Festival Theatre. Does Bob like opera?'

'Bob likes most music, except Wagner. Have you any idea how long *Tristan and* bloody *Isolde* lasts? Going on for six hours, and I couldn't dare fall asleep, or it would be all over the gossip columns. That one's for the arts minister.'

'Very good,' said Lena. 'I thought I'd give her this last one too. It's only just come in and it's very short notice, next Tuesday. It's an art exhibition, in a new gallery down in Home Street. It's of work by a Scottish-born painter, just back from the US; she studied there and exhibited in New York and Washington. Her name's Caitlin Summers. Her agent says that if you'll agree to open her show it'll help him make a big splash in the press and get her the attention she deserves. She's very new on our scene, though, not really your weight.'

Aileen smiled. 'My weight, is it? I put on a couple of pounds on holiday, but I hoped it wasn't that obvious. What the hell? I can't be turning everything down. Tell them I'll do it. What else is there?'

'That's it, boss. The rest is pure gossip.'

'You'd better pour us a drink, then. There's some white wine in the cold cabinet. In fact, do you fancy eating somewhere quiet a bit later on? I'm a single woman for the next few nights.'

'That would be good. Just like old times.'

Aileen watched as her assistant drew the cork from a bottle of Cloudy Bay. 'What's the goss, then?' she asked.

'Fresh from the Crown Office,' Lena replied, as she handed her a glass. 'The Lord Advocate called to tip you off before it breaks in the media. It's a bit of a misfortune for the police in Dundee, where Bob's pal's the deputy. They have a big drugs case in the works. The man they've got for it is being tried for murder first, but they had this as a back-up. There was a big row when you were away: they were ready to begin the murder trial last week, but the Crown forgot to get the accused to the court. The judge gave them pelters.'

'No wonder. So, what have the police cocked up?'

'They've lost the evidence in the drugs case, a serious amount of heroin and cocaine. It's gone missing, assumed stolen from the evidence store in the Tayside Police headquarters. The Lord Advocate said the Crown Agent nearly split his sides laughing when he heard about it.'

'I'm not surprised,' said Aileen, 'and I know why. You tell the Lord Advocate from me that if Mr Dowley does any side-splitting in public, I will ask Sir James Proud to send me a copy of a so-far confidential report he has sitting in his office, with a view to disciplinary proceedings. We'll see if the so-and-so finds that funny.'

Eighty-one

'But where does it take us, Jack?'

'I don't know, boss,' said McGurk, 'but it's interesting, is it not? It's enough for me to take another look at stuff we put away earlier, looking for long shots.'

'You do that; meanwhile I'll start compiling a list of male officers who've crossed paths with Theo over the years. Sauce is already looking into Mae Grey's family background. We know she still has a mum, because she mentioned her, so chances are there's a dad as well, and given that she's mid-twenties, he needn't be old and decrepit.'

'I hope he thinks to check on any brothers as well.'

'I've told him to. You sure Lisanne doesn't have any?'

'She told me she's an only child, and that her mother's a widow.'

'Okay,' said Stallings, as her phone rang, making a mental note to check anyway. She picked it up.

'Inspector,' a firm voice said, 'Arthur Dorward, bearer of positive tidings.'

'About what?'

'That shirt your lad had sent across from Gayfield. I haven't had time to do any definitive tests yet, but I'm pretty confident it was dumped by the guy you're after. I've analysed the blood that was soaked into it and it's A negative, the same as your victim's.'

'But how many . . .'

'Would you like to hear the odds? Seven per cent of the population have A negative blood, so it's thirteen to one on that it's his. I'll be able to tell you for certain once the DNA testing's complete.'

'Thanks, Arthur,' said Stallings. 'That's a step forward: it tells us where the killer went after the murder. It's a pity it doesn't tell us any more about him, though.'

'Don't you be so sure. This man might be thinking he was clever cutting the labels off, but if he'd really been smart he'd have turned it inside out and removed his personal traces as well. When my people had a good look, they found four oxter hairs.'

'What?'

'Ah, sorry, Inspector. I forgot to make allowance for your Englishness. Oxters would be armpits to you. Three of the hairs have roots, which means they can be used for testing. Find me the guy, and I'll prove he wore this shirt when he killed PC Weekes.'

Eighty-two

Her Majesty's Honorary Consul in Monaco was not used to evening visits from British police officers, bearing copies of international warrants. Looking at the nervous little man, Skinner was not sure that he was used to anything disturbing his sunny days.

He was an expatriate named James Major, who maintained a small law office on the second floor of a building in rue des Orangers, not far from the port. The official crest above his nameplate at street level implied grander surroundings than those in which the Scot stood.

'What is it you're telling me?' Major asked.

'There's a man we've been after,' Skinner replied, 'in connection with the death of a colleague of mine. He disappeared a few months ago. Since then we believe he's found himself a new identity. His parents are flying down here tomorrow: we're not certain, but we believe there's a chance that he'll show up here to meet them. If he does, I'm having him.'

'Why are you telling me? This is a police matter.'

'I'll be meeting them in the morning. I'm talking to you to warn you that later this week, you could have a British citizen in jail here awaiting extradition. That will definitely be a Foreign Office matter. Unless I'm mistaken, in this part of the world, that means you.'

'Extradition's way beyond my remit,' the man spluttered. 'I'll need to take advice from the consulate in Marseille.'

'You can take advice from the Foreign Secretary's mistress for all I care. If this man turns up here, I want him back in Britain as soon as possible after his identity is confirmed.'

'Are you sure you have the authority to do this?' asked Major, officiously.

Skinner stared at him. 'Am I what?' he whispered.

It dawned on the honorary consul that he might have drifted into dangerous waters. 'It is rather off your beat, that's all.'

'Sunshine, this man killed one of my officers, someone I've known all through his career, someone I considered a friend. In his pursuit, there is nowhere, absolutely nowhere, that is off my beat.'

Eighty-three

'Do you have anything planned for tonight?' Becky Stallings asked.

McGurk smiled. 'Do you mean, am I seeing Lisanne? If so, the answer's no.'

'Cooling off, or just getting your breath back?'

'The latter, I hope. It's taken us both by surprise.'

'Have you spoken to Mary about it? I know your separation's been friendly so far: you want to make sure it stays that way.'

The sergeant gave her a curious look. 'Are you speaking from experience?'

'Yes,' she admitted. 'I don't talk about it very often, but I was married once; it ended twelve years ago.'

'What happened?'

'Your story in reverse; it was him that couldn't stand the job. I nearly gave it up for him, but at the last minute I decided that I'd rather give him up for it. We agreed that it was best for us to go our own ways, and we separated formally. We were the best of pals for a while, and then it all went tits up.'

'You went out with someone else and he threw a moody?'

Stallings shook her head. 'Entirely wrong. He got himself a new girlfriend, about six months down the line. When he told me that he was in love with somebody else and planning to marry her when he was free, I just blew up in his face. I took myself completely by surprise: I didn't want the guy, and yet I was jealous as hell. We barely spoke after that, and I haven't seen him or heard from him since the divorce went through. No Christmas cards, nothing: he could be dead.'

'And if he was?'

'Now? I wouldn't care. Eventually I worked out why I reacted as I did. He had a new relationship going, but nobody had given me as much as a look. It kicked me right in the self-esteem. I went without for three years after that, mainly because I didn't think there was any point in going out looking. So you be careful with your ex, Jack, if you want to keep her as a long-term friend.'

'Thanks for the advice, Becky. If Lisanne and I do get serious, I'll break it to her gently. But I think she'll be all right. Last time I visited her, to pick up some stuff I'd made room for at my place, I had a headache and went looking in the bathroom cabinet for paracetamol. Didn't find any, but there was a not-quite-new Gillette Fusion razor in there, and a can of shaving foam.'

'What did you do?'

He grinned. 'I was needing a shave at the time, so I had one.'

'God, did she notice?'

'Oh, yes. She blushed bright red, we had a laugh, and I wished her all the best. What about Ray? Does he know about your past?'

'Yes, we had a tell-all session early on. Fancy a pint with us? I'm meeting him in Ryrie's Bar.'

'I'll pass. There's something I want to go back over.'

'Okay. Mind if I go ahead?'

'As if I could.'

She picked up her bag and headed for the door. McGurk waved her on her way, then picked up a videotape from his desk and walked over to the player. He was about to plug in the cassette when the phone rang. He picked it up: 'CID, Detective Sergeant McGurk.'

'Sergeant,' said a clipped, cultured voice, 'I'm glad I've caught somebody. This is Michael Colledge. I'm at Stansted Airport where I've just met my son. I've been told that you need to interview him. I understand that, but poor old Dave's still shocked, having only just found out about Sugar. I propose to take him home with me tonight, and bring him up to see you tomorrow.'

'That's fine, sir.'

'We'll catch the midday shuttle. Should be with you about two, if you tell me where we should come.'

'We'll send a car for you, Mr Colledge.'

'Not blue lights, I trust.'

'No,' McGurk assured him, 'we'll be discreet. Sir, the interview's no more than a necessary formality, but would your son like legal representation?'

The Shadow Defence Secretary chuckled. 'I'm a QC, Sergeant. I think I can fill that role myself.'

Eighty-four

The small piece of Margaret Rose Steele's soul that remained incurably romantic was disappointed. When Bob Skinner had told her of Adrian St John's discoveries, and of Davor Boras's interesting trip to Monaco, she had seen herself flying south in the seat next to the DCC, headed for a confrontation that she had done much to create.

The rest of her, the greater part of her that a lifetime of personal tragedy had made dourly realistic, knew that she could go nowhere near it. She was recovering from major surgery, she had a child to look after, but most of all, she could not rely upon her self-control if their quarry was run to ground.

So she sat at home in Gordon Terrace and fretted. Bob had called her, as he had promised, reporting that he had put the honorary consul on standby, and that Mario McGuire had met with the commander of the Monégasque police, to advise him of their presence and of their purpose. She had been encouraged, and yet she had sensed that somehow he was less certain, less confident than he had been that morning.

With Stephanie fed and readied for the night, she held her in her lap and picked up the television remote. She joined a holiday programme half-way through, watching a package on Jamaica, but imagining Monaco instead.

It was almost over when the telephone rang. Bet had gone out to meet an old school friend, so she laid the baby in her cot and picked it up.

'Maggie?' Maurice Goode's voice was unusually hesitant. 'Sorry about the hour. It's for a colleague again; this time it's the guy who took over my old job. I might as well go back on the crime desk. That bastard doesn't seem to have a single reliable contact.'

'I think I prefer you where you are, Mo,' she told him. 'You can do less damage there. What is it? Another highly placed source claiming to know who blew up Lord Darnley?'

'This isn't a source. It's an anonymous tip-off.'

'You know how much they're worth.'

'That's exactly what I said, but the editor wants it checked out because of what the caller said. I told them to take it to the force press officer, but the boss said that if it was true Royston wouldn't admit it. The informant's claiming that Bob Skinner's been suspended from duty, and that he's under investigation.'

Maggie gasped. 'That's all bollocks,' she snapped. 'I've spoken to Bob twice today. I know exactly where he is, and I know exactly what he's doing . . . and before you ask, I'm not going to tell you. But, believe me, he is on police business.'

'You're certain?'

'You calling me a liar?'

'Sorry, Maggie, of course not.'

'Just as well. You go back to your editor and your colleague and tell them they've been had. Tell them this too. You know Bob's daughter?'

'Not personally, but I've heard of her.'

'In that case you'll know she's a lawyer, with the biggest firm in town. If you or anyone else runs that story, you'll find out how she reacts when anyone has a go at her dad.'

Eighty-five

'**D**o you think we'll be in trouble with the Northumbria force for this,' asked Mario McGuire, seated opposite Skinner in a restaurant in the place des Armes, 'since Stevie died on their patch? Not that I give a damn if we are, you understand.'

'Only,' the DCC replied, 'if Les Cairns and his chief want to get involved in a public row that'll very quickly focus on their failure to achieve in three months what our Maggie did in three days, armed with no more than a phone and a computer. But if they do kick up a fuss, I reckon we're on pretty solid ground. He was one of our officers, killed in the line of duty. As far as I'm concerned, that gives me the right to investigate his death, regardless of where it happened, and to pursue suspects as far as we have to. I ran that thinking past Gregor before we left and he agrees with me.'

'Did you tell him where we were going?'

'No, the fewer people who know that the better. If word got to that bastard Dowley, you never know what he'd do, especially after what Aileen told me when I spoke to her five minutes ago. Someone's nicked a drug haul from the evidence store in Dundee. He was going to have a ball with it, until she told the Lord Advocate to stop him.'

'Revenge on Andy?'

'What else? Aileen was talking about firing him, but I persuaded her to back off. Instead the Lord Advocate's going to give him a lecture about pissing in the right direction from now on. If that doesn't work, he'll wind up on the bench in Stranraer Sheriff Court.'

He stopped as a waiter approached to take their orders. Skinner had just chosen a focaccio when his mobile sounded. They were seated in an archway, in the shadow of Monaco's great rock, and so he walked away from the table to take the call, in search of a stronger signal.

'Boss?' McIlhenney's voice was staccato, but understandable. 'You need to hear this. I've just had a call from Mags.' He relayed the story of Maurice Goode's approach, and of the way in which it had been dismissed. 'What's all that about?' the superintendent asked.

'How many enemies have I got, Neil? Tell Andy about it, and make sure that anybody else who asks that question gets the same response. You'd better brief Alex too, just in case somebody's silly enough to run it tomorrow. If that happens, I will want her involved. Apart from that, fuck it. Thanks for letting me know.'

He replaced his phone in his trouser pocket and rejoined McGuire. 'Routine,' he announced, picking up his beer.

'So we're all set for tomorrow,' said the head of CID. 'Do you think he'll show?'

'Let's hope so,' Skinner replied. 'It's a gamble, us coming here, but it's one we had to take.'

'On emotional grounds?'

'Operational. Let's keep emotions out of this. All the same,' he admitted, 'I wish I was more certain. There's something about the whole equation that doesn't sit quite right, just a small piece that's out of place. I wish to hell I could spot it.'

Eighty-six

'Morning, boss,' Jack McGurk called out from his desk, as Becky Stallings walked into the CID room.

She stared at him: his clothes were crumpled, and familiar, and a shadow showed on his chin. 'Have you been here all night?'

'Yup,' he replied, 'but not awake, not all the time at any rate. I had a kip in one of the cells. Not too bad, actually; it felt strange, not having my feet hanging over the edge.'

'Are you trying to ramp up the overtime?'

'No, just trying to fit some pieces together. Before I forget, we had a call last night from Mr Colledge, MP. He's been reunited with his tearful son: they're flying up at lunchtime. I said we'd send an unmarked car to meet them at the airport.'

'Have we got an unmarked car?'

'I can dig one up if you want, but I thought . . .'

'You're right,' said the inspector. 'I should pick them up myself. It might help the boy's memory if he sees that he and his dad are getting VIP treatment.'

He followed her into her small office. 'I'll come with you. I've never met a shadow defence secretary before.'

'How did he sound when he called?'

'Co-operative, and more than a bit relieved to have his son back home.'

Stallings smiled, as she threw a copy of the *Scotsman* on to her desk and hung up her jacket. 'I wonder if young Dave's told him the story of his trip to Holland yet. He thought his squeeze had changed her mind so he went to the most famous red-light district in Europe to get his ashes hauled. Boys will be boys.'

'And that's all this one is, too; just a kid, for all he's a big lad.' He picked up the newspaper and glanced at the front page. 'What the hell's this?' he exclaimed, holding it up for her to see.

'What? "Returning Artist Gets First Minister Plaudit"? Caitlin Summers? Never heard of her, but she must be good if Aileen de Marco's endorsing her.'

'No, not that.' McGurk straightened the paper, so that she could see the lead story.

She blinked at the banner headline. 'Jesus. "Red Faces for Tayside Cops. Who Let the Drugs Out?" Blimey, that's a warning to us all. Someone's nuts are in the wringer, for being that careless.'

'If it's carelessness,' the sergeant murmured, as he read the story. 'The biggest hoodlum in Dundee's going to be the beneficiary of this. They've got him on a twenty-year-old murder charge, but he'd probably have got longer inside for the drugs.'

'You think somebody's been bunged? I didn't think that happened in Scotland. I thought you were all too tight with the bawbees.'

'Why go to the expense of a bribe, when a simple threat to chuck acid in someone's wife's face is just as effective?'

'Either way,' Stallings pointed out, 'it'll get the media off our backs for a day or so. Their pain, our gain.' She looked at McGurk. 'If you're coming to the airport with me, a wash, a shave and a change of clothes won't do any harm. Nip off home for a couple of hours.'

'Be sure,' he told her, 'that's on my agenda. But before I go, come back through here and take a look at what I've been doing for most of the night. Once you've seen what I've found, I don't think you'll have any problem signing my overtime claim.'

Eighty-seven

'This couldn't have happened at a worse time,' said Skinner.

'Would there have been a good time?' asked Andy Martin.

'Of course not. Sorry, Andy, that was a thoroughly selfish thing to say. You've got to stay in Dundee, no question. My apologies to Graham Morton for depriving him of your presence when it was obviously needed.'

'I can't see that my presence would have prevented what's happened, but I'll know better when I've had a look at the situation. It could be that my chief will be asking yours to return the favour, by sending us somebody to do an outside investigation job.'

'I'd come myself, if he asked, but it might not be the time. Have you heard what happened last night?'

'The anonymous call? Yes, Neil rang to let me know. Maggie seems to have nipped it in the bud, though.'

'So far, but I wish to Christ I had access to the *Scotsman*'s telephone records, to see if the call could be traced to its source.'

'Fat chance of that. There are still some working phone boxes.'

'Yes, I suppose. It didn't exactly make my night, though.'

'Think positive, man.'

'Help me.'

'The call is proof that someone's setting you up, to embarrass you at the very least. There's half a dozen people within your set-up who could know of the link between you and these murders, and I guarantee you it's none of them.'

'Dowley?'

'Dowley is an insecure, arrogant son-of-a-bitch with an apparent down on the police, but he isn't professionally suicidal. No, I reckon the guy who made that call has the blood of at least five people on his hands. I can't see how he could have done the sixth, but let's leave that aside. I wasn't sitting on my hands yesterday. I had a consultant look at the full autopsy report on Ballester, and I asked Prof. Hutchinson for an opinion as well. They both agreed that the condition from which the man suffered would have meant he couldn't have hit a bull on the arse with a banjo, far less hit a moving target with a hand-gun. Old Joe told me that if he'd done the PM, he'd have told you that straight away.'

'Magic,' said Skinner. 'Have we got egg on our faces, or what?'

'Less than you think. You found the gun, the trophies, a shed-load of evidence that pointed straight at Ballester. I'd have written it up exactly as you did. What I'm seeing is that Dražen Boras planted it all, that he's your killer, and that he's still out there. You exposed Ballester's death as murder, not suicide. You came within an arse-hair of catching Dražen in London. Now he's on the run, with a big down on you. My money's on him as last night's mystery caller.'

Although it was afternoon in Monaco, and although it was a cloudless day, a light came on in Skinner's brain, so bright that it almost blinded him. 'Fuck!' he whispered. 'That's a very sound theory, Andy,' he said, 'but you forgot a couple of things.'

'What?'

'I'll tell you after I've spoken to a bloke called Ignacio Riesgo.'

'Who the hell's he?'

'Tell you later. I've got to go now. Things are happening.'

'Bob, where the hell are you?'

'Right at this moment I'm in a café outside the Monte Carlo casino. Can't you hear the seagulls?' He snapped the phone shut and concentrated his attention on what was happening across the concourse on the driveway in front of the Hôtel de Paris.

Two people had emerged from a white stretch limo: a blonde

woman, elegant, slim, middle-aged, and a stocky, balding man, with powerful shoulders and a hook nose. 'Hello again, Davor and Sanda,' Mario McGuire muttered. As two porters descended on the boot of the vehicle, a third person, another man, emerged from the front passenger seat, wearing a pilot's uniform and carrying a briefcase. He trotted around the car and fell into step behind the couple as they walked into the hotel.

McGuire started to rise from his chair, but Skinner stopped him with a hand on his forearm. 'Let them check in,' he said. 'Our contact inside will tell us when they've gone upstairs.' His mood seemed to have changed completely. 'I know what'll happen next.' He sighed.

They waited at their table for ten minutes, until the DCC's phone emitted its 'text received' signal. He flipped it open and read. 'It's clear,' he announced, standing and striding off without a glance at his companion.

A woman was waiting for them in the doorway; she wore the Hôtel de Paris livery, but they knew she was no receptionist. Inspecteur Rosalie Gramercy was their Monégasque police liaison, assigned to them that morning by her commanding officer.

'They have registered,' she said. 'I handled the paperwork and saw all the passports. Monsieur and Madame Boras, and their pilot, Captain Ross Wallace. He is occupying the single suite.'

'That's it,' Skinner exclaimed, 'the piece of the jigsaw that didn't fit. The rooms were booked by Continental IT: the reservation is subject to scrutiny by the company's auditors, and Dražen has bugger-all to do with it. They're probably down here for a couple of days at the tables.'

'No.' The Scots looked at their escort as she spoke. 'There is a reception tomorrow evening in the Hôtel Hermitage, given by the presidency of the republic of Bosnia and Herzegovina. They are the principal guests.'

'How do you know this?'

The *inspecteur* smiled. 'Madame Boras told me. I asked her why they were visiting. She is a pleasant lady.'

'And tougher than she looks,' McGuire murmured. 'She wouldn't let Davor go off to be fêted all on his own.'

'No,' said Skinner, 'and she wouldn't write off her son for the rest of their lives either. Rosalie, could your department get a sight of the guest list for that reception?'

'We are responsible for security,' she replied, 'so we may have it already. I can check.'

'Then please do so. You know the name of the man we're after.'

'Riesgo, *oui*. I have checked with Reservations here and there is no separate booking in that name.'

'Except,' McGuire interrupted, 'if Davor and Sanda's accommodation was booked by their firm, then his might be corporate as well. His company's called Fishheads dot com.'

She pulled a face at the strange name. 'That will be easily remembered. I will check here and in every other hotel in the principality.'

'Thanks,' said Skinner. 'Get in touch when you have information for us, either by mobile or at the Columbus. We can't hang about here, in case Davor, or his wife, comes back down and spots us.'

Eighty-eight

The first thing about Davis Colledge that struck Becky Stallings was his height. It was not that he was a giant: at a little over six feet tall he was probably of average size for a well-nourished teenager. No, the oddity was that he was almost a foot taller than his father. The Shadow Defence Secretary was no more than five feet four inches tall; glancing down surreptitiously, the inspector noticed that the heels of his black patent shoes were almost as high as hers. After setting eyes on the towering McGurk outside the airport, the Member of Parliament seemed to go out of his way not to stand close to him.

'Was your flight okay?'

'Fine, thank you, Inspector,' Michael Colledge replied. 'The national airline still has a lot going for it. I did once fly on one of these budget jobs, on a parliamentary delegation. Not an experience I care to repeat.'

'But I imagine that Davis had to use one yesterday, to get back from France.'

'Needs must. These operations are okay for students, I suppose. My attitude is that if someone refuses to give me a seat number, I refuse to get on his damn aircraft.' He paused. 'But that's of no consequence: we're here to talk about your investigation into Sugar's murder. In the light of the death of this man Weekes, is it now closed?'

'It isn't closed until the procurator fiscal says it is, sir. That's the way it works up here. One of the things that's been holding us back has been our inability to interview Davis.'

378

'I understand, but reading between the lines, I'll guess you're getting close to a solution.'

'Literally, a solution, Mr Colledge; you have to remember that now we have two murder inquiries in progress.' Stallings turned to his son, as she opened the rear door of her car for them to enter. 'Yesterday must have been a horrible day for you, Davis.'

'Frightful,' said the younger Colledge. He seemed subdued; his eyes were those of someone in his mid-twenties rather than a school leaver, with dark shadows underneath. There was a maturity about him, an indefinable confidence beyond his years, and undeniable attractiveness in his blond good looks. Since the start of the inquiry she had been privately sceptical about the idea of Sugar and him as a couple, but now that she had seen him Stallings could understand her being drawn to him. *I could fancy some of him myself*, she thought.

Still, his other features attested to his youth. He had gone for a few days without a shave, she guessed, but the growth on his jawline was soft and downy. Although he had a substantial frame, his body was lean and bony, with some filling out yet to be done. There was his clothing too. In contrast to his father's lightweight summer suit, shirt and silk tie, he was clad in an Aerosmith T-shirt and faded denims, with a lightweight rucksack, part of the uniform of modern youth, slung over his right shoulder.

'It must have been a terrible shock, to learn of Sugar's death like that.'

'It was,' he murmured.

'Yes,' McGurk agreed, as he folded himself into the front passenger seat. 'You must have gone through the gamut, right enough. Shock, then grief, and a bit of guilt too. Am I right, Davis?'

'Guilt?' the boy replied. 'Yes, you're right. I thought she'd dumped me. I went off to Amsterdam to get my hole, to spite her, and all that time she was lying dead. I'll always feel guilty. I should have known she'd never let me down.'

'Language, Dave,' his father interjected. 'A lady is present.'

For a moment the boy looked puzzled, as he ran through what he had said, until he recalled his slang. 'Oh, yes, sorry, Inspector.'

'That's all right,' she said, from behind the wheel. 'It's well seen you've been educated in Scotland. I don't think I'd ever heard that phrase until I came up here. Tell me,' she continued, 'did you ever discuss your relationship with Sugar with any of your classmates?'

'It wasn't a secret.'

'So some of them would have known you were going away together?'

'Yes.'

'So might you have felt a little bit humiliated when she didn't appear?'

'Humiliated? No, I'll never see most of those guys again, my school friends. I'm going to art school, and most of them are going to uni. But wait a minute, if you're suggesting I'd been bumming about the two of us, no way. I don't brag about scoring.'

'Sorry. I wasn't suggesting you did. You were angry, though. We've seen the picture you left in Collioure,' she explained. 'You certainly look angry in that.'

'Yes, I was,' he admitted. 'And I'm guilty about that as well.'

'When did you finish it?' McGurk asked.

'Just before I left. I suppose I thought that if she did turn up, ten days late, it would be the first thing she'd see and serve her right.' His face twisted, as if in self-loathing.

His father leaned forward. 'It occurs to me, Inspector,' he began, 'that this journey into the city is probably unnecessary. I'm sure that your conversation with my son could take place in the airport's VIP lounge, or in that hotel we've just passed.'

Stallings looked in the rear-view mirror, angling her head slightly to catch his eye. 'You know, sir,' she said, 'you're absolutely right. That should have occurred to me. But we're on the road now, so we might as well carry on.'

Eighty-nine

The afternoon was at its hottest, but it can be virtually impossible to hail a taxi on the street in Monaco, and so by the time they reached the foot of the Avenue d'Ostende, Skinner and McGuire were both happy to see the shade offered by one of the bars along the quai Albert I. They ordered two mugs of Heineken and collapsed into chairs, looking out into the harbour, which was dominated by the bulk of the *Lady Moura*, a private yacht large enough to have a helicopter parked on a pad at the stern.

'You know,' said McGuire, wearily, 'this guy could come and go without us having a bloody clue. Look at that thing there. Do you reckon that everyone who flies in there clears Customs?'

'No,' the DCC agreed, 'and there's no way we'll get a search warrant for it either.'

His colleague pointed to the sky. 'Do you reckon those are gulls up there, or could they be wild geese?'

'That's a possibility,' Skinner admitted. 'If it turns out that way, I'll pay for this trip as penance for dragging you away from important business in Edinburgh.'

'This is important.'

'So's the reopening of the Ballester investigation. Andy's got proof that he didn't kill any of those four people.'

'Fuck!' McGuire whispered. 'You have to be kidding, boss. Tell me you're kidding.'

'How I would love to, but I can't.'

'But all the evidence was there, at the scene of his death. He must have had an accomplice.'

'Mario, you've been over those inquiry files, over and over. In your wildest, can you see any of them as a two-man job?'

'No,' he admitted. 'That's not a runner: which means that Dražen planted all that stuff.'

'Aye, that's how it looks.' The big DCC drained his glass in a single swallow. 'But that's all in Scotland and we're here. Decision time. Another here, or do we go back to the hotel?'

'To be honest, boss, I feel the need of efficient air-conditioning.'

By a small miracle, the first car they saw as they stepped on to the nearby boulevard was a taxi, with its light on. McGuire gave the driver no choice about picking them up by stepping into the roadway and stopping it. Less than five minutes later, it pulled up outside the Hôtel Columbus.

Heavy-legged, the two Scots climbed the steps to the lobby. Skinner was leading the way into the bar, to the right of the reception desk, when McGuire grabbed him by the arm, stopping him in mid-stride. He turned, to see his colleague wide-eyed.

A man stood a few feet away; his back was to them, as was that of the woman by his side. He was six feet tall, with wide shoulders and a narrow waist. He wore a white T-shirt, decorated with a logo, a quotation from something or other, and below it, in large letters, the word 'Margaritaville'.

They stared at him for a second or two, no more, before Skinner pulled his head of CID after him, inelegantly, into the bar, out of sight.

Ninety

'You were right, Mr Colledge,' Stallings conceded. 'We should have used the airport facilities. I'm afraid this isn't the nicest interview room in Edinburgh.' She sniffed the air. 'I'll swear I can still smell Theo Weekes in here.'

'You had him in here?' Davis asked. 'In this room?'

'Yes indeed,' said McGurk. 'We gave him quite a grilling, didn't we, Inspector?'

'Not quite the thumb-screws but, yes, he had a very detailed interrogation.'

'And yet you didn't charge him with murder,' Michael Colledge remarked.

'Again, sir,' Stallings explained, 'we don't lay the charges, the fiscal does.'

'I am aware of the differences between Scottish and English criminal procedures.'

'I'm sorry,' she said. 'Of course you are, you being a barrister. But the same rule applies on both sides of the border, the basic one about being innocent in the absence of proof of guilt. Weekes was charged with what we know he did, but we were a step or two short of doing him for killing Sugar.'

'What did you lack?'

'A murder weapon for one. An eye-witness for another. We could prove he was there, but not that he shot her.'

'But he was your only suspect, right?'

'At this moment . . . probably. That's one reason why we needed to talk to your son.'

'You don't think I killed her?' the youth exclaimed.

'Don't get excited,' McGurk told him. 'Let's get that formality out of the way. Did you?'

'No! I did not.'

'Where were you at half past eight on the last morning of the school term?'

'Probably cleaning my teeth after having a shower.'

'Did anyone see you?'

'Warty Armstrong, one of the lads.'

McGurk smiled. 'I don't suppose he was christened Warty.'

'Sorry, Warren.'

'He'll confirm your presence in school at that time, you're sure?'

'Absolutely.'

'Fine. See? I told you it was a formality.'

'Does that mean we can go?' Davis asked.

'Not quite. We need to ask you about Sugar. How well did you really know her?'

'Very well. We were . . .' He stopped. 'I don't know how to put it without sounding silly.'

'Just say it as you feel it,' Stallings told him. 'We'll tell you whether it sounds silly or not.'

'Okay, we were in love.' He glanced sideways at his father, as if to gauge his reaction, but he was impassive.

'Nothing silly about that,' she retorted. 'So am I. Sergeant McGurk might be too. Did Sugar ever talk to you about her life before she met you, about people she knew, people she didn't like, people she might have been afraid of?'

'Only one.' The young man's answer was almost a growl. 'That man Weekes. Sugar wasn't afraid of him . . . she wasn't afraid of anything: you could see that in her work . . . but he upset her.'

'Are you sure about that?' McGurk asked. 'She had no enemies, no rivals?'

Davis looked at him, with a hint of scorn. 'Creative people don't have rivals,' he said. 'Colleagues, more like. We all do our own thing, in our own way. Each one of us is unique. As for enemies: you didn't know her, or you'd know how laughable that idea is.'

'Apart from Weekes?'

'Apart from him, although I don't know if you'd call him an enemy. He was somebody from her past who wouldn't let go.'

'Did she talk to you about him?'

'She told me all about him. She told me that they had been engaged once, but that she had chucked him.'

'Did she tell you why?'

He nodded. 'He gave her a dose, the bastard. He'd been two-timing her and he passed on a disease he'd caught off some slag. She told him it was all over, but he wouldn't go away. There wasn't a week went by without him phoning her. She told him to stop, but he didn't and she was too nice to do anything about it.'

'Did she tell you what his job was?'

'No, she never mentioned it. I never knew until Dad told me. He must have been good at it, though, because he followed her. More than once, she'd see him at places she'd gone, or she'd see his car parked near hers.'

'When you were with Sugar,' Stallings asked, 'were you ever aware of him following you?'

'No, but he must have done, because he knew about us.'

'Are you sure?'

'Yes, because of that time at the Gyle.'

'Weekes told us that Sugar agreed to meet him there,' said McGurk. 'Is that true?'

The young man gasped. 'That's bollocks!' he exclaimed. 'She went shopping there one day; she had just parked and he pulled into the bay right beside her. He jumped out of his car and came straight up to her, shouting at her.'

'Shouting what?'

'Stuff about me, about the two of us. She said he called her a fucking cradle-snatcher, and said a lot of other obscene stuff, about her and me. He told her to stop seeing me, or else.'

'Or else?'

'That was what she said he said. That was when she lost her temper; she told him that the two of us were going to France for a month, and that she was looking forward to having safe sex for the first time since she'd met him. Then she told him that he could fuck off, got back in her car and drove away.' He paused. 'When she told me about it later on, she was still shaking with anger. It's the only time I ever saw her like that. Weekes killed her. I don't care about proof; I'm telling you, he killed her.'

'But, Davis,' Stallings began, 'after that, when Sugar didn't appear in France, weren't you worried?'

He shook his head. 'No, I wasn't. It never occurred to me that anything could have happened to her. To tell you the truth, once I'd had a few days to think about it, I began to wonder whether she still felt something for him, after all. If people can get so worked up about somebody, doesn't that mean that deep down they care about them? I read that somewhere, in a psychology book.'

'Maybe. But if it's any consolation, there's no evidence of that in Sugar's case.'

'In a way,' said Michael Colledge, 'that's good to hear. I'm sure Dave will take some comfort from it.' He gazed at the detectives. 'That covers everything, does it not? I don't want to rush you, but I have to get back down south. The House is still in session.'

'There is just one thing I'd like to revisit,' Stallings replied. 'Davis, can I go back to the time when you discovered that Sugar was dead? Tell me once more, please. When was that?'

'Yesterday, when I called Mr Skinner. He told me.'

The inspector straightened slightly in her chair. She looked from son to father. 'At this point, gentlemen,' she said, 'the interview must proceed under formal caution. Davis, I have to advise you that you do not have to say anything, but it may harm your defence if you do not mention when questioned something which you later rely on in court. Anything you do say may be given in evidence.'

'What the hell?' Michael Colledge exploded. 'What is this?'

'It's necessary, I'm afraid, sir. There are matters we have to raise. Davis, when you were in Collioure did you ever go on the Internet?'

'Yes,' the young man blurted out. 'I used a café.'

'Inspector,' his father intervened, 'I must insist on a few words in private with my son.'

'I'm not going to allow that. At this point, sir, you're here as his legal adviser, at my discretion.'

'Then this interview is at an end. Come on, Dave.'

'You can go, Mr Colledge,' said McGurk. 'He stays.'

'Have you any idea who . . .'

'Please, sir.' The sergeant sighed. 'Don't insult us by finishing that sentence. Davis,' he continued, 'the Internet access you mentioned. Was it one of those places where anyone can walk in off the street?'

'No,' the young man replied, carefully and quietly. 'The guy was fussy; he made you sign in and give your passport number every time you logged on.'

'Yes; apparently he has a fixation about paedophiles using his kit and him getting the blame. Your name and passport number are both in his book. You used the place five times; three of those were during your first week there, on the Wednesday, Friday and Saturday. The other two were on Monday and Tuesday of last week. Is that correct?'

'Yes.'

'What did you do when you were on line? What did you look at?'

'Just stuff. YouTube, music sites.'

'Did you send any emails?'

A brief frown registered on Davis's forehead. 'I sent three to Sugar, the week before last, asking where she was.'

'Are you sure you didn't send four?'

His face reddened. 'Sorry. Yes, I sent another last Monday. It wasn't very nice. I was angry with her by that time.'

'Was that before you visited the BBC website?'

'What?'

'You heard him,' said Stallings. 'Was it before?'

'What do you mean?'

'Davis, you're a bright guy, but maybe not as bright as you think. Web browsers leave a history. Our French colleagues looked at the terminals in your café on the days you were signed in. Last Monday somebody logged on to the BBC News page that reported the discovery of a woman's body in Edinburgh. The next day there was a session in which someone logged on to the *Evening News* website and then to the BBC again, to a report which said that the body had been identified as that of Sugar Dean.' The young man's head was bowed: his father was silent, gazing at him. 'Why did you lie to us?' the inspector asked.

'When?'

'You told us that you learned of Sugar's death yesterday, from Mr Skinner. Davis, the café owner has said that at the end of your last session, you left in a highly agitated state.'

'I'd had a big bet on a horse. I lost a lot more than I could afford. It must have been somebody else who was looking at the BBC.'

'You were the only British user of the café last Tuesday. Most of the others were French; the rest were German and Czech.'

'Tough. One of them must have spoken English.'

'I have to point out,' Michael Colledge murmured, 'that you have no evidence of prior knowledge of Sugar's death.'

'How many juries have you known in your career, sir,' asked the inspector, 'who wouldn't have accepted those circumstances as proof? But let's leave that to one side,' she went on. 'Next morning, Davis, you left Collioure. You've told us that you went to Holland, to frolic among the sex workers of Amsterdam. We know that you flew there on Thursday. How many nights did you spend there?'

'Three. I took the train back to France on Sunday, overnight.'

'What was the name of your hotel?'

He blinked. 'I can't remember.'

'That doesn't surprise me. I don't believe you were ever there.'

'That's preposterous,' Michael Colledge shouted, but Stallings could see uncertainty and fear in the little MP's eyes.

She pressed on. 'This is what I think happened,' she said. 'You never went to Amsterdam. Instead you crossed to the UK last Thursday, as a foot passenger on an overnight ferry. You did that rather than fly, to avoid airport security and to avoid leaving your name on a flight manifest. When you landed in Britain, you probably discovered that we had a man in custody in connection with Sugar's death. Maybe that threw you a bit, but as soon as his court appearance was reported by our national broadcasting organisation, you knew that he was out on bail, and you knew who he was: Theo Weekes, the man you believe killed Sugar.' She looked at him. 'Care to comment?'

'No comment,' he answered.

'Noted. So you headed north, having turned some of your euros into sterling, not using your debit card. We think you came by bus, and reached Edinburgh on Saturday. You knew where Weekes lived; the papers told you that. You know your way around Edinburgh, so you took a bus out to the west of the city. You probably hung about for a while, watching from a distance, getting the lie of the land. While you were there, John Dean arrived. You may well have seen his altercation with Weekes; if you did, it would have left you in no doubt about what your man looked like. The police turning up didn't help you, but you were patient enough to wait. After a while, another man arrived, got out of his car and banged on Weekes's door until he answered.'

'Inspector,' Michael Colledge intervened. She held up a hand to silence him, and continued.

'That was when you made your move. You took the path that leads to the back of Weekes's place. He had gone inside; the back door was open, and you waited, until the shouting inside had subsided and until you heard the front door slam. Then you went inside. When Weekes came into his kitchen, you were there, with a big diver's knife that you had bought for the purpose. You stabbed him with it. He didn't have a chance to defend himself, for you were all over him with the blade, stabbing any part he didn't shield, and slashing at him. He staggered away from you, into the hall, and eventually went down, on to the carpet, where you cut,' she made a sudden, violent movement, 'half-way through his neck, causing the blood to gush like you'd struck oil. You stuck the knife in his eye for good measure, and that was that. You'd taken revenge for Sugar.'

'Inspector,' the politician repeated. His face was chalk white. 'You can't be suggesting my son did that. I'll have your job, woman.'

Stallings picked up a bound folder from the table and tossed it to him. 'That's what he did,' she told him. 'Those are photographs from the crime scene and from the post-mortem. The autopsy report's there too. Take a look.'

'Brutal, I'm sure,' said Colledge, ignoring it, 'but not proof. Evidence, please, Inspector, Sergeant.'

'We really don't want to fuck up your son's life,' McGurk told him, sadly and sincerely. 'I wish we didn't have any. The trouble is, we do.' He stood, and stepped over to a video-player and monitor, set up in a corner of the room. He pressed a button and a series of jerky images appeared on screen, people, some descending from a bus, some waiting, some stepping on board. A second bus appeared: more passengers stepped off. McGurk pressed a remote and froze the image of a tall young man. He wore a baseball cap, with the letters FDNY, cut-off jeans and a pale blue T-shirt, and carried a rucksack over his shoulder. 'You, Davis,' he said.

'That could be anybody,' the Shadow Defence Secretary exclaimed.

'But it's him.' He ran the tape again, until he froze it at a second

390

image. The same young man, same baseball cap, but wearing a black T-shirt and denim shorts. 'And so's that,' he said, then reached down, took a clear plastic bag from under the table, and held it up: it contained two items of bloody clothing. 'The first of those shirts was found yesterday, in a bin in George Street. The denims turned up this morning, in a skip behind a building in York Place. That's Weekes's blood, and in both garments we found some DNA traces that weren't his. I'll need a sample from you, Davis, but we both know what they'll confirm, don't we?'

The boy, for that was what he had become, stared stonily ahead.

'You're left-handed, aren't you?' McGurk asked him.

'Yes,' his father replied for him.

McGurk turned over a print that had been lying face down on the table. It showed the painting that Davis had created in Collioure, the one in which he held a gun . . . in his left hand. 'He caught the inter-city bus out of town on Saturday night,' he said to the MP. 'We have a witness who places him at the bus station, then there's the driver. Ferry across the Channel, train back to Collioure and it all looks as if he's been in Amsterdam getting his end away, just like the story he made up.' He resumed his seat. 'I'm sorry, kid.' He sighed. 'I really am.'

'I'm not,' the younger Colledge replied harshly. 'Weekes is dead, and that's all that matters to me.'

'But, son,' said Stallings, 'there's no evidence that he killed Sugar. In fact, we don't believe he did.'

'That doesn't matter either!' he retorted. 'Even if he didn't, if someone else did, don't you think he thought about it? He was an animal, an evil bastard, Sugar told me. He deserved to die, and I'm glad I killed him.'

Ninety-one

The bar was empty of customers, and the bartender was absent. The two Scots found a table, out of the direct sight of the check-in desk, but from which they could watch it, reflected in a mirror.

The man was smiling, relaxed, as he signed in, and took his key card from the receptionist. He glanced to his left, in the direction of the elevators, then turned, with his companion, and walked towards them.

'Well?' Skinner asked, as he passed out of sight. 'Was that him?'

'If it is, he's changed, or he's been changed, a lot,' said McGuire. 'There's the beard, for a start, and the glasses; his nose is different too, narrower, and his ears. You have to remember that I met the guy very briefly, and that he was sitting down all the way through our conversation. But the ears are the biggest change: Davor's ears stick out, if you've noticed. They're not quite in the Dumbo class, but pretty prominent. When I saw him, Dražen's were the same. Now they've been pinned back, literally.'

Skinner's mobile sounded. He fished it out of his pocket. 'Yes, Rosalie,' he answered. 'Yes, thanks. We've just found that out for ourselves. Can you get down here? . . . Good . . . Yes, bring back-up, but be very discreet.'

As he repocketed the phone, he saw that his companion had left him and walked round to Reception, where he was in conversation with the clerk. 'Yes,' the DCC heard her say as he approached. 'That is the name: Ignacio Riesgo. He's in room five two four.'

'Who's the woman?'

'Her name is Chandler Lockett.'

McGuire laughed. 'He and Richards must really be buddies. Ifan's lent him his girlfriend for the occasion.'

'What do you think?' Skinner asked. 'The *inspecteur's* on her way; do we wait?'

'She's got a gun, we don't.'

'Let's hope it doesn't come to that.' He turned to the duty manager behind the desk. 'Has his case been taken up yet?'

'No.'

'Then hold it for a minute and get me a porter's jacket.'

The man looked at him doubtfully. 'I don't know about that, sir.'

'It's either that or armed police go up to get him. Will the boss fancy that?'

The manager reached a decision. 'Maybe I can find a jacket to fit you,' he said, then stepped through a door to his right. He came back within a few seconds, holding a brown tunic. 'This is the biggest I have.'

'That'll do.' Skinner took it from him and slipped it on; it was a tight fit, but he managed to fasten the buttons. 'Gimme the cases,' he ordered. The manager pointed at a trolley beside him, laden with two suitcases and a vanity bag. He nodded and pushed it towards the lift.

'Fifth floor?' McGuire asked.

'Yup.'

He pressed the button. 'I don't know about you,' he said. 'I've spent most of my career listening to you complain whenever you have to be in uniform, and now look at you. Nice gear, but it's not your colour.'

The lift came to a halt and the doors opened. The floor layout was the same as theirs, one below: Skinner pushed the trolley along a corridor to the right of the small lobby area. The door was the fourth along. He stopped outside it, allowing McGuire to pass beyond him, then rapped on it twice, not too hard, not wanting to sound like a cop.

'Who is it?' a male voice called.

'Baggage.'

The door opened and he found himself face to face with a man he had never met. 'Come in,' said Ignacio Riesgo.

As Skinner pushed the trolley through the narrow opening that led into the suite, he passed the bathroom door. It was ajar and he caught a glimpse of the woman inside, in her underwear.

'Just dump them on the bed for now,' he was ordered.

'Si,' he said, and unloaded the vanity case, then the suitcase below it. The man was watching him. 'Como es tu culo?' Skinner asked.

He shrugged his shoulders. 'Yes, that's fine,' he replied.

The DCC grinned, and nodded at a point behind him. He turned to see the bulk of Mario McGuire facing him.

The head of CID did not possess the hand speed of a Floyd Patterson, but when he threw a punch, there was something inevitable about it, a certainty that it would land. The blow hit its target flush on the chin. It lifted him off his feet and flung him backwards. He would have hit the floor, had not Skinner caught him, twisted him round and flung him face down on the bed for McGuire to seize his wrists and secure them with plastic cuffs.

'What the . . .' A small female scream came from behind them, as Chandler Lockett stepped out of the en-suite, naked.

'I'd get back in there if I were you,' Skinner told her. 'We're the police, and your man's in the process of being nicked for murder.' He looked down at the captive. 'Isn't that right, Dražen?'

'My name is Ignacio Riesgo,' he hissed.

'Panamanian?'

'Yes.'

'In that case you need to brush up on your native language. I just asked you how your arsehole was, and you didn't bat an eyelid.'

Ninety-two

'I meant it, you know, what I said to Colledge. Usually I get a real buzz from a clear-up, but not this time.'

'I know what you mean, Jack,' Stallings told her sergeant, 'but we don't get to pick and chose our perps. Sometimes we have to lock up people we'd rather not.'

'His father seemed to think he's got a chance of an acquittal.'

'That's not what his eyes were saying. He knows how it'll go. Tell me, why did you recommend that he engage Frankie Birtles to defend his son?'

'Two reasons,' said McGurk. 'She's pretty damn good, and also, when it comes to consider a tariff on the life sentence, the judge will read something into the fact that although Weekes was her client, she was prepared to speak for the lad who killed him.'

'They won't plead it down to manslaughter?'

The big sergeant grinned. 'In Scotland that's culpable homicide, boss: and not even in England would this be a plea bargain. The boy has to be charged with murder. It was all premeditated. He tried to make it look as if he'd never been within five hundred miles of the crime scene. On top of that he stabbed him twenty-seven friggin' times. Best he can hope for is no minimum sentence. That'll leave it up to the Parole Board; if they're sympathetic, he might just be out while he's still in his twenties.'

'He wasn't wrong, you know. Weekes was a truly evil bastard. God, maybe he did kill Sugar after all.'

'Maybe he did. Probably he didn't. Possibly we'll never know one way or another.'

'Are you going to see Lisanne tonight, to tell her what's happened?'

'I'm going to see her anyway. Theo's well in her past now, and this investigation is in ours too, more or less. She and I can look forward now, and see what's there for us, see if what you suggested to young Davis turns out to be true.'

Ninety-three

The honorary consul was more flustered than any human being Skinner had ever seen. 'Are you sure?' he demanded frantically. 'Are you sure? Because if you're wrong, if you've had an innocent foreign national arrested, you'll have caused an international incident.'

The DCC laughed. 'That's pitching it a bit high, chum. But don't you worry, we're not wrong. Miss Lockett knows exactly who Señor Riesgo really is, and she's telling it all to Inspecteur Gramercy, even as we speak. We don't even have to wait for the DNA match. Dražen's done and he knows it. You can tell Our Man in Marseille to get the wheels turning. I want my Northumbrian colleagues to be able to take this guy out of here tomorrow.'

'But, assuming I accept what you're saying, what about his father? He'll make a God Almighty fuss.'

'He won't say a fucking word. If he does, he and his wife are admitting that they knew who the new director of their son's company really was, and that, even for parents, puts them in big bother. Even if the courts didn't do anything to them, the City would ostracise them. So on you go, Mr Major, do your job and get the wheels turning. Tomorrow, remember; he goes back tomorrow.'

As Her Majesty's representative left, Rosalie Gramercy came into the room in police headquarters. 'Chandler is co-operating,' she told them. 'She told me that she was Dražen's girl all along, and that being seen with his friend was just a front. Do you want me to charge her?'

'Hell, no!' Skinner laughed. 'She's told you what we wanted to hear. You can give her free chips in the casino, as far as I'm concerned. We would like to see him, though. We've got something we'd like to put to him in private.'

'No problem. I'll take you to him.'

Dražen Boras was being held in a secure room on the top floor of the building. The Scots had seen many hotel suites that were less well appointed, but they knew that he would be on round-the-clock watch, and saw that the basic principle of removing anything that might be used for self-harm was being observed.

As they looked at him, they were surprised by his serenity. He still wore his gaudy shirt, but within it, his demeanour seemed to have changed. 'How did you find me?' he asked.

'Dedicated research,' Skinner told him. 'You don't speak Spanish, so where did your name come from?'

'One of my DEA handlers in the States came up with it.'

The DCC was rarely surprised, but his eyebrows rose. 'DEA? Where do they come into it? I was told that you and your father had CIA connections.'

'We do, but recently I have been helping in other ways. There's a drug route through the Balkans. My business has made me well placed to track it, and that's what I've been doing.'

'Don't trust your friends,' Skinner told him. 'Especially when they're spooks. The name, Dražen.' He explained what it meant. 'Somebody was having a laugh.'

'If I ever see him again,' Boras murmured, 'that laugh will be cut short, along with his throat.'

'You never will, chum. Even as we speak, every record of you is being wiped from their files. Your old man will find he's no longer useful either. He should watch his back from now on: a man like him has more enemies than brain cells. He may find himself on the list for a polonium sandwich.'

'My father will be all right, sir.'

'But not you, Dražen,' said McGuire. 'You're going down for life for what you did.'

'I'm admitting nothing, friend.'

'I didn't expect you to,' Skinner told him. 'But you know what we have on you and you know where it will lead. However, that's all for discussion back in Britain. We're on foreign soil here; none of this conversation is on the record. That I promise you.'

Boras looked him in the eye for several seconds. 'I think I believe you,' he said. 'In that case, I am truly sorry for what happened to your officer. You know what was meant to happen and that was not it.'

'I know. Your dad's two operatives were meant to be caught in that trap. You couldn't be sure you'd bought their silence for ever, could you? Listen up, Dražen,' he continued, 'I know that you'll admit to nothing on the record. To do so would incriminate your father, and for all that you've been supposed business rivals, you won't do that. So here, and nowhere else, I want to ask you one question. Why did you kill Daniel Ballester?'

Boras's eyes widened; he stared at Skinner in astonishment. 'Because he murdered my kid sister,' he exclaimed. 'You know that.'

'He was a nasty muck-raking journalist out to make trouble for your dad and you,' said McGuire. 'That could have been your motive.'

'He was a pipsqueak. We'd already taken care of him professionally. In revenge he killed my sister and her friends, including poor little Amy Noone. I liked little Amy. I tell you . . . off the record . . . I've never killed anyone, apart from him. I didn't imagine I'd enjoy it, but I did. It was good to watch him strangle and shit himself as he died.'

'So that was your only motive?' Skinner repeated.

'Absolutely.'

'In that case, I'm even more sorry for you. Ballester didn't shoot Zrinka, or anyone else. You killed the wrong man. And you know what? You're the second guy today who's discovered he's made that mistake.'

Ninety-four

The artist known as Caitlin Summers looked out of the window of her new home. Never in her wildest moments had she ever dreamed of waking up in a Stevenson lighthouse, but that was what she had done less than an hour before.

At first, when they had told her of the accommodation that had been rented for her, she had feared that she would have to maintain the light, and had been relieved to learn that it was no longer operational.

She sipped from her mug as she surveyed the seascape, looking north along the coastline towards Dunbar, the nearest town. The view to the south was less attractive: Torness nuclear power station was never likely to be short-listed for a Design Council award. Still, she had seen uglier structures, and uglier people, in her time.

Her sudden fame had taken her by surprise: she still marvelled at the skill of her managers in securing the First Minister to open her exhibition, with the attendant publicity it had brought. But that was their job, she supposed; just as she had hers.

She checked her watch: it was time for her morning appointment. She finished her coffee, rinsed out the mug and slipped on her waxed cotton jacket. 'Well, Caitlin,' she said aloud, 'let's see what wildlife we can spot this morning.'

A soft wind was blowing off the sea as she stepped outside; the tide was on its way in. She picked up her pace quickly as she headed north, hoping that she would reach the fossilised remains of the prehistoric forest that she had been told about before the water covered it. The team from the BBC news programme *Reporting Scotland* had suggested it as the ideal location for their interview.

A few seagulls greeted her as she walked along the grassy path, above the narrow beach. 'Sorry to disturb you, birdies,' she told them. 'You're probably not used to human company out here.'

The coast was wild and desolate. There was not another soul in sight and yet, somehow, she did not feel in the slightest alone.

Ninety-five

In full uniform, Deputy Chief Constable Andy Martin sat in the well of the High Court in Dundee with a growing sense of horror as an usher in the corridor outside called out, for the third time, the name of the chief prosecution witness.

The jury, eleven men and four women, had been empanelled the day before, and had heard opening speeches by counsel for the Crown and for the defence. They sat in two rows, some displaying signs of impatience, one or two showing signs of bewilderment. The judge, Lady Broughton, sat sternly above them, dressed in the wig and red robe, trimmed with white fur, that was the traditional uniform of the Scottish Supreme Court bench. The prisoner, Cameron 'Grandpa' McCullough, sat in the dock, stone-eyed and impassive, flanked by two huge constables as he watched the majesty of justice implode.

Martin knew what was going to happen. He knew that when police officers had called at the Aberdeen home of Carmela Dickson, John McCreath's widow, to collect her and her sister for their big day, they had found the house empty. The shouting in the corridor was a charade.

Ten minutes after he had been sent to summon Mrs Dickson, the usher reappeared and whispered in the ear of Herman Butters, the Advocate Depute, who sat at a table, facing the judge, his wig pushed forward until it almost covered his eyes. He nodded and the official withdrew. Slowly, reluctantly, counsel rose to his feet. 'My lady,' he began, 'I regret to inform you that the principal witness for the Crown has failed to appear.'

'The whole of Dundee must know that by now,' said Lady Broughton. 'Are you telling me that, for the second time in as many weeks, you are unable to proceed?'

'Regrettably, I am. The Crown offers no evidence against the prisoner.' He resumed his seat.

The judge glared at the dock. 'Please stand,' she snapped, not trying to hide her anger as the accused stood up. 'Mr McCullough,' she told him, 'you lead a charmed life. Fate, or someone playing the part, seems to have intervened on your behalf. The case against you is deserted *simpliciter*. The jury is discharged. Ladies and gentlemen, I apologise for this inexcusable waste of your time.' In the public gallery a few cheers broke out. She silenced them with a glare, then looked back towards the Crown table. 'Mr Butters, there remains the matter of the charge on which the prisoner was remanded last week. Do you have a motion to present?'

'Yes, my lady, I do. I regret to advise you that we are no longer able to proceed with that charge either. The indictment is withdrawn.'

Lady Broughton's eyes were like ice as they swept back to the dock. 'In that case, Mr McCullough, you also are discharged and are free to leave. But before you do, let me make two things clear to you. I do not believe in luck when it comes to criminal matters, and I have a long memory. Good morning.'

The room rose as she did. She turned to leave the bench; as she did she caught Martin's eye, and gave an almost imperceptible nod. He read her intention: as the court emptied, he followed her through the side door into her chambers.

By the time he entered, she had divested herself of her robe and wig, revealing long legs in a dark trouser suit, and was standing before a wall mirror rearranging her short auburn hair. 'Lady Broughton,' he began.

There was no preamble. 'I hope you're as angry as I am,' she said. 'When I see a man like that walking out into the sunshine, I . . . Oh, dammit, Andy, you know what I mean.'

'I know, Phil. Trust me on that. My chief constable would have been here to face the music himself, but he's taken personal charge of the investigation into the disappearance of McCullough's white powder from a secure store. God, is he on the warpath! He's suspended half a dozen people, three officers and three civilians, pending the outcome.'

'Any progress?'

'One of our civilian clerks went on holiday on Friday: a Polish guy. He told colleagues that he was going on a package to Ibiza from Edinburgh. He didn't. His bidey-in swears she doesn't know where he is. Whether she's lying or not, we don't expect him back at work any time soon. Our opposite numbers in Krakow . . . that's his home town . . . are looking for him over there.'

'Do you think you'll find him?'

'I can't say. By now he could be deep under a house, or an industrial unit: Grandpa's a very thorough man, and there's plenty of new building going on in the region.'

'The man . . . your Polish clerk . . . must have had help, surely. That's a lot of drugs to walk out of the door.'

'Like I said, we've got half a dozen people under investigation, but it's possible he did it alone. The packages were replaced by look-alikes, full of talc and flour; it could have been done over a period, probably was.'

'How was it discovered?'

'The stuff was reweighed: routine, to guard against people nicking small quantities of coke as party treats. There was a discrepancy, so we took a closer look.'

'Too bad. Maybe if nobody had checked . . .' the judge chuckled ironically '. . . but forget I said that. Anyway, the defence would have been bound to ask for another look. Do you think McCullough's counsel knew those witnesses weren't going to turn up?'

Martin frowned. 'Are you asking me if I think Sally Mathewson's bent? For if she did, that's what it would amount to. If she had knowledge of that, then as an officer of the court she'd have been obliged to declare it. Grandpa would know that; he wouldn't have taken the risk.'

'What about the witnesses? That really is bad, Andy.'

'I know,' he replied. 'And I accept the blame on behalf of the police service, even if it was the Aberdeen force that lost them, and not my people. They were regarded as being at risk, and they should have been kept under observation all the time. Graham Morton's pursuing that as well: he's going to ask the Inspector of Constabulary to investigate.'

'The chief up in Aberdeen won't like that.'

'Tough. He'll have to go along with the request.'

'Do you think they're dead?'

'I wouldn't put anything past Grandpa. They could be under the same house as the Pole . . . or he could just have paid them all to go away for a while.'

'Whatever he's done, I hope you can nail him for it . . . not that I'll have anything to do with future proceedings. I went too far with my closing remarks; they won't let him appear before me again. I'd be a walking ground for appeal.' She sighed. 'What the hell? I'm out of it all for a while from the end of this week. The Court of Session's on vacation and so are Gregor and I: we're off for three weeks.'

'Mario McGuire and Neil McIlhenney won't like that: they've just made an arrest in the Weekes murder inquiry, and the Dean case is still open. They don't have a lot of confidence in your husband's deputy.'

Lady Broughton smiled. 'Nor in the Crown Agent, from what Gregor tells me. Well, they're just going to have to get by. We will be on the golf course in Spain.'

'Are you renting?'

'No, we have a house, in a complex called Torremirona; it's near Figueras.'

'Enjoy yourselves, then. I know that part of the world.' He laughed. 'I'm sure the Glimmer Twins will be thinking of you.'

Ninety-six

'Gregor,' Skinner asked, 'can you see any way that we can try Dražen Boras in Scotland rather than England?'

'I wish I could, Bob,' the procurator fiscal replied, 'but I can't think of a precedent for it. He committed both murders in England; that's where he has to be tried. If anything, history undermines you. The Lockerbie bomb wasn't planted in Scotland, but it exploded here and the victims died here, so this is where the Libyans were tried.'

The DCC paused to consider the point. 'Could we argue,' he continued, 'that DI Steele was a Scottish police officer in hot pursuit, as part of an investigation into crimes committed in Scotland? Let the English try Boras for the Ballester murder, fair enough, but could we have him for Stevie?'

'I could put that argument forward,' Gregor Broughton conceded, 'but it would be risky, even if I won. If he was prosecuted in the High Court, his counsel would probably argue absence of jurisdiction before the trial even got under way. If the judge overruled him that decision would be subject to scrutiny, and might be set aside. You have the probability, maybe the near certainty, of a conviction in Newcastle, or wherever they try him, and the real possibility of an acquittal in Scotland.'

Skinner sighed into the phone. 'Okay, they can have him.'

'A wise decision, especially if you want to maintain friendly relations with your colleagues in Northumberland.'

'That's not an issue. I spoke to Les Cairns, my opposite number, last night. He'd have done the same thing in my shoes, and we both know it. The way things stand, he'll take all the credit, having done bugger-all of the hard work. All he has to do is send a couple of officers down here to collect Boras, once the court formalises his extradition.'

'And all you have to do is get on the plane . . . or are you and Mario taking another day or two down there?'

'Hell, no! He has to get back to deal with a very shocked Shadow Defence Secretary. Me, I have to . . . I just have to get back, that's all. Things to do.'

'Mr Colledge, QC? Yes, I have the papers on my desk, ready for a remand hearing in an hour or so. I must say, if he thought he was representing his son's interests during that interview, he made a real Horlicks of it, allowing the lad to confess on tape.'

'From what I've been told, his confession was all over the clothing he dumped.'

'Oh, yes, he's had it, no doubt about that. Daddy's already asked for a meeting with the Lord Advocate.'

'Gavin's not going to agree, is he?'

'No, no. He's referred him to me; I'm seeing him this afternoon. I know how it will go. He'll ask me about a plea bargain, and I'll tell him that I can only discuss that with his son's legal team.'

'He wants to see Mario and me too, to go over the evidence once again.'

'Are you going to do that?'

'He is; I'm not. Like I said, I have other things on my plate.'

'Yes.'

Skinner sensed the fiscal's hesitancy. 'What's up, chum?' he asked.

'I was just wondering whether those things might include the backwash from a call I had this morning, from a *Scotsman* journalist.'

'What did he want?'

'He asked me about you. He said that the redtops may be getting ready to run a story about you being implicated in two investigations, one being run by your own force and the other by the police in Spain. The suggestion is that you've been informally suspended.'

'What did you tell him?'

'After I'd picked myself off the floor and got my laughter under control I told him to bugger off.'

'Thanks, Gregor.'

'Somebody's making mischief for you, Bob.'

'Don't I know it,' Skinner replied. 'Someone close, too: I can sense it. There is nothing worse than being betrayed by a friend.'

Ninety-seven

'**D**o you think glass ceilings exist any more?'

'Why do you ask that?'

Alex Skinner reached across the table for the bottle of St Émilion and topped up her goblet. 'I'd have thought that was obvious. Here we are, two women having dinner together, not a man in sight. I'm still well short of thirty and I'm an associate in the biggest law firm in Scotland. Two days ago, I had a phone call from the chair . . . another she . . . of our most serious rival, asking if I'd like to join them as a partner. For your part, you're still well short of forty: you're our nation's First Minister and we're sitting in your official residence.'

'I suppose,' said Aileen de Marco. 'Yes, if a Martian bloke was teleported into this room he could be forgiven for thinking that we're equal shareholders in humanity, and maybe even the dominant half of the species. But drop him into my home city, Glasgow, and he wouldn't think that. He'd see the pubs, filled with so-called alpha males while Mum stayed at home with the weans. He'd see the hookers in the red-light district, selling sex to sad or voracious men, then giving much of their money to their pimps and the rest to their drug pushers, none of whom are likely to be female. He'd see foreign girls in sweatshop jobs, thinking they were lucky to have them. He'd see wee neds on the street corners, tooled up, learning to be just like their big brothers and even their dads, bad news one day for their womenfolk. He'd see refuges for battered wives. Would he see a single refuge for battered husbands?' She peered over the top of her glass. 'Would . . . he . . . fuck.'

'Maybe Martians don't have blokes,' Alex mused. 'Maybe they're . . . androgynous . . . hermaphroditic.'

'Then they can go and screw themselves.'

'Stop right there!'

Aileen giggled. 'Yes, maybe that was taking it a bit too far. Mind you, why does Doctor Who always regenerate as another man? Why does he never turn into a woman?'

'If he did she'd probably make a hell of a mess the first time she went to the toilet. As for his first period . . . Jesus, the mind boggles. Can you imagine David Tennant with PMT?'

'No. Definitely not. As for the standing up or sitting down bit, though, I don't think he does. I don't go all the way back, but I'll bet you, in forty years, or whatever it is, of travelling through space and time, the old Doc has never once taken a piss. Speaking of which, is that bottle empty?'

Alex picked it up and shared its contents between them. 'It is now.'

'Will I open another?'

'Better not. School day tomorrow, and all that.'

'What did you say to her?'

'Who?'

'Your rival firm's boss. She who tried to lure you?'

'I told her thanks but no thanks, that I'd stay with Curle Anthony and Jarvis for a bit longer.'

'And how did she take that?'

'She told me she wouldn't ask again.' Alex smiled, a little crookedly. 'I told her there was something illogical in that. If they want me now, I said, then in a couple of years' time, when I have more training and experience behind me, they should want me even more. So she left the offer open.'

'Did you tell your boss?'

'No. It would only cause bad feeling between the firms.'

'Maybe you should,' Aileen suggested. 'He might offer you a partnership straight away.'

'He has done already or, rather, he's promised me one; when the time is right, he said.'

'In that case, why don't you tell him that the time's right for your rival?'

'He'd think I was blackmailing him. Anyway, I like doing what I'm doing at the moment. A promotion would change it.'

'You sound just like your dad.'

'That's a compliment.'

'It's meant to be. He has your reluctance to move on, but there comes a time when you have to, or spend the rest of your life wondering. His has come now.'

'Not yet,' said Alex. 'Sir James retires next year, doesn't he?'

'Not any more. He goes next month.'

'And will Pops . . . ?'

'He's promised me that he will.'

'He's made his mind up? How did you manage that?'

'I suppose you could say there was a bit of mutual blackmail involved.'

Alex peered into her glass. 'I see. He's doing that for you. So what are you doing for him?'

'He's supposed to tell you that.'

'God,' she gasped, 'you're going to marry him.'

Aileen nodded. 'Is that okay with you?'

'Are you asking me for his hand? Of course it is . . . as long as I don't have to call you "Mother". Sarah had a brief flirtation with that notion, after my brother was born.'

'No, "First Minister" will be fine. Seriously, though, you don't mind?'

'I couldn't be happier for both of you. You're made for each other. Here, you're not pregnant, are you?'

'Jeez, no. Your dad has enough children as it is.'

'Only three of his own. Mark's adopted, remember.' Alex paused. 'Have you done due diligence on each other, told each other all your secrets?'

'He knew most of mine before we started to get serious. But, yes, he's told me all of his . . . including his dalliances, between his two marriages, and even during his second.'

'Mark's mum?'

'Yes. He doesn't think you know about that.'

'Sarah told me, one time when she was mad at him. Did he tell you who the mystery woman was too?'

'What do you mean?'

'There was somebody, when I was fourteen. I never found out her name. He hinted at her on Sunday, but he still kept it to himself.'

'Yes, he told me about her too.'

'Was she married? I wondered that, afterwards.'

'No,' Aileen replied, 'but she married someone else, and that's how it finished.'

'Who was she?'

'Now that, I don't think I can tell you. I'm a politician, Alex; I know the value of trust between two people, and I'll never do anything to put that at risk.'

'That's good . . .' said Alex '. . . because I'll always trust you.'

Aileen glanced at the clock on the sideboard. 'Speaking of Himself,' she said, 'he should be home in triumph now from his trip to Monaco.'

'Yes, was that a result or not! Maggie will be so pleased to see that man put away for the rest of his life.' She paused. 'You said he's going home, not coming here?'

'Yes. He told me he's got one more thing to sort out, and that it might mean an early start. Once it's done, and here I quote him, he'll be free to concentrate on the next stage of his career, and of his life.'

Ninety-eight

Caitlin Summers smiled as the interview began. It was the third time she had watched it, having recorded the original transmission on the Sky + box that she had discovered as an added bonus when she had moved into her new home.

'Why this location?' the BBC arts correspondent asked. 'Isn't it a bit of a contrast from your last home in the United States . . . New York, wasn't it?'

'That's right, and the choice is quite deliberate. I'm a creature of extremes, a risk-taker, and I like to think it shows in my work.'

'Being an artist in Scotland has been a risky business lately. I suppose you're aware that three young painters have been murdered this year.'

Caitlin watched herself smile mischievously at her female inquisitor. 'Are you saying I'm live bait?'

'Hardly, but doesn't it worry you?'

She saw her face grow serious. 'How many soldiers have died in Iraq this year? Do armies knock off when a man is killed? Should I set my work aside because of some nutcase? Should I abandon my walks every morning, and shut myself up in my lighthouse? No, thank you. As I understand it, two of those crimes have been cleared up, and the third might have been. If there is still a madman out there, tough.'

'Going back to your past career, you've exhibited in several major cities, and now you're coming home. Where to next?'

She was about to hear herself reply, 'Glasgow, probably,' when her mobile rang. She picked it up and checked the caller ID.

'Hi,' he said. 'I just thought I'd call to see whether you were okay.'

'And I am.'

'Listen, I know that this leap into the spotlight has been very sudden. I just want to say that although it's going to look good on your resumé, if you feel you've been rushed into it, you can still back off.'

Caitlin laughed. 'And miss the chance to meet the First Minister, the second most famous Scotswoman, after Lulu? No chance.'

Ninety-nine

Maggie sat and gazed at the television as the ITN newscaster read the story. 'A man detained in Monaco yesterday has been named this evening as Dražen Boras. It was revealed that the business tycoon was wanted for questioning in connection with two murders, including that of a Scottish police officer. It is understood that Boras arrived in the principality under an assumed identity and was on the guest list for a reception to be given by the president of Bosnia.

'His father, the billionaire Davor Boras, is also in Monaco to attend the same reception. He was said by an aide to be astonished by the turn of events. In a statement issued on his behalf, he said that he and his wife had had no contact with their son since he left the United Kingdom, but felt confident that he would successfully defend the charges made against him.

'The Foreign Office said this evening that extradition proceedings were expected to be swift and that Boras would be returned to Britain on Friday.

'A spokesman for Northumbria Constabulary said that the arrest was the result of a joint operation carried out with colleagues in Scotland, two of whom are understood to have travelled to Monaco to liaise with local officers.'

The background changed. 'In London today . . .' the announcer continued. Maggie pressed the off switch on her remote, and let out a huge sigh.

'You are wonderful,' said her sister. 'You did all that, and you never left the house. You must feel . . . Christ, Margaret, I have no idea. How do you feel?'

'Flat,' she replied. 'I wanted to be there, Bet. I wanted to see his face, to watch his eyes as he realised that he'd been nailed.'

'That couldn't be, and you know it. Mind you, I thought that a little public credit would have been in order.'

'No, that can never happen. I should never have been allowed anywhere near the investigation.'

'It might still leak out. Your friend from the *Scotsman* knows you were involved, and so does the woman you told me about, the stockbroker.'

'Mo won't say anything; I'm too good a contact to lose. As for Jacqui Harkness, if she does say anything I'll claim that I was after a stock-market tip when I approached her. My part in the arrest will stay secret, and I'm fine with that. But I did so want to confront the bastard.'

'Then you'll just have to do it in court.'

'Oh, I will. I'll cheer when the sentence is passed.'

'And when he gets out, are you still going to kill him?'

Maggie smiled. 'No, I was joking when I said that. Anyway, I probably won't have to. I've just given Mo Goode the story of his life. I've told him that Dražen and his father have been agents for the CIA in the Balkans and that the Americans helped him escape and set him up with his new identity. I've also told him to take a look at the LTN Trust in Bermuda and see where it leads him.'

'Can he run a story like that?'

'Too bloody right he can. And when he does it won't just be Dražen who's in trouble. He and his father will both be on the run from their own countrymen, and with their cover blown, they'll find that they've run out of influence in America. Even if Davor isn't incriminated in his son's trial, he'll need to hire a private army afterwards to protect him.'

She looked at Stevie's photograph on the sideboard. 'That's as much as I can do for you, love,' she said, 'but I reckon it's not bad.'

One Hundred

And Caitlin walked out again, along her beach path, for the fourth time since she had moved into the lighthouse. Yes, it was lonely, but she was content, for there were the birds. There were the gulls, and there were those that she now knew to be gannets, thanks to her afternoon visit to the Sea Bird Centre at North Berwick. She had been recognised there, from the television interview. When the manager had asked her if she would be prepared to help with fund-raising by staging a show there, she had replied, regretfully, that her work was not suitable for the venue, given the limitations of its hanging space.

She had spent the rest of the previous day logged on to her website, which had registered more than a hundred hits following her media coverage. Her work was displayed there, and her biography: single, born in Largoward thirty-one years earlier to an English father and a Fifer mother, educated in Canada and at the New York Academy of Art; successful exhibitions in Toronto, Québec and Calgary, as well as in major American venues. She had received twelve feed-back messages, and she had replied to them all, including the man with the Australian Internet address who had asked her to marry him. She had told him to send a photograph. The others had been innocuous, most of them from people wanting to know where they could buy her work.

She was still smiling over the Australian as she closed the door behind her, but soon she had left him behind, as she listened to the cries of the gulls and watched the plummeting of the gannets, and the darting of the occasional puffin. They were good company, and so were the voices in her head.

The voices were always with her in the outdoors. Most people would have thought her crackers, told her to get a life, to seek help, but she liked the voices. They were her friends, they gave her comfort, they helped her plot every step she took, every path she trod. She listened to them as she walked, her hands plunged deep into the big pockets of her canvas jacket.

On previous mornings she had walked for four miles, to the site of the fossilised forest and a little beyond, then back to the lighthouse, trying not to look beyond, to the great grey mass of the nuclear power station, where two reactors supplied the energy to power huge turbine generators. This time, she had decided, with the consent of her voices, to walk all the way to Dunbar, although the second part of the journey would be even more isolated. She would be doing it only once more, maybe twice, before she had to concentrate on other things. 'Mustn't get too set in our ways, must we, Caitlin?' she said, to the voices as much as to herself.

She walked on until she reached the petrified forest or, rather, the spot on which it had once stood, where now only holes in the ground remained to show where the trees had been, inland in those times, before the North Sea had encroached. She stopped, and looked at it for a few minutes, stilling her voices until she was ready to go on.

The terrain changed as she neared the Burnmouth Estate, where a modern forest grew. Caitlin knew her history: she had heard of the decisive battle at which General Leslie's Cromwellian army had defeated the Covenanters before going on to punish the rest of the area for their insurrection. Three and a half centuries later, the place still had a dangerous air about it.

The path seemed to level out, then led on to a small beach, with the wood close by. As she stepped on to it, she thought she heard a crunch behind her, but she resisted the temptation to turn round. A little further and Dunbar golf course would come into sight.

And then one of the voices in her ear spoke again. It was the South African and this time its tone was different, no longer laughing, no longer soothing: instead it was urgent.

'We have a man in sight, behind you. He mustn't close on you! Go now!'

Several things happened at once.

The woman known as Caitlin Summers threw herself to her right. As she landed on the sand she rolled over and came up to one knee, her right hand clear of her jacket pocket and clutching a pistol.

From somewhere behind the tree-line an amplified voice boomed, 'Armed police officers! Stand still immediately. Put both your hands on your head. Do not move, repeat, do not move or we will shoot.'

The figure at the centre of it all paused. He looked at the woman on the beach, his eyes hidden from her sight by the enveloping hood of a light grey cotton garment. He saw the gun in her steady shooter's grip, pointing at his chest. Then, slowly and carefully, he spread his arms out wide, then brought his hands together, interlacing his fingers as they met.

He stood like a statue as the woman rose from the sand and as Ray Wilding and Griff Montell emerged from the wood. The two detectives held their weapons on him as Wilding approached him and patted him down until he reached the right pocket of his jacket from which he removed a silenced pistol.

As the sergeant pulled the man's arms behind his back and cuffed him, a fifth person stepped out of the trees. He walked slowly towards the prisoner; as he reached him, he took hold of the hood, and pulled it backwards, revealing his face.

'Old friend, old friend,' said Bob Skinner, sadly. 'What the hell has all this been about?'

One Hundred and One

The Crown Agent was at his desk glowering at a pile of papers that had come to him in his deputy's absence; bloody man wasn't due back for another week, and with Broughton going off too, things could only get worse. That assistant of his couldn't be relied upon either. If she had shown a little common sense, the shit-storm of the previous week would not have descended upon his head.

Top of the list, of course, was the prosecution of the Shadow Defence Secretary's son for murder. The indictment would have to be absolutely flawless. He could not bear to imagine the consequences if a young man who was as guilty as sin managed to walk free as the result of a technicality. And that bloody woman Birtles was just the type to throw open the door, if it was left even the slightest bit ajar.

It had never occurred to Joe Dowley that he was a misogynist, but he was. He was of a school, greatly diminished in numbers, but still alive and whining, that regarded women as professionally inferior. He bowed his head, sometimes literally, to the Lord Advocate, and the Lord Justice General, but he held the First Minister in barely disguised contempt, seeing her as the result of a period of ridiculous tokenism in parliamentary selection. As he glanced at the photograph of the Queen, which had been placed on the wall by one of his predecessors, and which he had been afraid to remove, he felt the usual frisson of irritation that she was proving so sturdy and apparently ageless.

He scowled at the phone as it rang, but picked it up. The caller was a woman. 'I have the Lord Advocate on the line for you,' she said . . . more than a little haughtily, he thought.

'Of course,' he replied, as if she had asked whether he was free to take the call.

'Crown Agent,' the principal law officer intoned as he came on the line. Dowley's heart sank at the formality of the greeting.

'Sir.'

'I have a task for you,' Gavin Johnson continued, 'and for you alone. It has priority over everything else. I need you to go to the police headquarters building down at Fettes, and sit in on an interview that will be conducted there. When it's over, you'll be given a copy of the tape. I want you to bring it back to me.'

'Who's the interviewee?'

'You'll find that out when you get there.'

'Are you sure this can't be delegated? I really am . . .'

'You, Joe. Nobody else, and go right away.'

One Hundred and Two

'You have to be kidding me,' said Martin.

'No, I'm not, but I am ringing to apologise for keeping you in the dark about certain things, even after you were given oversight of the inquiry. If I'd been able to tell you face to face, Andy, I would have. I wasn't keeping you out of the loop.'

'So what was it that I missed out on?'

'On Monday,' Skinner told him, 'I set up a black operation.'

'Under cover?'

'Anything but: it was so far out there I'm still amazed that we got away with it, but we did, all the way. Have you seen anything in the papers lately about an artist called Caitlin Summers, big name in the US, come home in triumph to Scotland?'

'Yes, I have. Isn't Aileen opening her exhibition next week?'

'That's what they said, but she won't be. Caitlin's a figment of my imagination, brought to life by Alice Cowan.'

'Alice? Special Branch Alice?'

'Yes. We gave her a butch punk haircut, dyed it peroxide, and stuck a pair of John Lennon glasses on her nose. Her own mother wouldn't have recognised her. In about half a day she became an internationally known painter, with a body of work that we borrowed from a graduate student in the art college, and presented as Caitlin's on a website our IT department put together for her. Then we set her up as living in a decommissioned lighthouse in East Lothian, and had her out walking the coast every morning. Our friends in BBC

Scotland even ran an interview with her on the evening bulletin on Wednesday.'

'You set her up as bait?'

Skinner laughed. 'She used that term herself in the BBC interview. Neil nearly burst a blood vessel when he saw it, but it worked. She volunteered for the job. There was no question of coercion or of her being punished for her leak to her uncle. There was also very little risk. She had a weapon, and she had two bodyguards every hour of the day and every step of the way, Ray Wilding and Griff Montell, both armed too. They camped out in the lighthouse, and they kept her under observation from the dunes when she did her walks. We hoped that if he turned up, he would try to take her where he did. It offered the best cover for him, but happily, it did for us as well.'

'And he surrendered when you had him trapped?'

'Thank God. Alice was under orders to take no chances, and the other two wouldn't have either. I had to take him alive, Andy, otherwise there might have been people afterwards who still thought it was me.'

One Hundred and Three

'I want you to understand, Mr Dowley,' said Chief Constable Sir James Proud, 'that you're here as an observer. You will take no part in the interview. You will not speak to the prisoner or to the officers who will be conducting it, whatever the circumstances. Understood?' The chief's customary bonhomie was missing: so were the chocolate digestive biscuits and tea with which he had greeted almost every visitor during his term of office. 'No McVities for him,' he had growled at Gerry Crossley.

'I'd understand better if I knew what was going on, Sir James.'

'Don't worry, you will as soon as you walk into that room. Once again, are my instructions clear to you?'

'Yes,' the Crown Agent replied curtly. 'Who will be conducting the interview?'

'Detective Inspector Rebecca Stallings and Deputy Chief Constable Bob Skinner.' Proud could have sworn that he heard a sudden intake of breath as the second name was mentioned. 'They're ready to begin, so let me take you there.'

The chief led the way out of his office, but not out of the command corridor. Instead he turned to his left, and walked a few steps to a small meeting room, where, unusually, a uniformed constable stood guard. Proud opened the door and held it. 'Your guest is here,' he said, as the Crown Agent stepped inside . . .

. . . then stopped in his tracks. Skinner and Stallings were sitting with their backs to the door, and a third chair was placed alongside

425

them. Facing them, staring at him as he entered, was Gregor Broughton, procurator fiscal for the Edinburgh area.

'Mr Dowley, Crown Agent, has joined us,' said Stallings for the tape.

'Sit down, please,' Skinner snapped. 'We've been waiting for you.' He turned and stared, hard, across the table. 'Once again, Gregor,' he continued, 'as I asked you on the beach, what the hell is all this about?'

'Aren't you simply going to ask me what I was doing there, Bob?'

'I saw what you were doing there. You were stalking one of my officers and I believe that you were about to shoot her. We found a pistol in your jacket pocket. You were dressed like a fucking hoodie, man.'

'I was dressed casually, yes, so that I could remain inconspicuous. I had no idea that young woman was a police officer because you chose to keep the facts of the operation from the fiscal's office. I had seen the way in which she was being exposed in the media, and I was so concerned that I went along there with a view to protecting her, if necessary. As for my dress, is that relevant?'

'You're not a police officer, Gregor.'

'I'm a concerned citizen, Bob, concerned about the inability of your force to prevent the murders of several young women over the last few months, and so lax that it has allowed a copycat killer to emerge, after the earlier murders were solved.'

'If only. You're wrong, they weren't solved.'

For the first time, Broughton's composure seemed less than complete. 'What do you mean? Those cases are closed.'

'No, sir,' said Stallings. 'They've been reopened as a result of new medical evidence indicating that Daniel Ballester could not have been the killer. I'm leading the investigation, which has now been linked with that into the murder of Sugar Dean.'

'Then link me to them, I challenge you.'

'I'll do that,' Skinner told him. 'We'll start with the most recent. When Ms Dean was killed, you were at Murrayfield Golf Club, and the Law Society's criminal justice event.'

'So were you, I'd remind you.'

'Yes, but while she was being killed I was spending a pointless half-hour on the practice ground, hitting golf balls. A couple of days ago, a colleague of mine found a green-keeper who remembers seeing me there. The same green-keeper has a hell of a good memory: he recalled seeing a man answering your description walking towards the clubhouse, along the side of the eighteenth fairway, that is to say, heading away from the place where the girl was shot.'

'I doubt if just "answering my description" is going to convince a jury.'

'On its own, probably not; so let's go back a bit to the shooting of Zrinka Boras. Again, I was in the vicinity, at home in Gullane, on sabbatical, very close to where the killing took place. But you weren't far away either, Gregor.'

He paused. 'Way back at the start of the inquiry, the investigating team asked local people if they could recall anything unusual that morning. Two of them recalled being overtaken between Gullane and Longniddry by a Saab 93 convertible, heading towards town and going like a bat out of hell. Yesterday I asked Neil McIlhenney to do a check with the traffic department. Your car was clocked by a camera on the A1 that same morning. It was referred to the fiscal in Haddington for possible prosecution; you're his boss, Gregor, so he did you a favour. He's just admitted as much. We haven't interviewed Lady Broughton yet, but when we do, I'll bet she tells us that you weren't at home the night before Zrinka was murdered. I believe you'd been stalking her for a while. That day you followed her, not knowing for sure where they were headed, from Edinburgh to North Berwick, where she and Harry, her boyfriend, ate, then back to Gullane, where they camped. And you took your chance. If they'd just gone back home, back to her place, those kids might still be alive.'

'Bollocks.' The prosecutor laughed. 'A speed camera near Tranent does not put me in Gullane. A jury would laugh at you.'

Skinner reached into his pocket and produced a clear plastic

427

envelope, with a piece of paper inside. 'No,' he admitted, 'but this does. You ate in the same restaurant in North Berwick they did . . . or someone did, and paid for his meal with your credit card. Is that jury still laughing?'

He stared at Broughton, who remained impassive. 'Let's go back to Stacey Gavin now. She died some time after eight in the morning, in South Queensferry. You live in Fife: you drive more or less past that spot on your way to work . . . and you were at work that day.'

'And where were you, Bob?'

'As it happens, that morning I gave evidence to a fatal accident inquiry in Fife, and drove close to the murder scene. You would have had easy access to the list of witnesses, Gregor. You could have known that.'

'Possibly, but the chain of coincidence extends further. As I recall, your inquiry revealed that you yourself own works by the first two girls murdered, Gavin and Boras.'

Skinner smiled. 'But you knew that anyway. Not long into my sabbatical you came out to Gullane to consult me about a pending prosecution. Both of those pictures hang in my living room. And you're an art buff, Gregor. I haven't been to your place, since I've never been invited, but Mario McGuire has, on business. You profess no knowledge of painting, but he describes it as being like an art gallery, with pictures all over the drawing room; quality, he says, and Mario knows his stuff. You knew what you were looking at when you saw my modest collection; you knew also, when you decided to make a comeback, that there's a piece of Sugar Dean's work hanging in this building . . . as there is in the Crown Office.'

Broughton chuckled. 'Looks as if it's either you or me, Bob. I suggest that the Crown Agent issues indictments against us both, then we'll see who the jury thinks is most likely.'

'You had a gun on the beach this morning, an illegal firearm. You were a member of Edinburgh Gun Club twenty years ago.'

'You're a police officer. You have access to guns. Indeed, you've killed at least one man that I know of. Let me answer your further point. You say that my gun was illegal, but I'll argue that I'm an officer of the law, like you, and that the laxity which allows you to carry a weapon also applies to me in times of extreme need, in the public interest.'

'But not in Spain.'

'Pardon?'

'You can't justify being armed in Spain. At my request, the Mossos d'Esquadra raided your house up in Torremirona yesterday. They found two starting pistols in the garage, both converted to fire live rounds. Of course, they didn't find the one you used to kill Nada Sebastian, the artist who was murdered within sight of my Spanish house. I guess you chucked that one in the sea. How many times have you been in my office, Gregor? How many chances have you had to see the picture of hers that hangs there? I didn't know myself that it was one of hers, but you clocked the signature and traced it to her website. Then you traced her, and you killed her, when I was there.'

'And when did I have the opportunity to do that?'

'When you were in Barcelona last week, on a liaison visit to the Catalan government. I've checked with the Catalan justice ministry; it ended on Tuesday, yet you didn't fly home till Thursday afternoon. My guess is you tracked Sebastian on the Wednesday, and then, next morning, you followed her again and shot her.'

Broughton leaned back in his chair, and gazed at the ceiling, before looking Skinner in the eye once more. 'And if I did all this, set you up in this way, why did I sign off on Ballester as the murderer?'

'Because you thought even that might implicate me. And also, probably, to show yourself what a clever bastard you are. But you weren't, you see, because that's where you nailed yourself to the fucking wall, that's where you made the big mistake that's going to put you away.'

'Do go on, my friend.' The fiscal yawned.

'No problem. You knew that we had Ballester in the frame, yes?'

'Yes.' Broughton nodded.

'Right, and then you heard that he was dead, swinging in his cottage in Wooler. You didn't stop to ask yourself why he would hang himself if he was innocent, as you surely knew he was. You seized the main chance, you drove down to the scene and when nobody was looking you planted all the evidence that was found there. That would have been easy to do. All of it was outside the house, outside the taped-off crime scene, and all of it was found after you'd been on the scene, none of it before.'

'As before, Bob, you're describing your own actions. You were there too, remember?'

Skinner leaned towards him. 'But I never touched Ballester's computer. I never laid a hand on it. You took that away from the scene. The local coroner went ballistic when he heard that, remember, so you had the hard disk copied and you sent the original machine back down south. When my guys looked at the copy . . . an exact copy, you told them . . . they found images, beautiful, caring photographs of the three dead girls, Stacey, Zrinka and wee Amy Noone, all taken, posed like angels, in the minutes after their deaths.

'Daniel Ballester couldn't have put them there, Gregor, because he couldn't have killed them. If you'd read his autopsy report carefully, you'd have learned that he had a physical condition that would have made it impossible. The only person who could have seeded that computer was their murderer, and the only person who had access to Ballester's machine, was . . . not me, not anyone else . . . it was you, Gregor. You killed them all, and that's how I will prove it, or prove enough of it to put you away until you're eating your dinner with a shaky fucking spoon! Go on, Prosecutor. What are my chances of a conviction, even before the world's most perverse jury? Go on, tell me!'

The deputy chief constable's eyes and those of his adversary seemed to lock together. To Stallings it was as if their intensity was sucking the air out of the room, until she realised that she was holding her breath.

Beside her Joe Dowley sat catatonic; she glanced at him and saw an expression on his face that was pure terror. She could see Skinner only in profile, and perhaps that was just as well. As she watched, Broughton, seated a few feet from her, slowly fell apart. First the confidence left his eyes, and then the courage, and finally the hope, until all that was left was despair.

'You can make a phone call,' said Skinner, quietly. 'Who's going to tell Phil, Gregor, you or me?'

'You'd better do it,' the beaten man whispered, only just loud enough for the tape to register. 'I couldn't find the words.'

'Okay. Interview terminated.' He looked to his right as he switched off the three recorders on the table, and removed the cassettes. 'Excuse us, please, you two. We've got enough for now. The next part's private, between the two of us.'

'Sir,' Stallings murmured.

'Jesus, Becky,' the DCC exclaimed. 'Relax, I'm not going to give him a doing.'

Doubtfully she left the room, taking the tapes and a still shaking Dowley with her.

Left together, Skinner looked back at the man he had thought he knew. 'So, Gregor, why?' he asked him, for the third time.

'They were beautiful, you know,' Broughton replied softly. 'You'll have seen those images. You called them angels, and others did too. I read the reports. You were all right. That is what they were. They were art themselves, dead, yet living art. I tried to make them something greater: not with a brush, for there I have no skill, but with my camera. There can be such beauty in death, Bob, in the perfect death. It's an art form, the purest, loveliest art form there is, and who better to appreciate it than those with art in their soul? As you have, for I've seen your taste, the things you possess. I know you can see the beauty.'

'I can see a very sick man, Gregor.' He paused. 'You must be aware that we are searching your house. The Lord Advocate gave us a warrant. Phil's in court, and your boys are being looked after while it happens. We'll find those images, but will we find any others, victims we don't know about?'

'Not there,' he said. 'You won't find them in my home, but sooner or later you'll search my office, and find my lap-top, my camera and a third gun in my private safe. You'll find nine, in total, including Nada Sebastian. Not just from Scotland, some from other parts of the world, where I have travelled, including countries where the penalty for such things is death, although I can't be extradited to any of them. It isn't just the art, you understand, it's the excitement too, the danger, and ultimately the thrill of the victory that's part of each creation.'

'Amy Noone?' Skinner asked. 'Why her?'

'You're on a roll, you tell me.'

'I will. I've read all the witness statements from those investigations. There's one with Amy, where she talks about the first time she, Zrinka and Stacey were all together. It was the final-year show, up at Lauriston, where the students sell their work. She said something about Stacey selling her last picture to a man. She said that he spun them a story about wanting it for his daughter's flat, and that he looked "as tough as fuck", as I recall. You're a pretty rugged guy, Gregor. That was you, trying to fit me up into the bargain. You saw that statement and you killed Amy because she could have identified you. Does that cover it?'

'As I said, Bob, it's your day.'

'Maybe, but there's one thing that's got me baffled. Why pick on me? Why try to set me up? Not even you would have anticipated that I'd be convicted for things I hadn't done, but enough smoke, even without fire, would have derailed my career, and probably Aileen's too. I suppose that's what those anonymous phone calls were about, you trying to kick-start that process. So why, Gregor, why me? We've known each other for twenty years. I've always regarded you as a friend. Tell me, please; I don't know and I can't guess.'

'I don't suppose you can, Bob. If it's any consolation, I've never regarded you as an enemy: as a friend, though, no, not for a long time; not since I found out about you and Phil.'

Skinner stared at him. 'That's it? That's why you've been trying to point my own officers at me in their investigations? Phil and I went out together . . . what? Twelve years ago now, before you and she were married, or even engaged. It wasn't a secret at the time, but I doubt if there's anybody in Edinburgh who still remembers it, apart from the three of us. I've never even told Alex about it, only Aileen. What's your beef? I didn't ask her to marry me, although I might have got around to it, I admit. You did, and she accepted. I was the one who got hurt, not you.'

'You think so? Remember when Ranald was born, our first?'

'Of course I do. We wet his head in Deacon Brodie's. Got it very wet, as I recall.'

'I told you he was carried full term . . . or, at least, I allowed you to assume that he was. Actually he was two months premature.'

To Skinner the room suddenly felt smaller. 'Now wait a minute . . .' he began. 'Phil and I didn't have that sort of relationship.'

'Never? Under oath?'

'Well, maybe a couple of times . . . just before it packed in. But you're not telling me that you and she were platonic.'

'No, I'm not, and our relations were within the time-frame. Phil never gave me the slightest hint that I might not have been Ranald's dad, but I'm afraid I always had that little niggle. Gradually I forgot about it, though, until last year, when something happened. Your daughter was attacked, and to help the investigation, she gave a DNA sample. Of course, the papers in the case landed on my desk. I'd never thought of having a test done until then, but I found the temptation too much to resist. I had comparisons run privately using your daughter's DNA, Ranald's and mine. Congratulations, Bob. Your sex with Phil may not have been very memorable, but for all that it was effective. You stole my son, you bastard.'

'Does she know?' Skinner whispered.

'No. She and Ranald must never know, but now that . . . now that it's all over for me, by God you should!'

'And you'll trust me to keep your secret, after what you tried to do to me?'

'You wouldn't hurt Phil. You wouldn't damage the boy.'

'How exactly would it damage him to know that the most notorious serial killer we've had in years isn't his dad after all? How much hurt do you think Phil's going to feel when I tell her about you? How is she going to carry on with her career, with her husband up before one of her fellow judges?'

'Bob, a few minutes ago you said you thought of me as a friend.'

'Fucking wrong there, was I not?'

'Maybe, but do this one thing for me. Keep my secret.'

Skinner glared at him. 'Okay, I will, if you do something for me.'

'What?'

'The psychiatrists are going to be crawling around inside your head for the next few weeks, Gregor. They may say you're nuts, unfit to plead. But if they don't, then the word you say is "guilty". You will not put Phil and her boys through the ordeal of a trial.'

'You're blackmailing me.'

'At the moment, pal, you're lucky that I'm not around this table disembowelling you with my fingernails. If you do that to your wife and family, what else do they have to lose? Do we have a deal or not?'

Gregor Broughton looked at him and nodded. 'We do. Tell me, Bob,' he added, 'since I can't be objective in this, you must have interviewed more than a few crazy people in your time. Do you think I'm one of them?'

One Hundred and Four

'Do you think he is?' Aileen asked him, her arm linked though his as they strolled past Gullane Parish Church.

'Fit to plead?' he responded. 'Sometimes it's hard to tell. Did he know right from wrong as he was killing those people? That's the test. Gregor's career, a very successful one, was based on knowing that very difference when it came to the cases he had to prosecute, so it may be difficult for him to offer that defence. On the other hand, this prosecution will be handled personally by the Lord Advocate; for practical reasons, he may be quite keen to accept it. Now ask me whether I think he's crazy. Absolutely not, but my gut feeling is that's what the outcome will be.'

'How did Lady Broughton take it?'

'She's a rock. Jimmy Proud and I went to see her together, in her office up at Parliament House. We told her what had happened and we played her a tape of the interview, then we sat quietly for half an hour while she persuaded herself that we were telling the truth.'

'Do you think she had any inkling that her husband was . . .'

'No, but neither did I until very late in the day. And, you know, if he hadn't made that mistake with the computer, nobody would have twigged. Not for a while at any rate. Phil's first reaction was to write out her resignation as a judge and hand it to the Lord President, but I talked her out of it.'

'What did you tell her?'

'That there was nothing to be served by allowing one very bad man to drag a very good woman down with him. Gregor's done enough damage. I hope I showed her also that her kids will need her up there as an example to them.'

'And Ranald?'

'Gregor's older son?'

'Except he's yours.'

'I've never met the boy; I feel no attachment to him, and I never will. I don't know why, but it's different from the way I felt about the kid Myra had aborted. As far as he's concerned, as far as Phil's concerned, he's Gregor's. As far as I'm concerned he's Gregor's. It all came down to racing tadpoles; mine won but the bookies paid out on the other.'

She laughed as she looked up at him. 'You can be a real romantic when you try, you know.'

'So I've been told.'

'How would you feel if we had a kid?'

'That's a question for you, just as much as me,' he told her, as they reached the door of the Mallard Hotel, where supper awaited, followed by the regular Friday gathering of the informal local group known to some as the Ten o'Clock Gang. 'But I'm not asking it, not for a while at any rate. Let's get married first.'

She nodded as he held the door for her. 'Let's do that,' she agreed. 'But first, Chief Constable-in-waiting, you have a promise to keep.'